Outstanding Praise for Lisa Black and her Gardiner and Renner Thrillers

"She is, quite simply, one of the best storytellers around."
—**Tess Gerritsen**

"Lisa Black writes with immediacy and unmatched authenticity."
—**Jeff Lindsay**

SUFFER THE CHILDREN

"With its solid grounding of information about child development, this fourth entry in the Gardiner and Renner series is instructional as well as being a well-plotted and -paced thriller with a pair of intriguing protagonists."
—*Booklist*

"A well-crafted thriller. Black keeps the suspense high throughout."
—*Publishers Weekly*

"In *Suffer The Children*, Black introduces a difficult topic and makes it come alive through her characters. The suspense builds to a well plotted climax that leaves the reader with something to think about long after the story ends! Black draws her readers into yet another must read!
—**Charles Todd,** *New York Times* Bestselling Author of the Ian Rutledge and the Bess Crawford series

"A timely and socially conscious psychological thriller that keeps Ms. Black at the top of her genre."
—*Florida Weekly*

"The surprising ending is sure to keep readers coming back for more."
—*Booklist*

"Black, a forensics investigator, skillfully portrays the stark realities of homicide cases in her latest thriller. In this series launch, she pairs Maggie with Jack Renner, a determined detective with secrets of his own who has no intention of allowing murderers to evade their punishment. A great choice for readers of psychological suspense, forensic investigations, and mystery."
—*Library Journal*

"A crime thriller with a sharp psychological edge running through it. . . . *That Darkness* left me thinking for days about the intricacies of the plot, the beauty of Lisa Black's writing, and the profound relationship between law and justice. Lisa Black, through her incredible characters and narration, shows the delicate balance between the two and how hard it is to know which side is the right one. With *That Darkness*, Lisa Black has written a book that everyone should read. But if you are a lover of mystery and suspense, this is an absolute must read."
—*Suspense Magazine*

Suffer
the
Children

Books by Lisa Black

*Suffer the Children**
*Perish**
*Unpunished**
*That Darkness**
Takeover
Evidence of Murder
Trail of Blood
Defensive Wounds
Blunt Impact
The Price of Innocence
Close to the Bone

Available from Kensington Publishing Corp.

Suffer
the
Children

LISA
BLACK

KENSINGTON PUBLISHING CORP.
www.kensingtonbooks.com

KENSINGTON BOOKS are published by

Kensington Publishing Corp.
119 West 40th Street
New York, NY 10018

All Kensington Titles, Imprints, and Distributed Lines are available at special quantity discounts for bulk purchases for sales promotions, premiums, fund-raising, and educational or institutional use. Special book excerpts or customized printings can also be created to fit specific needs. For details, write or phone the office of the Kensington special sales manager: Kensington Publishing Corp., 119 West 40th Street, New York, NY 10018, attn: Special Sales Department, Phone: 1-800-221-2647.

Kensington and the K logo Reg. U.S. Pat & TM Off.

ISBN-13: 978-1-4967-1358-2
ISBN-10: -1-4967-1358-3
First Kensington Hardcover Printing: September 2018
First Kensington Mass Market Printing: September 2019

ISBN-13: 978-1-4967-1359-9 (ebook)
ISBN-10: 1-4967-1359-1 (ebook)

10 9 8 7 6 5 4 3 2 1

Printed in the United States of America

To my parents—
I am so lucky to have had you.

Suffer the little children, and forbid them not, to come unto me.
                    —*Matthew 19:14*

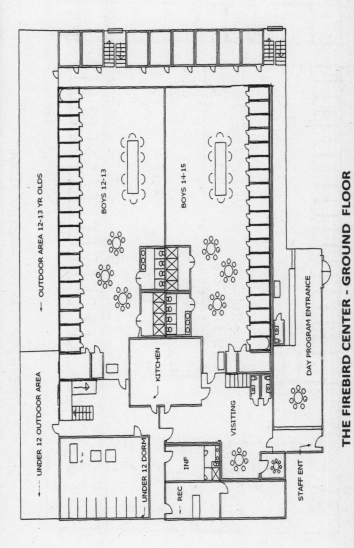

THE FIREBIRD CENTER - GROUND FLOOR

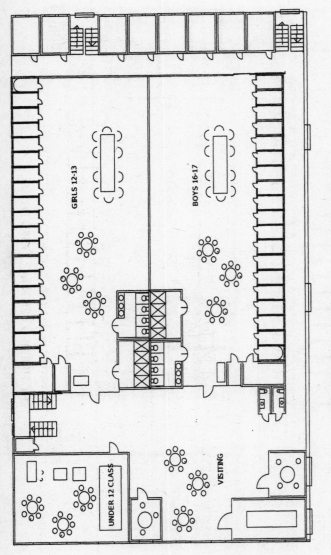

GIRLS 12-13

BOYS 16-17

UNDER 12 CLASS

VISITNG

THE FIREBIRD CENTER - SECOND FLOOR

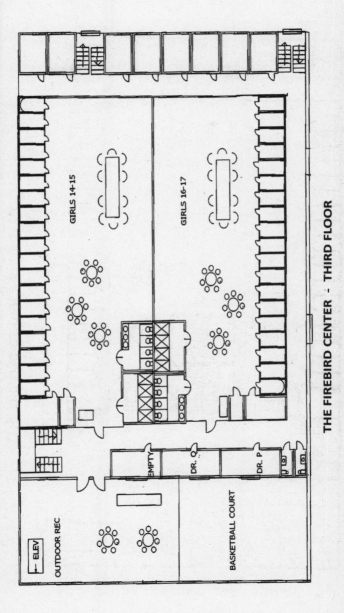

THE FIREBIRD CENTER - THIRD FLOOR

Prologue

Rachael hated kitchen duty. Bad enough to be locked up in this hellhole but then to be put to work like some sort of slave—ridiculous. They said it was all about learning responsibility but she knew it was about the damn free labor, that's what it was about. She already knew everything she needed to about responsibility. She knew who had been responsible for her being shut up in here, and why, and how. Washing dishes until her fingers got pruney would not deliver any further insights about that.

She let the door slam behind her and moved across to lean her arms on the railing. The stairs looped down and down into a vortex of emptiness, which seemed to be the perfect picture of her life at the moment. Everything had been stripped away, piece by piece. First her mother, then her father, then her own body, taken and ripped and seared by this shithole of a universe.

No, wait. That last one wasn't due to the universe. That could be wholly set at *his* feet, and when she got out of here she would see to it that he paid in blood, lots of blood, more than he had ever broken out of her.

The universe, well, its debt had mounted—time for it to start paying. Emptiness had gotten boring.

She didn't feel the movement behind her until just before it struck.

Chapter 1

It was an old-fashioned stairwell, with wide steps, painted iron pipes for railings, and a rectangle of wasted space down the center. Plenty of room for the body to fall, perhaps the entire three stories. The final impact left a spray of blood from the girl's head across the worn terrazzo tile.

Maggie Gardiner stood with a camera in one hand and a crime scene kit in the other, surveying the lifeless body and the hallway around it. Simple, as crime scenes went. No furniture, no wet grass or old clothes, no useless debris to be sorted from vital clues. Empty steps and what remained of a child who had suffered the misfortune to land on her head instead of her feet.

Around this very ordinary stairwell sat the Firebird Center for Children and Adolescents, otherwise known as the city's juvenile detention facility—only six or seven blocks from Maggie's lab in Cleveland's Justice

Center complex. She had never been there before. It smelled of disinfectant and Pine-Sol and years of mass-produced food, and the fluorescent fixtures kept it thoroughly bathed with a yellowish light. Maggie had been there for ten minutes and hadn't seen a child yet, but the air hummed with ambient noise. The various floors bulged with classrooms and restrooms and dormitories for juveniles ranging from under ten years of age up to seventeen.

The staggered bedtimes for the various dorms had not yet arrived and, freed from classes, the young people had a precious hour or two to amuse themselves at high decibels. With the doors closed it sounded as if she were in the center of a beehive. Maggie hated bees.

She also hated prisons. She'd been in plenty, processing the occasional death in custody or more often collecting hair and saliva swabs from arrested suspects, but had never reconciled herself to getting locked in with a teeming mass of dangerous and angry people. And now—even worse—a teeming mass of teenagers.

"Her name is Rachael Donahue," the director said, Mark Palmer, PhD. He stood to Maggie's left, not rushing her. He looked about sixty, was gray haired and a few inches shorter than herself, and seemed genuinely saddened over the death of a child who had been put in his care.

The Firebird Center, he had told her upon her arrival, was a care facility for children in crisis. Every resident (not inmate, he made clear) had been the vic-

tim of physical or sexual abuse at worst or extreme neglect at best. Some had not committed a crime, only
run away from the abuse, though most had. The center
strove to counsel both the resident child and their families until the child could return home, or until the child
could be matched with a foster family in cases where
their home situation could not be rehabilitated. At the
same time their educational requirements were maintained, since schoolwork usually became the first fatal-
ity of crisis. Getting back on the track toward college
or vocational training would get more difficult with
every day lost.

Maggie steered him back to the physical layout of
the building. They would need to know how Rachael
came to be in the stairwell in the first place.

Along with the dorms and classrooms the center had
meeting areas for legal representatives and family
members, areas for intake, as well as areas for the staff
to write reports and eat lunch and for the live-in dorm
"mothers" and "fathers" to sleep.

Doors were locked. Some residents *could* leave, but
only for certain reasons, and the times were strictly
monitored. The children weren't prisoners . . . and yet
they were.

And so, temporarily at least, was she.

Maggie hefted the camera with the large lens and
heavy detachable flash and began to document the
scene. She would photograph and measure and collect
and the detectives, when they arrived, would ask the
questions—yet she inquired, "How long has she been
here?" of director Palmer, simply to keep him from

getting bored and wandering away. After all, he had the keys to those locked doors.

She had actually meant to ask how long Rachael Donahue had been at the facility, but he said, "It couldn't have been more than ten minutes. The kitchen had brought dessert to the under-ten group and returned with the empty trays, through this door here. They had loaded up dinners for the next group into the dumbwaiter and one of the staff came out to go up and unload, and found her."

Maggie began close-ups of the still form. The inmates—residents, she corrected herself—apparently didn't wear uniforms. Rachael was dressed in tight jeans, black hi-tops, a pink tee, and an oversized red and purple flannel shirt. She had three rings on each hand and three earrings in each ear, with dark purple polish on her bitten nails. Dark chestnut hair—the same color as Maggie's—appeared to be shoulder length and layered into unruly waves, now soaked with blood. It had begun to thicken and clot. Her clean face was turned toward the ceiling, forty feet overhead, with eyes closed, long lashes against creamy skin.

"She was fifteen," the director said, answering a question Maggie hadn't wanted to ask.

In another world, a more just world, the girl would have been the apple of some parent's eye, instead of dying alone behind locked doors in a government facility.

Maggie looked up through the spiraling steps. "Where would she have come from?"

"Fourteen to fifteen girls are on third-floor north.

She should have been in the common room or her bedroom. Erica—Ms. Washington—released her to report for kitchen duty. She must have fallen right after that. We have outdoor rec on the roof but I've already asked Justin and he said he didn't see her, and she wouldn't have been able to get into the other units, the other age groups."

"Released her?"

A pained look crossed the director's face. "The doors to the units are locked, of course, from both inside and outside."

But it's not a prison, Maggie thought.

"Else we'd have chaos. They're children, after all, made to go through doors they're not supposed to go through. All our dorm mothers and fathers have a clunky set of keys at the moment, but eventually we'll go to key cards. Then the doors will open automatically if a fire alarm goes off, lock automatically if there's an active shooter situation or something like that, but the system is under construction. The whole *building* is under construction. I'm sure you noticed all the scaffolding and new drywall on your way in."

"Yes."

"We're a work in progress, in more ways than one. But only for a few more months. Then we'll be the most secure juvenile facility in the country as well as the most therapeutic." He rubbed one rheumy blue eye. Then as if avoiding the sin of hubris, added, "Not taking anything away from my colleagues in other states, of course."

"Of course," Maggie said.

"I'm pushing hard. We're having an open house next week for the state budget committee. The federal system is finally throwing money at the mental health care crisis and we have to grab every dollar we can before their attention fades. You know how that goes."

His fellow government employee said, "Sure. Can we take a look at the video?"

Director Palmer followed her gaze to the dark half-bubbles embedded in the ceilings at each landing and winced.

Maggie did too. "They're not recording?"

"They don't even have cameras in them. Those are supposed to be installed next week, and the control panel the week after that. The manufacturer tells me that in these increasingly paranoid times, surveillance systems are selling like a cure for baldness—that's their excuse for taking so long to get all the components on-site."

Maggie couldn't imagine any kind of detention facility operating for five minutes without comprehensive surveillance, but then juvenile justice programs seemed to exist in a permanent state of experimentation.

She took close-up photos of the girl's hands, as best she could without touching them—Maggie could not move or "molest" the body in any way until the Medical Examiner's office investigator arrived. But the backs of the girl's fingers gave no signs of defensive wounds, blood, or hair. If Rachael Donahue had struggled with anyone before plunging over the railing she had done it without chipping the purple polish on her nails. She might have jumped. Three flights of steps seemed an iffy method of suicide, but would that calculation have occurred to a teen? Surely fifteen was young enough to play, perhaps try to walk on the railing or jump from one landing to another. And, of course, perhaps she had been under the influence of drugs and thought she could fly.

"Why was she here? At the facility, I mean," Maggie asked.

The director fumbled with a lifetime of protecting the civil rights of his underage charges. "Rachael? I don't think I can . . . I mean, I know you'll have to . . . I've never had an accident like this in our history." This realization brought him up short. "Never. I've lost a great many clients *outside* our walls, of course—the world is a dangerous place for a child—but under our care, no."

Rachael had ruined his perfect record, and he seemed to allow himself one fleeting moment of self-pity before admitting, "Rachael had anger issues."

"Oh." Maggie didn't ask anything more. She had already done more of the detective's job than she should, and if Rachael had been fighting with someone, that would be their job to discover. Detectives, as a group, could get pretty persnickety when someone ducked past the crime scene tape into their territory.

Instead Maggie began to walk the stairwell, photographing as she went. At first she used a flashlight to examine each riser for shoeprints and disturbances in the dust, but quickly surmised that a great many people used the stairwell every day with marks on top of other marks from one end of the tread to the other. Maggie gave up, telling herself that any particular set of prints wouldn't prove much.

So she took pictures of the steps. She took pictures of each door she encountered, without attempting to open them. Some had a great deal of noise and movement behind them, some—such as the one labeled MAINT.—dead silent. She closed her fingers around the handle to 12–13 BOYS but it didn't budge. What she guessed to be the twelve- to thirteen-year-old males' dorm could not be entered from the hallway, only by pressing the button to the left of the door and having someone inside allow admittance. She didn't push the button.

Maggie took pictures of a long, dark hair caught where the pipe that formed the upper rail on the second landing screwed into its stanchion, the threads still rough after decades of repainting. She tucked the hair into an envelope, but the resolutely bare tile and solid barrier of the railing refused to give her any clue as to whether the girl had fallen over here, had hit her head on the railing during a fall from the third floor, or the hair had been clinging there for months.

Maggie continued upward. The third-floor landing proved equally unhelpful.

She leaned over the railing to take a photo of Rachael's body at the bottom, lying perfectly centered in the rectangle of open space. It could have been the promo shot for a horror movie, the teen star flush with the beauty of youth cut short to be resurrected in the sequel. But this was all too real, and there would be no resurrection for Rachael Donahue.

The final door felt cool to the touch and the voices beyond it seemed distant enough. The plaque read REC.

12–15. This latch turned with a light application of gloved fingers and Maggie peeked out. Cool September air brushed over a group of six boys playing basketball, their forms visible against the lit windows of the office buildings across the street. A trim young man with a sweatshirt and goatee watched them, shouting a word of either advice or encouragement. Three boys lounged around a table, also watching. It would have been a peaceful picture of youth at play if not for the razor wire atop the chain-link fence, which in turn topped the knee-high brick wall ringing the roof. If Rachael Donahue had wanted to commit suicide, Maggie now saw why she chose the interior stairwell over the outside roof. She wouldn't have been able to get over that.

"That's the younger kids' roof," Dr. Palmer said. He stood at her elbow when she had thought he had stayed at the bottom of the stairwell. When her heart receded from her throat she told him she could see that.

"Sixteen to seventeen have a separate court and roof area behind the classrooms. Under twelve have our little patch of grass below this." He added, "Children need to be outdoors—it's a very basic desire and it's good for them. Burns off extra energy and they learn to appreciate fresh air. But it's so hard to find outdoor spaces in the middle of a city, and even harder to make them truly secure—so we converted the roof. No trees, but after the reno we're going to ring the patio area, where those boys are sitting, with potted shrubs. Same thing on the other roof." He looked at her expectantly.

"That will be nice," Maggie said. She let the door shut with a heavy *clang* that echoed down the stairwell and seemed to reverberate in her ears.

"It's not much, but . . . And in a city where it's cold six months out of the year the weather creates a problem. Residents have to have warm clothing, bulkier stuff, boots, rain gear and we don't have storage space for all that. It would be easier to keep them inside all the time, but . . ." His voice trailed off as they crossed the second-floor landing.

"Are the boys and girls always separate?"

"Not in classes. Co-ed classes are normal, and it's important to keep the surroundings as normal as possible. Otherwise we keep them segregated even during recreation, except for the under-twelve group. We have to be practical."

And unexpected pregnancies would be anything but.

He went on: "It's difficult to make a facility this large homelike, so we went the other route and made it school-like. Kids are *used* to school, and keeping them in that sort of mind-set will make reentry easier."

"Reentry?"

"When they go back to their actual home, their regular school. Their 'normal' life. Unfortunately, for so many of them, their lives have never been what we'd call normal. That's why we always work from the basis of 'what happened to you?' rather than 'what did you do?' Frankly, America locks up far too many juveniles, especially considering that the majority of them have committed nonviolent infractions, like truancy and running away. Violating probation and such."

Maggie said, "And the children here?"

He blinked at her. "Here?"

"Nonviolent offenses?"

"Well, no."

She glanced at him as they reached the ground floor.

"This facility specializes in high-risk clients. The kids who have resisted more community-based interventions."

She tried to sort out that verbiage. "So—"

The doctor sighed. "Some of their crimes have been violent, yes. But it has been shown over and over that with an intensive yet secure program their lives can still be turned around. I can personally attest to amazing strides with a number of our charges."

They stood in front of the girl's body at the bottom of the steps, frozen into her final and hopeless position. "And Rachael? Her crime was—?"

"Murder."

Maggie blinked. "She killed somebody?"

He nodded, shaggy graying hair falling around his downturned face. "Two people, actually."

Loud footsteps abruptly sounded behind them, causing Maggie's heart to pound again. She really hated prisons.

But a middle-aged black woman led in two detectives she knew, and well. The red-headed Riley and his partner, Jack Renner. Maggie knew more about Jack Renner than she would have ever wanted to, and her life had been turned inside out because of it. In the span of a few months they had accumulated a number of experiences together, all of them bad.

Well, nearly all.

But for once she didn't cringe at the memories he brought into the space with him. For once she felt just a little glad to see him.

Jack might have a lot of issues, but should they be suddenly set upon by a teeming band of wilding teenagers she felt fairly sure he would do his job and at least attempt to protect her. Even though her death would remove a serious complication from his life.

Still.

Fairly sure.

Chapter 2

Damon got up from the floor to follow the first big person to the door. She had brought the food to him and the other small persons, as they did a couple of times every day. Damon loved the food, which was unlike anything he had ever eaten. It took him a while to get over the different sensations of it—sometimes hot or wet or soft instead of dry and crunchy—but the tastes made it all worth it. He especially liked the little things they would give him after he ate the hot wet things, usually cool and soft and sweet. The big persons called them things like "cookies" and "brownies" and something amazing called "ice cream" but Damon thought of them as wonderful. He couldn't form the words but he could think them, and he thought them a lot.

The other words didn't make much sense to him, but he didn't worry about that. This new world didn't need to make sense; he only cared that it existed. The sights and smells and colors and sensations were a constant delight of new experiences. He liked the other small persons, ones like himself, like his brother had been. He would watch them as they listened to the big person say words he didn't understand and then draw in their books. He would laugh—in itself a new and bizarre eruption—at their expressions and their mannerisms. He rushed at them and touched them, their clothes, their hair. At first they had not liked this and pushed him away, but after some time they'd gotten used to Damon. Now when he touched they just brushed him off like a pesky fly.

Damon avoided the big people, only because they *were* big, staring down at him from an imposing height that made his stomach quaver. They forced him to do things, like take his clothes off and get under a big faucet of water, or at least put his hands under the faucet, and stick a thing in his mouth and rub his teeth with it. But those things didn't actually hurt, so it didn't bother him so much anymore. And the big people also gave him food.

But right now he wanted to get past this one.

Beyond the door was a place that led to other places, like outside where the bright light shone and there was stuff growing out of the floor. All of them went there every day, but he could see the place outside the door went in other directions as well and he wanted to see them. There might be other small people, and more food. But the big people wouldn't let him. They caught him by the arm or the shirt if he tried.

However, every night one of the big people took the stuff that the food came in, and the metal pieces that the other small people used to eat that food instead of using their fingers like Damon, and carry it out the door. Damon might not be able to form words, but he could plan.

He hovered behind her, rubbing at his nearly bare head, waiting until she opened the door, her hands full of the tray, then—go!

He ducked under her arm and shot through the opening. But he didn't get far.

There were other big people in the place outside the door, some he hadn't seen before. One who was *really* big, and one who had brown stuff growing out of her head that he liked. He liked the color without knowing why, or what color actually was. He had only become aware of color recently, since it had always been so dim where he used to live, but in this new world the lights were always bright. Sometimes a little too bright for his eyes.

They all stared at him, but he had grown used to that.

The big person called, "Damon!" which he knew, from experience, meant him.

He should run, but curiosity about these new big people kept him from pursuing his curiosity about other new places. Plus the air smelled like . . . almost like his brother had, at the end. Only the faintest whiff. It came from the white thing on the floor. It seemed long and stiffish but not solid, and had one of those magic fasteners like on the clothes the big people put on him.

He moved closer. The big people did nothing to stop him, and *his* big person had to set the tray down before she could catch him. Big people always did that—set things down instead of simply dropping them. He didn't know why yet.

The stiffish white thing had a person inside it. Not quite a small person like himself but not a big person, either. The face didn't move, didn't blink even though Damon stood right over her. He had seen this before. It meant that, like his brother, this person wasn't going to move ever again.

He put a hand on the person's face, pressing the cheek and nose. It still felt warm and very soft. He knew that would change after a while.

The big person with the hair he liked put both her hands on both his wrists, not tight, but to pull him away from the person in the bag. But he had given up looking for new places to look at this instead and didn't want to go back to the other small people so soon. He knew what to do about that.

He whirled and kicked, knowing from her grunt that his foot had landed well on her shin. Then he drew one skinny arm back and punched her in the stomach. This knocked her back a little, so he followed up by pushing with both arms until she snapped against the wall.

But then the *really* big big person grabbed his wrists from behind, just as the first one had done but now so tight that it hurt. And he didn't pull Damon softly like his usual big person did; this one jerked him off his feet and dragged him over to the door to his place. Damon's big person opened the door and the other one dropped him back into the midst of the other small people just like the food would be dropped down the steps where he used to live.

Damon wound up in a heap, grinning at the other small people's surprise at his abrupt leaving and even more abrupt coming back. He hadn't gotten to any new places, but it had been worth it. It had *so* been worth it.

As usual, Jack had barely acknowledged her presence at first, but now he asked if she was all right. Maggie took in some breath and said she was. Only a little startled, though she didn't admit it, unaccustomed to being physically attacked at a crime scene even by pint-sized assailants.

"It sounded like your head clunked against the wall."

She had to smile at that. "Just a little clunk. No major damage."

"If he's an example of the clientele, maybe a dead girl isn't so surprising," he said in a low tone. Out of earshot, Director Palmer eyed the tall detective as if he could guess his thoughts.

The Medical Examiner's office investigator arrived, and with Maggie he took a closer look at the eyes, neck, and hands of the dead girl. He shifted the clothing and checked the pockets, finally rolling her over, taking care to control the mess that spewed from her broken skull.

No signs of strangulation, no apparent bruises. No damage to the teeth or mouth. Bra and panties present and in place, giving no signs of sexual assault. Shoes clean, lacking, say, damp asphalt, which might have come from the roof. Pockets empty except for a woven string bracelet and a gold-plated ring too big for any of her fingers. It could have been a man's wedding band, worn and scratched and without engraving.

"That's very curious," Maggie said aloud, examining the ring against the latex surface of her gloved hand.

"We're going to need this girl's history," Jack said to Dr. Palmer. "Family, parents, siblings, where they are, how she came to be here."

"Of course. The file will have all that."

"Her dad's in jail." The woman who had accompanied them spoke without inflection. Her name was Erica Washington and she was the "dorm mother" for the fourteen- to fifteen-year-old girls—at least on Monday through Thursday. Another woman stayed, twenty-four hours, Fridays through Sundays. Dorm mothers—fathers for the boys' sections—provided guard duty; counseled; broke up fights; observed who ate well and who didn't, who made friends and who didn't, who slept through the night and who didn't; moderated family meetings and goal progress; and supplied extra attention for those who had no family support as well as a shoulder to cry on, all administered with a stern sense of discipline to the ten to twenty kids in their section. Then they got to go home for a few days to take care of their own families and their own kids and their bills and their homes and their lives. In short, they did a job Maggie wouldn't have considered taking on for a million dollars a month.

Ms. Washington continued, speaking to no one in particular, her eyes on Rachael as the body transport team arrived to move the girl to a gurney. "Her mom took off years ago, no one knows where, dad got twenty for armed robbery. Grandfather got custody and then raped her daily from the age of ten. She started running

away, spent her thirteenth and fourteenth birthdays on
the street before beating up another girl in a dispute
over shoes they'd stolen from Kohl's. Officers took her
back to her grandfather. She got a kitchen knife and
slashed the man's arm before the cops had even pulled
away from the curb. I think the ring is her father's,
though she never exactly said."

"How long has she been here?" Riley asked. Suspects often made the mistake of underestimating
Thomas Riley, with his growing paunch, thinning
hair, and the way his clothes seemed rumpled even
when they weren't. But that underestimation was, indeed, a mistake. Maggie wondered how he must be
feeling inside, looking at the body of a girl not much
older than his two daughters.

Ms. Washington told him, "Three weeks. Three weeks
and two days, I think."

"She friendly with anyone?" Jack asked.

A hint of a smile played along the woman's lips. "I
wouldn't call it friendly. There were girls she tolerated
more than others. She had a lot more interest in the
boys, common for a girl with her history. Common for
fifteen-year-old girls period. But we keep a tight clamp
on that."

The ME staff wheeled the body of Rachael Donahue out of the area. The girl could now leave the facility, though probably not in the way she'd hoped for.
Or perhaps she had, Maggie thought. They had found
nothing to rule out suicide.

"Where does she sleep?" Jack asked.

Erica Washington looked at him as if that should be
obvious. "In her room."

"Can we see that?"

The woman exchanged a brief glance with Dr. Palmer, and then led the way to the third floor.

And they plunged into the teeming band of wilding teenagers.

Chapter 3

A large, well-lit open area took up one half of the space, and a row of doors lined the other half. These were apparently the dormers, each with a single bed, desk, chair, throw rug, and a window with no bars but a rugged sturdiness that made Maggie think bars weren't necessary. A wall unit of cubes held folded clothes and toiletries, leaving everything visible with no doors behind which to hide contraband. Small shelves were present to display personal items, but no one seemed to have many of those. Most of the doors were open but some were not. All smelled of TV dinners past overlaid with perfume, body spray, and nail polish.

In the open area four round tables sat in a line with six folding chairs at each. A one-piece washer and dryer combo had been installed in the corner next to a sink and counter. Beyond them a low wall of plant holders created a casual conversation area, with more comfortable armchairs grouped within. Each had already been claimed by a different girl, and those who arrived too late, or too low in the pecking order, sat on the rug. As one they stared at the visitors.

"We want the kids to socialize with each other," Dr. Palmer said as he slipped into tour guide mode as they walked. "But at the same time we keep the age groups strictly separated. Too much damage can result when you throw a twelve-year-old in with those in their late teens. It also allows for closer monitoring by counselors. This section is fourteen and fifteen." He gestured past the tables and conversation area. "On the other side of this wall are girls sixteen to seventeen. There are mirror sections on the floors above and below with boys and the younger girls. Classrooms are at the east end of the building." As they passed a doorway he pointed to a small—very small—room with a coffee table and three chairs. "Each section also has a room like that one for one-on-one counseling and sometimes for meeting with family members or legal representation, though usually that's done in the first-floor visitation area. And we have one at the end of this row that's kept completely empty. Kids can use that for meditation."

"They meditate?" Riley asked.

"Time-out," Ms. Washington clarified.

"We call it meditation," Dr. Palmer said. "If they are upset, sad, or angry, they can go in there for as long as they need until they get themselves under control. Anger especially—they all have anger control problems after what they've been through in their small time on this planet. We try to teach them to deal with it more constructively, or at least less violently. But sometimes they just want to be alone. Doesn't everyone?"

Palmer walked a few more steps, keeping to the wall opposite the conversation area, the better to speak without being overheard by the girls around the conversation area, who watched the group progress, their wary expressions hardened into near permanence. They didn't look like prisoners in worn but varied clothing. One wore all-black. One wrapped an oversized Hello Kitty sweatshirt closer around her thin frame, and one wore a blouse trimmed with lace. Their skin color ran the gamut. The hint of fear and anger glinting from their eyes formed the only consistent characteristic among them. They made thirtyish Maggie feel old. And uncomfortable.

"Boys are on second. Under twelve occupy our west wing. At eighteen we have to find other arrangements for them. When someone reaches a birthday they move to the next section, no exceptions. It breaks up any little cliques or gangs that tend to form. Most of these kids come from gangs, so they gravitate right back toward that structure when they get here."

"It also breaks up friendships," Ms. Washington added.

"Which is unfortunate," Palmer agreed. "But socialization is a double-edged sword. I said we wanted to mimic the 'real world' as much as possible for the residents, and kids are used to being around other kids, school, home, neighborhood. But they also encourage each other's self-excusing behavior—that all adults are unfair, we don't understand, and so on. We want to encourage the kids to develop relationships with more pro-social adults, which will serve them far better in the long run."

He stopped. "This was Rachael's room." The end of the sentence turned up in a questioning tone, and Ms. Washington nodded her confirmation.

Maggie turned the knob, as gingerly as before.

The standard bed, desk, and chair did nothing to suggest why their occupant had come to a violent end. The bed had been made, not well. Very little rested on the shelves; instead Rachael's possessions and most of her clothing lived in a layer across her desk.

Maggie photographed the room, then by unspoken agreement began to shake out and refold the clothing. It would seem less a violation to the girls in the armchairs—watching through the open doorway—if a woman did it, she thought. Apparently the detectives agreed because they spent the time asking questions of Palmer and Washington.

Or perhaps, Maggie thought, that's an old lady's assumption of a bygone attitude. Perhaps any interference by an adult represented a violation to these children, just one more in their long and tragic history.

She started with the few clothes in the wall unit, found nothing of interest, and moved on to the desk.

"They all have their own rooms?" Jack asked Dr. Palmer.

"Yes, we insist on that. The county is always trying to send us more but I won't let them bully us into overcrowding. If we're going to help these kids we have to provide a specific and intensive—anyway, yes, their own rooms. Teens need the security of having a door they can close. For many of them the Firebird Center is the first time they've been safe. Ever. And they can't heal until they feel safe."

Maggie said, "But you—"

"The doors don't lock," Ms. Washington said, as if she had read her mind. "If a child is a danger to themselves or is being oppositional, we have to have a way in."

"But that's a last resort," Palmer insisted. "You'll see in the under-twelve section there is no fourth wall, so the rooms are more like cubicles. That's because smaller children are not used to being alone—especially ones from a low socioeconomic status who usually have a passel of siblings piled into a small space. They get scared in a strange room by themselves. But teenagers want the privacy."

Maggie had refolded most of the clothing and piled it neatly in the wall unit. The worn T-shirts and pajama pants seemed clean of bloodstains, mysterious notes, or, indeed, anything else.

"Over fourteen have to do their own laundry," Ms. Washington told her, again as if reading her mind. "They use the unit in the common area. We insist on them making their beds and keeping the rooms relatively neat as well. Many have never been taught basic hygiene, so we have to introduce it."

Riley gazed back at the group of inmates, a lion tamer to the lions, who had relaxed enough to converse among themselves yet without breaking their scrutiny of the interlopers. Hushed tones, hard looks, and the occasional giggle arose from their midst. "All these girls—do they argue?"

"They're teenagers. They argue about everything. Rachael more than most."

Jack asked her to expound.

"She didn't like the food. She didn't like the other girls. Her teachers picked on her—not admitting that she didn't pay attention in class or do her homework. She had an aunt who drove up here from Wheeling who wanted to get involved. She had suffered from the grandfather herself. We hoped that would prompt a bond, but Rachael blamed her for not intervening sooner." Ms. Washington paused. "Can't really blame her for that one."

Maggie folded a neon orange bra, size 30C. "The aunt knew?"

"No, but the kid wasn't in the mood to be understanding. Adults seem omnipotent to children, and they resent us when we're not."

Riley asked. "How did she get along with staff?"

"Hated everything and everyone."

Dr. Palmer said, "That's completely typical, especially with a new arrival. What these kids are looking for, who they're starving for, is someone who won't give up on them. Each person they've encountered has turned into a disappointment until it's easier to reject you so that you can't reject them first. They keep pushing you away with preemptive strikes, seeing if you'll stick."

Having finished with the clothes, Maggie moved on to the smaller items on the desk, Jack watching over her shoulder. Two photos, printed on regular paper about three inches square each. One showed Rachael and another girl in Public Square, scrunching up their faces for the camera. She had had at least one friend, once. In the other a little boy, perhaps three, gazing up at the lens with a solemn expression, arms wrapped around a filthy stuffed horse. Neither Ms. Washington nor Dr. Palmer could identify the kids in the photos.

A handful of jewelry that had tangled together—all battered costume pieces. A drinking cup, empty. A spiral-bound notebook labeled SCIENCE without a single entry on any page. Another labeled ENGLISH with doodles, tic-tac-toe games (played by herself against herself, to judge from the pen ink and handwriting), and the occasional class note. Rachael had apparently found the word *ellipsis* and its plural, *ellipses,* either interesting or amusing and decorated their definitions with many dots. A small fringed bag with lip gloss, a state ID card, and a crumpled-up letter from the aunt who said she knew how Rachael felt and only wanted to help.

"She rejected the aunt but kept her letter," Jack observed. "Seeing if she'd stick."

A paper clip, a movie theater ticket stub dated two months before, hair scrunchies, eyeshadow, a small plastic bucket holding toothbrush and skin cream.

Maggie tried to think of what had been in her bedroom at fifteen. At least four times as many clothes, pictures cut from magazines, stuffed animals she refused to part with (and still hadn't), bottles of perfume, records, books, statues, knickknacks, a radio shaped like an old-fashioned telephone that she liked to pretend was her very own phone in her very own apartment, to which she would move after graduating from college. School records going back to first grade and an elaborately decorated sheet of paper reading "Alex Stay Out" taped to the outside of her door, which her brother had, of course, ignored on principle. A very ordinary and, she thought, very boring existence, without runaway mothers and incarcerated fathers and a monster for a grandfather. *There but for the grace of God—*

Jack and Riley checked the bed, lifting the mattress, the usual hiding place for everyone from small children to death-row inmates. But Rachael hadn't secreted anything under her mattress. Perhaps she had learned the futility of trying to hide from a system that had control over every single aspect of your life. Or perhaps she had nothing worth hiding.

"We search their rooms twice a week," Ms. Washington told them.

Dr. Palmer agreed. "It's regrettable, since we're trying to establish trust with them. Without trust we can't possibly develop a relationship, and without a relationship we can't approach rehabilitation. But we have to balance caring with safety. We try to do it subtly, when they're at class, so most of the time they can't even tell."

"It used to be every week," Ms. Washington said. "But we upped it after an overdose last month."

Riley perked up like a dog getting a whiff of beef jerky. "A kid overdosed?"

"A boy in the sixteen-to-seventeen group—Tyson, Derald Tyson. Lord knows where he got the stuff. Probably bought it off a day student. The metal detector can't pick up string needles or powders."

Dr. Palmer said, "Drugs are the second-biggest scourge we have to deal with here, after abuse. Virtually every child we get has some sort of history with mood-altering substances. They're pervasive in the schools. Plus most of them got some diagnosis along the line—every tenth child in America is now on some kind of psychotropic medication—so their addiction of choice is or was legally prescribed."

"Nothing here but Pepsi," Maggie said, pulling an empty can from under the desk. She used her flashlight to confirm it held nothing more dangerous than sugar residue inside.

Ms. Washington frowned. "Don't know where she

got that. Must have talked one of the other girls out of it. She certainly didn't earn it."

Dr. Palmer explained, "We use little things like that as rewards. The kids buy privileges back with good behavior. It develops self-discipline and teaches that they can control their destiny."

"Both carrots and sticks," Jack said.

"Um . . . you could put it that way. Not ideal for their dental health, perhaps, but there have to be some joys to balance the sanctions."

"Why was Rachael here?" Riley asked.

Dr. Palmer hemmed a bit as he had with Maggie earlier, until Riley pointed out that the right to privacy died with the person. "After the incident with her grandfather, Rachael had been placed in foster care. Her social worker put her with a wonderful couple who already had two other girls and who assured Rachael that she would never, ever have to see her grandfather again except to testify at his trial. Her life should have been looking up at that point. But one day at dinner her foster parents were trying to teach her how to load a dishwasher and the father patted her on the shoulder, that's all, and with his wife and the two other foster kids in the room. Rachael grabbed a steak knife from the sink and threatened to, um, cut his balls off and make him eat them."

"So she came here?"

"No . . . the foster parents had seen reactions like that before. They took it in stride—just got extra careful around the cutlery," the doctor said, huffing to himself as if this were a joke he'd told before. "But a week later Rachael was hanging around with some kids from the neighborhood and word must have been spread about the incident. They started to tease her. Rachael had already found another knife and stabbed four of them before the screaming prompted a neighbor to call nine-one-one."

"Four," Jack said, with his usual lack of inflection. He had often shown a virulent—and, Maggie knew, violent—empathy for the victims. Rachael, perpetrator and victim in one, must challenge that mind-set.

"She lashed out," Dr. Palmer said. "One wound went into a girl's side and it nicked the heart. She died before the ambulances arrived. A second girl had slashes to her arm and back. A boy had a minor cut to his arm."

Ms. Washington put in, "She chased him through four yards. She told the cops she needed to take care of any witnesses."

"Yes, um—and the last girl took a stab to the back. I don't know where the blade went in but she bled out in the ambulance."

The detectives were silent. Then Jack said, "And then she came here."

"With blood still on her clothes," Ms. Washington confirmed. "But at least they'd taken the knife away."

Dr. Palmer frowned.

"Where was she going to go from here?" Riley asked. "What was the plan for her, um—"

"Treatment," Dr. Palmer finished for him. "This is not punishment. The children here are exactly that—children, who have been abused and violated and neglected. Most, as I said, have a diagnosed mental disability along with substance abuse issues. We do what we can with those issues as we try to get them back on an even keel and to set them up for successful reentry into a more 'normal'—and I put that word in quotes—life."

The cops' expressions didn't change. "And what was going to be the next step in her treatment?" Riley asked again.

"Rachael had not yet been adjudicated. Her next hearing is scheduled for . . . I don't know—"

"Next Wednesday," Ms. Washington supplied.

Palmer nodded his thanks. "The prosecutor, as always, wanted her tried as an adult. The public defender, as always, is overwhelmed and has only been here twice that I know of—"

"Three times."

"Since Rachael got here. Meanwhile we immediately put her in classes with therapy once daily and more upon request. As far as I know, Rachael never requested."

Ms. Washington confirmed this with a shake of her head.

"Or cooperated much during the sessions. But that's common for new arrivals. They stonewall, waiting it out, assuming we'll give up. As I said—they're looking for someone who will stick."

"Any incidents in the three weeks she'd been here? Between her and other kids?"

Riley looked at Ms. Washington but Palmer answered. "No. Little bit of shoving, trash talk—as usual for the 'new kid.'"

"She was trying to carve out her territory?"

Ms. Washington said, "More like the other girls were establishing theirs. Just playground stuff. Rachael wasn't much of a joiner. She talked tough enough that they settled down and let her cohabitate, if not exactly let her *in*."

Dr. Palmer assured them, "We want to make sure no one is isolated by the others, but adults interfering often makes things worse."

"She would have picked up friends eventually," Ms. Washington said with an assurance born of years spent observing teens. "She didn't care much either way— with the adjudication hanging over her head, probably saw no point in getting comfortable. Kids with these backgrounds learn real quick to sort out the temporary from the semipermanent, and they don't waste time on the former."

Maggie took a close-up shot of the two-month-old ticket stub, in case the detective wanted to run it down later, see who she'd been with. Rachael had hung on to it, so perhaps it served as a memento of a special afternoon. *Insidious 5* at four-ten p.m. So the girl liked horror movies. You'd think her own life had been horrible enough.

Meanwhile Riley apparently wanted to separate needles of fact from the haystack of social theory: "So she didn't get in any fights, no physical violence or complaints of same?"

The doctor and the dorm mother both said no.

"Any fights between any other kids? Not involving Rachael?"

"No . . . not in this unit. In the under-twelve group—"

"Damon," Ms. Washington interjected.

"*Damon*. He's a—challenge."

"The Damon we just met downstairs?" Jack asked.

"The same. But Rachael shouldn't even have known of that, much less been concerned about it."

"What did Damon do?" Riley asked, apparently out of curiosity.

"He bit a few of his groupmates, tried to choke one. He is, as I said, a challenge. But that's the under-twelve group."

Ms. Washington said, "He scratched Trina, just lunged at her for no reason when the groups were passing in the hallway. But Rachael wasn't even there."

"Then why did he want to see her body?"

"Damon would want to see *any* body," Ms. Washington said. "He has none of the usual filters or instincts, but he couldn't have known it was Rachael. He couldn't have known Rachael period."

They seemed confident on that point so Riley moved on. "Okay. Any other conflicts going on in the building?"

They seemed to consider, then said no. No physical violence worth mentioning.

Maggie had untangled most of the jewelry into cheap bangles; three necklaces with a Chinese character, a quarter moon, and a small stone bear, respectively; hoop earrings, skull earrings, earrings with dangling cats; and a ring with a scratched stone of purple glass. No piece appeared special to its owner, left as they were in a jumble. Not like the gold ring she apparently made a habit of carrying with her, hidden, kept in a pocket. Not hung around her neck with one of the chains, as women often did with a ring important to them.

"We're going to need to talk to the other girls," Riley told the administrators.

"Mmm," Ms. Washington said.

"Mmm," Dr. Palmer said. "That could be problematic. Nearly all of them have legal cases pending—"

Riley said, "They're not suspects. We aren't sure a crime has even been committed—this is most likely a case of suicide, and—"

Dr. Palmer's eyes widened. "Of course it's suicide! What else would it be—well, unless she tried walking on the railing or something like that. Reckless behavior is quite common for these kids—so death by misadventure, yes, quite possibly. An unfortunate accident." Having worked that best-case scenario out in his head, he visibly relaxed his shoulders.

"Yes," Riley soothed. "So all we want to ask them about is Rachael. Not their own situations. No legal worry in that."

"I understand that," the doctor said with a touch of asperity. "But these girls have also been traumatized—Erica, what do you think?"

"They'll be fine," she said, and led the detectives over to the conversation area.

Chapter 4

They pulled chairs over from the dining tables, all the adults, even Maggie. She didn't have anything else to do and had no interest in trying to find her way out of the building without an escort. The doctor and the dorm mother clearly would not be leaving their charges in the company of homicide detectives without supervision.

The conversation area, however, had been closed in by a low wall of planters with only two openings. Riley grabbed that one open space, and no one else felt inclined to walk to the other side of the ten-by-ten area to settle in the opposite opening, so the rest of the adults sat outside the cozy square, gazing at the girls inside over low shrubs with yellowing leaves and dry soil.

Nor did any of the girls offer their seats, or even shift their comfortable positions. Don't give an inch, they seemed to have learned. Too often in their lives miles had been taken.

Riley introduced himself, Jack, and Maggie. Maggie

received softer, more interested glances than the cops did—not because of her gender but her occupation. Most teens were *CSI* fans in some way, and that bestowed her with a desirable but probationary judgment of "cool." Maggie encountered this combination blessing/curse attitude often, and this time felt grateful for it. She would be given a mental pass until she disappointed them by not actually *doing* anything "cool."

The cops, of course, had their own predetermined judgments, not nearly so friendly. Riley spoke in a calm, matter-of-fact voice but he was a cop, a man, and an adult. They owed him nothing.

He had two daughters now approaching their teens; Maggie wondered what he must be thinking. She would expect this entire facility to be one of the worst nightmares of any parent—*Is my kid going to wind up here?*

But he kept any internal turmoil to himself as he told them that Rachael had died, apparently having fallen in the stairwell. Not one girl batted an eye. The one in the Hello Kitty sweatshirt paled and pressed her fists to her mouth. Another raised one eyebrow. Another smirked. They had already known, from that institutional osmosis that winds through any organization, or surmised it from the presence of cops in Rachael's bedroom.

"I know she hadn't been here that long, but what can you tell us about her?"

Blank stares.

"We'd appreciate anything you could tell us about her life before she came here. What did she like to do, who were her friends?"

Nothing.

Then as if a bubble burst, several spoke at once.

"She was a bitch," the girl dressed all in black said. She had dark hair chopped at the jawline and a lot of eyeliner, fingernails bitten to the quick, and an oddly stiff manner of sitting, with both feet on the floor, hands on her knees. But she must have done something good because she held a can of Sprite Zero in one of them.

Ms. Washington said, both gentle and warning, "We respect each other here. Everyone has problems."

"Exactly," the girl replied. "And she didn't care about anybody's but hers."

An overweight girl with dark black skin and a royal blue T-shirt said, "All she *did* care about was boys."

"She was mean." This came from a tiny girl with a mop of dark hair, wearing flannel lounge pants with a Halloween theme of spiders on them. She sat on the rug between an occupied armchair and the coffee table, heaped with old newspapers. She had not once looked up at the cops.

The Hello Kitty girl said, "She wasn't always mean. If something struck her funny, she could laugh."

Of everything Maggie had seen and heard that day, this came close to breaking her heart. *She could laugh*.

A slender black girl with her hair in spiky pigtails said, "She stabbed a bunch of people."

Riley asked, "She told you about that?"

Universal eye roll. "Every day. Like that made her so, so tough."

Dr. Palmer said softly, "Hurting people is nothing to be proud of."

"I stabbed someone, too," said the girl wearing royal blue.

"You had reason," the girl in black said.

"Everyone has reasons," Ms. Washington reminded them. "But we need to act with—"

"Had she been here before?" Jack interrupted. "A prior—"

"Incarceration?" the girl in black finished for him. "You can say it. Nice jacket, by the way."

This had to be sarcasm. He wore a brown blazer that made him look like a college professor, the kind who didn't grade on a curve. "Had she?"

After a pause the girls collectively shook their heads. Rachael hadn't said, they reported. As far as anyone knew she had not been in custody before.

"Had anyone here met her before? Knew her from—"

"The real world?" The girl in black again. "You can say that, too."

"Did you?" Jack asked, skewering the girl with his harsh gaze, one that Maggie had seen too many times and that still made her stomach tremble. But either this girl had been made from sterner stuff or for all her hard-won street smarts she had no ability to sense what lay under Jack's surface.

But Maggie knew. She knew that Jack had murdered a number of Cleveland's worst criminals—and those in other cities as well—in the name of sparing their future victims. Until she had both stumbled onto his secret and created one of her own. Now they were locked into an uneasy pact of mutually assured destruction. She couldn't begin to heal until he left town, and he couldn't leave without attracting attention. Neither of them wanted attention, so Maggie remained in a daily fog of second guessing.

The girl said, "No. Never saw her before."

The other girls all agreed, with apparent sincerity. They had not known or heard of Rachael before she arrived there, and didn't have much interest in her either. As Ms. Washington had said, they all had problems.

"Did she know anybody else here? Either staff or residents?"

The shy little one on the floor spoke to the rug. "She knew a kid in the day program."

"Who?" Riley asked, his voice gentle.

"A boy."

"What's his name?"

The girl shrugged. In the armchair behind her, the girl with pigtails leaned forward and patted her shoulder. "Tell them. We don't care about no boy we don't know."

Still not looking at them, but with more resolve in her voice, the girl said his name was Luis Borgia. "He's been coming here for a couple months. Her first day in class they started talking about a neighborhood around West Thirty-Seventh and he asked about some people they knew, sounded like other kids."

"They hook up?" another girl asked, zeroing in on the more interesting gossip.

"Not here. But friendly. They used to talk through the whole class until Ms. Wallace made Luis sit up front. They'd still say hi before we have to sit down. Last Tuesday she asked him to bring her some cigarettes but he said his social worker would kill him and there was no place for her to smoke them without getting caught anyway."

"Did Rachael get mad?"

"She was kind of pissed but said good-bye to him okay at the end of the day."

"Anything else you can tell us?"

The girl hadn't stopped staring at the rug through this entire recitation. "She was on meds but wouldn't take them. She didn't trust doctors, I think. She'd throw them down the sink in the lav. She *said*, anyway."

"Damn waste," the girl in black complained in a tone of great disgust, and dropped the empty Sprite can into a small waste bin.

Ms. Washington said, "Self-medicating is all about avoiding the world instead of living in it."

"Recycling," Dr. Palmer reminded them.

With a put-upon sigh the girl both rescued the can from the bin and placed it by her feet for later disposal, and piped down about the benefits of drug use.

Riley said, "She carried a gold ring in her pocket. Anybody know who that belonged to?"

The girl on the floor hazarded one quick glance up at their faces, as if she found this interesting. But the other girls shook their heads, and so did she.

"Is that all you can tell us?" Riley asked.

"Yep."

The girl in pigtails beamed down at her charge as a mother at a precocious child. "See? She sees everything."

"What about Rachael's movements today?"

One girl giggled, finding "movements" obscurely

funny. But the rest complied, as if they'd made an un-spoken decision that they had resisted authority long enough and could now be helpful without losing face. The day had been routine—washup, breakfast, English class, math class, midmorning snack, group therapy, lunch, science class, outside games, life skills class, indi-vidual therapy meetings, dinner, rec time. Rachael Don-ahue hadn't seemed any different today than any other day, meaning she remained uninterested in classes and dorm mates, complained about the food, and didn't ap-pear to have had any breakthroughs with her therapist. ("Usually we come out either crying or smiling when we've made progress," one girl explained helpfully.) They had gathered where they now sat after dinner, waiting for the evening's round of family meetings, homework help, and kitchen duty assignments. They had not noticed Rachael in particular and had no idea when she left for kitchen duty, not even the observant little girl on the floor.

"About six," Ms. Washington said. She remembered only that for once Rachael had gone without complain-ing about "slave labor."

No one said so but it seemed accepted that while de-scending the stairwell Rachael either dawdled in some reckless manner or decided she couldn't face one more class, therapy session, or dirty dish. These girls had gotten familiar with both death and despair and found neither surprising.

The detectives wrapped it up and thanked the girls for their time. A few mumbled, "You're welcome," but most just stared. As a unit the adults in the room traveled out the door and into the stairwell for a quick huddle. Without any sign of foul play the cops leaned toward a conclusion of accident or suicide, and for the moment it seemed that all that could be done had been done.

Jack asked if the therapist might be available, but she had gone home at five.

"We'll also want to talk to this Luis," Riley said. "And by the way, what's the day program?"

"We have approximately fifty kids who come in for classes, counseling, and individual therapy services but don't live in," Dr. Palmer explained.

"So Luis Borgia would only be here during the day?"

"Yes."

"Any chance he hung around after class?"

"No. They're checked in and out of the building by the day program director. He would have alerted me if a student had not been accounted for."

"We'll come back tomorrow and talk to him," Riley said. "I'd rather have that conversation in one of your counseling rooms than in the kid's kitchen."

"They're different on their home turf," Ms. Washington said in apparent agreement. Then without a good-bye she returned to her girls while Dr. Palmer guided them down the steps. Riley asked about Rachael's kitchen duty.

"We give the older kids chores. It teaches them to take some responsibility for their surroundings, to cooperate with others, gives them something constructive to do with their time, not to mention teaching basic hygiene. Kitchen duty is mostly washing dishes, sometimes cleaning the cooking areas."

"Let's check in with the kitchen staff, see if she ever made it there," Riley said.

"I already have, but you're certainly welcome to as well. They should still be here."

Dr. Palmer guided them to the source of the mass-produced food smell. The kitchen had red tile on the floors and walls, no windows, and barely stretched to twenty by twenty feet, crammed with stoves, ovens, refrigerators, and freezers. It seemed clean enough, though the insufficient lighting didn't stretch to the back corners. Every surface, as in most industrial kitchens, seemed to be coated with a layer or four of decade-old grease. Two giggling cooks stacked plastic quart containers in a freezer, while an older woman who didn't appear to have anything to smile about scrubbed a stove.

Dr. Palmer said, "As you can see, it's not remotely adequate for a facility this size. Justin is working on our proposed budget and writing in a special capital expenditure to expand and update the kitchen—Justin Quintero, my assistant director. I've tasked the poor boy with getting every dime he can out of the state. We don't even have GFI-protected outlets in here, so every week I'm on the roof resetting the breaker. And, more importantly, how can we teach these kids about proper nutrition when we don't have enough refrigerator space to store fresh fruits and vegetables? They're getting way too much starch now and at least one-third of them are technically obese."

The cooks had straightened up in a hurry upon seeing their boss, and stowed the last of the containers. They had not seen Rachael at all that day, but knew exactly who she was—the one who did nothing, complained about everything, and flounced around as if she were a long-lost princess waiting only for her true identity to be revealed.

The microwave stopped humming, beeped, and the older woman removed a coffee cup from it. She visibly inhaled the scent of reheated caffeine and it stimulated her enough to add, "These kids are put on different custodial duties for two weeks at a time. Yesterday when she left she said she wouldn't be back, but she was supposed to have today yet."

"Did you ask her what she meant?" Riley inquired.

"Wasn't that interested."

"Was she angry? Upset?"

One of the cooks said, "No, she said it like you'd tell your boss you need next Tuesday off. We just ignored her."

"You should hear some of the excuses these kids come up with," the other one put in.

"And you didn't see her at all today?"

All three shook their heads in unison.

"Did she complain about anything in particular the last couple of days? Especially yesterday?"

The two younger cooks exchanged a glance. "What, you think she killed herself?"

"You don't?"

Put on the spot, one said, "I don't know. I guess I didn't think of it like that—she never seemed serious about her griping. She never seemed serious about anything. She said her father was going to come and get her and they were moving to Montreal."

"Like, Canada?"

"Yeah. I asked once if that was where she was from but she said no. She didn't seem to know it was in another country, just liked the name. I told her it was cold there and that stumped her for a while, but then she said, 'Well, I'll buy me a fur coat.'"

"Brainless little brat," the older woman said, without rancor. "Most of them are. Sad."

The cook who had found the body had gone into the hallway to check the dumbwaiter for dirty dishes. She didn't even know if there had been any, or if there were now. It might be weeks before she stepped into that hallway again, she added to the older woman in a warning tone. The older woman's expression gave nothing away, certainly not the promise of temporary light duty.

She hadn't seen or heard another person in the hallway at any time. She'd exited the kitchen, seen Rachael, and screamed. The two other cooks had alerted Dr. Palmer, and there her involvement had ended.

They thanked the kitchen staff and followed Dr. Palmer to the exit. As he opened the door to the street he said, "I hate to be callous, but does this have to be in the paper? Or on the news? We have an appropriations hearing coming up in Columbus and this tragedy would not help. Firebird Center is unique in the area and—"

"The report is public record, but other than that we don't alert the media," Riley assured him.

"Oh, good," he said. "It really is regrettable about Rachael."

He said this with sincerity. Then he gently shut the door, leaving them on the sidewalk.

"So the dad was going to bust out of jail, rescue her,

and they'd make a run for the border together," Jack summed up to Riley in a quiet tone.

"Yeah, but was that her plan or her father's?"

Maggie drew deep breaths of September air. Somewhere on the other side of tall buildings, the sun had reached the horizon, turning the streets to a misty dark. The Firebird Center provided a caring, intelligent, and above all safe place for children with bad histories to heal and hopefully progress toward a constructive and happy life. A good place. But still a prison place, and no one inside wanted to be there.

"What do you think?" Jack asked her as Riley checked his phone. "She took a swan dive onto the concrete?"

"Could have. She could have thought her life had gotten too messed up to ever fix. Or she tried to balance on the bannister."

He snorted. "Why on earth would she do that?"

"Because even though she'd seen and done more than any person should, she was still a kid. And that's the kind of thing kids do."

"You can't examine anything . . . test anything. . . ."

She couldn't help smiling as she shook her head. "No, Jack. Forensics can tell you she went over the railing. It can't tell you why."

He stared up at the building, not at all satisfied with this answer.

Neither was she.

From the conversation area, Trina watched them go, feeling both relief and apprehension at their departure. Relief because they were done asking questions, and she hated answering questions. Apprehension because they were the cops. Cops were supposed to protect people, right? This entire facility was sort of an extension of the cops, the state, the court, and yet no one had protected Rachael.

Which meant no one would protect her.

Chapter 5

Friday

Rick Gardiner, Maggie's ex-husband, sat at his desk in the homicide unit, staring into space. Not an unusual position for him, but whereas he usually thought on the Indians' chances for a pennant this year or what to have for dinner, this time he considered one of his open cases: the vigilante murders, in which several of Cleveland's worst had been summarily executed by an unknown killer. Rick had no problem with said killer's choice of victim, which ranged from a murderous human trafficker to a woman running an illegal and torturous mockery of a nursing home. But he did have a problem with the case being dumped in his lap. The killer seemed to have moved on, dooming the investigation to failure, and the chief didn't want the open file to ruin the clearance rate of the detectives he liked. Why not let the high-profile disaster whittle Rick's record instead? Fabulous.

Mostly due to a pesky but hot reporter who tended

to share her information without noticing she didn't get much in return, Rick had followed up on the vigilante's final victim, the woman guilty of severe elder abuse and murder. She had apparently operated, under various names, in Phoenix, Chicago, Atlanta, and maybe Detroit. And in these same cities there had been unsolved execution-type murders. Rick couldn't decide what that meant. The woman's motive had been purely financial, and the vigilante's motive seemed to be purely, well, altruistic, for want of a better word. Why they coincided in so many places could only mean the vigilante had been pursuing her and chronically failing. Until they reached Cleveland.

Rick had thought he'd had a lead in Phoenix, but it hadn't panned out. Officially. But he couldn't quite let it go.

He picked up the phone and dialed a homicide detective in the Valley of the Sun. The guy answered on the first ring and Rick wondered if his luck had finally hit an upswing. "Daley."

Rick reintroduced himself and reminded him of the conversation they had had about a vigilante's actions in the Maryvale precinct.

"Yeah," the detective said, not so chatty this time around. With the three-hour time difference between Ohio and Arizona he had probably just walked in, wanted to check his e-mail and get a cup of coffee before starting his day. Did guys drink coffee in such a hot climate?

Daley said, "You sent me a sketch for the little girl who got a look at who might be your vigilante guy, the one who killed our coyote–slash–child molester. But she said no, not him. What else . . . ?" He didn't finish, too polite to ask, *What the hell do you want now?*

"I'm just . . . I wanted to ask. . . ." Rick knew what he wanted to ask but couldn't think of a discreet way to word it. Finally, he abandoned that better part of valor. "Did you guys ever have a guy named Jack Renner working for you?"

"Working for—you mean a cop?"

"Yeah."

Detective Daley gave this a quick mull. "Doesn't ring a bell with me, and I'm coming up on my twenty. Was he with Phoenix PD? Or the county—Maricopa Sheriff's Office?"

"I don't know."

Again, a short silence. Somebody asking questions about a crime or a suspect was one thing; someone inquiring about a fellow cop, even one he didn't know, hit the pavement on a whole different stretch of road. Of course a cop also did the inquiring, but still— "Why?"

I don't know that either, Rick thought. *I only know that Renner said he'd never been in Arizona and then used the same term you had, which is apparently native to that area. Oh, and I think he's got something going with my ex-wife. She says no, my partner says no, everybody says no, but I see a vibe going on between them that is more than "Hey, did this latent print match my suspect?" That means any trouble I can make for Jack Renner is a good thing.*

As long as it doesn't make trouble for me as well.

"Long story," he told Daley. "But I heard he may have worked a case that fits with mine. I wanted to ask him about it."

"Oh. Okay. When would that have been?"

"Around the same time as that coyote was killed."

"Well, I had already been in homicide for, what, fifteen years by then and I've never heard of him. If he was county you'll have to call them."

"Okay . . . could you check with your HR? He might have been on the road"—meaning regular patrol officers or "beat cops"—"or special ops, who knows."

"Sure," Daley said without enthusiasm. "I'll get back to you."

"Thanks," Rick said, let Daley get to his coffee or Coke or whatever the hell you drink in the mornings when it's a hundred degrees outside. Was he, Rick, really thinking of a fellow cop as a suspect in the vigilante murders? And if Renner did it, did he even want to know? Only the scum of the earth had been killed, the same people a jury would have sentenced to lethal injection if given half a chance. Did Rick really want to be the guy who fingered another cop, dragged the whole department through the mud, put Cleveland on CNN in the worst way possible?

But did he want to let a case he could solve sit on his books, making him look like an idiot? Leaving Renner free to sniff around Maggie?

His partner, Will, returned from the copy machine, and noticed Rick's hand still resting on the desk phone. "What'cha working on?"

"Nothing," Rick said.

That morning Jack and Riley returned to the Firebird Center to speak with Rachael Donahue's therapist, who looked, Jack thought, like a therapist. Dr. Melanie Szabo's graying hair fell to her waist, lavender eyeshadow framed eyes the color of faded jeans, and an ankle-length multicolored skirt adorned with looping patterns and sequins gave a splash of color to the tan walls. The death of her patient gave her the sniffles and she held a lace-trimmed handkerchief to her nose, clutching a nearly empty water bottle in the other. Jack expected her to smell of patchouli, but instead caught a whiff of something floral, sweet, and expensive.

They spoke in a tiny conference room used for legal counsel, off the main visitor's area on the second floor with nothing but a small table, a few chairs, and a blue recycling bin. The staff preferred to keep the officers away from the residents, which suited Jack. After speaking to Rachael's peers the prior evening he didn't see any need to revisit that particular lioness's den. But Melanie Szabo, through her sniffles, praised their discretion. "You know how it is! Any disruption to the routine spreads out like ripples in a lake. The teachers have a hard enough time getting traumatized and suffering children to concentrate on lessons. It's so important to try to keep them on pace with others their age. Delinquency and academic failure are joined at the hip."

She probably began every session that way, Jack thought, by telling the other person something good about themselves. Smart, as far as it goes, as long as she doesn't devolve into one of those types who believe the answer to all childhood ills is good self-esteem. The "ill" children he encountered seemed to have way too much esteem for themselves already, and none for anyone else.

"Tell us about Rachael," Riley began.

Szabo did not hesitate, showed no concerns about patient confidentiality—not when her patient had died and had no one else in the world to speak for her. "She was not suicidal. Not at all. She seemed determined to attack the world and carve out a place for herself in it. Fierce, I call it. But not in a good way."

"What does that mean?" Riley asked, as usual ready to sit and listen for as long as it took to learn something helpful. He had so much more patience than his partner, Jack thought.

She tucked her hair behind both ears and talked with her hands, the handkerchief fluttering from one set of fingers only to be plucked by the other as from a magician's wand. "These kids are here because their lives have gotten out of control. Their own control as well as society's. They have been raped, beaten, drugged, abused, and neglected to the point that they finally pushed back. Most detention facilities—in the name of protecting society from these violent predators—simply isolate them further at the one point in their life where they desperately need connections and support. That does not help *anyone*. All it does is shove the kid farther down the spiral, almost guaranteeing that they will wind up behind bars for a good portion of their adult life. This isn't bleeding heart talk. Crunch the numbers and you'll see that it's a whole lot less expensive to pay for a couple years of intensive therapy and intervention instead of decades of incarceration. The reality is, in 2001 serious juvenile crime rates were essentially the same as they had been in 1981, but the number of youths confined in juvenile residential facilities doubled. *Doubled.* Society doesn't need to be protected from these kids. The kids need to be protected from society. Protected from us."

Dr. Szabo might appear to be an aging flower child, but she talked as fast as a day trader.

"So we've heard," Jack said.

"Punishment doesn't work. Programs that focus on interpersonal skills and anger management do. Behavioral training, like stress inoculation. Positive reinforcement with graduated sanctions. Basically, we have to teach them *morality*. It's an old-fashioned word and an old-fashioned concept, but like all fundamental truths we eventually come back to it. Caring about other human beings is where all civility begins and it's a learned response that we have to teach."

"Because their parents didn't," Riley said.

"Nine times out of ten, yes. Their parents didn't. Sometimes they're abusive, often they're too wasted to notice they even have a child, or alternatively they want to be the kid's best buddy instead of their parent. They let day cares, schools, and prisons teach their kids what they should have been teaching them."

"And Rachael?" Riley prompted.

"Rachael," she said, nodding to concede that she had gotten off topic. "All these kids want is someone to tell them that they have value, that they matter, and we have to do that first. Only then can we get into what's been done to them and what they've done to others. We have to acknowledge their pain—this isn't coddling. It isn't being all touchy feely and agreeing that they couldn't help taking a knife to their mother."

"I get that," Riley soothed.

"You try to get it, I see. Your partner doesn't."

Jack cleared his throat. "I understand that they've been through a lot."

"A lot? Some of the things I've seen and heard in this place give me nightmares. Anyway, what we try to do here, above all, is be honest. About what has been done to them as well as vice versa. I needed Rachael to talk about her mother, what she remembered of her. Her father, her grandfather. Who ought to be boiled in oil as far as I'm concerned, but that's a topic for another discussion." She gave them a wry smile. "*Then* we would move on to Rachael's violence. The fights, the threats, the kids she stabbed. Because we *do* need them to take responsibility for their actions. Need them to acknowledge that what they've been through may be a reason but it's not an excuse."

"And Rachael?" Riley repeated.

"Nowhere. I got nowhere. Nothing but bravado and arrogance—which isn't such a bad coping mechanism. It's better than cutting or clinical depression. But I needed her to stop coping and start dealing. In a safe place where you have support, that's where it's time to start dealing.

"She refused to speak of her grandfather, other than to say she wished she'd killed him. Can't blame her for that. But she also professed no interest in her absentee mother or her dad in jail. All she would say about the kids she'd killed was, 'They deserved it.' I'm used to kids stonewalling, arguing, manipulating. They don't understand subtlety at that age and they're not super good at reading faces—though these kids are better than most, since their survival often depends on it—

but they're still kids. So if one tactic doesn't work they veer into another, obvious as hell. I didn't worry at first, with Rachael. There's always a testing period, waiting to see if I'll be judgmental. If I'll tell them they're bad seeds. If I have the slightest clue what I'm talking about. If I can be easily conned. If I give a shit."

"If you'll stick," Jack said.

She beamed at him as if he were a student showing unexpected improvement. "Exactly. I go in knowing it's going to be a process to bond. Without a strong bond to an adult the kid isn't going to make progress. It's as simple as that. Some take days to trust me, to start really talking. Some take weeks, some take months. I figured Rachael for the latter."

Jack said, "Dr. Szabo—"

"Call me Melanie. I don't stand on ceremony." She tossed the now-empty water bottle into the recycling bin, making the shot easily.

"Um, yes—what *did* Rachael talk about?"

"Not much. Better at asking questions than answering them. Was I married, how long had I been a shrink. Which exterior doors were locked, had anyone ever jumped from the basketball court—"

"You think she planned to escape?"

"All these kids plan to escape. What else do you think about when you're behind locked doors? But I told her there would be no point in running away. She'd been doing that all her life and it hadn't served her well. She didn't seem serious, just yanking my chain. But about her, her life, her goals . . . nothing. She'd sit in the chair and stare at the wall behind my head. Or she'd stare at *me*, try to freak me out. One time she got up and did a handstand against the wall, as easily as a gymnast; they're so flexible at that age. Stayed a minute, then let her feet fall, then retook her seat as if nothing had happened. Kids do a lot of wild things in therapy—that was a new one."

Riley said, "She carried a gold ring in her pocket. Did she tell you who that belonged to?"

Szabo's eyes widened slightly. "No. I never saw anything like that. She didn't mention it."

"Was she close to her father?"

"Didn't talk about him, as I said. I asked, she ignored me. I asked when he would get out, she shrugged. I asked if that meant she didn't know or didn't care. She shrugged again." Szabo gave them a rueful smile and her shoulders sank a bit. "See what I mean? Therapy hadn't been especially productive for Rachael. I figured it would take time. I figured we *had* time."

Jack asked, "Where is her grandfather now?"

"Jail. Permanently, or at least for all intents and purposes. The judge gave him twenty, which at his age is a death sentence. Hooray hooray. Five years too late for Rachael, though."

Jack couldn't think of anything else to ask. Riley finished up with, "Is there anything else you can think of that we ought to know?"

Melanie Szabo thought, frowned, thought again. "Only that I'd like to think Rachael had a chance. A chance to leave the violence behind. A chance to heal all those wounds and get a decent life for herself. What we would call a 'normal' life. Everyone deserves normal. But you know, I don't think that ever would have happened. I would never say a kid is a lost cause . . . but after years and years of working with these kids every day, you get a feeling. Instinct. I don't think Rachael would have ever achieved 'normal.' The damage was just too great." She teared up again. "Poor kid."

Chapter 6

Assistant Director Quintero found them a different small counseling/legal services room to interview Luis Borgia. The day students, he explained, were kids who had been kicked out of public schools and had legal procedures pending. Some were chronic runaways, and some had committed nonviolent offenses. Most had technical violations, parole offenses, curfew breaking, truancy, explained the slim young man. Justin Quintero was a dark-skinned guy of about thirty-five with the cheekbones of a *GQ* model. He stood in the separate entrance area for day program students, on the south side of the building. Teaching staff checked each day student in every morning and out every night. Over twelve would be given breakfast and lunch in the visiting areas with the residents in their age groups, with therapy sessions carved out from study times. After classes ended they would leave the building and go home to, one hoped, their families.

"There's no need to put these kids in custody. Their acting out is always—*always*—a cry for attention, and if we respond by isolating them, well, that just starts the downward spiral. These late teens, early twenties are when kids usually grow out of delinquency even without intervention, so—sorry, I'm lecturing." He checked in the final youngster, who appeared to be about six to Jack, but he tended to underestimate ages. Every person had begun looking young to him. Rookie cops didn't seem old enough to date a girl, much less carry a gun.

He and Riley walked with Quintero as he escorted the under-twelve group from the entrance foyer to their separate breakfast area. The teens were left on their own, but since all restricted areas were locked they'd be safely funneled to their classes. Quintero herded the very young ones with an ease born of practice, and indeed, they seemed to be a fairly typical group of kids, energetic and griping at the same time. One demanded to know what they'd be having for breakfast and proclaimed that it had better not be eggs. Another pointed out that eggs were baby chickens and that was gross. A girl said the eggs weren't baby chickens and never would be so it wasn't gross as long as they were cooked, because that "got all the germs out." A little boy with dark shadows under his eyes said nothing at all. A little girl with stiff pigtails talked quietly to herself.

After they'd been turned over to the under-twelve unit, Quintero guided the cops back. The building could be confusing, Jack saw. There were so many rooms, an intake office, a shower/locker room for incoming residents—no doubt where they had washed the blood off Rachael Donahue upon her arrival—an infirmary with two beds (now empty), and a room storing new clothing in a large range of sizes, should it be needed. Three separate large rooms, resembling inexpensive hotel lobbies, for family meetings (even for parties, Quintero explained, so an extended family group could have a private area). Many small rooms used interchangeably for lawyers or counselors. A tiny break room with lockers for staff. An industrial kitchen with heavy locks on its doors to be opened only by kitchen staff or administrators (liability, Quintero explained, because of the heating elements and cutlery—not because the county worried that the night nurse might make off with a box of English muffins).

Jack said, "I thought most of the resident kids had committed violent crimes. Isn't there a worry putting the regular—I mean sort of regular—students with—"

"No. Well . . . it's not that simple. Not all residents have had violent incidents, and some day program kids have. A few residents have nowhere else to go and are here for a few days pending assignment to a foster home. Some of the day kids have committed assault or robbery, but their home situation is relatively stable and they're pending adjudication. Out on bail, in other words."

Juveniles weren't "convicted" when found guilty of a crime, they were "adjudicated." And then they weren't put in jail, they were put in detention, and usually only for a few months to a year. For offenses committed before age eighteen, they could be held only until they turned twenty-one.

Quintero said, "Our main focus with the day students is to keep them *out* of custody and instead work on their mental health and their family's parenting abilities. If all goes as it should they may stay out of jail permanently. Meanwhile they're closely monitored and can keep up with their schooling, which is another reason to do everything to keep these kids out of the usual incarceration—the late teens are when the brain is most primed to learn critical thinking and decision making. Slapping them in jail where they'll get a rudimentary and regimented education is just dooming them for life."

He found them an available counseling room and ushered them inside, still talking. "We work very hard to find exceptional teachers. Usually no one is jumping at a chance to teach at a juvenile detention facility, but once they get here they find it better than the average public school. We give our teachers above average pay and every administrative support we can to retain them, and to spread the word."

"What's this kid's story?" Riley asked.

"Luis? Runaway. His mother's boyfriend was, let's say, *problematic*. To avoid going home Luis would hang out with lowlifes, where he racked up a few minor drug charges. But his parole officer got Children and Family Services involved, his mother kicked the boyfriend out, and she and Luis are trying to make better choices. He misses his stepbrother, but otherwise he's been doing well here." As he shut the door he added, "Very well."

Jack finished the unspoken warning: "So we shouldn't screw him back up."

Riley slapped his notebook on the small table. "If they don't salvage these kids, it won't be for lack of conviction."

The lavender walls held no decoration except a poster of a beach with crystal-clear water, framed with lightweight plastic. Worn but clean carpeting reached the walls. No windows. "The tables are all round here. Did you notice that?"

Riley nodded. "More inclusive. Less confrontational. Plus kids won't stumble and hit their head on a corner."

"They're teens, not toddlers."

"Yeah, I know, but that mind-set . . . it never really goes away. I still hesitate when I set the table for the girls. Is Hannah old enough for a serrated knife?" Riley, divorced, made every effort to stay in his daughters' lives.

"Must be tough when you grill steaks."

"I'm a cop," Riley said. "Who can afford steaks?"

Luis Borgia studied the two men. The tall one looked tough, kind of like his stepfather but with even more muscle to back it up. The shorter one could easily be outrun—Luis had outrun a lot of cops, and felt confident in this assessment. But for once he didn't have to. For once he could talk to cops with nothing to hide, no reason to worry. That was weird.

And he still worried a little, of course.

White guys. He knew they looked at his dark hair and olive skin and put him in a category somewhere below black guys and bikers. This made him angry. Most things made him angry.

Justin Quintero said, "Here is Luis. He said he's okay with talking to you without me in the room, so I'll leave you to it."

The guy ducked out like his pants were on fire and shut the door, leaving Luis behind.

He took a seat without waiting to be asked, feeling it important to establish that he wasn't nobody's bitch and wasn't going to be pushed around, not this time.

They were good-cop, bad-copping him, the big one just staring at him, arms crossed, and the little one being all friendly and shit. Luis's brother Esteban had clued him in to this technique. He wished Esteban would be at home to rehash this with, but he had had to leave with his *hijo de puta* father.

Meanwhile the short one, he gave Luis their names, some blah blah blah that Luis didn't listen to. The guy even apologized for interrupting his school day, as if Luis were so concerned about his grades that he might worry about missing algebra. The idea made Luis laugh, but he stifled the smirk. Guys usually hit you when you smirked. His stepfather always had.

He wondered how Esteban was getting on now that he didn't have Luis and his mom to absorb his father's blows. Luis had begged the social workers to keep an eye on the kid. They said they would but Luis didn't believe them. Without an adult making a complaint, Esteban would be on his own.

He forced his mind back to the present. *No one is going to hit you here*, his healthy brain said.

That might be what the docs say, his not-healthy parts argued, *but they ain't in this room now, are they? And these cops know they're free to question you without a parent or guardian present and without reading your Miranda rights because you're not arrested or in custody*. Though of course he *was* in custody while in the day program, as he had been required to attend by a judge's order and his movements were supervised. Either way, he'd better be careful.

But unless these guys were idiots they had already checked with the teachers and found that Luis had been gone from the building before Rachael left the dorm unit and therefore couldn't have had anything to do with her death. Even if he *could* have somehow gotten to the northwest stairwell when all the day program areas were concentrated in the east and south parts of the building. So he had nothing to worry about.

And he did want to know what had happened to Rachael. If one of those other bitches had pushed her—

"Did you see Rachael yesterday?"

"Yes."

The short one asked about her "state of mind." He told them, "She seemed fine. I mean, normal. Complained about the homework, said the bitch—oh, sorry, that's what we call her—"

"That's okay," Riley assured him. "I had teachers I didn't like when I went to school, too."

Thinking of this old guy as a person his age made Luis smile. "Rachael said having to read a whole chapter was bullshit and she didn't do it. She never did her homework, really. I started because my mom makes me now—anyway, I sat by her at breakfast and she told me about the new *Star Wars* movie. She'd read about it in the paper. They get newspapers in residence because they want you to be aware of what's going on in the world. But they don't like girl magazines, 'cause they say they're unrealistic—which I guess they are. But Rachael'd read the paper a lot. She hated school but she wasn't stupid—she knew a *lot* of stuff. She was . . . cool."

He was talking too much. They could probably see that he'd wanted in Rachael's pants since they were ten, before he even knew what girls *had* in their pants. He'd had girlfriends since, but Rachael had always been more than that. She'd been a *friend*, not just a girlfriend. And it sucked that the state took her away and made her live with that dirtbag of a grandfather.

"How did you and Rachael meet?" the cop asked.

"We lived in the same building when we were kids. On Thirty-Seventh. That was before her dad went to jail. He'd been in jail a few times but just for, like, a couple weeks. He didn't tell anyone about Rachael so she'd stay by herself until he came back."

"How old was she then?"

"Seven, eight, I think. We're the same age. I'm two and a half months older. She'd come over when she got hungry and my mom would take care of her." They would play on the monkey bars at the end of the street, walk to the ratty school, and try to lift candy from the 7-Eleven but the old guy there always caught them. He'd hide in her apartment when his real dad beat up his mother, thinking he could still hear her crying through three apartments of walls, hating himself for not protecting her. But Rachael convinced him not to, that it would just make his dad more angry, that he would just get hurt as well. She used to hang on his arm to keep him from leaving.

That was why he had healthy parts of him, and unhealthy parts. Seeing his mother bleed and not be able to get out of bed for days and, later, take up with another man who did exactly the same thing had created unhealthy parts. Those parts made him angry all the time and made him yell at his mother and take drugs and beat up other kids who didn't want to buy the ones he sold. The unhealthy parts weren't his fault but they were his responsibility.

The healthy parts of him were the ones that wanted to take care of his mom, that liked playing baseball, that were smart enough to know he needed to get a real job someday so he'd better graduate from high school. Every day he learned more how to listen to the healthy parts and not the other ones. When Dr. Szabo first told him about the parts he thought it was stupid, something you'd tell little kids, but then he began to see how it explained a lot of things. It made sense. Luis liked things to make sense.

"And then her dad went to jail for a long time?" the short one asked.

"Yeah. I tried to get my mom to adopt her but she said we couldn't, the court wouldn't give her to us with my dad's record." Though he knew it didn't have anything to do with her numerous domestic violence reports—she just didn't want another mouth to feed; the relationship between him and his mother remained a work in progress.

He had found Rachael again only to lose her permanently—another reason sadness gripped his heart. "They sent Rachael to her grandfather, who was a—" He couldn't think of a word bad enough to do justice to Rachael's violation.

"Yes, we know. So the next time you saw Rachael—"

"Here, in class. When she got here a couple weeks ago."

"Since that time have you seen her outside this building?"

Was this guy stupid? "No. She can't leave. The residents can't leave. It's a jail." *Duh*.

"What did she say about being here, at Firebird?"

"Hated it," Luis admitted immediately. "Hated the food, hated the classes, hated the other kids. She kind of liked her room, though."

"Really? Why?"

"It had a door. All Rachael wanted was to find a place where she could live alone, without anyone else. I think that's why she talked to me." Luis watched his fingers, clasped in his lap. "I think, like, the best time in her life was when her dad went away and nobody knew about her and she could just live in her apartment by herself. Do whatever she wanted, go where she wanted."

"Sure," snorted the big one, "until the building shut the utilities off and she ran out of food."

"She was ten," Luis reminded him. *Idiota.*

"Did she get along with the other girls?" the short one asked.

"No. I mean, she thought they were lame." Rachael thought everyone was lame, except him. Kinda except him.

"Any fights? Beefs?"

"Nah. I think she shoved someone when she first got here, but that wasn't nothing. She pretty much ignored them." The other girls, he meant. Not the boys.

"What about the staff?"

Luis gave him a shrug, the universal kid gesture to demonstrate *don't know and/or don't care and/or that's not important.* "She didn't say nothing."

"Ms. Washington?"

"Called her a bitch, too. But nothing, you know, *specific.*"

"She carried a gold ring in her pocket. Do you know who that belonged to?"

"Huh? No. I—I didn't know she had . . ." *From some guy? Or had she stolen it? Knowing Rachael—* "Look, what *happened* to her? Why did she fall?"

"That's what we're trying to find out."

Luis didn't think they were doing much of a job, but he didn't say so. They were trying (his healthy parts said), so he should help them. If Rachael had a ring from a boyfriend she would have shown it to him. That would be Rachael. "She probably stole it. She must have done a few burglaries, maybe a lot. Everyone does."

"Everyone?" the one guy pressed.

"Yeah. Everyone." Luis felt the anger welling up. Rachael had helped his loneliness for his absent stepbrother and now she was gone, too, and the adults were as clueless as ever. "You . . . you don't get it."

"Get what?"

"What it's like being from my generation."

"That's a lot of syllables," the big one muttered. The little one frowned at him. The bad-cop/good-cop thing again, which didn't fool Luis one bit.

He said, "You don't get that every day we go to school and wonder if somebody's going to shoot us. Maybe over drugs or girls or money or maybe for the hell of it, like those psychos who bring AK-47s and try to kill all the jocks. You want us to focus on getting good grades and following the rules and living up to our potential, but for us, we're just trying to stay alive."

That shut them up for a minute. Then the big one said, "Morality and survival are sometimes mutually exclusive."

Luis studied his face for signs of sarcasm, but he didn't seem to be yanking Luis's chain. "Yeah. That's it."

After that they let him go, gave him a card and said that if he thought of anything else he should call. Luis threw the card out in the visitor's area before returning to class—if he got jumped on the way home he wouldn't want to look like a snitch. If he thought of anything he could tell a teacher to get hold of them but doubted that would be necessary. They would write Rachael off as another bad kid and forget about her. No point getting angry about it, that was just the way it was.

It occurred to him that he had talked to cops without being, or getting, in trouble. He hadn't gotten in a fight and they hadn't threatened him with juvie. Maybe Dr. Szabo was right.

Maybe his healthy parts *were* winning.

Outside on the sidewalk Jack drew a deep breath. "We done?"

"I think so. Autopsy said no drugs, no weird bruises. No one heard a scream or saw an argument. Doing a headstand in therapy. You think she was fooling around on the railing and fell?"

"It makes more sense than anything else. She didn't sound suicidal or even depressed."

"Their moods turn on a dime at that age, though," Riley said. He waved to a motorcycle cop cruising by, eyed a hot dog cart across the street, and then plopped into the driver's seat of their assigned car. Jack settled opposite him. "I speak from experience. And not that it's a consideration but it doesn't do anyone any good to have her go down as a suicide, least of all those kids in there. Suicide can be contagious."

"More things point to accident anyway. She'd been cocky, forward looking, possibly athletic, and not interested in kitchen duty. It's a lot easier to picture her deciding to fool around on the bannisters instead of figuring out that she'd never dig herself out of the sinkhole life had thrown her into."

"Yeah. I'll tell the ME we're good with death from misadventure. I'm sure they'll agree. Ready for lunch? That hot dog smell got me going."

Jack said sure, glancing up at the stone building as they pulled away. He didn't expect a return visit to the Firebird Center anytime soon.

As usual, he was wrong.

Chapter 7

Monday

Maggie taped one end of a bright pink string to the wall, rubbing the piece of duct tape to be sure the string's end wouldn't escape. Then she dabbed a chunk of the tape to the other end and held it out—gently—with one hand while holding a protractor to the wall with the other. When the extended string made an angle of thirty-two degrees she attached the free end to a vertical metal rod protruding upward from a heavy metal base, making sure the angle stayed at thirty-two. All was well for a moment, but then the end taped to the wall snaked through its duct tape anchor and fell to the floor. Maggie breathed out a quiet and uncharacteristic swear word.

"This is the part they never show you on TV," her boss, Denny, agreed. He used a disposable pipette to douse a different section of the wall with Amido Black, trying to darken a pair of bloody handprints. The Amido Black would turn the red ridges to a deep black. If the friction ridge patterns were clear enough to com-

pare and didn't belong to the victim, they had to belong to the killer.

Maggie used the protractor again and retaped the
string. "That's because on TV they have cool lasers and
foggers and a set of twenty-five tripods and they do it all
in high heels."

"That's your problem. You're not wearing high
heels."

"It's bad enough in boots." She sat cross-legged on
the floor in worn BDU pants and department-issue
steel-toed shoes, her back curved in a hunch to be able
to view the bloodstain directly on without skewing the
loupe's perspective. Her neck ached. The hardwood
planks hadn't been swept and certainly not washed in
months or years, but at least without carpeting she didn't
have to worry—or so she hoped—about fleas. The cockroaches had disappeared into their cracks and would
stay hidden as long as she kept moving.

She moved on to the next bloodstain, holding a
rounded plastic magnifying loupe to the red spot on the
wall. Bloodstains when they struck a surface at a less
than ninety-degree angle formed an oval shape. Divid-
ing the width of this oval by its length gave her the
angle at which the drop hit the wall. The loupe had a
built-in scale to measure with. She did the math on the
wall in pencil, next to the drop. Any new owners
would have to paint the wall anyway and a few pencil
marks would be the least of their worries compared to
all the blood and especially the Amido Black. That
stuff stained like the dickens.

Her problem lay in that after a drop hit the wall,
while most of the blood would instantly stick, momen-

tum would push the still-liquid extra bit farther to form a tail. This tail could obscure the exact end, and therefore the exact length, of the drop. Even half a millimeter changed the angle by more than a few degrees. Between this lack of precision and the duct tape and carrying the heavy rod bases up two flights of dingy apartment steps, she couldn't help thinking there had to be a better way.

Denny doused the wall again with tap water, rinsing off the excess Amido Black. It pooled in a gray mess mostly caught by a wad of paper towels at the baseboard. He made a satisfied little sound, meaning that a sufficient amount of ridge detail appeared and could be able to be compared to a suspect's known prints. The forty-year-old mother of three had been taken to the Medical Examiner's office for her final appointment with a doctor—a forensic pathologist—but with luck her blood remained to tell them who had killed her. So far everyone's bet rested on an abusive ex-husband.

"So you're back with Dr. Michaels again," Denny said.

Ping. The next string also slipped from its duct tape, possibly because Maggie's hand had twitched. "Yes. *Again.*"

"You don't have to sound so aggrieved. The department is trying to make sure you're okay with two different people nearly killing you in the past, oh, six months. Three, if you count the guy who shot at you on Euclid."

"That one doesn't count. He wasn't aiming at me," Maggie said, knowing that might not be true.

"Besides, I thought you said you liked her."

"She's a nice lady. I'm sure she's an excellent doctor, too. But I don't need her and I'm sure many people in this county do, so I hate wasting her time."

"Very altruistic of you," Denny commented, pointedly neutral.

"Okay, I hate wasting mine, too. Damn. Can't we at least get those little plastic anchors with sticky wax?"

"Tried 'em. They pull off even more easily than the tape. And before you mention lasers again remember that in order to photograph the cool lights in the cool fog we'd have to cover all the windows to get it dark in here. I know how much you love doing that when we spray luminol."

She didn't admit that, yes, by the time they did all the prep and set up all the tripods and blocked out all the light, cool lasers would take longer than the tape-and-protractor route and still be harder to photograph. But she'd rather talk about forensic equipment requests than her visits with the department shrink. Dr. Michaels seemed an excellent psychologist—certainly good enough to figure out that Maggie still kept a whole lot of things locked inside herself. And Maggie didn't need anyone getting near her with a key.

"Well, just do the mandatory. No going around that."

"Yeah, I know."

Denny squinted at the wall, his black skin glistening in the stuffy apartment. "I've got most of the interdigital here."

"Good."

"Let's hope it's his and not hers."

"The odds are good. There's no more blood in the

hallway and this is the only spray on the walls. With
that huge pool by the couch—she went down and stayed
down. She didn't stagger around the place."

"Just make the meetings," Denny said, veering between topics again. "Don't keep blowing her off like
last time."

"I won't." She could do it now. Maggie had gotten
better at maintaining the boxes in her head, allowing
only one open at a time. When she had to talk to the
good doctor she would keep certain experiences shut
and latched. Like the moment she knew the identity of
their vigilante killer. The moment a defendant died of
anaphylactic shock at his own trial while she testified
against him. The moment Jack didn't really need to kill
the man who had been strangling her, but did anyway.
The moment she, Maggie, had killed someone. She
could keep those boxes closed and separated now, she
thought.

At least most of the time.

Did this mean she had grown cynical? Cold? Numb?
Or more understanding of reality and its limitations, the
knowledge that rules that should be hard and fast weren't
so hard or so fast, when it came right down to it?

"If it's any consolation, I think you're fine, too,"
Denny said. He used a shutter cable to snap photos of
his enhanced blood print without having to touch the
camera and possibly jostle it.

"You smooth talker you."

"I mean you seem more, um—normal."

"Gee, thanks."

"I mean . . . right after the vigilante murders you
were, you seemed, pretty—spaced out. I know that really
shocked your system."

Maggie pressed a piece of tape to the drywall, focusing on the tip of her finger as it rubbed the silver backing. She had thought she'd done so well, hiding the doubts and the mad thoughts that tumbled up and down the rabbit hole, telling herself that some day her heart would stop pounding all day every day, an exhausting *thud thud thud* she thought must be audible to those around her. She had tried so hard to act, think, be utterly normal, be just like she had been every day Before even as her life now existed in After.

Denny said, "But lately you've been back to—well, just you."

His words stumbled a bit; neither of them liked to speak of personal things. When every day they saw other people's lives laid bare, the people in the forensics unit kept their own partially covered. Light things were discussed at work—the Indians, diets, in-laws, and the ever-changing weather—and that worked for them. The sunniness kept them balanced and did not lessen the fierce bond they felt that matched that of cops or soldiers or maybe teachers. Maggie, for instance, knew that she would take a bullet for Denny or Carol or Josh or Amy without regret or hesitation.

Of course this was a largely pointless concern. Forensic techs didn't arrive on the scene until long after the bullets had stopped flying. Usually. At least until she had met Jack Renner.

"Good," was all Maggie said.

Neither one of them looked up from their individual tasks.

"How's Alex?" Denny suddenly asked.

"Fine. They had a lull in the gigs so he's taking the kids to Disneyworld. He says I should join them."

Watching her two tiny nieces whirl around in teacups with their ever-patient parent would be a nice time. Dragging Alex onto Space Mountain one more time would be fun. Eating French fries while debating Belle versus Anna would be . . . *normal.*

It might also convince her brother that there was absolutely nothing wrong with her, that she had not changed in any way. She knew he had suspicions.

Denny had met her brother. "Alex at Dizzyworld. I can't picture it."

"Hey, just because he's a musician and has never owned a tie doesn't mean that he only eats raw foods and wears hemp clothing and won't let the girls watch television." Although she wasn't entirely sure about the television part.

"You should go."

"You telling me to take time off, boss?"

"Not *too* much time. But yes, I promise we'll survive without you."

She had attached enough strings to the rod to feel comfortable with their convergence point. She stood with one shoulder to the wall and photographed her witch's broom of angles, then had Denny hold up a stiff tape measure to demonstrate the distance from the wall and the distance from the floor. It seemed a perfect match to the stab wound in the prone woman's back.

"He got her here," Maggie summed up, pantomiming the killer's slash. "She crawled away and started for the kitchen, trying to escape, get out the apartment door. She fell or he struck her again here, in the middle of the room."

Denny finished, "She went down next to the couch.

Three wounds in the back, throwing these droplets onto the cushions, then she bleeds out. He stumbles toward the hallway, slaps one hand on the wall there, washes them in the bathroom sink—hence the positive phenolphthalein at the drain—and leaves the apartment."

It had taken them approximately two hours of work to establish this scenario and chances were it would prove completely useless. Knowing where the victim had been stabbed didn't tell them who stabbed her. Unless her ex-husband could be found with her blood on his clothes, or an alibi didn't check out, or some other form of additional evidence came to light, the forensic information might not help the case at all. Or he might claim self-defense and the sequence of events inside the apartment would be of great interest to both prosecution and defense. Either way, Maggie and Denny had gone through the process and reached their conclusions, and the criminal justice system would have to take it from there.

Maggie said, "Okay. I'll just swab a few of my stains and then I think we're done here. I'll have this written up in time for lunch."

Her phone rang and she checked the caller ID. "Or maybe not."

Justin Quintero met them under the admiring eye of the receptionist—admiring for him, she barely glanced at Jack and Riley—and shook their hands with a firm grip. "Detectives. I want to thank you for your discretion. So far this tragedy has stayed off the radar of the local news."

"That's not up to us." Jack didn't feel any responsibility for the Firebird Center's relationship with the media or the success of their proposed budget. The cops had returned to pick up Rachael's personal property, especially the gold ring. Her father in jail thought it might belong to him—or he wanted to scavenge any item from his daughter's life that might have street value in the event of his release. Either way the county prosecutor had been trying to make a deal for his testimony against his coconspirator on an armed robbery charge, and thought that a goodwill gesture on the part of the police might tip the scales toward cooperation. The homicide chief, whose only talent lay in schmoozing the power structure, did not want to miss an opportunity to do a favor for the prosecutor. *So now we're bloody couriers*, Jack thought.

Justin Quintero said, "I know, but still—we're fighting for these kids as hard as we can, and any misstep could give the state a reason to nickel-and-dime us. Not that Rachael's death is a misstep, of course. It's a great pity." He guided them up the hallway, but at the next door a small brown force threw it open and barreled out, running straight into Jack.

"Damon!" A woman in white scrubs pursued, so Jack grabbed what felt like shoulders, their tiny bones shifting under the skin. The kid formed a blur, all arms hitting and legs kicking—capable of some force, as Jack's shins found out the hard way.

"I guess he's feeling better," Quintero noted.

The nurse wrestled her young charge back into the room, apologizing to Jack as she did so.

"That's okay," he said. "We've met."

Quintero shook his head. "That one's always going

to be limited. All the therapy in the world can't fix a background like that."

They continued on toward the stairwell.

Riley said, "Mr. Quintero—"

"It's Doctor, actually, but I try not to put on airs. Justin will do fine."

"I hate to be a wuss, but doesn't this place have elevators? My back is killing me. I spent two hours last night putting together a bookcase for—um, a bookcase."

"This is a very old building. An elevator was added, but it's on the other side of the building. Strictly for staff only and operated by keys, which we all have."

"The kids have to walk, huh?"

"Aside from the few disabled ones we have, yes. They need the exercise—not easy to get, cooped up in one city block. And of course we don't want them anywhere where they can't be observed."

Jack asked, as they reached the staircase, "When are your cameras going to be operational?"

He expelled air with an audible *pfft*. "Good question. Dr. Palmer asks every day. But when you have to go with the lowest bidder, sometimes you get the lowest results—that's why he needs me. We're trying to construct a first-class facility here with a fourth-class budget. Let me give you some background."

Let's not, Jack thought to himself.

"Youth crime began skyrocketing during the eighties. People panicked that we'd have roving bands of wilding teenagers by the nineties, and built all sorts of juvenile detention facilities. Then despite all predictions in 1990 the juvenile crime rate began to fall. But society believes what it believes regardless of facts and the number of kids in custodial settings doubled."

"We heard that from Dr. Szabo," Jack said, to hurry him along.

"Cool. Now a chunk of these kids were incarcerated for technical offenses, things like parole violation and public misdemeanors. States all over the country built megajails for juveniles, except for Missouri, which somehow figured out long before the rest of its neighbors that smaller, local facilities are much more effective for turning kids around and reducing recidivism. Taking a kid halfway across the state to lock him up with no one else except other incorrigibles to socialize with only turned them *less* law abiding, not more."

One flight down, the woman in white scrubs hurried along with a tiny black girl, the woman explaining in a breathless voice, "She was tryin' to catch the ball an' it hit her finger and bent it way back and she thinks it broke—"until the *clang* of an exterior door cut her off.

The noise covered the sound of the phone in Jack's back pocket vibrating. The phone that wasn't issued by the police department—the burner phone bought with cash with a number that could never be traced to him. The phone he used to look up places and people he would never be able to explain away to a board of inquiry or a jury. The phone Riley had seen on occasion but never commented on, assuming that Jack used it to text another man's wife or the chief's daughter, or someone equally scandalous. Just as Jack never verbally observed that Riley had bought several new shirts lately, changed his aftershave, and apparently started going to a professional barber instead of the vocational school shop. All these things heralded a new girlfriend, but Jack didn't ask. If he asked for a confidence, one might be expected in return.

"All locking kids up does," Quintero was saying, "is makes them more likely to get locked up in the future. So the pendulum began to swing the other way. In 2008 Ohio had eight major custodial juvenile detention facilities. Today we have three. This is a good thing, keeping secure placement only for the most violent and serious offenders—except that there're still forty-five hundred juveniles adjudicated for felony offenses every year. We're at maximum occupation every minute. *Every* minute. Hence, the dog and pony show next week to convince Fiscal Operations to give us more money, so that we can be a properly secured and effective facility instead of a Cracker Jack box with only two working cameras."

"I'm going to use the men's room," Jack announced, his voice echoing slightly in the deep stairwell. "I'll catch up."

"It's back by the reception room—" Quintero began, but Jack had already turned. He heard the young man explaining to Riley how DORC budgeting staff would be coming to see how well they'd done with the miniscule budget they had, and hear how much better they could do with something like realistic funding.

Once ensconced in the narrow hallway by the entry door, he checked the Missed Calls log. A Phoenix area code.

He returned the call. When a woman answered, he said, "Emma."

"None other," Emma replied. "What's up, cuz?"

Jack sidled over to be able to see into the reception area. Empty except for the administrative assistant working busily at her keyboard. He sidled back before she noticed him. "Not much. What's up with you?"

"*Why are you whispering?* I can barely hear you."

"I'm in a prison and I don't have much time."

"Wait, you did just say you're in *a* prison, right, not *in* prison? Because those imply two very different situations."

"What do you want, Emma?"

"Well, sorry. I tried to soften the blow, but if you're in such a hurry—Giles died."

"Oh." His father's brother. Giles had taken him fishing, loaned him well-worn Zane Grey books—which Jack had only skimmed, though even at twelve he appreciated the gesture—and taught him how to make chili. "I'm sorry to hear that."

"The funeral's on Wednesday."

"I'll try to make it."

His cousin gave a snort. "Like you tried to make Aunt Betty's ninetieth? Or my daughter's wedding?"

"I'm sorry." *I'm sorry, but I left my old life behind when I started this . . . this . . . and that includes the people in it. I can't bring my darkness into a circle of good, decent human beings who still believe I'm the man they used to know.* "But things are really busy here."

"How is San Francisco?"

"Hilly and expensive. Emma, I have to go. Give Bethany and Frank my love."

"All right. But seriously, cuz—just think about it, okay? No one has seen you for so long. What did you do, join the CIA? Are you waterboarding terrorists at Gitmo or something?"

"No . . . no. I'll try, but right now I have to go.

Sorry." He hung up before she could play any more of the family guilt card. Because it might work. He *did* have a family, people who had given him birthday gifts and attended his high school graduation. Helped him learn to ride a bicycle. Came to his wedding.

But that had been before.

Across the hall, he heard a thump in the infirmary. The beast-child playing while the keeper was away.

Inside the homicide unit at the Justice Center, Rick Gardiner considered his takeout options. Chili dogs or Chinese? He had packed on weight without Maggie's horrid "healthy" crap to eat all the time, but if he smoothed his shirt down over the growing belly he still looked good, right? General Tso's Chicken called his name and he stood up just as his phone rang. Detective Daley from Phoenix, Arizona. With the three-hour time difference he had probably just finished breakfast.

No chatting this call, but he sounded friendly enough. "I checked with HR, and no Jack Renner on the job here, ever. And before you ask, I went you one better and called the county, too."

They must have a lot of spare time in Phoenix, Rick thought. Or were super nice.

"Negativo there, too."

Huh. Maybe he was wrong. Renner could have picked up the phrase from someone he knew and that someone had lived in Phoenix. Maybe he saw it on a TV show— who the hell knew.

Daley listened to the silence for a split second, then asked, "Anything else?"

"Um . . . no. I guess not. Thanks for your help, though."

"No worries," the guy said, and hung up.

Well that was that. A bizarre hunch that didn't pan out. Might as well pick up his General Tso's and forget about it.

But Rick continued to sit at his desk, tapping a pen against its metal surface.

Chapter 8

Maggie met Jack and Riley on the sidewalk outside the Firebird Center, the concrete path interrupted by a sunken circle of dirt that held a sickly-looking tree of indeterminate family. Its scattered brown leaves crunched under their feet.

"What's up?" Maggie skipped any preamble.

Riley said, "Another dead kid."

"A fall?"

"Don't know. We were waiting for you." Now he knocked on the door and a worried-looking, overweight blonde peeked her head out. "Are you ready?"

Yes, they confirmed.

She ushered them inside, holding the door and glancing up and down the street as if she expected antenna vans from every major news team to careen up the street with tires screeching. Either that or a phalanx of angry parents with pitchforks and torches. She shut the door behind them with a decisive thud.

In the kitchen farther up the hallway some sort of vegetable and pasta concoction had been cooking that made Maggie glad to think about her crisp tuna and broccoli pita chilling in the small fridge back at the lab. They passed Reception, which held benches and a desk with office equipment. An effort had been made to make the place look welcoming—new tan paint, earth-toned abstracts, and comfy couches—but these careful choices appeared to be lost on the teenage girl lounging against the cushion. She had her legs straight out in front of her and her face turned to the ceiling to demonstrate her sense of utter ennui. She wore enough eyeliner to resemble a raccoon, skintight leggings, and a push-up bra under the tank top proclaiming "Bitch" in tiny pink rhinestones. It had stains across it, something orangey like old food or vomit, which also didn't seem to concern her. A cloudy fake diamond the size of a dime hung around her neck. Maggie wondered if she had arrived to fill the vacancy left by Rachael Donahue.

The "receptionist," a matronly black woman with a stylish scarf and perfectly coiffed hair, would most likely be a social worker responsible for assessing the needs of the new resident: medical care, clothes, social work, school level. No small task—it had already been made clear that these children's lives were myriad and complicated and always, in some sense, tragic.

Though right now the girl didn't look tragic. She just looked bored.

The blonde used a key to open the infirmary door, again scanning the area for potential witnesses. Once inside, however, Maggie could see why.

The infirmary held only a small desk, two beds, and a door leading to a small lavatory. A dark, unnaturally still form occupied one bed.

The dead boy.

"That's him," the woman said, twisting her hands together. "I really don't know what happened."

Now Maggie noted her ID badge hanging from a lanyard around her neck: CATHY BRANDRETH, R.N.

Maggie began to snap pictures, capturing the room from each wall, the other three adults shuffling to keep out of her lens, not always with success. Riley asked Nurse Brandreth to bring them up to speed.

"Tawanna sent him down here on Saturday. He had a small fever, a hair over a hundred, and acted as if his throat hurt. General malaise—some of these kids, lying around like a slug is their normal operating mode. But Tawanna said Damon usually bounced off the walls, so if he didn't seem to feel like doing anything, he really didn't."

Maggie moved in closer to the boy. He wore a gray T-shirt and rested on his back, face turned toward the ceiling. A sheet covered his lower half while a thermal blanket had slid to the floor. A small wooden puzzle with colored shapes sat on the table, a glass of water next to it.

The boy's eyes were open in a startled look of pain or surprise, hands clenching the sheet to his chest. White foam flecked his lips and filled his mouth.

Poison. Or some kind of overdose. Or some odd physical ailment Maggie did not recognize.

"I had him lie down for a while, gave him two Children's Tylenol and a peppermint candy. You'd be amazed what a peppermint candy can cure. But when I checked an hour later the fever hadn't gone down so I gave him a rapid strep test, which was positive, so I had the doctor on call stop by. They're usually in on Tuesdays and Thursdays. He came Saturday evening, brought him liquid amoxicillin, fever came down that night, general malaise persisted. The other nurse—Sheba—noted the same. Damon seemed back to normal this morning but I was keeping him here for another day, making sure the antibiotic had knocked it out. With all these kids in close quarters, we can't let something get around." Her voice had grown steady during this recital. She knew her job and felt comfortable in her expertise.

"Roger that," Riley said. "Anyone else in his . . . group . . . sick?"

"Nope."

"No reaction to the amoxicillin?" Jack asked.

"No, he was fine with it. Four teaspoons a day. Grape flavored, so he swallowed it no problem. I gave him the morning dose, he had breakfast, no fever, but I wanted to keep him out of class one more day. I didn't want to expose the day students to him or vice versa, in case anything lingered or his immune system was still weak. I gave him the morning dose, came back and he was"—her voice caught—"as you see him."

"Came back from where?"

She kept staring at the dead boy as she spoke. "The twelve to thirteen outdoor rec. The play area—it's a little fenced lawn on the north side. They have outdoor games, kickball, not really kickball but a combination of games and calisthenics . . . games, not sports. Sports are too competitive and they're trying to foster cooperation, which for some of these kids is an entirely new concept." She put a hand to her face. "Sorry. I'm babbling."

Riley, of course, soothed. Jack simply waited. Maggie wondered if he knew how intimidating his waiting face could be.

But Nurse Brandreth wasn't looking at him anyway. "It was about ten-thirty. Marley—from the twelve to thirteen group—came to get me. They'd been kicking a ball around and a girl fell and jammed her finger. No real damage, basically a little rubbing and patting and assuring her that it would be fine. I put a Band-Aid on it to make her feel better and came back. I couldn't have been gone more than twenty minutes."

"Was this after you'd given him the amoxicillin?" Maggie asked.

"Yes . . . immediately, I guess. I remember I was capping the bottle when Marley burst in, all red faced." She turned from Damon's body with an abrupt twist and strode the four steps to her small "station," a desk with wall-mounted cabinets behind it. She opened one and reached—

"Don't touch that!" Maggie cried.

The nurse jerked her hand back as if the bottle of liquid antibiotic might grow teeth and bite her. Maggie moved closer. The brown glass surface bore a printed label with the boy's name—Damon Kish—and the contents and dosage information.

"Is that cabinet kept locked?" Riley asked, as Maggie photographed the bottle.

A long pause. "It locks. I keep all of them locked most of the time."

"Today? Before you gave Damon the morning dose?"

Another pause, during which she undoubtedly saw her career passing before her eyes. "I don't always lock them when I'm here, and it's mostly too high for the kids to reach . . . the littler kids . . . unless they stood on the chair, I guess, and I'm usually in here every minute when I have a patient." She gestured to another door and added, "*This* one . . . that's always kept locked. It's got the Ritalin and the antidepressants, anything that has street value. So many of these kids come in with their own scripts." She tugged on its handle before Maggie could warn about fingerprints. Still secure.

Riley asked again, "And today? The cabinet with the antibiotic?"

Her shoulders sagged. "No, not today. I had to unlock it for his morning dose, but I didn't . . . what do you think, someone tampered with it? With what? What could they have put in it that would kill a kid like that, practically instantly?"

"I don't know. Do you have any toxic substances in these cabinets?"

She thought. "No. It's all basic first aid stuff."

"Was the twenty minutes the only time you left the room since the morning dose?"

Her tone dipped several degrees farther into misery. "No. I popped in and out to get some coffee from Reception, to get a report from the fax machine on one of the kids that juvenile detention sent over. I went to the ladies' room once, maybe twice. I got Damon's breakfast from the kitchen, took the tray back. . . . I can't even guess how many times I left." She added, "I got a Fitbit for my birthday. I'm trying to up my daily steps."

"I understand," Riley said, but his verbal empathy did not seem to comfort her. "We're going to have to take the bottle, of course, and Maggie will fingerprint that cabinet."

I guess I'm fingerprinting a cabinet, Maggie thought. *And the water glass, the nightstand, and the door-knobs* . . . She thought of something else. "Is this room locked when you step out?"

"No. If he had some sort of medical episode and started yelling while I was on the other side of the building, the other staff would need to get in here." She slumped into her desk chair. "It's never been a problem before. Ninety-nine percent of the kids are under supervision at all times."

The thrust of the building's design, Maggie thought, was to keep the adults safe from the kids, and to keep the kids safe from other kids. Keeping the kids safe from the adults ran a very distant third.

The kids, after all, had the proven history of violence. Though obviously the twelve- to thirteen-year-old Marley had been running around on her own, so exceptions were made.

The two detectives continued questioning the nurse while Maggie opened all the doors except the one locked cabinet. She took photographs of each one, as soon they would be covered in black powder and look quite different. The cabinet doors themselves were smooth and white—an ideal surface for the black powder—and she pulled one piece of tape after another off with patterns of fingers and palms. She spread each piece on a glossy white fingerprint card. Trying to identify them all would be a nightmare given the number of staff and residents *and*, since they were right next door to reception, any visitors, family members, legal counsel, and relatives dropping off or picking up.

She spread another piece of tape over another set of blackened ridges.

Riley's phone rang and he answered it, then asked the nurse if she would guide in the medical examiner's investigator. As soon as she left the room, Jack moved to Maggie's side.

"Poison?"

"I think so. I can't see another reason for an otherwise healthy kid to drop dead, but we haven't examined the body yet."

He waved at the basket labeled DIABETIC SUPPLIES. "What about insulin? Could that have killed him within twenty minutes?"

"You're assuming it was added to the amoxicillin bottle?"

"Yes. You're going to fingerprint it?" It still sat on its shelf.

"Of course I am! But I want to superglue it. I'm not quite willing to go with simple black powder for that item. And swallowing insulin wouldn't have any effect; the stomach acids will just break up the proteins. That's why it has to be given by injection."

He continued to scan the shelves. Riley joined them. "What about the Ritalin? If someone had a key."

"It's a stimulant. . . . I believe it's possible to overdose on it but I don't think you could fit enough in a"—she checked the dosage on the amoxicillin bottle—"teaspoon to kill someone so quickly, even a skinny little kid like him."

Riley, having pulled on latex gloves, gingerly poked through a basket labeled MISC. "What about Lanoxin? Anything?"

"Digitalis," Maggie said. "Odd thing to have around for kids."

He read the label. "It's two years old. Probably left over from a staff member. Would it kill?"

"It could, but again I have no idea how much would be needed, or if it would fit in a teaspoon. You'd have to crush up the pills and hope they dissolve in the antibiotic. They might just fall to the bottom."

"Antifreeze?" he suggested. "I know that's poisonous."

"Do you *see* antifreeze?" Jack asked.

"It's got to be somewhere in the building. Or in the trunk of somebody's car."

"Causes vomiting," Maggie said, "and wouldn't work that fast."

"We only have her word for that twenty-minute time frame," Riley pointed out. "Maybe he *wasn't* perfectly fine when she left the room."

Jack said, "And it sounds like the other nurse had all night to work, probably without interruption."

"This is all guesswork until we get the toxicology results," Maggie warned them.

"Or we turn him over and find a knife in his back."

She added, "Exactly, and there were also several opportunities for Damon to get up, come over here, stand on a chair, and help himself. He wasn't that sick anymore, certainly capable of getting up and around."

"Boy, I'll say. He was certainly up and around when we got here. Came out swinging just like before."

"Wait," Maggie said. "You were *here*? When he died?"

Riley explained how they had come to retrieve

Rachael's possessions, and Damon had seemed more than all right. "Quite energetic, in fact. Nearly knocked my partner down." Suddenly he asked Jack, "Did you see anyone?"

"What?"

"I just realized, that nurse went past us on the stairs, then you had to visit the little boys' room. Did you see anyone?"

"No. No one in reception either, just the woman at the desk." He spoke stiffly, oddly. Maggie noticed but couldn't interpret what that meant. But then she couldn't interpret much of anything when it came to Jack. He had his own unique configuration.

"See the kid?" Riley asked his partner.

"Nope. Door was closed. And shopping at the drugstore while the nurse was out sounds exactly like what that kid would do. I'm surprised he lasted two days in here without either biting her or setting the bandages on fire."

Maggie said, "Here's the thing. I don't know what in these cabinets could be a potential poison or not, or if there is such an item it could have been given to him by someone else or he took it himself. We really won't know until the autopsy is done, toxicology results are in, and/or I can give them the amoxicillin bottle for analysis. In the meantime—"

"In the meantime this is a crime scene," Jack finished for her.

Riley said, "We need to lock it down, seal all these cabinets."

Maggie said, "Which means the nurse doesn't have access to her supplies, or the kids to their own medications."

"What a mess," Riley groaned. "The nurse will have all sorts of reasons why we can't do that, most of which will be true and accurate. But at the same time she is officially number-one suspect, so what do we do?"

"Tell Patty to start preparing a court order for us," Jack said.

"We have to ask our de facto boss to start our paperwork. We'll have to put lovely red tamperproof tape over all these doors. A bunch of juvenile delinquents are going to be without their meds, and we'll have to pull a patrol officer off the streets to sit here and guard the scene. Patty's not going to be happy about this one and neither is Nurse Brandreth. Ain't nobody going to be happy about this one."

Jack said, "But if we don't, then we're sloppy, careless investigators who let a killer walk free because we didn't care about some little psycho kid."

"I can process everything here," Maggie said. "It's just going to take a while. We'll have to fingerprint all the bottles, then verify the scripts, then count all the pills and determine if there are any missing. If I can get Josh or Amy over here with the portable chamber and maybe some iodine fuming wands, I might be done in here by . . . dinnertime."

"That's not too bad," Riley said.

"Dinnertime tomorrow," Maggie clarified.

The official number-one suspect reappeared with the ME investigator, this time a tall blond man with a slight limp. He took the same type of overall photos that Maggie had and then concentrated on the small, still form.

Removing the sheet revealed no surprises. The boy wore pajama pants along with the gray T-shirt and had kicked off white socks. The investigator took careful note of the boy's eyes, with no petechiae, which might indicate strangulation, and his mouth, with no damage that might indicate smothering. The foam suggested poison or overdose but could result from other events as well.

The pathologist would need the amoxicillin bottle, and Maggie promised to hand-deliver it after she processed it for latent prints. Try as he might, the investigator could not talk her out of handing it over now.

"You really think someone poisoned this kid?" he asked her.

"I don't know. But I'm not going to take the chance."

He suggested finding a fresh plastic urine sample cup and pouring out the liquid antibiotic, then she could keep her bottle and he could have the amoxicillin, but it wouldn't have been possible to get the lid off without touching the bottle and she didn't want to take even that small chance of disturbing the only trace of a child killer. *If*, of course, there was a fingerprint on the bottle and *if* the bottle contained poison and *if* the poison had killed Damon Kish.

They finished the examination of the body. Damon did not have a knife in his back or any other sign of injury. His dorsal surfaces had begun to turn a cherry pink as the blood obeyed the law of gravity and pooled to coagulate. The upper thigh on his right side had a healing road rash from hip to knee. The nurse said it had been from falling in the outdoor play area the day before he'd come down with the sore throat. She'd cleaned the scrapes and spread some Neosporin over the area, not for the first time. Damon tended to run into things full tilt. "I guess no one ever taught him to be careful. No one ever taught him *anything*."

She stepped out to escort the body removal team, who gently ushered Damon into the same type of body bag that had so fascinated the boy only a few days before. Maggie wondered if in some other dimension that would come as a comfort to him, the boy with a curiosity about death being able to experience it for himself. She hoped so. She hoped that he would find the next world more comforting than the last.

The detectives wanted to talk to the boy's dorm "mother" as well as get his complete social and medical history from Dr. Palmer. They slipped past the nurse as she scanned the hallway to make sure the coast was clear of children or parents before the body could be spirited out of the building. She made them wait as the girl who had been in the waiting room when Maggie arrived now followed a woman past the door. All the makeup had been scrubbed off and damp strands of hair clung to her neck. The dirty clothes had been replaced with a soft T-shirt and thin sweatpants, tennis shoes, and a stack of other clothes carried against her chest. She still wore the fake diamond on its chain, but that seemed to be the only thing left of the earlier persona. The bravado and contempt had been washed away with the eyeliner, and now she seemed soft, more than a little apprehensive, and about five years younger.

As Damon left the building, Dr. Palmer arrived. He had been at a county government meeting and had returned as quickly as possible; his graying hair had been tossed by the wind and a haphazard pile of binders threatened to slip from his arms.

"Please come into my office," he said upon seeing them, and bustled away without waiting for an answer. The cops glanced at Maggie, then abandoned her. She turned to Nurse Brandreth.

"This is what we're going to have to do," she began.

Chapter 9

Dr. Palmer's office spanned perhaps ten feet from one wall to its opposite, with even less between the other two. It perched on a corner of the third floor with a view of the rooftop basketball court, currently empty. He waded between an overstuffed bookshelf and the cartons stacked on the side of his desk to reach his chair, an ancient leather thing with stuffing bursting out of one seam. The room smelled like it looked, of old books and damp shoes and years of brown-bagged ham on rye. The shelves held tome after tome, magazines, loose Xeroxed articles, and the occasional family photograph. Nothing that told Jack much about the man, other than he didn't care much about appearances or self-aggrandizement. There were no framed diplomas, photos with city leaders, or awards.

"Sorry the place is a mess," he said, apparently automatically and without much real regret. He let Jack and Riley move file folders off the two folding chairs between the door and the desk.

"That's okay," Riley said as he positioned himself. "It's nice to see a work space that looks like a work space. No crayoned stick-figure pictures stuck to your filing cabinet with magnets, though."

Dr. Palmer gave his own office a quick survey, as if only now realizing that for a man who had devoted his life to children he had nothing childlike there. Nothing breakable, nothing that could be hurled by an irate youth, though many texts appeared heavy enough to do real damage. "No, I guess not. Kids are never in here—they meet with their therapists and teachers and dorm parents, and those adults in turn meet with me. I guess you could say I'm once removed. My position here is purely administrative and research oriented. I'm doing a study on early childhood outcomes, which has turned up some quite fascinating—"

A knock sounded at the door and the slim young black woman they had last seen trying to keep Damon from escaping his dorm area entered. She spoke a bit breathlessly to Dr. Palmer: "Cathy said you were back. I can't believe Damon's gone. He wasn't that sick. She said it was just strep."

Dr. Palmer stood and leaned across his desk as if trying to comfort her. "I know, it's a great shock. Come in and sit down, my dear. This is Tawanna Cooper, one of Damon's dorm mothers. She's been a great asset to us for, what, about four years now?"

Jack gave her his chair, which allowed him to both stretch his long legs and stand in the corner, back against the bookcase, the better to observe both the administrator and the social worker while Riley held their attention. Not that he expected to learn much. They both seemed discombobulated by the boy's death.

"He had been making progress," Tawanna Cooper sniffed, dabbing her eyes with a delicate touch of tissue. "He actually wrote some of his numbers the other day. And he patted Mariana's shoulder when she was crying over her spelling test. That indicated such a leap in his capacity for empathizing—"

"Let's go back," Riley interrupted. "You—"

"I took him to the infirmary on Saturday. He was lying around and picked at his food—usually he sucked everything down like a whirlpool. His forehead felt hot to me so I took him down to Cathy. She said it was strep. I think he picked it up from a day student—"

"Possibly the one he bit," Dr. Palmer mused, apparently to himself.

"—because no one else in my unit had it. Anyway, that was . . . the last time I saw him." Again she sniffed.

"Why was he trying to get out of your room on Thursday?" Jack asked.

"When? Oh, that was you—with Rachael's body. Damon did that often, really. When he felt bored or particularly energetic. He would often throw himself at doors just to see if they'd open. Not surprising, really."

"Why is that?"

The young woman and the old doctor exchanged a glance. Then Dr. Palmer took a deep breath as if about to begin a long story. Which, as it turned out, he was.

"Damon came to us about two months ago, from Geauga County. They found him in a big old house in a fairly isolated location. No one knew that the woman had had two children, or that she kept them locked in the basement."

"Wow," Riley said.

"Damon and his brother. We don't even know what the brother's name is since there were no records of anything. We only guess at Damon's name because the mother had written it on the calendar, then never flipped to the next month. When authorities entered, the ten-year-old calendar was still hanging in the kitchen. The brother had been younger. No record of the father or fathers, no indication of a man living at the house at all.

"The woman died from some natural cause, heart attack, I think. A mailman noticed the mail piling up in the box, police did a welfare check, found her body in the kitchen and Damon in the basement. Its door, I guess, looked like something you'd see in a castle in an old movie—an inch-thick hasp and padlock. They found Damon and his little brother. The brother had been dead for at least a year, possibly three or four."

Hence the fascination with death, Jack thought. "Did he eat him?"

Three heads swiveled to look at him as if *he* had grown three heads. "*What?*" Riley asked.

"I mean, kid stuck with no food . . . did he resort to cannibalism? Is that why he bites?"

"No!" Ms. Cooper seemed aghast while Dr. Palmer stifled what sounded like a chuckle, and said that all children bite.

Ms. Cooper said, "No, no. Damon wasn't starving. Underweight, certainly—he barely weighed over fifty pounds. But he wasn't abused, physically, in the strictest sense of the word. He had no broken bones, no deep bruises, no internal injuries. She apparently threw food down the steps and water dripped from a faucet. Blankets in the winter, etcetera. He came here in fairly decent health even with the persistent malnutrition." A frown puckered her perfect skin. "At least as far as could be told—who knows what was hiding in his body that wouldn't have been found during a basic checkup."

"What killed the brother, then?"

Another exchanged glance.

Dr. Palmer said uncomfortably, "They can't really be sure. So much time had passed and the body had mummified."

"But—" Jack prompted. Obviously, there was a *but*.

Ms. Cooper said in a low tone, "There were broken bones in the face and chest."

"How old was he?"

"About six months. Impossible to know how long he had been in the cellar with Damon."

"So the assumption—"

"We can't make any assumptions in that case," Dr. Palmer said. "It could have been the mother. The fractures might not have been serious and the baby died of malnutrition. With a boy of about seven trying to feed a baby water and crunchy dog food, it would have taken a miracle for that baby to survive."

Jack said, "Or the seven-year-old got tired of listening to the crying and belted him a few times."

Dr. Palmer said, "Or the mother literally threw the baby down the stairs with the dog food and Damon did what he could for him. It's impossible to know."

"Then why was Damon here?" Riley asked. "At this facility?"

They seemed to find this a confusing question. "Where else could he go?" Dr. Palmer asked. "Obviously the average foster family wouldn't be equipped to handle him."

"He attacked other children while he was here?" Jack asked. It seemed the kid had been dangerously off the rails but they couldn't find a politically correct way to say so.

Dr. Palmer admitted, "Well, yes. Aside from the biting and scratching, he threw a bowl of hot soup at a little girl in his group. He twisted a boy's arm hard enough to sprain it. Lord knows he's hit Ms. Cooper here enough times. So I guess you could say that."

"How else would you say it?"

The doctor and the social worker took a moment to think, as Jack watched a group of older boys, big enough to be the sixteen- to seventeen-year-olds, gather on the rooftop basketball court. It seemed like any other pickup game, the boys talking, laughing, obviously teasing each other, dribbling a worn ball in an absent manner, the game only a cover story for the real purpose of forgetting their problems and issues for a half hour.

Then Ms. Cooper said, "It's kind of like how your cat can be purring and rubbing up against you one minute, and then the next it decides that your ankles are a cosmic threat and must be scratched to death. Unpredictable. Damon wasn't dangerous, Detective—he was *feral*. Out of control one moment, quite docile the next, especially if you were giving him something good to eat."

"Why wasn't he removed from the group?" Riley asked, somehow without making it sound like an accusation.

Dr. Palmer said, "Because no one anywhere can—could—spare a staff member to be one-on-one with him twenty-four/seven. The only alternative would be to lock him in a padded room somewhere, and further isolation was hardly the answer."

Ms. Cooper added, "He had ten years of socialization to catch up on. We had to start somewhere."

"Did he have a problem with anyone or any aspect of the program in particular?" Jack asked. Damon may have died by misadventure or some bizarre medical condition, but it could easily be a case of homicide, so he might as well ask the usual questions. "Did he have any particular complaints?"

Ms. Cooper said, "Damon didn't speak."

Jack felt himself blink. "Not at all? Didn't at least grunt, or scream?"

"Nothing."

The cops digested this. Riley asked, "Couldn't or wouldn't?"

"Couldn't," Dr. Palmer said. "The brain isn't all ready to go at birth. It continues to develop neurological connections and abilities—which if they're not developed within the first two years will most likely never develop at all. In real life, Tarzan never would have learned to even say, 'You Jane.'"

Ms. Cooper said, "There were cruel experiments with animals that showed if their eyes were sewed shut for the first few months, they were permanently blinded."

"So Damon never learned to talk?"

"No." As if it had just occurred to him, Dr. Palmer said, "If the brother had been closer in age, perhaps they would have developed their own language. *That* would have been interesting."

Ms. Cooper said, "But by the time the brother came along Damon had already lost the ability. It's also possible any sound made was met with punishment—we don't know when in his development he was imprisoned. At any rate, even with normal physiology Damon became permanently mute."

Dr. Palmer said, "The brain needs stimulation to develop proper channels of functioning. This is why early childhood intervention is so important. Programs like Head Start are already too late—we need family counseling to begin the minute a woman gets pregnant. They don't have to play Mozart to the baby in the womb—just talk to it once it's born. Look at it, respond to it. Very basic, basic things that involved parents do automatically."

Ms. Cooper said, "We see this all the time in our family counseling and intervention services—these people aren't bad parents because they're bad people. They're bad parents because they never experienced a good one. With a little guidance and support they can make great strides, and in turn so can their children."

Jack thought this all sounded quite logical, but he had spent most of the lecture watching the boys on the other side of the window. They had settled into an actual game now, the players focused on either making a basket or blocking the guy with the ball. The most assertive player appeared to be at least a hundred pounds overweight. Two listless boys hunched in plastic chairs, twitching and occasionally scratching—Jack guessed meth use. A tall kid with light brown skin and more enthusiasm than talent liked to celebrate his team's scores by leaping onto the chain-link fence that separated the court from empty, open air.

"So Damon couldn't speak. At all," Riley said, sounding a bit stunned—and no doubt wondering how they were ever going to find out what had been going on in the kid's life without any sort of communication from him. No text messages, diary entries, past conversations to go on.

Dr. Palmer was still on early childhood development.

"Physical and mental abilities have to be stimulated after birth in order to develop. When a baby cries and its mother comforts it, eventually the baby learns to self-soothe and self-regulate their emotions. When the baby's cry is ignored and as thoroughly as Damon's obviously was, that isn't learned. Given that he also didn't have the greatest nutrition in the world, it's no surprise that he had less IQ, less self-control and equanimity, and more extreme reaction to stimuli."

Ms. Cooper interrupted her boss. "But he could learn. With the lack of language, obviously, it was so difficult to teach anything. I usually had to resort to hand gestures, but his eyes would light up when he figured out what I was trying to communicate to him. We even did the house-tree-person test. Sort of. I had to leave out the tree."

"The what?" Riley asked.

Again the glance from Ms. Cooper to the doctor, this one with a slightly pitying cast to it. She said, "It's a tool developed by a psychologist named John Buck in 1948. It is designed to give us an estimation of the child's intelligence and personality, though we use it mostly to identify possible problem areas. We give them a crayon and a piece of paper and tell them to draw a house. That's it. They can take all the time they like and of course artistic ability is not what we're looking for. Then we ask questions—there's a large catalog of questions you can ask, but since we focus on possible trauma and abuse as well as the child's history we ask things like, Who lives in the house? Who comes to visit? Where does everyone sleep? Are they happy? We look for what's missing: Are there windows, doors? Or for what's added: Is there a lump in the lawn that looks like a dead puppy? That gives us a direction to ask more questions. A child who was beaten in the garage every night might draw the garage and then scribble it out. An abused kid who grew up in apartment buildings might put windows for every apartment except their own."

"Okay," Riley said. "Damon—"

"Next we have them draw a tree. Does the tree have leaves? Is it a large, healthy tree or a few sticks? What's around it? With Damon I just skipped the tree. With a child raised in a basement—I didn't think I could get that idea across. I had to draw myself in my house, and had started drawing myself in our under-twelve unit before he understood that I meant the *dwelling*. He was actually quite bright, given the circumstances. Such a pity." She nearly sniffed again. "If he had only had a normal existence I think he would have been a really smart kid."

The basketball kids had ended their game, the fence climber jumping down to give a teammate a friendly— or unfriendly, Jack couldn't tell—shove.

"So—" Riley tried.

"The third part is the person," she went on. She enunciated each word in a way that made Jack think she had spent a bit too much time talking to small children. "It's okay if their person is a blob with stick limbs. We look for, does the person have hands? Hair? A mouth? Are they smiling? Then we ask, Who is the person? Do they have a family? And so on."

"And what did Damon draw?" Riley asked quickly.

"I can show you," she said, rising, her posture as perfect as it had been while seated. "You can see his cubby, too—I mean where he slept. Though it won't tell you much. He didn't have much of anything."

"What about the children?" Dr. Palmer asked.

To the detectives, she explained, "Many of these children have been physically or sexually abused. They often find grown men intimidating—but I think a short visit that doesn't involve them personally, and of course I'll explain that you are helping us, might be good for them. One more step in getting them to accept the idea that not all adults will hurt them."

Dr. Palmer nodded his bow to her judgment, and the cops left the room.

Chapter 10

They followed the teacher to the opposite side of the building and down two floors to the under-twelve dorm area. School time had paused for lunch and about twenty kids clustered at round tables eating macaroni and cheese, overseen by a slender young man with sandy blond hair and a vaguely tense expression. The smell made Jack's stomach rumble, wanting food, any food. They fell silent as soon as Ms. Cooper led the cops into the room and, staring back at them, Jack had the uncomfortable feeling that he could read each one's history. None had a sweet bedtime story to tell. Some of them seemed wary but curious, more or less typical of energetic children. Some squirmed and shot hostile looks, waiting for the confrontation, waiting to have to fight their way out. One little girl looked at them appraisingly, almost seductively, her dark eyes sweeping them from hair to shoes. Many went still as stone, faces blank but eyes watching the cops' every move from the door to near the tables where Ms. Cooper introduced them, to the open cubicle where Damon had slept his nights.

"As I said, he didn't have anything," Ms. Cooper explained as Jack poked around in the rumpled bed-clothes and largely empty shelving. Exactly three sets of T-shirts, knit pants, socks, and little-boy briefs had been neatly folded. A newish but scuffed pair of tennis shoes sat under the bunk. A plastic cup, scratched and opaque with age, sat on the small table that served as a nightstand, next to a battered red cushion and a bracelet with large plastic beads. "To remove him from that basement, they had to trap him like a wild animal. They couldn't ask what he wanted to take with him so they grabbed a few things that were by his blankets. He doesn't show much interest in them, though, so I can't—couldn't—tell if they had any sentimental value."

Riley looked around. "And this is it?"

"This is it. When a kid spends ten years locked in a basement, he doesn't accumulate a lot of stuff."

A shout from the room outside distracted them, ac-companied by the thumps of thrown items. Then a howl went up that raised the hairs on the back of Jack's neck. He looked around the wall of the cubicle to see a book come sailing out of another one. A teddy bear, a pillow, and what looked like a dress followed.

The blond man at the tables with the children stood up, warned the children to stay in their seats, and went to deal with the young ravager. The children at the ta-bles continued to eat, while craning their necks to see the show. Some looked frightened. Some quivered with excitement at the commotion.

A small girl of perhaps eight burst from the space, managing to throw a good-sized book at the closest table while running full tilt for the door at the same time. The book fell short. The man pursued her. She had dark hair in need of a comb and bare feet, a T-shirt and jersey pants covering her thin frame.

She reached the door, turned the knob desperately. It didn't budge, and she gave up in order to face the teacher/therapist. Unlike Damon, she was not remotely mute. "IhateyouIhateyouIhateyou!" erupted, loud enough to rattle the high windows. She added a few choice curses with words a girl her size should never have heard, much less mastered.

The teacher held out each arm to block her in, but quick as a sparrow she faked left, darted right, and went under his elbow. She plowed into a play area in the corner of the room, snatching every toy that came to hand to lob at the man. In the midst of this carnage came giggles, as if she were having a wonderful time.

"Um," Jack said to Ms. Cooper, "should we—?"

"No. He can handle Martina."

And indeed, the man caught her, and more deftly than Jack would have expected he swung the little girl around and hugged her from behind, wrapping her arms across her own stomach and holding them there. Then he dropped to the ground, pulling her with him, and hooked his own calves over her shins, gently pinning her in place. She shrieked and squirmed but could not extricate herself.

"Does this happen often?"

"Once or twice a week. It used to be once or twice a day, so we're making progress."

Riley had come out to observe, with darting glances as if staring might be rude—not that the girl seemed to care. She was too busy yelling to even notice their presence. "What is her story?"

Ms. Cooper said, "We don't know. She was found

on the street about a year ago, filthy and starving. We never tracked down her parents. She won't talk about any memories she has, probably repressed most of them. We can only imagine."

With her limbs pinned, Martina could only move her head. She made full use of her neck muscles, pulling her chin down to her chest to get as much momentum as possible before snapping her head back. The guy turned his face from one side to the other to protect his nose but after one particularly savage attack Jack heard a crunch that might have been a cheekbone, or the cartilage protecting his carotid.

"This is the problem," Ms. Cooper said absently, and in what seemed to Jack like a vast understatement. "She's so desperate to belong, to have someone care about her, but so discouraged by whatever pain and rejection she's suffered in the past. So she rejects you before you can reject her, before she's tempted to feel close to anyone. Her subconscious believes it's easier that way, to get it over with. She's dying for someone who won't shove her away, and instead makes it impossible for anyone to pull her close."

"A self-fulfilling prophecy," Riley said.

"Exactly. You see this all over in life, the girl who keeps burning through fiancés, the boy who gets his dream job only to send his boss a stupid e-mail. Unfortunately, Martina's reaction is much more intense."

The girl's flailing hadn't weakened. Jack couldn't help but stare at a grown man getting the snot kicked out of him by an eight-year-old girl. She nearly lifted him off the ground with her contortions.

"Do you have a lot like her?" Riley asked.

"Traumatized kids? Yes. Ones who throw such spectacular meltdowns? Only a few. At least she doesn't work on getting the other kids to join in. We had one a few years ago. . . . Compared to him, Martina is in the peewee league. She only resembles a tornado. He reached category five . . . put holes in cement walls, chipped the linoleum, threw adult-sized chairs ten feet."

"What do you do when they get too big to pin?" Jack asked.

A touch of uncharacteristic hopelessness colored her eyes. "They go to jail. Or, if they're lucky, a residential treatment program."

"*In* the prison," Riley clarified. There were no longer "hospitals for the criminally insane." Prisons had their own designated areas.

Ms. Cooper said, "That's Martina's future if we can't get her healthy. She'll have issues into adult life, no doubt, but if we can redirect her rage into less destructive outlets, she may be able to have some semblance of what we'd call a normal life. Maybe, here and there, a moment of actual happiness—before her childhood is gone completely."

"What did she do?" Jack asked.

"Martina? Nothing, actually. Nothing criminal other than the kind of assault you just saw. She's here because there are few other facilities that will take her on the public dime. Fostering hasn't worked out—it's extremely difficult to deal with kids coming from this kind of abuse and neglect. Everything that is, well, normal doesn't apply to them. Some people think all they need is love. Some people think all they need is discipline. They're both wrong." She paused, apparently trying to summarize human development in a few sentences. "All the things we take for granted—eating regular meals, hugging people we love, going to the bathroom *in* the bathroom—those aren't as instinctive as we think. We were taught all those things by our parents. So severely neglected kids come into a foster home. A hug makes them scream. They defecate in their bedroom. They steal food no matter how many times you explain that there is plenty of food and that stealing will be punished because no matter how much they may want to please you they have to put their own survival first. Buying them toys does not produce gratitude because they don't understand the concept of giving. They don't want to wear a coat when it's cold or else they insist on having one when it's warm. They eat until they're sick, or won't eat with the family at all. They want to be loved, Detectives, but they make that so very, very difficult."

As if to emphasize the point, Martina let out another scream and twisted to bite her captor's shoulder.

"Come with me," Ms. Cooper told them. "I'll show you that drawing of Damon's."

She led them past the eating kids again, making Jack pity the really quiet ones. The cops had entered and nothing bad had happened. They had finally unbent enough to spoon in another mouthful or two, but now his glancing approach turned them back into statues.

"Under-twelve isn't separated by gender?" Jack asked the woman, out of earshot of the kids.

"No. Aside from not having the space or the staff, it's a conscious decision. Very young children are accustomed to being around other people and other children all the time. Their young ages are a chance for us to get them in the habit of cooperative, consistent socialization. And most of them are prepubescent so the threat of sexual activity isn't as heavy as it is with the teens. Not that that necessarily counts for anything these days, not when grade school kids have oral sex. But they're so closely monitored here that it hasn't been a problem."

"What is the age range?"

"Right now everyone I have is under ten. Damon was actually my oldest. The youngest is six."

"A six-year-old?" Riley couldn't help reacting.

"She stabbed her baby sister to death," Ms. Cooper said as she pulled out a ring of small keys.

"Oh."

Martina's wails began to subside, with more seconds elapsing between the head butts.

Ms. Cooper unlocked a low horizontal set of drawers that doubled as a credenza.

"That's one heavy-duty file cabinet," Riley observed.

The dorm mother chuckled. "It has to be, surrounded by small children every day. Look at my desk—I think it could be used as a barricade against an invading Viking horde if necessary."

Jack watched the children pile their empty dishes onto a tray on a counter near the door, though their teacher still sat with Martina in the corner. He couldn't pick out who might be the youngest murderer in the group; they all seemed tiny to him, too young to cross the street by themselves, certainly too young to be incarcerated for violent crimes. "And everything locks. Is that to preserve each child's privacy or to keep the rubber bands and tape from appropriation?"

"Both. We're in a fishbowl here, as you can see. Transparency is important—these kids have been abused and traumatized by adults doing hidden, mysterious things in secret. We want there to be no secrets in their spaces. Plus I can't keep an eye on them if I disappear into an office all the time." She found Damon's file, re-locked the drawer, and sat at her desk. She gestured toward the various free chairs, but they tended to be undersized and Jack didn't trust his bulk on them. He and Riley simply leaned over her desktop.

"This was his house drawing." She pushed a sheet of construction paper toward them. In red crayon Damon had sketched a square with a complicated gable roof represented by angular peaks. It had three windows and a door with what looked like a detached garage in the back. Simple, but the lines were straight and firm. Jack had no background to judge average ten-year-old artistic ability, but it didn't look half bad.

"I offered him other crayons but he stuck to mono-chrome. Usually we take that as a red—no pun intended—flag. Red and black indicate aggression, so if a child uses those colors in particular areas of the drawing, we pay attention to it. But in a case as unusual as Damon's, I hesitate to make the usual assumptions." She glanced at the picture again. "Of course, the house *had* been his prison, so maybe he knew exactly what he was about."

"Okay," Riley said.

"This is the interesting part. I got these crime scene photos from the county sheriff's office. I didn't show them to Damon, of course."

Jack looked at a photograph of an old-fashioned

basement, with bare wood walls and a dirt floor. What looked like a plow sat in one corner, with one handle used as a clothes pole. Shelves held dusty boxes, jars of old screws, and a box of cereal. A rectangle of blankets must have been Damon's bed. Next to it lay another pile, the edge of the flash barely illuminating the tiny, desiccated form of what had been Damon's brother.

In the corner, Martina's noise lowered to a keening moan. Over it, the teacher instructed the other children to get out their spelling books. Some skipped off to comply, while others ignored him and headed for the toys.

"And this was the house." She slapped another photo on top of the basement one. The house loosely represented in Damon's picture, a small two-story structure with a gabled roof. "He only saw—as far as we know, of course, but I doubt the mother took him out for picnics in the yard if she didn't even speak to him enough to develop even minimal lingual skills— he only saw this house for a few minutes as county authorities were dragging him away. Think of that, a kid who'd been locked up for ten years, who couldn't have known other human beings existed. They wrapped him up in restraints because he reacted as any other wild animal would when cornered—hissing and scratching."

She gazed at them. "My point is that he would have had only a glimpse of this house in the midst of overwhelming physical and mental upheaval. Yet he got the details right—three windows, the door on the left side, the garage in back. Two bushes at the corner."

The two detectives compared the photo and the drawing, acknowledging that, yes, that was rather amazing.

Regret welled up in her voice. "As I said—very bright. I wonder what he could have done if he'd only been born to someone other than a monster."

"Did he draw the basement?" Jack asked.

Ms. Cooper shook her head. "I couldn't figure out a way to communicate that request to him. I gave it a few tries but I couldn't be sure he understood that the basement was underneath the house. I also couldn't be sure if he didn't understand me or he simply didn't want to draw his own prison. I didn't want to push him."

"What did this drawing tell you?" Riley asked.

"Other than that he was incredibly observant? Not much—or, not much that I could discern. This test isn't a series of checkboxes. So much comes from the child's body language and their response to questions, or lack of same—just like adults. What they don't say is more revealing than what they do say."

Rather like myself and Maggie, Jack thought. There were worlds of things that they didn't say, that she didn't ask. Where had he come from? Why did he start—why couldn't he stop—feeling it to be his job to rid the world of predators? She knew pieces and parts of the story but seemed too afraid to ask for all of it.

Or too sensible. What she didn't know, she didn't have to torture herself over for not revealing.

She was in a hard and miserable spot. So was he, by extension. One pang of her conscience could compel her to expose him. Herself too, of course, but he could see her disregarding that. He needed to get himself out of it. If not the spot, at least the city.

Ms. Cooper was explaining that Damon's bizarre background made the test difficult to interpret. "Did he leave out the basement? Did he not make a connection between the house and the basement, perhaps thinking they were two different structures? Did he not consider his imprisonment traumatizing but assumed everyone lives that way? Damon was a medium physical challenge, but a large mental one. I had been contacting nationally known child psychologists trying to get them interested in his case, but so far . . . most responded but thought they'd stop by while on a lecture tour, that kind of thing."

Riley said, "You skipped the tree. Did he draw a person?"

She pulled another sheet of crayon-covered construction paper from the file. "I asked him to draw himself—by drawing myself and then gesturing the connection. His eyes would light up when he figured out what you were trying to say, and he liked to draw, a new experience for him where his lack of speech didn't matter. I would let him draw during classes because, frankly, trying to teach long division to a kid in Damon's situation . . ."

In green crayon, Damon had drawn a sturdy boy in a T-shirt and pants, with curly hair. He had spent some time on the shoes, adding each grommet and twist of the laces. But—

"No mouth," Riley said aloud.

Ms. Cooper shook her head. The figure had eyes, ears, a nose, even eyebrows—but the lower section of the face sat empty of crayon marks.

Jack asked, "How much would he have recovered, of, um, functioning? Would he ever have been . . . normal?"

"Normal isn't a word we use around here much, Detective, but . . . other than speech, physically normal. Mentally? You hear about 'attachment disorder' and the like and you probably think it's just the latest line of psychobabble—"

Jack said nothing, because on the whole . . .

"—but the orbital frontal cortex acts as a control center over the sympathetic and parasympathetic nervous system. Children who are deprived of attachment as infants most often have a lifelong inability to regulate primitive negative states. They may *truly* not be able to help it." Her fingers made air quotes around the last six words. "Then if there had been drugs or alcohol in utero—before he was born—and certainly we saw evidence of lifelong malnutrition, he'd almost certainly have less IQ, less self-control and equanimity, distractibility, and oversized response to stimuli."

As abruptly as Martina had begun her fit, she stopped, her body going limp. She sniffled and began to cry.

"So he'd have been violent?"

"Not violent, feral. We sometimes think that nothing in the first two or three years of life can hurt us because we don't remember it, but that isn't true at all. In utero, infancy and toddlerhood—the brain is still forming, and both the quantity and quality of its tissue and chemistry can be altered by trauma, malnutrition, and neglect."

So the kid was pretty much a total loss. Jack asked, "Did Damon have an assigned therapist?"

Martina had quieted and now watched a boy building a wall using foam bricks. The young man took his legs off of hers, one by one.

Ms. Cooper brushed Damon's paperwork back into its file and carefully locked the cabinet. "Yes . . . we schedule the under-twelve group a little differently than the other units, try to keep their environment as stable as possible. Most of them have lived with a revolving door of adults, extended family members, different schools. . . . Anyway they have me; my counterpart, a teacher who lives in Friday, Saturday, and Sunday—I teach about half the subjects, she takes the other half; and Hunter there is our child psychologist." She nodded toward the slim young man as he now let go of Martina, letting her slide from his lap to the floor and releasing her arms. He stood up, quietly, gingerly, watching for her to continue with the fit. "He fills in the gaps and meets with the children individually, over at that table in the corner."

"No secrets," Jack murmured.

"Most of these children have been abused by men, so they are much more comfortable within sight of their playmates, or . . . fellow residents. On the other hand, they have to discuss very painful topics, so in that way the openness isn't conducive. No one likes to cry in public, not even small children."

"That's a lot of kids for only three of you to handle," Riley said, observing the group.

"Half of these are day students. They come here for breakfast and go home about four p.m. Only ten of them are residents. That's our maximum."

"Sad that there're ten kids in this city who can't live

with their own families," Riley murmured, no doubt thinking of his own daughters. Hannah would be celebrating her twelfth birthday next week. Natalie would be upstairs in the fourteen to fifteen unit.

Ms. Cooper gave an unladylike snort. "Are you kidding? We have fifteen more on a waiting list. Damon's little cubby will be filled as soon as we clean it out. There're another fifty for the day program. But Dr. Palmer won't let them overcrowd us. You can't put kids' lives on an assembly line—there's no one-size-fits-all fix. They're all different because all their stories are different, so all their problems are different and all the solutions have to be different."

In the play area the psychologist walked away slowly, to wipe a drop of blood from a scrape on the corner of his mouth with a napkin before helping the children still at the tables to move their reusable lunch dishes into a deep plastic bin. Without being told they tossed any empty plastic cups into the blue recycling bin near the door.

Martina didn't acknowledge the doctor's absence but continued to watch the boy with the blocks. Then she rubbed her teary face with one hand, like the tired child she was. She picked up a plastic car and ran this along the wall of foam bricks. Jack wondered if ancient tales of demonic possession were actually the acting-out of traumatized children. It would explain a lot.

"And how did Dr. Hunter get on with Damon?" Riley asked, picking up on the touch of professional rivalry.

Ms. Cooper wasted no time in clarifying that Hunter

was his first name, his last was Kohler, and he hadn't made much progress. "Getting Damon to sit still for anything was extremely difficult. Hunter couldn't find a way to communicate with Damon. He proved too much of a challenge."

This time her sniff had nothing to do with grief.

Chapter 11

Maggie's coworker Josh had arrived with the extra lab equipment and he and Maggie had divided the work. She set up the portable superglue chamber and put the amoxicillin bottle and the glass from Damon's bedside inside it, then placed a foil dish of powdered cyanoacrylate on the hot plate. While that fumed she texted her brother that while she loved Disneyworld as much as the next Mouseophile, she would have to check the on-call schedule.

The iodine processing of the other bottles took place in a small venting hood. If prints appeared in a purplish color she photographed them, then passed the finished item to Josh. He would count the pills, capsules, and ounces of medication remaining, then examine the records and the calendar to determine if these counts were short. They worked in silence, broken now and then by Josh's Bluetoothed conversations with his fiancée about wedding cake flavors and when his crazy Uncle Leo should be cut off from the bar.

Even without this the area didn't prove very quiet. Because the infirmary sat next to the reception room, there seemed to be a constant flow of adults and children in and out of the building. Now that Damon's body had been removed Maggie left the door open for the detectives to return. Nurse Brandreth had been persuaded, without much difficulty, to take a break and sit next door with the receptionist, to whom she could be heard recounting the entire day thus far in excruciating detail. A health inspector had arrived to be escorted throughout the building; the kitchen staff took delivery of another gross of unbreakable plastic plates, questioning whether "unbreakable" was really supposed to mean "unbreakable" because so far many had not lived up to this description; and the mother and father of one Marlon Butts arrived in separate visits to demand that the county relinquish custody of their child since they had been released from prison, and not to listen to the boy's grandmother as she had been diagnosed with Alzheimer's, dementia, delirium tremens, and/or antisocial personality disorder and besides had never liked them. During both visits the receptionist had had to call one of the building's two security officers, and Maggie wondered why she had not met these officers previously. It turned out that they needed to stick close to the several consistently violent residents in the building and since Rachael's death had appeared to be an accident and Damon's a medical event their presence had not been required. Or requested. "Doc Palmer keeps us on a pretty tight leash," the officer told Maggie after sticking his head in to see what was up. "These poor deprived children don't want us pigs around. Probably because most of them have a record as long as your arm. And if you don't mind my asking, what the hell are you doing?"

She laughed. After placing several prescription bottles inside an acrylic case that sucked fumes up through a particulate filter, she had filled a glass tube with iodine crystals and glass wool. It looked like a cigar tube, but open at both ends. One end had a stopper with a small open tube through it, to let the fumes out, and the other had a stopper attached to a rubber hose. Maggie would blow into this end of the rubber hose, which would push the iodine fumes from the crystals out through the other end and onto the pill bottle. Her hand around the tube would warm the crystals so that they sublimated, or turned into gas without melting into liquid first. She explained this, then admitted that it *did* look funny.

"It looks like you're smoking a hookah. But if anyone asks, I'll tell them you didn't inhale."

"I wouldn't want to do that. The iodine fumes are, um, slightly carcinogenic."

The eyebrows on his round, black face crept upward and he made no attempt to come any closer, leaning against the doorjamb instead. He nearly filled the entire opening, and she expected he could subdue unruly residents without much difficulty. His name badge read, COGLAN. "Proving once again that OSHA doesn't care about us public servants."

"The fume hood catches it all . . . I hope. It may be an old-fashioned technique but it works, and it works on almost all surfaces, even problem ones like money or painted drywall. On top of that it disappears in a few hours, so the nurses won't have to deal with a bunch of dirty medicine bottles." She moved a fumed bottle to where she'd placed her camera on a short tripod, to photograph the print. The curved surface wasn't helpful, so she took several shots, rotating the bottle. A program could "stitch" them together into a flattened version of the print if necessary, but unless Damon turned out to have something called risperidone in his system, she would be disregarding this bottle's prints anyway.

"Disappears," Officer Coglan mused.

"Which also makes it handy for use in IA or other hush-hush investigations." She meant Internal Affairs or spy-type things, where the cops could go into an office or home and process the area for prints, but when the target arrived hours later all trace of the processing would be gone.

"I'll have to keep that in mind." He asked what had happened to Damon, and she told him they didn't know yet.

He said, "Not surprising. Not often we get a kid who *literally* bounces off the walls. We'd have to hold on to the back of his shirt like you'd hold a dog by his scruff. Went through at least seven of his shirts that way. Had to—couldn't grab his hair. That had had to be shaved because of the lice."

"I heard he was quite a handful."

"Eh, I didn't mind him. He was easy to figure out once you realized he was like a squirrel you'd cornered in your garage. And he didn't talk, which also made him a hell of a lot easier to get along with."

Maggie laughed and passed the bottle off to Josh, still discussing cake frosting with his girlfriend. He had started out by insisting he didn't care about flavoring as long as it wasn't lemon, but then had some objection to every suggestion offered. Strawberry was for little kids. Licorice was weird. Vanilla was boring.

Coglan said, "I couldn't get too mad at him for being what he'd been raised to be. A lot of the other kids here, though . . . it gets hard to feel real bad about anything you do to them."

"How so?" Maggie asked, wanting to know what might be "done" to them.

He rubbed his face and his voice lost its boisterous quality. "Most of them think that if they ask you to pass the salt and you say there isn't any on the table, the logical response is to beat the shit out of you. Simple as that. Normal teenage trash-talk is grounds for instant retaliation. Last week we had one girl choke another because the first implied that the second's shirt might be a little too small. It took me and another guy to pull her off."

Hmm, Maggie thought. *Dr. Palmer and Ms. Washington hadn't seen fit to mention that when asked about recent violence.* "That wouldn't have been Rachael Donahue, would it?"

"Scanning the memory banks . . . don't recognize the name . . . oh, is that the chick that did a header in the stairwell last week?"

"Yes."

"Nah, I hadn't run into her."

The iodine smoke raised a good latent on a nearly empty bottle of Ritalin, and Maggie placed it under the camera.

Officer Coglan continued to shoot the breeze, taking advantage of a new grown-up on his beat. "I decided to work here because, well, I got sick of the prison, but mostly I thought I could give back a little. I grew up in a crappy neighborhood, I ran with a gang, I got arrested at thirteen. I thought I could say that I know where these kids come from, show them that I could pull myself out so they can, too."

"That's a great thing." Maggie finished with the Ritalin. Behind its spot sat a yellow box of EpiPens. It had no sticker to indicate that they had been prescribed to someone in particular, so they were probably kept on hand as a general first aid item. Oddly, the box had been opened and the pens protruded from its top.

"Yeah, except—some of the stories behind these kids make *my* hair curl. They can look at you with eyes so dead it gives *me* the creeps. I get that these kids have bad things behind them, but that doesn't change the fact that they're as sneaky and lying as a guy who's done twenty on death row. They've been in the system long enough to learn what to say, how to act in front of who. With each other they're all the baddest mother in the valley. With their social worker it's all wah, wah, my daddy beat me. In court they're deprived and depraved and have deep mental issues, anything to stay out of adult court. Usually kids are bad liars, even ones who have been arrested and NTA'd out the wazoo."

He meant issued a Notice to Appear, a "ticket" for minor offenses like small drug possession or traffic fines. It gave the person a court date to go in front of a judge, but the person wasn't officially arrested, fingerprinted, or detained.

The EpiPens distracted her. They came four to a box, snug in their outer cases, and not looking much like pens at nearly half a foot long and as big around as a quarter. She breathed iodine onto the box. Nothing.

"But every kid in this building can look you straight in the eye and convince you the sky is green. It's scary. *They're* scary. And as many hours as Doc Palmer and all the shrinks and substitute moms and dads put in here, they can't fix that. Once a kid has been programmed to never give a shit, they aren't going to turn into some sweet, caring type. They're going to rob, beat, rape, game the system, take drugs, sell drugs, and generally be a toothpick in everyone's eye until they overdose in an alley somewhere, and the only thing we can do is hope that happens sooner rather than later."

An accurate assessment, Maggie suspected, but the human being in her didn't want to admit it. So she said nothing, occupied with the obviously used EpiPens. The outer carrying case of each pen had a flip top that had been opened—and had to stay open since the pen tips had been extended and were now too long to fit. That happened when an injection was made. The needle retracted after use but the orange tip mechanism remained extended. The opposite end, missing its blue safety cap, protruded from the carrying tube and in turn the box.

In the doorway, Officer Coglan shifted and his voice took on a less personal quality. "Mrs. Sherman." A female voice answered him, but Maggie couldn't make out the words.

Why keep a box of used EpiPens?

"Family counseling is part of the program," she heard Officer Coglan saying, in a stilted way that implied he had had this conversation before, and more than once.

Perhaps the nurses kept them to remember to reorder, or as part of some inventory tracking system. But she hadn't run across any other empty items, and there were no fresh EpiPens to be found. Only a still-sealed box of EpiPen Jr.

"Got no right to keep my kid."

"Your kid nearly killed someone."

"He didn't have no choice, that other boy comin' at him. You still got no right to lock him up—"

"The state says we do."

"—and tell me I'm a bad parent. I raised four other kids and half of my sister's—"

"And three of them are in jail. Just sayin'."

Maggie glanced up to see her now, in the hallway, a bundle of swaying cloth and scarves, hair curled to a perfect coif atop her head.

The foam in Damon's mouth could have come from a heart attack brought on by a large dose of epinephrine. Or maybe from anaphylactic shock, as the throat closed up and breathing got difficult.

In the hallway Mrs. Sherman said, "So I'm a bad person, now? I'm the villain? I gots to have some little college intern telling me how I ought to run my house?"

Coglan's voice leaked a pained patience. "Everyone can use help in raising kids. I've got two myself, and there's lots of things I could have done better—"

But, Maggie knew, anaphylactic shock typically brought on vomiting and skin changes, and Damon hadn't shown any signs of that. And the ME investigator hadn't seen any signs of injection. She held one of the pens inside her fume hood while trying to juggle the iodine wand and its hose with her free hand.

"I don't need no help. My mama raised me the same way and I turned out all right."

"Um, yeah—"

"People in my neighborhood tired of the county tryin' to tell us who we gots to be."

"I get that. But this is about what's best for your son, right?"

"I'm his *mother*. I *know* what's—" Mrs. Sherman insisted, and then her voice became lost in the hum of the fume hood as Maggie processed both the pen and its protective outer tube with iodine.

No fingerprint ridges turned brown for her. She tried the other tubes and their pens. Nothing.

Maggie pulled off her gloves and called the ME's office, where a kindly diener told her what he could.

Officer Coglan reappeared in the infirmary's doorway. "Once again the world should be safe from the wrath of the Sherman Tank for the next half hour or so. She's shut in a room with the therapist and her kid, and whatever they pay that therapist, it ain't enough. I know it ain't easy to let someone tell you how to be a parent. I've been there—though usually it's my own mother telling me, so I guess that's different . . . or maybe just as annoying but in a different way. But you gotta do it. You gotta listen. Because it's amazing how much a little family counseling can make a difference in what a kid is doing. Being aware of the problem is half the solution and that sort of—"

"Do you know where the detectives are?" Maggie asked.

"No, I don't. Want me to find 'em?"

"Yes, please," Maggie said. "I need them. I need Jack."

Chapter 12

At that moment Jack and Riley were hanging around Melanie Szabo's door like two tardy students who needed a permission slip signed. A few minutes after the half hour the door opened and the tiny girl who had been sitting on the floor in the fourteen- to fifteen-group room came out. She froze when she saw them, fight-or-flight instincts clearly battling. To judge from the expressions flitting across her face she assumed they had come for her, then doubted, then felt sure of it—

"We're here to see Dr. Szabo," Riley assured her.

That didn't seem to comfort her any, yet with a glance back into the room behind her, she squared her shoulders and stepped closer to them. The tiny gesture made Jack respect the kid; he hoped she could defeat whatever demons had hounded her into a life of violence.

"Rachael had a boyfriend," she whispered.

And before they could follow up she had skipped away, as lightly and abruptly as a deer in the woods.

Melanie Szabo appeared in her doorway. "Detectives? Can I help you? I heard about Damon—that's awful. Poor kid."

Riley did his usual glad-handing, sorry-for-interrupting intro.

"No worries. My next appointment is a dawdler. He's probably still perfecting his jump shot."

Riley explained that they had heard about the house-tree-person test and would like to see Rachael's. The therapist seemed surprised by the request but promptly found Rachael's file in her overstuffed cabinet. It rested in a corner of the room next to a small desk that looked more like a drafting table; it held a laptop and monitor. Some thought had been given to making the therapy office nonconfrontational. No large desk for her to sit behind as they conversed; two padded office chairs faced each other over a circular throw rug, with a third and fourth chair tucked against the wall if needed. No framed diplomas on the walls, only an abstract poster in muted colors. A box of tissues and pads of paper and pens for those residents who found it easier to write than to talk and a blue recycling bin. But no personal items, no family photos, knickknacks, stuffed animals, takeout menus. Jack wondered if it had been designed to keep the child's focus on their own personality rather than the therapist's. More than one therapist used the room, so maybe they weren't encouraged to tailor it to their own tastes.

And perhaps the doctors kept the surroundings generic for more practical reasons. Perhaps they had learned from prison guards that anything learned can be used against you. Never let them know where you live, what you drive, who your family members are, where your kids go to school.

Or they didn't want to leave objects around that could be easily picked up and thrown.

While he puzzled this out, Dr. Szabo spread a piece of white copy paper on the table for their perusal.

Rachael had used a pencil to sketch a two-story house with columns flanking the entryway. Windows had four panes and shutters and curtains hung inside them. The door had panels and an elaborate knocker. Several trees with big fluffy tops flanked it. A girl stood beneath one, with long hair and a long dress, both of which blew in an unseen wind. One spiny hand rested gracefully against the tree trunk.

"Huh," Riley said.

"What does this mean?" Jack asked the therapist, to cut to the chase. Playing amateur psychologist had never interested him. Actions were much more important than thoughts.

"Good question. This test can get harder to interpret the older the subject is. Teens, especially, can be unpredictable. Some resent doing it at all because drawing pictures seems like little-kid stuff, so we let them pick their own paper and writing implements. No crayons, that's too babyish. I give them colored pencils. The colors can be significant."

"So we heard," Riley said.

"Some get sneaky and try to draw what they think you want to see. Whatever will make us go away and get off their back. Some leave things out because they don't think they have much artistic ability and don't want to be embarrassed."

"Okay. So what did this test tell you?"

Szabo hemmed and then asked what they noticed, ever determined to teach.

"It looks fine," Riley said. Jack refused to play.

"Exactly. It's perfect. Beautiful house, beautiful lawn. There's a chimney with smoke coming out, which indicates a warm, inviting home. There's a knob on the front door, which could mean she *wants* to go in the house. The windows are uniform. If one was colored in with black or red, that could indicate abuse occurred in that room but the rest of the house was okay. On top of the nice, warm home we have a pretty girl with nice hair and clothes. Even a sun shining in the sky. I'm surprised she didn't throw in a unicorn."

Riley said, "It's too perfect. Rachael is trying to convince you that there's nothing wrong with her."

"She's trying to convince herself. This certainly isn't *her* home; she lived first in a crappy apartment, then in a falling-down bungalow in Garfield Heights somewhere. This is a fantasy. Maybe it's a picture she saw once—I don't know. The long dress, something she'd never wear in real life—like a princess or a girl on the cover of a period novel."

"But the girl doesn't have a face," Jack pointed out.

"Yes! That could be interpreted a number of ways. I asked her what the girl looked like, trying to draw her out—no pun intended! She said the girl was too far away to see clearly, then said she couldn't draw faces very well. Rachael knows this isn't her life, never was, never could be. She keeps trying but can't really see herself as the girl in the picture."

"Sad," Riley said.

"So much about these kids is sad, Detective. If you let it, that vortex will suck you down. The real challenge is to find the life, the joy in them. Plug them back into that resilience."

"We heard about Rachael's boyfriend," Riley said.

"Huh," Melanie Szabo said, settling back into her chair. "I didn't. I asked her about boys, if she had anyone special. She gave me that nineteen forties Bette Davis enigmatic smile."

"And that meant?"

"That she didn't but wanted me to think she did. Rachael had an arsenal of deflections like that. Why . . . why are you asking about Rachael, anyhow? I thought she was ruled an accidental death."

Good question, Jack thought. *Ask my partner, who's suddenly insatiably curious about the inner workings of teenage girls.*

Riley said, "It was. I just—"

"There you are!"

They turned. A mountain of a black man in a type of uniform said, "You're from CPD? Your forensic girl is looking for you."

They thanked Melanie Szabo for her time and left her to the lanky young boy who wandered in for his appointment.

I oughta have my head examined, Rick Gardiner thought to himself. This was crazy. A city full of suspects and he found himself looking at a cop. And most of his belief that the guy was dirty stemmed from the fact that said guy had something going with Rick's ex-wife. Rick wasn't stupid. He knew that suspicion could be swaying his perception to ridiculous lengths. No question.

But a cop as the vigilante killer made sense in a lot of ways.

And what the heck, he didn't have anything else to go on. The killer had been a ghost. The victims had had no connection with each other, operated in different theaters. A gang leader, a drug dealer, a child pornographer, a Eurotrash human trafficker. They had no clients, victims, or suppliers in common.

They only thing they *had* had in common was the cops. So maybe he wasn't so crazy after all.

Okay, *maybe* some arch villain had tried to corner the market on each and every brand of vice the city had to offer. Maybe he even had a cool nickname and Rick would need Batman to come and rout the guy out.

But in the meantime, he couldn't make himself give up on Jack Renner. The victims hadn't begun to turn up until after Renner joined the force. Who but a cop would be able to set up that murder room and not leave a print or some touch DNA on an old envelope or something that Maggie would find—

Maggie.

A cold feeling washed over him. It took his breath away, his body's reaction stunning even himself. All those things could have disappeared from the lab—

No. Maggie hadn't processed the murder room; that had been one of those other idiots, the girl or the boy.

Though Maggie would have access to anything they brought back. She could alter, ruin, or make things go away entirely.

No. Not Goody Two-shoes Maggie. Not covering up multiple murders committed *by a police officer* for chrissakes. She wouldn't even let Rick double-claim his 1040 expenses.

Not possible.

Get your head straight, Gardiner. You've got a case, you've got a hunch, you can either act on it or throw it out for good.

He stood up.

"Where ya headed?" his partner asked.

"HR."

"Going to polish up your resume?"

"Not mine," Rick said, and headed for the elevator.

Quentin Sherman listened to the math teacher with surprising interest. Not that he let on—anyone who glanced his way would see his face frozen in the same sullen mask he wore like a suit of armor. Never let anybody know what you were thinking. Never let them get too comfortable. Never let them forget who's boss.

One-Eye had taught him that.

Quentin stared at the teacher as if deciding where to put a bullet, but actually he thought of uses for calculating a percentage change. New minus old over old, then multiply by one hundred—and he could calculate how much sales from each corner had increased or decreased. He could make a rule: Decrease by a certain percent, and you get a beating. Increase, you get a bonus.

Motivating his employees could be a problem sometimes.

One-Eye had run the gang in his neighborhood, the gang that beat Quentin bloody once or twice a week during his ninth year. It had been worth it, though. When he kept coming around despite the beatings, One-Eye knew he'd be a good soldier and let him in. Which was all Quentin had wanted.

Quentin had exactly enough self-awareness to know that he represented a walking cliché. No father, grew up in a falling-down pit of cockroaches and fleas, a mother who brought a revolving circle of "uncles" into the home—at least in her younger years—and who told him he was stupid and ungrateful and should have been aborted but would fight others bloody if they dared to criticize him. Joined a gang because without it he would have been entirely alone. Rose up the ranks, bided his time, struck when One-Eye violated his own rule and got too comfortable. He let Quentin get too close, close enough to put a .38 to the back of One-Eye's head and leave his body in an alley to be blamed on a rival gang. It had been the old man's own fault for letting his guard down. Quentin only did what One-Eye had always told him to do, and any remorse felt would have been as phony as a knockoff perfume.

No one ever found out about that. But let him pistol-whip some white boy who couldn't pay his dealer and suddenly the cops dumped him into this low-rent version of juvie hell. Now he had to waste every day pulling on his dick while outside there was money to be made. He ached with the frustration until he wanted to put a beat down on every person in sight. Even his therapists. *Especially* his therapists, since they recognized the cliché just as he did. He could feel their utter disinterest in every session.

The sessions themselves were torture—so many better things he could be doing: having some girl, smoking some crack, eating a decent burger. He would have had a better time in a real prison, and it would sure as hell impress his boys much more than this stupid juvie halfway house. When he came out of a place like the

Youngstown supermax no one would dare to do to him what he'd done to One-Eye. But when he got out of this place he'd have to watch his six like never before. His crew might be thinking they could forget him, move on to the next king of the shit pile.

This kiddie pen sucked. No wonder the shrinks didn't care about nothing.

Depending on how things worked out, though, their interest might be perking up.

Nobody forgot about Quentin Sherman.

Chapter 13

"What's up?" Jack asked as soon as the two cops returned to the infirmary.

Maggie held up the object in question by one end, the brownish iodine still clinging to its surface in vague swipes. Josh had taken over the fuming for her, making slow progress through their office full of possible weapons. She didn't want to stop looking merely because she might have found it. "This is an EpiPen. Used in case of anaphylactic shock." She didn't add that she knew he knew all about anaphylactic shock after the untimely death of a criminal defendant over the summer.

"So?" Jack asked.

"It's empty."

"And?" he asked more warily.

"Someone used it, put it back into its outer plastic tube, put that back in the box, and put the box back into the cabinet."

"Is that weird?" Riley asked.

"Did Damon die of anaphylactic shock?" Jack asked.

"Yes, and no. In that order. I called the ME—they

aren't going to get to the autopsy until tomorrow, but they did an external exam and there's no sign of any allergic reaction. No skin rashes, no swelling of the throat, etcetera."

"What we first thought, then? Poison?"

"Maybe. He could have had some bizarre abnormality, given the malnutrition and lack of medical care in his life to date. Or he could have been injected with four doses of epinephrine, which might threaten a grown man with heart seizure. Certainly it would do a number on a skinny ten-year-old."

Riley had been peering at the object in her hand. It was a rather confusing item, labeled from top to bottom with instructions and warnings. The bright orange tip put one in mind of a glue gun rather than a medical device. "How can you tell it's empty?"

"To use one of these, you have to take the blue cap off the end first."

"What blue cap?"

"Exactly. It's missing. Then you jam it into the victim's thigh and the needle comes out automatically, the mechanism pumps the epinephrine into their system. It's a single-use item, no way to refill or reuse. See this little window here? It would be clear if there were still solution inside. It turns this grayish color after emptying."

"You know a lot about EpiPens," Riley commented.

She couldn't help a darting glance at Jack. He would know she thought about that day in the courtroom, but she said, "I had to use one on Amy a couple of years ago when we were processing a house and disturbed a beehive in the wall."

"So someone used the pen and put it back instead of

throwing it out," Jack said, his tone adding, *That doesn't prove much.*

"All four. All four in the box are empty. It's their whole adult supply. There's no way the staff would use them and not order more—they'd never risk being without one."

"Can you tell when—"

"No. So they *could* have been sitting there for a while and no one ever noticed because they never needed them—but they haven't. You can see from the expiration date on the box that they received this last summer. I asked Nurse Brandreth and she said she last used one on a sixteen-year-old with a peanut allergy two years ago. So this box should hold four unused pens."

"We're taking this nurse's word for a lot of stuff," Jack said.

Maggie nodded. "Yes, but I'm not seeing any reason to doubt her. I've been going through these cabinets for an hour—everything is categorized, labeled, neatly stored. This infirmary is organized and well run. This entire building seems aware of how iffy the funding is for places like this and being careless with drugs could get them shut down. The nurses have to dot every *i* and cross every *t*."

Riley said, "Just suppose . . . she thought the kid was having an allergic reaction, for whatever reason, panicked, and used too much EpiPen. Kid dies, she panics again and pretends she's got no clue what happened."

Maggie disagreed. "She'd have to be completely incompetent, which she does not seem to be, to overuse the epinephrine to such an extent. On top of that you wouldn't even use a regular EpiPen on a child Damon's size—you'd use this." She held up a different box, labeled EpiPen Jr.

"Are those—"

"Full. Not used. They were sitting right next to the adult ones, so even someone who wasn't medically trained would figure out the right box."

"Any prints on the used ones?" Jack asked.

"None. On anything—the box, the outer plastic tubes, the actual pens."

"Which doesn't make any sense if they were used legitimately."

She said, "Maybe—molded plastic isn't exactly the best surface. It's not as smooth as it looks. But since to use one you're supposed to hold it in your fist and jam it into the thick muscle for a few seconds to a minute, you would think I'd at least find smears."

"The killer wiped it."

"Okay, wait," Riley said. "Does that thing have a needle?"

"A pretty big one."

"What kid sits still to get poked with a needle *four* times? Especially this kid—it'd be like trying to give a cat a pill. Four times. Wouldn't he—oh."

They explained to Maggie that Damon could not speak.

"The perfect victim," she said. "He can't call for help, and even if he groaned loud enough to attract attention or had an incredible constitution and survived, he couldn't tell anyone what happened."

Jack said, "His abilities were so backward, he would never have been able to explain . . . well, except for pictures. He could have drawn it."

Riley said, "His teacher said he was super obser-vant. *If* he had survived, he might have been able to identify the killer. But would his killer have known that, or counted on it? Is that why the overkill? Or was it someone who had no idea how much epinephrine it takes to kill a ten-year-old?"

Maggie said, "That I can't tell you."

Jack pointed out, "The investigator didn't see any injection marks."

"No, but he had that big scrape on his thigh, from the playground fall. The injection marks could have been hidden in that. The pathologist is going to check for them."

"How long would it take the kid to die?" Riley asked.

Maggie said, "I really don't know. That's doctor ter-ritory. But I'd guess that by the last one or two, Damon would have been in pretty bad shape."

"Twenty minutes. Someone had to come in, find the Epi-Pens, hold the kid down, and inject him four times. That took a while."

Jack said, "Not that long. A couple minutes, maybe, assuming they knew where the pens were and didn't have to browse through the medicine cabinets looking for something lethal."

Riley said, "Assuming they didn't have to catch the kid first. It might have been someone he trusted—at least until that first needle hit his skin and he went into Tasmanian devil action. Or he might have been sleep-ing, then ditto. It took a marching band to wake up my kids at that age."

He paced in a wide circle. Jack rubbed his face.

"We're going to have to do a timeline," Riley said.

"Of everyone in this building," Jack said.

"Without cameras or prints—no one needs a key to get in the door—it's going to be back to the Sherlock Holmes crap. Next we'll be looking at cigar ash and the train schedule."

"That's very literary," Maggie said. "But only a few have a reason to be in this room, and anyone else should have a hard time explaining it if their prints turn up."

Jack said, "If they had the sense to wipe down the pens, they would have wiped anything else they touched . . . or could always say they popped in for an aspirin or something."

Riley said, "Working here, these people probably go through a bottle a day."

Maggie said, "But that still eliminates the kids— they're all locked down, aren't they?"

Riley said, "Yes, but between classes and meals and kitchen duty and day program kids, bathroom breaks, hall passes, lawyer and family visits, I'll bet the degree to which the inmates run this prison is a lot higher than you'd think."

"And they're the killers," Jack said.

Riley looked up at the ceiling, where an empty black half circle bubbled out of the surface. "Why oh why couldn't this supercomprehensive camera system already be installed?"

"Maybe it is," Jack said. "Let's find out for sure."

He took Maggie with him, just in case video existed and anything appeared on it that he didn't want Riley to see, as unlikely as that seemed. Riley had never asked about his extra phone and wouldn't start now. Probably.

He also had little skill with most video systems and wanted to save a return trip to the reception area to fetch her. Dr. Palmer himself guided them to the tiny room on the third floor, tut-tutting about the lack of progress on the renovations, only to be called away by the demands of someone a frazzled therapist referred to as the Tank. Riley had been left in the reception area, getting a staff schedule with entry and exit times.

The third-floor room had been set up with four monitors on a cheap laminate desk, a keyboard, a mouse, a manual, and a bank of DVRs on mounted bases on the wall. When Maggie touched the mouse the monitors sprung to life with a series of boxes, sixteen on each monitor. Most were blank.

Jack said, "Huh. Got something."

One square on one monitor showed the visitor's area, where a woman had brought a small, decorated cake to a young Hispanic girl. She smiled shyly as the woman cut slices with a plastic knife. Maggie's stomach rumbled.

"Hungry?" Jack asked.

"Yes."

The next two monitors were blank, but the last one had three squares functioning. The camera squares had no identifiers, no time stamps. One showed a patch of grass, fenced with ten-foot chain link topped with a discreet ribbon of razor wire. At first glance it might look like an ordinary school's play yard. Maggie had gotten oriented enough to guess aloud that it was the recreation area for the under-twelve group. The second viewed the sidewalk and entrance door by the receptionist that they had used on all their visits.

The last showed a wide entry lobby with an exterior

door and a wide counter that cut the room nearly in half. It funneled the occupants through a metal detector.

"Where's that?" Maggie asked.

"The day program entrance. Serving the slightly less violent children."

"You're not crazy about this place, are you?"

"I'm all for trying to rehabilitate juvenile delinquents, but I can't believe they have much of a long-term success rate."

She slid into one of the chairs, provided for security guards who hadn't yet been hired. "You have to try."

"Sure. There's nothing here that can help us," he added, fighting a sense of relief. Even if there happened to be a camera covering the reception area hallway, Riley wouldn't have seen anything except Jack speaking on the phone—hardly a suspicious activity. But he might ask who had been on it, and then Jack would have to lie, and then he'd have to remember the lie so he could stick with it, and those little details could pile up until one day they fell over and crushed him. No thanks. Best to keep himself as much of a blank as possible. "Let's go."

She didn't move, staring up at him.

"What?"

"Does this place present a—a dilemma? For you?"

After one surprised second he snorted. "What are you asking, Maggie? If I'm planning to kill any of them? They're kids."

"So was—"

"No, okay? No." He couldn't help glancing at the hallway. He feared being overheard and that fear made him annoyed, almost as annoyed as letting Maggie Gardiner into his life in the first place.

Not that he had had much of a choice.

But letting her get—what, comfortable?—enough with him for a little philosophical chat about whether he should have an age limit to his target list—no. He couldn't allow—

"It's the old question," she went on. "If you could kill Hitler as an infant, would you?"

She turned to the monitors instead of facing him, as if that would make the conversation more dispassionate.

"Would *you*?" he countered.

"Yes. But in that case we know the future. Here we don't, though according to Officer Coglan most of them are already stone-cold psychopaths."

He kept his voice level. "Stay out of my head, Maggie. My reasoning doesn't concern you. You can't—"

"There's no one but me," she said without heat.

He stared at her. That weight on her shoulders . . . only she knew what Jack was. Only she formed a gossamer wall between wholesale murder and the rest of the world.

He had no idea what to say, because, of course, she was right. If his goal was to save future victims of violent crime, then finding a nest of raptor eggs and himself with a stone in his hand presented him with a clear choice: eliminate the ever-widening ripples of future burglaries, rapes, assaults, abused babies, and murders in one application.

Was this a dilemma? Or an opportunity?

He said to her, "You're missing the important point—"

"What is this kid doing?" She pointed to the video of the day program entrance. A tall boy in the uniform of his peers—oversized sports jersey, ball cap cocked at an angle that only looked cute on a toddler. "He walked in from the outside and is just standing there."

"Probably waiting for a friend," Jack suggested, pathetically grateful for the change in topics.

"He keeps moving around behind the outflux of students."

"Outflux?"

"It's like he's trying to avoid the guy behind the desk." A man in a uniform similar to Officer Coglan's stood watching the young people leave, occasionally talking to one or fielding a question once they were on the other side of the counter. Most of the kids seemed like any students at the end of the school day, hustling out of the starting gate without a backward glance. But two boys exited the metal detector, made definite eye contact with the waiting visitor, then moved away from the detector to the unoccupied end of the outer floor.

A fourth boy in the parade of kids glanced at all three, then stopped and stepped out of line for the detector so that he remained on the inside of the security zone. Jack recognized him as the particularly active basketball player, but right now he kept his energy burner hidden, his movements furtive.

As Jack watched, the two boys at the far end of the room seemed to be speaking loudly to each other. The first pushed the second with a theatrical shove of fingers to shoulders, then let his hands fly. The second got up in his face.

"This is a setup," Jack murmured to himself.

As soon as the officer leaned over the counter, apparently to threaten the boys to behave or else, the visitor in the corner near the metal detector tossed a package to the boy waiting behind it. It flew smoothly over the four-foot-high barrier between the detector and the wall. The waiting boy caught it with both hands, secreted it inside the pocket of his hoodie, turned, and walked back into the interior rooms in one fluid movement. The kids around him had undoubtedly seen this exchange—a pair of girls whispered, a boy's gaze followed the package but then he moved forward and out the door. No one alerted the guard, still talking to the two boys faking a fight. No doubt seeing that their purpose had been achieved, they now apparently agreed to a truce and left.

"What do you think that was?" Maggie asked Jack.

"Nothing good."

He ran out the door.

Of course, she followed.

Chapter 14

They moved hastily through the third-floor visiting rooms, empty except for the two people with the cake and a paunchy man in a suit speaking to an apparent client. Both he and the girl looked bored and impatient.

Jack did not have a gun, Maggie remembered. Law enforcement officers (LEOs) were required to check weapons in locked bins at the reception area, standard procedure for entry to any prison, jail, or custody location. It could prove too easy for the residents to grab one from a distracted LEO.

Maggie couldn't be sure he knew where he was going—but the classrooms and the day program entrance were on the east side of the building. The boy with the package couldn't go far.

Jack could have called for the security guards—except they didn't all have the same radios, as cops would, and he didn't know the number and didn't have time to stop and find out.

They passed a tiny office and Dr. Palmer looked up from his cluttered desk. As they sped past Maggie barked out a call for help, hoping that her voice would convey the urgency.

Her mind returned to Jack's lack of a firearm. There could have been anything in the package so surreptitiously passed into the secure zone—a knife, a drug shipment for a resident, money for same, a set of skeleton keys, a secret cell phone, even cigarettes. All of which Jack could easily handle with a boy of less weight and height than himself. As long as it wasn't a gun.

Please don't let it be a gun, she prayed, as they darted in and out of the empty third-floor classrooms.

Jack took the stairwell in the center of the hallway, Dr. Palmer trying to catch up to them.

On the second floor they found the boy, in the last classroom to the north. And he wasn't alone.

Jack entered, then stopped dead, causing her to run into the back of him. Over his shoulder she saw the boy who had caught the package.

And of course it *had* been a gun. She knew that because he now held it in his hand, extended, aimed squarely at the face of a young Hispanic man.

The little girl who had sat on the floor when they questioned the group about Rachael cowered in the corner, on the same side of the room as Maggie and Jack.

The boy with the gun swiveled to point it at the intruders. Jack held up his hands.

"No problem," he said in a calm voice. "We just wanted to see what was going on."

"I'm goin' to kill this—" The boy ended with an unpleasant and incestuous epithet. "That's what's going to happen."

"Maggie, get out," Jack said quietly, without turning his head or lowering his hands.

The kid said, "Yeah, Maggie. Get out."

"Okay. I will. If she can come with me." Maggie nodded to her right, toward the girl in the corner. On her left she glimpsed Dr. Palmer hovering in the hallway, out of sight of the boy with the gun.

"You know what, forget it. Ain't nobody goin' nowhere. Y'all can watch when he die."

"Maggie," Jack said.

"Then I'm just going to wait over here with her." She tried to keep her voice as low and calm as his, and moved slowly, her hands in view, toward the girl. Jack reached one arm back to catch her but she sidled around him and made it to the corner, the barrel of the boy's gun trained on her the entire time. She could see his finger on the trigger. She could also feel Jack's murderous glance at her and understood it—she'd just violated one of the rules of hostage negotiation: never give them another target.

In the hallway, Dr. Palmer said something to a handsome black man, who trotted away with silent footfalls, no doubt to summon the guards and probably the police.

Maggie reached the girl, both of them facing forward, hiding nothing. She kept her hands up. "Are you okay?" she asked quietly.

The girl shook her head in quick jerks as she trembled from head to toe. She wore mascara, Maggie could see, but no other makeup. Her sweater hung on her, jutting collarbones emphasizing her spindly frame. Her dark hair seemed to have been cut with a pair of garden shears but somehow suited her. She smelled of a fruity body spray and sweat.

"What's your name?" Maggie asked quietly.

She could hardly hear the answer. "Trina."

"Well, Trina, we're going to be all right. That's Jack, there, and he will take care of this."

And she prayed that this would prove true. From what she had seen of Jack, negotiation did not seem to be his forte. Neither were teenagers. *Homicidal* teenagers—doubly bad.

"So what's going on?" Jack asked. "Why do you want to shoot Luis?"

"You know him? Not surprisin'—little narco."

This caught Maggie as well. The targeted boy must be the friend of Rachael's whom Jack and Riley had interviewed.

"He didn't tell us anything about you. I don't even know who you are."

"You don't need to." He hadn't lowered the gun, now back on Luis, who stood absolutely still but without raising his hands. The expressions flitting over his face ranged from angry to frightened to defiant.

Jack said, "Come on, you're a student here, right? Everyone in the building knows who you are. Clue me in."

"I'm Quentin Sherman. Q-ball to my friends, which this guy ain't."

"Interesting to meet you, Quentin. What's your beef with Luis?"

"He knocked my sister and her little baby down."

Luis spoke, angrily: "I didn't mean to. I was robbing the place, had to get out of there. She was just in the way."

"You ran over my nephew! Kid had blood all down his face."

"I bumped into them! It's not like I beat down on 'em. Get a grip."

"Okay," Jack said. "So—"

"And you ain't apologized!"

"I was runnin' away, dude! I didn't have time for no apologies!"

"You gots time since, ain't you? Been three months. She ain't heard from you. I ain't heard from you."

"And that's it?" Jack asked, but they weren't listening to him. The gun had not wavered.

Next to her, Trina continued to tremble and Maggie put an arm around her thin shoulders. The girl looked up at her in amazement.

"Why should I apologize to you? I didn't do nothin' to you."

"That's my family. You disrespect *them*, you disrespect *me*."

"Why the hell you deserve respect? You ever show me any?"

"Why the hell should I? You knock down babies and don't even say—"

"You boys talk a lot about respect," Jack said, without raising his voice. "You never seem to figure out that it's not a right. It has to be earned."

Sherman said, "We *do* know that, Mr. Adult. But everything we do to earn it, you tell us we ain't supposed to do. We ain't supposed to fight. We ain't supposed to get with girls. We ain't supposed to speak up. We act like guys an' you say we gots ADD and drug us."

"How about you act like an adult? Do the homework. Get a part-time job. Clean up after yourself at home."

"Yeah, that's the other thing you tell us. Go to college, get a job, and make lotsa money so you can have a nice house and a nice car and dress nice. But I ain't going to go to no college, and there ain't no good jobs. It all a lie."

Switch tactics, Jack, Maggie thought. *You're not going to get anywhere by trying to tell a teenager not to be disappointed in the world around him.*

He did. "Quentin. You have to ask yourself—is this really worth it? You're in a building you can't get away from. If you harm Luis you'll be instantly arrested, if not by me then by Officer Coglan. You'll be looking at armed assault and you know they'll try you as an adult."

Quentin Sherman listened without any sign of softening, but Maggie felt pulled by the smooth reason of Jack's voice. He had coaxed a variety of hardened criminals into his net only to execute them, quietly, humanely. He must, she realized, be quite persuasive when he wanted. A chameleon-like quality, and one she would not have expected.

"And I'm sure Luis is willing to apologize to your sister."

Maggie felt a vibration as the girl under her arm shook her head. "He won't."

"Why not?" Maggie whispered.

"He just won't. They're men. They can't back down."

And indeed, Luis did not pick up on the offer. He appeared to consider but then reject the idea, preferring to lose his life than his street cred.

"It's a guy thing," Maggie agreed. "Just usually not with such lethal results."

Quentin's arm with the gun tightened ever so slightly.

Why doesn't it get tired? Maggie wondered. She doubted she could hold a three-pound weight that steady for that long.

"Is this about Rachael?" Jack asked.

The other four people in the room stared at him. But the one with the gun seemed the most confused.

"Who the hell's Rachael?" Quentin asked.

Luis spoke, his tone exasperated. "No, and it's not about his little nephew, either. It's about Tyson."

Maggie scanned her memory banks to see why that name sounded familiar. Derald Tyson, the boy who had overdosed?

Quentin's form took on a stiffness that made the slightly undersized assassin even more ominous, his voice as hard as steel. "I know you sold him the stuff that killed him."

"I didn't," Luis insisted, almost as firmly. But he had begun to sweat, beads forming along his hairline.

"What the hell you cut it with, hey? Fentanyl? Why you kill him?"

"I didn't. I don't do that anymore."

"Your crew do most of Ohio City, everybody know that. Killin' off most of your customers—that's how stupid you are."

Maggie knew that heroin overdose deaths had sky-rocketed in the past few years, but didn't keep up with which gangs operated where. "Is that true?" she asked Trina, to distract the girl from her fear. The girl whispered back that she didn't know.

The room felt airless, and with two teenage boys leaking testosterone the locker-room smell began to accumulate. Neither Riley nor Coglan appeared in the doorway, and she wasn't sure what they'd be able to do when they did arrive. The classroom had only one door and would be immediately visible to Quentin upon entry.

Jack asked, "This is Derald Tyson? The boy who overdosed last month?"

Quentin didn't bother to look at him. "Yeah."

"I didn't sell him anything," Luis insisted to Jack. "I didn't even know the kid."

Quentin said, "Why you lookin' at him? I'm the one you gotta convince."

Luis wasn't having any of that. "I don't give a shit what you think. I didn't pass Tyson nothing." For a fifteen-year-old with a gun in his face, he showed amazing fortitude. Or foolishness.

Jack said, "So you were close to Tyson. I get that."

Quentin scrunched up his face in extreme annoyance. "Don' say it like that. Like I'm some kinda fag. He was in my crew, that's all. A man's gotta look out for his crew. Anyone mess with him, they mess with me."

"I didn't pass anybody in this school nothing," Luis continued to insist, adding plaintively, "I'm trying. I've been trying."

To get off drugs? Maggie wondered. *To get out of the criminal trade? To pull himself out of the downward spiral into which he'd been thrust, probably since birth?*

Jack said to Quentin, "He was in your crew, okay. So why didn't *you* get him what he wanted?"

This stopped the boy. The gun lowered a few inches as he searched for an answer. "'Cause he didn't ask."

"Why do you think that is?" Jack asked, exactly as Dr. Michaels and her colleagues would. Let the patient reach their own insights—

"I don't know. Mebbe he figured I couldn't get it 'cause I'm stuck in here too. Didn't ask 'cause he didn' wan' embarrass me. Tyson thoughta stuff like that, man. Course I *could* have, gotten whatever. If I wanted."

"He didn't ask me for nothing," Luis stated again. "I don't know where he got the stuff. I probably never said ten words to the guy."

"Your crew sells the shit. You the only one here from your crew," Quentin said, his forensic evidence neatly aligned. The gun came back up.

What does this kid do, Maggie thought, *two hundred push-ups a day?*

But Jack kept trying. "Quentin, you'll wind up in adult prison. Your nephew will be graduating from high school before you have any hope of parole. Is that really what's best for you? Is that really worth it for some petty slight and an accusation you can't be sure of?"

The gun arm remained stock-still. Quentin turned his head to Jack, to Luis, then slowly back to Jack.

"Yeah," he said. "I think it is."

Then he pulled the trigger and shot Luis Borgia in the face.

Chapter 15

Trina screamed. Maggie shoved the girl behind her without thinking. Jack's whole body gave a twitch as if quaking with the urge to run at Quentin, wrest the gun from his hand, but then stalled as the weapon turned to him. It swung toward Maggie and Jack tensed again, but then Quentin decided to prioritize the threats and aimed it back at Jack. About two seconds had elapsed, but they felt like eons.

In the silence that followed, Luis Borgia groaned.

Jack apparently decided to cut out the chitchat. If Luis could hold on, perhaps they could get medical help in time. "What's your end game here, Quentin? What do you want?"

"I want to take everyone down wit' me."

"If you really wanted to die today, you would have done that already."

"I'm gettin' to it." His gaze flicked to Maggie, and Trina behind her, as if deciding whom to shoot first.

"What was your plan for getting out of this? Shoot Luis, drop the gun, melt back into the crowd of students before anyone knew it was you?"

Maggie thought, *Tell him—*

"You're unlucky enough that this is one of the few rooms in the building with a working camera. The video has already recorded you shooting Luis. You can't get out of this."

Quentin looked up at the dark bubble in the ceiling. He fired off two rounds at it, missing both times. Gangbangers didn't get in a lot of range time. That was why they relied on sprays of overkill instead of sniper-like shots. The air clogged with that metallic-smelling smoke and Maggie developed an instant headache as she wondered if the video system even *could* record. With their luck, the cameras only viewed and didn't save.

Behind her, Trina clung to her back with both arms, a little whimper escaping her lips with each *boom*. Who knew what traumas the girl had already survived in her life, and here was this petty gangbanger undoing any progress that the center had been able to achieve in helping her overcome them. Maggie's fear dissipated. "Stop it!"

This interruption surprised Quentin.

She said, "Let Trina get out of here. You're terrifying her."

"Not my fault she's here," Quentin said. "She was hangin' around linin' up Luis."

"Fine. But let her go now."

"You might as well get them both out of here," Jack said to Quentin, calm, man to man. "You're in a room with one door and three cops and a security checkpoint on the way to the only exit. Unless you expect James

Bond to drop from a helicopter, you're not going any-where."

"I am as long as I gots you all," Quentin said, in a confident tone that wavered only a little. Obviously, he had no clue how to get out of the situation he'd created but couldn't let himself admit it. He'd die rather than back down, probably figuring he would do that today anyway, so might as well do it on his own terms—or whatever nonsense teenagers told themselves when they had no real concept of mortality. She knew the whole thrust of hostage negotiation is keep them talk-ing until they accept that they are not going to get a fast car and a million bucks and a police escort to the airport, and give up, but right now they didn't have time for the hours or days that would take. Not when Luis Borgia lay bleeding out on the schoolroom floor.

In the hallway outside the door Maggie saw Riley and Officer Coglan, with Dr. Palmer hovering behind them until Riley shooed him away. Riley caught her gaze. He held up one finger with a questioning look. She dipped her chin, and wondered if Coglan had a weapon, or if Riley had retrieved his.

"Let's do this," Jack was saying. "Give me the gun and I'll ride with you to the police department. I'll make sure you're treated with respect, as a man. Then these women can leave and the medics can see to Luis. I'll tell the prosecutor's office you cooperated. They'll give you the best deal you can get."

Luis Borgia gave a rasping sigh, which seemed to fill every corner of the room. It made the back of Mag-gie's neck tingle. She could see only parts of him, with all the desks in the way, but caught sight of his left hand twitching in spasms. The kid was dying.

Quentin didn't jump at it, but his tone of voice said his brain mulled it over. "I'm not plannin' to go to no jail."

"Come on, Quentin, you know how the world works. You know there's not going to be probation and community service for this. You done the crime. Now you've got to be a man and take the time."

Pretty smart, Maggie thought. He made giving up sound macho. And she thanked him for referring to herself and Trina as women and not girls.

Then Quentin said, "Then it might as well be worth it." And he shot Luis Borgia two more times.

At the first retort some animal instinct took over Maggie, and she dashed for the exit, dragging Trina behind her. Halfway there she heard the second shot and saw a blur as Jack leapt onto a desk to launch himself at Quentin Sherman.

She shoved the small girl into the waiting arms of Riley and Coglin. Then she heard the third shot.

And she turned and ran the three feet back into the room, shouting his name.

In a pit of overturned desks, Jack and the boy struggled. Jack was on top but Quentin was strong, and still had the gun in his left hand. To Maggie's relief, neither appeared to be bleeding and a hole spiderwebbed through one of the windows. She took one step onto the same desk Jack had, then down the other side of it.

Jack straddled the kid, holding both arms to the floor but with difficulty, and couldn't keep them still.

Maggie stomped as hard as she could on Quentin's

left wrist. With both hands she wrestled the gun out of his hand, fighting the fingers that closed around it like metal prongs. She had to wrench it sideways to get the index finger from the trigger guard and couldn't be sure she hadn't broken it. Not that she cared.

With the gun free, she stepped back, stumbling over Luis's body. She didn't point it at Quentin, didn't have to. Coglan and Riley now reached either side of him and together the three men hauled him to his feet. He stopped resisting as the cuffs were snapped on. He had maintained his stubborn manhood and now could take the consequences with his head held high. He said nothing, only drank in Luis's still form as Coglan shuffled him from the room.

Maggie dropped to the floor and pressed her fingers to Luis Borgia's neck. The first bullet had entered his right cheekbone, below the eye, creating a neat hole but bulging the eye out in a reddened, grotesque bulb. The other two shots had entered his chest, only a few tablespoons of blood circling each to dye his white polo shirt. He had died very, very quickly after that.

Jack stood over them, catching his breath. "Anything?"

She shook her head. Then she stood up as well. There would be no more urgency required on Luis Borgia's behalf.

"You all right?" Jack asked.

Her body started toward him, and she realized that she intended to give him a hug. She intended to throw her arms around him in massive relief that that third shot had not gone through his head or his heart or any other vital organ. The realization made her stop as if hitting a glass door she hadn't known was there. She sucked in air. "Uh—yeah. You?"

"Peachy," he said.

During the short elevator ride, Rick Gardiner had formed a plan, founded upon the twin rocks of bureaucratic sprawl and the lack of curiosity on the part of the average civil servant. He calculated those two things alone gave him a 95 percent chance of success.

The woman behind the desk hung up from arguing with either her husband or her child about what to make for dinner and greeted Rick wearily. She appeared to be having a not-so-great day, perhaps feeling more than a little beaten down by life. As long as he didn't tick her off, he figured, she raised his odds to ninety-nine.

"Hiya, slim," he said, friendly but not loud, and despite the fact she needed to lose about thirty pounds.

It worked. About half the lines in her brow smoothed out.

He spun her a tale about how the Ohio Association of Chiefs of Police were considering making Jack Renner Detective of the Year for his work on "that missing kid case" and—

"What missing kid?" the woman asked.

He shouldn't have made up a case involving a kid. Chicks always wanted to know about kids—but it had to sound spectacular or it wouldn't warrant an award. "I don't even remember; it was way back in spring. Anyway my boss wants to have a little bio prepared in case he's got to, you know, make a speech about good old Jack."

"Oh." And the thick clod stood there like she couldn't figure out the rest. But at least she'd forgotten about the fictional missing kid. Probably had enough trouble with her own real ones.

"So I need his resume or whatever, where he was born. Vital statistics kind of crap."

"Oh. But I can't give you his file."

Rick waved his hand as if that was the last thought on his mind. "Of course not. Just tell me the highlights and I'll jot 'em down. Make my boss happy and I can go back to real work."

She considered this, but not for long. Police departments handed out nearly as many awards as Hollywood so the request must have seemed routine to her. And if not, she had too many of her own problems to bother asking questions about his. She shuffled off to get the file.

She returned only after opening three huge file drawers and answering two phone calls. The counter hid Rick's tapping foot. He didn't need another cop walking in and asking what was up, especially one who might know that police chiefs association awards were given only to police chiefs, and then in spring, not fall.

The thin manila folder plopped onto the desk behind the counter and she flipped it open to start at the back, locating the application. Renner must have filled it out online because the responses were printed, not handwritten—this made them easier to read but not as easy to pick out. Plus they were upside down.

"Minneapolis," the woman said aloud.

"What?"

"Born and raised, apparently. Worked for Minne PD

for twenty, then came here. Who moves to Cleveland from Minneapolis?"

"Someone looking for warmer weather?" Rick suggested, leaning over the counter to scan the documents. He needed Maggie for this—she could be sitting on the other side of the breakfast table and read stuff out of the paper upside down faster than he could right side up. But of course, he wouldn't want Maggie for this particular project. He didn't want to think about where her loyalties lay these days.

"Was he a detective there, too?" he asked the woman.

"Yeah—property, then vice."

"Okay. What about personal stuff. Kids? Wife?"

"We can't ask that on the application," she said as if he went beyond stupid. "Why don't you just ask him?"

"I have to keep it hush-hush. It's supposed to be a big surprise to him when he wins, *if* he wins. He may not. The boss just wants to have the bio prepared in case."

"Oh, yeah."

Her phone rang again and, glory be, she moved a few feet away to answer it but left the file open. Rick peered mightily, trying to concentrate on the words, then gave up and managed to turn the file around without attracting the clerk's attention. He jotted down the dates of Renner's employment with Minneapolis PD. He also noted the name of Renner's supervisor there.

The spaces below were blank. He had listed no other police departments prior to Minneapolis, or even a gig twirling ice cream cones at the local Dairy Queen. Not that surprising, since he'd put in the full twenty at the PD. Cops often did that, got their pension from one place and then moved to another for some supplemental income or because they realized fly fishing or golfing all day, every day, might not be the life for them. At least not yet.

The spaces in the "Military" section were all blank.

Under "Education" he had listed a high school—Southern, no, Southwest—but no college. Rick would have figured the smarmy Renner for a degree, but nothing. So he went right into the force, spent twenty years, moved to Cleveland for whatever bizarre reason, gave up on retirement and applied to Cleveland PD. Nothing suspicious.

He scanned for any other useful information. The HR flunky was right—the Equal Employment Opportunity department wouldn't let employers ask for birth date, marital status, or ages or existence of spouses or children on an application. They could, however, get the social security number. Rick carefully wrote 2-8-8-4—

The woman behind the counter slapped the file shut, obviously noticing its position had changed but just as obviously opting not to make a fuss about it. "Anything else?"

Rick forced a smile. "Any awards or commendations they can mention? Something to fancy it up, let the police chiefs know they awarded the right guy?"

She picked up the file so she could flip through it out of his sight. "Nope. A certificate for marksmanship training."

"Nah," Rick said. "We all got those."

"That's it."

Big smile. "Okay. Thanks for helping me out."

At the door, her voice stopped him. "Hey."

Turn slowly, keep it casual. "What, babe?"

"If he wins, make sure we get a copy of the award certificate. For his file."

Rick promised he would absolutely do that.

Chapter 16

It was 10 p.m. by the time they finished with the reports and the questions and walking the Bureau of Corrections as well as an official from the charter school system that provided the teachers through the events of the afternoon. Maggie and Trina sat at a table in the second-floor visitor's area. They had the large room to themselves and their voices all but echoed over the empty tables and worn linoleum. The older woman from the kitchen had done what she could by supplying them with coffee for Maggie and hot chocolate for Trina until Maggie felt ready to jump out of her skin and the girl risked diabetes.

Trina had been shuffled in for an emergency session with Dr. Szabo, and Ms. Washington had hovered for most of the afternoon as a stoic foundation of support. Trina said she had still been in the room finishing up her notes, but Maggie suspected that the girl had been chatting with Luis. Bad luck for both of them, to linger until Quentin could find them alone.

Maggie herself had given her statement several times over, had assured her fellow technician Josh of her continued well-being, and had been sheltered from the media outlets gathered in the street outside to report the latest "school shooting," which technically this wasn't. It had taken place in a schoolroom, Maggie puzzled to herself absently, but it was more along the lines of a fellow prisoner getting shanked in the shower.

This led her to wonder why Quentin hadn't smuggled in a knife, which would have been silent to use and given him a much better chance of wandering off into the crowd long before anyone discovered the body. Perhaps he didn't have the nerve or the skill to carry out hand-to-hand attacks. Or he feared getting blood on his clothes, which he couldn't explain or hide. A gun meant his getaway had to be like lightning, but it would leave no evidence on him except microscopic traces of gunshot residue, easily washed off his hands in the men's room.

Whatever. She had the feeling Quentin Sherman had never been an especially deep thinker. And he *was* only fifteen years old.

"Trina," Maggie said. "You told Detective Renner that Rachael had a boyfriend. Was that Luis?"

Exhaustion had been catching up with the girl, but now her eyes snapped open. She gazed at Maggie as if she had single-handedly rescued her from a dragon and a burning tower.

"No. Uh-uh."

"So who was it?"

Trina ran thin fingers through her shiny hair, which stuck out at odd angles. She had a bracelet tattoo of either barbed wire or twining ivy, Maggie couldn't tell, which looked as if it had been accomplished with ball-point pen. Her nails had been chewed to stubs and her cuticles were red and raw. Maggie had no idea how Trina came to be a resident at the Firebird Center, and didn't want to risk their cautious rapport by prying into her trauma.

"I don't know—I mean I don't know his name. She wouldn't tell me. She said he was older than us and drove a Lexus and had a big house. He was going to kick out his wife and bring Rachael home to live. He was going to get her out of here—legally, not like helping her escape or anything, because he could afford famous lawyers, special guys from New York."

"Was it someone she met here? Or from before she came here?"

"She didn't say, exactly." Trina pulled her knees to her chest in one effortless motion, the fingers of each hand toying with her earlobes as she thought. "But I kinda thought she meant someone who worked here."

"Any kind of description? What he looked like? Hair color, eye color?"

Trina shook her head no to each, adding, "She said he was hot."

That let Dr. Palmer out. On a hotness scale Maggie wouldn't have put him remotely near the flaming end, and she doubted a fifteen-year-old would feel differently. Though women looked at attraction differently when they found someone who treated them with respect and love.

Rachael's therapist and dorm mother were both female. Ditto for the kitchen staff, at least the ones Maggie had met, though they must have others for a twenty-four/seven operation. And could a school cook convince a girl that he could afford fancy lawyers?

Possibly. A smooth-talking grown man could convince a vulnerable teen of just about anything, as the sad history of pedophilia showed.

She asked Trina, "What about teachers? Any male teachers that she could have been referring to? Pardon my grammar."

This made Trina smile, a quick, furtive flash of grin before giving the question serious consideration. "We only have one man teacher, Mr. Lewis. He teaches English."

Maggie remembered Rachael's fascination with ellipses. "Is he hot? Would you think so?"

Trina said no, with that quick grin again. "His nose is all smashed-like and his hair sticks out. He smells like sausages."

"So, not so much, then," Maggie concluded, and this thrust Trina into a fit of giggles, fingers covering the lower half of her face, chin tucked behind her knees, her eyes dancing with delight. Maggie joined in, thinking they were probably both punchy from the adrenaline valley and lack of food. But there were few things more enduring than females giggling about males, and she didn't try to fight it.

"What about Dr. Quintero?"

"Who?"

"The assistant director. He works with Dr. Palmer."

The girl shook her head. "I don't know who that is."

Ms. Washington came into the visiting room to collect Trina, saying it was high time she got to bed. The girl gave Maggie a look that said she felt reluctant to leave her new friend, which Maggie understood. They had a bond forged in fire, and it felt wrong to turn one's back on it.

Kind of like how you feel about Jack popped into her head without warning.

Meanwhile Trina had leaned over the table to say, "Will you come back and visit me?"

This caught Maggie by surprise. "Yes. Of course. Sure . . . actually I might be in and out here for a few more days anyway, given recent events."

The girl got to her feet under Ms. Washington's watchful gaze. "You have to get on the reception list. Then they have to clear you."

Firm now, Maggie said she would take care of it. Trina's face lit up and she all but skipped toward the door with her dorm mother.

What have I gotten myself into? Maggie thought, feeling in no way equipped to serve as mentor for a traumatized teenager with at least some kind of serious criminal history. *Someone who will stick.* She started to pull her own knees to her chin, then shook it off and stood up. Her body wavered slightly as the caffeine overreacted to the change in position. She tried to walk it out while draining the last dregs of the coffee. This left her standing between the garbage and recycling bins debating where a Styrofoam cup fell. Most Styrofoam was recyclable but most facilities were curiously reluctant to accept it. She could take it to the local grocery store along with her old meat trays but didn't feel quite that dedicated to the cause at the moment, given everything else that had gone on all day. On the other hand, she could crumple and shove it into her crime scene kit between the camera and fingerprint powder, or choose the half-assed method and drop it into the recycling bin for the authorities to figure out.

As she puzzled over this she glanced down into the

blue bin and forgot all about the recyclability of Styrofoam.

Maggie pulled on a fresh pair of latex gloves, crouched, and poked around under the accumulated water bottles and pop cans. A minute later she stood and gazed at four small blue objects in her palm.

Jack approached from the hallway, looking for her. "We're about done," he said. "What are those?"

She didn't look up. "Our missing EpiPen caps."

Maggie stored the caps carefully in an evidence box.

Jack asked, "So this person kept the caps, but then decided to dump them in the recycling? He, she, really wants to save the planet?"

"Who knows? He might have put them in his pocket, then discovered them later and wanted to get rid of them in case we decided to search people. All the trash cans here are the standard open-topped household cubes—you can easily see inside, so he wouldn't have wanted to throw them out in the infirmary. If we assume Damon's death was deliberate—and that's still a big if—he would have been hoping we didn't even notice the EpiPens."

"So he took the caps with him but didn't want to take the risk of throwing them out in his own work space. Instead, a common area, which is, of course, not monitored on security video . . . wait, it is. We saw it on the monitors—"

"No, the camera gets that half of the room, not the through traffic along this wall. If we're lucky we might get pictures of who passed through, if they stepped past, say, this point"—she traced a line on the linoleum with her toe—"but we won't have a shot of someone dropping four little items into this bin."

Jack said, "Damn."

"We'll try touch DNA on them, and hope he didn't wipe them off as carefully as he wiped the EpiPens."

"Okay. Is the Luis crime scene all done?" he asked.

"Staties took it over, with my abundant blessings. Meanwhile, Josh wrapped up the infirmary and took everything back to the lab. We've got a ton of prints, none of which we can do anything with unless you can get a warrant to seize or copy all personnel records of Firebird staff. Job applicants won't be in our fingerprint database. The kids we should have, at least the ones with arrests."

"Which is all of them," Jack muttered.

Dr. Palmer, apparently having aged a decade or two since that morning, entered with Riley and Justin Quintero. "I think we finally have the residents calmed down for the night. Most of the day students were already out the door—that's a mercy."

Maggie asked, "The boys who smuggled in the gun—"

"Your people"—she assumed Palmer meant the police—"have already picked them up. I'm so glad I didn't let the construction people disconnect the day entry area camera until they had a new one in place. We don't know the boy who first brought the gun in, however; he isn't one of ours. But Mr. Sherman's gang is a good-sized one. Unlike me, he has no shortage of personnel." He gave an unhappy chuckle at this witticism, and Maggie felt like patting him on the shoulder in sympathy.

"You know all about Sherman, then," Riley said.

"Oh, of course. We know all about all of the children here—it's impossible to help them without knowing the history. I had a bad feeling Mr. Sherman wasn't going to make it."

"He's the one still alive," Jack pointed out.

"I meant make it as in find a way out of the thug life. We're not trying to turn these kids into perfect ladies and gentlemen; we're not that naïve." He sat down heavily, as if his aging legs could no longer hold him. "But if we can keep them out of custodial care, show them a way to live other than by hurting people—that's the goal. It saves society a mountain of pain and hurt and, not to mention, money. But the best way is to identify at-risk youth before they even take their first breath, and intervene then. Not eighteen years later."

"How, though?" Maggie asked.

"Simple. Are the parents poor, unmarried, have been in trouble with the law, have addiction issues? Do they come in turn from parents in the same boat? Were they shuttled from extended families to foster homes and the like? Do they have mental illnesses or issues? Do they have trouble holding a job or show poor judgment in caring for the children or pets that they already have? It's not hard to spot a problem area. Those families need home visits with a social worker—not to judge them or to tell them what to do, but to answer questions, guide them to resources, simply listen to their thoughts and concerns. To provide support, not censure. It is amazing the change that we can make in a family, that they can make in themselves, if they're simply given a little guidance and support."

"Is it a lack of funding?" Maggie asked as Jack shifted impatiently. He didn't seem to have a lot of time for social theories other than his own. And it *had* been a very long day.

"It's a lack of *will*."

"And funding," Quintero put in. "Despite the fact that Ohio spends two hundred and fifty million dollars on juvenile justice every year, too much of it is still sometimes put into projects that don't work, or 'get tough on crime' policies that lock up too many kids while cutting staff at the same time."

His boss went on as if without interruption, eyes focused on the middle distance. "This intervention system needs to be mandatory, and society resists mandatory when it comes to children. America sees child rearing as one of the few bastions of personal independence left. As long as it doesn't result in serious physical harm, no one can tell you what to do with your kids. Certainly not when or where to have them, even though doing exactly that would immeasurably improve the lives of everyone here, most especially the kids. In some states you have to have a home visit before the animal shelter will let you adopt a puppy. But you can push out a baby without so much as a driver's license." He glanced up. "Yes, I sound like an Orwellian nightmare."

"No," Maggie said. "You sound frustrated."

Justin Quintero said, "We'll make it, Doc. We'll wow the budget folks with our success stories until they give us the funding package just to make us stop talking. Then this place won't have any dead zones or security loopholes. Come on, I'll walk you folks out."

Maggie couldn't resist poking her head into the infirmary to apologize to Nurse Brandreth and her counterpart, a slender black woman with graying hair, as they gazed unhappily at the black-powdered cabinets. Damon's bed had been stripped to the mattress and not remade.

"We tried to get everything back in its original place," she told them, and they said they understood but would still have to do a complete inventory. And send an order upstairs for more EpiPens.

Meanwhile Riley warned Quintero, "No chance of keeping this out of the paper."

"I know . . . and the doc has worked so hard on this. Talk about burning the midnight oil—but, hey, the paper doesn't deliver on Tuesdays, so maybe there's just a chance we can schmooze some promises out of the board before it lands on their doorsteps Wednesday morning. And maybe they won't watch the evening news. Maybe," he repeated with an air of hopelessness.

Riley chuckled as Maggie rejoined them in the hallway.

Quintero said, "I know, I'm an optimist. In this business you have to be, or we'd all have shot ourselves years ago. Everyone wants violent kids in custody but they also want us to be able to do it for the same money as intervention programs and community diversionary tools. It can't be done. Our day program is fabulous for keeping kids *out* of incarceration, increasing their chances of staying out, but it's not the same thing as having someone in custody twenty-four/seven. The amount of resources needed increases exponentially. Staffing is seventy percent of the costs. If we can't show real results for the investment—"

The outer door of the hallway opened and two uniformed officers escorted a cuffed Quentin Sherman back into the Firebird Center.

"What the hell?" Riley demanded.

The kid grinned at them. "Hey, thanks for the welcome back. Nice to know you miss me."

"What is he doing here?" Jack asked the cops.

"They don't have any place else to put him," Quintero explained wearily, and Maggie wondered if he had been trying to get them out of the building before the prodigal's return. "The juvenile ward at the jail is full and under eighteen can't be put in the general population. He's already known here and it's a secure facility."

"But he *killed* someone today." Jack seemed to be speaking through gritted teeth.

Quintero gave him a somewhat pitying look. "Nearly every juvenile here has at least tried to kill someone, Detective Renner. Many have succeeded."

The cops hustled Quentin Sherman away. As he passed Maggie he gave her a smile, his eyes as dead as a shark's. She itched to move backward, to step away from his body heat or at least out of kicking range, but didn't let herself. She stayed still and maintained eye contact, and hated every minute of it. As they turned the corner she let out the breath she'd held without realizing it.

Quintero hustled the two detectives and Maggie out the door—probably to avoid listening to the protestations they were too stunned to voice. Prisoners were human beings, with mass, who took up space. If the space wasn't available, it wasn't available. But Maggie had never before seen a killer escorted back to live at the scene of his crime.

"What now?" Riley asked.

Jack looked down at her. "Let's get Maggie something to eat."

"Good idea," his partner said. "I'm about to pass out."

Chapter 17

They went to the Hofbrauhaus, one of the few options still open at that time on a Monday night, and even there an unhappy waitress told them they would close in fifteen minutes. Riley asked her to bring them whatever they still had that hadn't been sitting under a warmer all day, and a couple of beers. Maggie changed hers to a Diet Coke.

"Don't tell me you're some kind of teetotaler," Riley groused.

"Not at all. I just don't like hops or fennel or whatever it is that gives beer its taste. But kudos for using an archaic word like *teetotaler* in a sentence."

She excused herself to wash her face in the women's bathroom, forgoing makeup for the slight refreshment the clean water offered. She returned as Jack continued to grouse—in his abbreviated Jackspeak—about Sherman returning to the center.

"As soon as they clean up Luis's blood he can go back to class, have lunch, play some basketball. Maybe he'll climb right over the chain link on the roof and we'll find him in the street." He set the bread plate down with a *clunk* and Maggie watched him over the hands she had loosely clasped in front of her mouth. The kid had gotten under Jack's skin. If Jack were left to his own devices, Maggie didn't want to place bets on Quentin Sherman making it to adulthood. He was safer inside the Firebird Center than out of it.

Though given recent events, perhaps not.

"Because there's so much *pressure* being a teenager nowadays," Jack went on, disgust in his voice. "Let him have one disabled kid and another about to go to college and then get laid off from the factory, and he'll find out about *pressure*."

His partner cleared his throat. "He's not alone."

This made Jack pause in the act of ripping a dinner roll in half. "Huh?"

"Kids. They all feel stress nowadays. Hannah takes it in stride but Natalie—she holds it in and then it bursts out in a bunch of words. I know it sounds crazy to people our age—we think kids are more spoiled than ever. They have whole TV channels, games, stores, parks, electronics all dedicated to them. Teachers and doctors are forced to cater to their every need. Society decided that they're the most important thing in the universe and they're all told that they're special, they can be anything they want, that they should reach for the stars. Great, right? But you have to look at the cost."

Jack waited, his face calming. Maggie listened.

"We parents think we're being supportive, encouraging the kids to be individuals, but the kids see a mountain of expectations they can't live up to. We send them to school to make friends, but the other kids aren't their friends; they're the competition and that competition gets fierce. They're as cutthroat as day traders who will exploit any weakness to get ahead. We tell them they're special, they're smart, they're great, they can do anything, but at some point reality catches up and they figure out they're not going to be a neurosurgeon and marry a supermodel and drive a Jag. Then they get scared. And *then* they get angry."

"But—" Jack began, and stopped.

"Us pre-Internet-world people think they're just whiny, weak, they want everything handed to them, they have no concept of reality. But it doesn't matter that we never really expected them to become rocket scientists. It's what the kid *perceives*, and to them this pressure is very, very real."

Jack said, "Okay, I get that. But most of the kids at that place—I can't see their parents expressing disappointment that they didn't get into Yale."

"True, but where parents don't create expectations, advertising takes over. Life is supposed to be all about becoming a rap star and buying your mama a house, or winning *American Idol* and getting an endorsement contract. Then you can wear the designer clothes and spray yourself with the designer perfume and get a boob job so that you'll look like the people those things are designed for. It's not just the girls who get their body image warped and not just young people. We scoff at these ads but then go on diets." He patted his beer belly. "Some of us, anyway."

The waitress brought the drinks and all three fell upon the glasses as if they'd recently crossed a desert.

Then Maggie said, "It's the unintended consequences of the self-esteem movement."

"Exactly," Riley agreed. "We were all better off when our parents were happy as long as we moved into the next grade. We weren't expected to get straight As and captain the T-ball team and take piano lessons at the same time."

"And heroes were baseball players who played for the sport and not a million a game," Jack said.

Maggie added, "And models were a size ten instead of two. So what's the solution?"

Riley said he didn't know. "But those days are gone, and they're not coming back. They had their own hazards, but at least more kids got killed outside of school than inside it."

Jack rubbed his face. "We're not done with the Firebird Center, are we?"

"Nope. I want to find out more about Derald Tyson."

"The kid who OD'd?" Maggie asked. "Why?"

Riley said, "This place now has four dead kids within a month. Either they're completely incompetent—and they don't seem to be—or they have a few employees who are completely incompetent. I think little Dr. Palmer needs our help."

"DORC is investigating," Jack pointed out.

"DOC—excuse me, Department of Rehabilitation *and* Correction—hasn't spent as much time there as we have. And we still have an active murder investigation going on."

Maggie pushed her hair behind her ears. Late-late-night dining at least had the advantage of a quiet environment since they were the only people in the restaurant. The waitress brought them plates of sausages and mashed potatoes, about the last thing she wanted to consume before bed both in terms of calories and digestion, but fuel was fuel and her body begged for some. It tasted great, too. "Damon's is the only death that's truly suspicious, and even that could have an innocent explanation. Damon couldn't communicate. It's possible that a staff member or even another child thought he was having some kind of allergic reaction and used the EpiPens. He couldn't describe how his speeding heart felt, so they attributed his distress to the anaphylaxis, administered more EpiPen, he died, and now they're too afraid to speak up."

Riley scowled. "And yet managed to give the kid four shots in the scraped-up area of his thigh, where the scabs would mask the needle tracks?"

"*If* that turns out to be the case. The pens are supposed to go into the thigh and through clothes. The person didn't have to see the scabs. I admit it's hard to picture. An adult would have—one hopes—the sense to grab the EpiPen Jr box, and at least would have yelled for the receptionist to fetch the nurse."

Riley said, "A kid could have wandered in to say hi to their pal Damon. Except Damon wouldn't have known anyone except in the under-twelve group, and I have a hard time picturing one of them having the presence of mind to find and use one EpiPen, much less four."

Jack said, "I have a hard time picturing either an adult *or* a kid panicking enough to overdose the kid but having the presence of mind to wipe their prints off the pens, the cases, the box, and probably the cabinet."

"True," Maggie said.

"Who would want to kill the wild boy?" Riley said. "He might have been a handful but no one seemed to dislike him. At least among the adults."

Maggie added a slice of sausage to a forkful of

mashed potatoes. "Anyone who knew his history felt sorry for the little guy."

They chewed in silence for a while, puzzling this out.

Then Maggie returned to her first point. "The other kids—Luis is hardly a mystery, he died before our eyes. Rachael was probably an accident—"

"Probably," Riley said.

"What about the hair from the stairwell railing?" Jack asked her.

"Not hers. A brown hair about the same length as hers, but the pigmentation is different. Also, I asked Trina about the mysterious boyfriend. She has only Rachael's word for his existence and he sounds like pure Rachael fantasy. Rich and hot." She gave them what details Trina could supply.

Riley said, "If she'd had more time she probably would have sketched him in next to the pretty house and the long flowing dress."

Maggie continued. "This Tyson apparently OD'd. Not really surprising if most every kid there has substance abuse issues. When they mix with the day students, it would be hard to keep items from being passed back and forth. A baggie of heroin would go through any metal detector." She suddenly stared at Riley's chest. "You have blood on your tie."

He looked down. "Damn. This is new."

The waitress had chosen that moment to stop by and now eyed the striped piece of material nervously. Riley distracted her by asking if she could find any strudel left in the kitchen, then went on: "Still. Four deaths in custody in less than a month? At a juvenile facility?"

"That's a lot?" Maggie guessed from his tone. She

didn't have a lot of experience with in-custody deaths, which alone told her that they were not common.

"That's a *boatload*. Now that the press has hold of the story, Palmer's life is going to become a living hell. 'Rash of deaths at juvenile facility.' Cue the 'we're too hard on the poor kids' people versus the 'zero-tolerance boot-camp' groups' letters to the editor. Throw in a couple of conspiracy theories and we'll make CNN."

Maggie continued to play devil's advocate, though in this instance she didn't believe her own arguments. "It still could be coincidence. Like most cancer clusters and things like that—sometimes it's just a run of bad luck. In this line of work it never rains but pours."

Jack agreed. "And this isn't a normal prison. It's a prison that's trying not to be a prison, so the inmates— I mean, the kids—have more freedom and contact with the outside world than a secure facility. Not just the day kids, either; there's family, counselors, lawyers. All of whom treat them like victims instead of criminals."

"They are victims," Maggie said.

"But they're also criminals. I asked about your new pal, Trina. Do you know why she's there? She put arsenic in her mother's sugar bowl. The woman's in an irreversible coma. Don't frown, I'm not trying to be harsh, but a high mortality rate isn't surprising given that this place isn't an alternative school or a halfway house for misdemeanor charges. It's a cesspool of violent impulses, that's all I'm saying. Oh, and that you shouldn't eat anything she offers you."

The waitress stopped next to his chair, bearing three plates of apple strudel.

"I didn't mean you," Jack assured her, but she gave

him a wide berth as she set the plates on the table. He waited until she walked away. "In light of that, four deaths in a month is not such a shock."

"It's not a secure place," Riley said.

"Which is DORC's problem to clean up. They're not going to listen to a word you say anyway. Bureaucracies aren't known for welcoming outside opinions."

Maggie continued to digest this information about Trina along with her strudel. Poison. Just what they had first suspected about Damon. Why would a little girl do such a thing? Did her mother abuse her horribly or just take away her cell phone? "Rachael suffered things I wouldn't wish on my worst enemy. Damon spent his life locked away. Sounds like Quentin joined a gang at, like, four."

"They had crappy lives," Jack said. "But a lot of kids have crappy lives, and they all feel that pressure we were talking about. How many end up as killers?"

"It would help if their parents had a clue. Or were old enough to have a clue." Riley ate half his strudel in two bites. "We should do it like China."

Maggie and Jack exchanged a glance. Perhaps Riley's blood sugar had dipped too low. "Restrict couples to one child?"

"Exactly. Less kids, more resources."

Maggie said, "If we did that, you wouldn't have Hannah."

He looked so stricken at the thought of life without his younger child that Maggie gave him the rest of her strudel.

He didn't abandon the theory, however. "A guy I know visited China for something or other—I think his son teaches English there. Anyway he said they *can* have more than one kid, they can have as many as they like, but you start paying the second they're born. In our country grade school and high school are free and you have to pay for college, so doofuses like me have a chance to save up for eighteen years to be able to afford it. There, grade school and high school cost a portion of your paycheck, and college is free."

"No one would be able to afford to have a kid until they were older—"

"And hopefully smarter, finished school, and, oh yeah, *employed*. It would cut the welfare rolls in half, instantly, let me tell you."

"Birth control via taxation," Maggie said.

"Harsh but effective."

"Unfortunately, it's very easy to get pregnant. What if someone did and then couldn't pay?"

"Aye," Riley said. "There's the rub."

"Did you just quote Shakespeare?"

Riley said he had, and wasn't that impressive.

Jack ignored them both.

Chapter 18

Tuesday

The next day Jack let his partner drag him back to the Firebird Center to ask about Derald Tyson and, at the same time, who might have wanted to kill a mute ten-year-old. DORC investigators had cleared the infirmary and turned to raking Officer Coglan and his coworkers over the coals as a biohazard team decontaminated the classroom. "Like these kids have never seen blood before," Jack said. He had no idea where the fourteen- to fifteen-year-old classes would be held that day but knew the staff would figure something out. The last thing they wanted was a group of teenagers with nothing to do. He wondered how they kept the kids busy over the weekends.

The receptionist escorted them to one of the small conference rooms tucked into a corner of the second-floor visiting area to meet Dr. Jerome Bellamy. The door was closed, so she asked them to take a seat in a row of cushioned seats, next to a small boy of perhaps six with smooth black skin and toddler-pudgy legs, which swung free over the floor. He glanced up at the men without concern.

Jack sat. "What are you in for?" he asked the boy, which probably violated HIPAA somehow but he didn't plan to worry about it.

Certainly the boy didn't mind. "I bit my brother."

"Really?" And they incarcerated six-year-olds for that? Jack had no clue how to respond. *Well, every kid does that? You shouldn't hurt your siblings, young man? Next time make sure he's in no shape to tattle on you?*

The boy didn't mind talking about it, however. "He deserved it, though. That's what I keep telling Doctor Bellamy."

"Okay. Why did your brother deserve it?"

"He ate my Lego."

Jack tried not to laugh. "Ah. How old is your brother?"

This represented a tough question and the kid screwed up his face as he worked out the answer. "I think he's almost one. He can't walk or nothing. And now he know, don't eat Legos no more. See?" He turned up a sly but visually adorable face to Jack's.

So his justified abuse of an infant had really turned out to be for the infant's own good. But even a six-year-old ought to understand a baby's lack of understanding, and Jack realized that this very small boy had already mastered the art of spin.

He no longer felt like laughing.

Ms. Cooper from the under-twelve group arrived to escort the boy back just as Dr. Jerome Bellamy opened the door. He did not resemble a therapist the way Melanie Szabo and the hapless young man in the under-twelve area did. Bellamy had perfectly cut blond hair and a suit that made Jack feel dowdy. He shook their hands with manicured fingers and smelled of something expensive. They were lucky to have caught him, he said. He only stopped in at the center twice per week.

"You're not on staff here?" Riley asked as they took seats around the tiny round table. Jack knew space and privacy were at a premium in the building but he wished all the spaces didn't seem so child sized. Claustrophobia set in as soon as Bellamy closed the door. No windows and, it seemed, little air.

"No, I'm in private practice, serving those whose parents can afford me." He spoke matter-of-factly, managing not to sound as annoying as he could have. The tight quarters didn't seem to bother him. "Derald and that short tyrant you may have seen leaving are— were—the only two boys. I've got one girl I'm taking over for our resident flower child. It's too bad about Derald, but—"

"But?" Jack asked.

"Not surprising. I'm pretty good at my job but I can only do so much. The younger they are, the easier it is to turn them around, and that's the whole idea here— they're not evil, they're not bad seeds, they're kids who started down a wrong path and no one stopped them. So they kept going. But convincing them to get off that path gets harder the farther down it they are."

"Dr. Palmer says intervention needs to start in the womb."

He leaned back in his chair, as relaxed as if it were a bar stool at his favorite pub. "Dr. Palmer's drunk the self-esteem Kool-Aid. It's the McGuffin these days, and yes, it's something to work on when you have a kid whose parents told him he sucked every day since birth. But even with not-great parents, let me tell you something about the self-esteem of the average baby, toddler, schoolkid. It's pretty darn good. They have the time and freedom to devote themselves entirely to their own causes. Bobby didn't steal from the corner store because he feels worthless or because he wants attention from Daddy. He stole because he wanted something and didn't have the money to pay for it. It benefited *him*. Children do things that benefit *them*. All we do when we say they need more self-esteem or they need more love or they need more attention is provide excuses to kids who are pretty good at thinking up excuses already."

Riley said, "For a child psychologist, that's pretty, um—"

"Harsh?" Bellamy shook his head. "It's not. Because the flip side of this is that children are naturally empathetic. Infants will share their toys with another crying infant. Like any other characteristic it will occur more or less—some people get along well with math and others with art, for example—but it can be taught to those who don't have a lot of it naturally. This is what I'm doing with the six-year-old. Like any toddler he screamed to get what he wanted, like a toy or ice cream instead of dinner. Most parents would put down a gentle foot but some parents—and teachers too—simply don't have a clue and give in to get the noise to stop. Well, it takes the average baby about two seconds to figure out that *this* works and then they're off and screaming."

"The Terrible Twos," Riley said, but he didn't seem to be exactly buying it.

"Yes, normal, kid—testing limits, etcetera. But the kids who don't get limits—"

"Keep going down that path."

"Exactly. Around three or four they start to enjoy it. Manipulating Mom and Dad is no longer means to an end; it's an end in itself. Why kids who aren't bullied at home still sometimes become bullies at school. It's a technique they stumbled on and it gave them a high. They become addicted to the power."

Riley guessed where this led. "And like any other addiction, they need more and more."

"Exactly!" Bellamy spoke with enthusiasm. Or perhaps he just enjoyed talking to grown-ups for a change.

"So how do you 'turn them around'?"

"Teach them empathy. Despite how they appear most of them are not actually sociopaths. They've just never thought about how their actions affect others. Every toddler lies and steals at some point—'I didn't take the cookie, my sister Susie did.' The worst thing you can do is say, 'Well, every toddler lies and steals at some point.' You can punish the kid, no cookies for a week, and that's good except that he might just decide to get better at stealing. He doesn't consider it wrong, just inconvenient if caught. Some parents say, 'Well, maybe I don't know who took it so no cookies for Junior *or* Susie for a week'—that's not so good because even Junior can figure out that's not fair, and if you're not fair, why should he be? And Susie might not benefit from such a lesson either."

Jack shifted impatiently. As he felt well past the age of starting a family, even if he didn't have such an unusual life situation, he didn't find the lecture relevant to him. And they hadn't even talked about Derald Tyson yet.

"The best thing to do if your toddler lies, cheats, steals? Burst into tears. Ham it up a little if you can. If just once they see how their actions are affecting you, they may do an instant one-eighty. Next, tell Junior he has to do something nice for Susie since he tried to frame the poor girl. Praise him when he does this nice thing. He gets a high. The goal is to train the kids to get the same high from helping people as they had from hurting them."

"I see," Jack said. "So Derald Tyson—"

"Of course, it's necessary that the kid cares how you feel. I try to make this connection to someone they already like. With small children it's usually a parent. They can feel quite strongly toward Mommy even as they make Mommy's life hell, or even if it's because Mommy gives them everything they want. There's a reason grandparents are often these kids' favorite people. No one's more indulgent than Nana."

Jack shifted in his chair, but Bellamy didn't seem to notice. "If they have no one who fits that bill then I try 'We need to be pals.' I spend a lot of time in sessions playing games with them—checkers, cards, Legos. They have to enjoy spending time with me. The one thing you can't fake is time, and it's what kids want from adults more than anything. A couple weeks of snapping plastic bricks together and Junior *cares* that I feel bad when he engages in antisocial behavior."

"So Derald Tyson—"

"Was, unfortunately, not a toddler."

Riley said, "So, another story?"

Now Bellamy sighed, crossing one slim ankle over the opposite knee. "You guys want any coffee or anything?"

"No, thank you," Riley said, as his partner ground his teeth.

"Well, I do. Give me just a sec, okay? The kitchen always keeps a pot ready for me."

And he disappeared out the door before they could protest. Only his suit jacket and briefcase, left behind on one chair, kept Jack from going after him. "What the hell? We listen to twenty minutes on the proper way to discipline a toddler and then he bails?"

"He's coming back." Riley nodded at the briefcase. "You don't think this was some code for 'I can't tell you because of doctor-patient confidentiality so I'm going to step out but conveniently forget my case files, wink-wink'?"

"No, I don't. He would have made sure to tell us he couldn't talk to us, and besides confidentiality died with Derald."

"Okay," Riley said. "Then he just wanted a cup of coffee."

"Or he just wanted to let us know that he's got a PhD and a roll of rich clients and we're lowly public servants."

Riley glanced over at his partner. "I'm beginning to think *you* have a self-esteem problem."

Bellamy returned, steaming cup in his hand. Apparently the short walk had sharpened his focus because he started to talk before his bottom even hit the seat cushion. "Okay, Derald Tyson. The perfect example of what happens to a Junior when Mommy and Daddy don't call me in time. Also the perfect counterargument to the belief that all criminally inclined children were neglected, abused, and unloved."

He sipped. They waited.

"I don't have his file with me so I'm going from memory, of course, but I can give you the gist: Derald was born to a couple in their thirties, very sweet people, Mom is a corporate travel agent and Dad is an exec at Lubrizol. Middle child. Would routinely hit his sister at the age of two. Big deal—what two-year-old doesn't hit their sister? Mine still raps my skull every time she sees me just to catch up. By three he's also beating up the neighbor kids. Now it's a little bigger deal. Mom and Dad spend a lot of time doting on little Derald to assure him that they don't love him any less just because he was born in between an older sister and a younger brother. So the beatings continue, and morale doesn't improve. Mealtimes are epic battles. Forget things like making his bed or combing his hair. A slight hiccup when he has to go to school but Mom and Dad tie the teachers' hands so tightly that they can only shift him to other classes and send him home, with great regularity. Arrested at the age of eight for public drunkenness—he ran out on a babysitter with a bottle of Dad's scotch. Parents get rid of alcohol in the house, he steals it from the neighbors and is arrested again at nine. Parents start a flurry of 'keep busy' activities, thinking they'll channel the aggression to more constructive traits. Horseback riding—he kicked the horse so hard that the instructor said not to come back unless he wanted to be tied up with a bridle. Soccer—try as he might, the coach could not convince little Derald the rules specified 'no hands' because, of course, rules were made to be broken. Karate—which he used to kick a schoolmate in the face, knocking out two teeth."

"Out of control," Jack said. "And the parents just let it happen."

"Yes and no. The parents would try to correct the behavior but not follow through with consequences. They'd say, 'Bad boy,' but not force him to correct the behavior or make amends, so he promptly tuned them out. He went down that path, and no one forced him to reverse course."

"How did he come to be here?" Riley asked, saving Jack from having to do so. No need to hear about every scuffle or stolen piece of candy in young Derald's misspent youth.

Now Bellamy hesitated, scratched one ear, shifted his feet. Things a psychologist such as himself would no doubt identify as delaying actions.

"That was me. In a way. Mom and Dad just knocked along, letting Derald dictate conditions in the household—in which, by the way, the other two kids are doing fine, proving once again that it's not all nurture, it's a bit of nature, too. The other two kids are a little spoiled and I feel sorry for whoever they marry someday, but hardly criminal and not violent. So far, anyway. They've learned to capitalize on the distraction Derald provides—with the parents spending so much time on the problem child the other two can pretend this neglect can only be fixed by expensive toys. But they're not violent, and actually the daughter is about the only support Mom has. Dad is a complete pushover, and when she tries to put her foot down he says she's being too harsh. But when thirteen-year-old Derald came within two minutes of completing a rape of a schoolmate, then told his mother that the girl had been asking for it and 'a man's gotta do what a man's gotta do,' she finally grew a pair of ovaries and hired me."

"And you fixed him?" Jack asked, trying to keep the sarcasm out of his voice, without success. He didn't really dislike this guy. He just wanted him to get to the point.

Without any humor at all, Bellamy said no. "In truth, I failed completely and it doesn't surprise me a bit. I knew I was in trouble the minute Derald walked into my office for the very first time. Usually kids—even tough, violent kids—are nervous. Hell, even violent adults are nervous when they're not hostile. Everybody is—you get used to that in my line of work. I meet my buddies' dates and there's that choking moment when they wonder if I'm analyzing them, if I'm going to report to my pal later or if they should be careful what they say so I don't think they're a neurotic idiot. But Derald? Sauntered in like he was taking a seat at his favorite bar. Plopped down, looked around, complimented me on the office, and asked how much I made in a year."

"Cocky," Riley said.

"They're all cocky, usually, unless they're so troubled they can't keep up the pretense. So I told myself it was bravado, a brave front, or perhaps the result of years of training himself not to feel so that he wouldn't feel bad. But I knew right away."

"Knew what?"

"That he was no such thing. He wasn't putting on a show for me because he wasn't troubled. He seemed relaxed because he *was*—he was the king of his own world and happy as a fu—happy as a clam. I have no doubt he slept like a baby at night while his parents stared at the ceiling and his sister locked her door. That kid was a stone-cold psychopath by the age of ten."

"So what'd you do?" Riley asked. Jack leaned forward despite himself as if watching a horror movie, knowing the monster was about to make an appearance.

"I tried. His parents were paying me, after all." He smiled, a crooked slash of leaking pain. "I told Mom and Dad not to get their hopes up, and gave it a shot. Talking, talking, talking. I tried playing video games with him, biting my lip at his smug smile when he beat me—because of course he beat me, he's a freakin' thirteen-year-old. You should have seen the look on his face when I finally bested him in one single game. Eyes flat, face still. Part of me thought great, he'll respect me now. Part of me thought I had just set the therapy back four months. Part of me thought he would stab me in the head with the game controller."

"Control freak?" Riley asked.

"Sociopath, in common parlance. Control is their drug. Anyway it wasn't all touchy-feely. I worked with the parents and even the other kids to set up a house plan, an organized structure of what we would expect from Derald and consequences for bad acts, reward the good ones, blah blah blah. I tried to get him to come with me to homeless shelters, old folks homes, to get him to view those less fortunate as needing his help rather than easy targets, but he always had an excuse to call it off. I talked about feelings and compassion and putting oneself in others' shoes until I got hoarse."

"Nothing?"

"Nada." He threw his paper cup into the garbage,

leaving a spray of dregs along the plastic liner. "He already had a home business of stealing and reselling jewelry, bicycles, anything he could pick up from the other kids at school. He'd use the jewelry to buy sexual favors from girls, having found that easier than raping them. All I could do was pray that he'd get locked up before he procreated and, as far as I know, he did.

"He found an inner-city gang to use as a source for drugs and guns, which he'd resell instead of use. He wasn't *in* the gang, he carefully explained to me. He used them. Any other kid I'd think yeah, sure, but him I believed. He also said he didn't use the drugs, and on that I think he waffled a bit, but he didn't show any signs of a hard addiction. More importantly, he had formed a mutually beneficial business arrangement that entailed a steady flow of firearms. Then I started praying he'd get locked up before he shot his whole family to death in the middle of some random night. The violence had grown on him until that cocky, relaxed attitude hardened into something cold and scary."

"And did he?" Riley asked.

"No, no, they're all still alive. But he did shoot two other kids who tried to rip him off, or he tried to rip off, depending on who you believe. Somehow no weapons were found near their bodies and they were both shot in the back, so the self-defense claim wasn't really going to fly. They were known gangbangers, the cop screwed up and didn't read his rights because he assumed the white kid had to be the victim—"

"I remember that," Riley said. "Rick Gardiner and his partner had that one. Didn't you assist?"

Jack said, "Yeah, I took a few of the witness interviews, went to the hospital for the victims' statements."

"Gardiner. No wonder it got screwed up."

Bellamy didn't seem interested in the police department's internecine rivalries. "Whatever the issue, they charged him as a juvenile. Mom and Dad wanted to post the bail and I convinced them not to, and called in a ton of favors to get him placed here. Hard sell—as desperate as those parents were they wanted to faint at the thought of their baby in prison. I wanted to faint at the idea of him going home, convinced they'd be dead in their beds the first night."

"And so Derald came to the Firebird Center."

"And died here," Bellamy said. "So now his parents are gathering lawyers to sue me, by the way. If I hadn't talked them into placing him here, their sweet baby boy might still be alive."

"Where'd he get the drugs?" Riley asked.

The young doctor let air escape from his lips like an agitated horse. "Who knows? I'm sure this place has its pipelines, like any prison. I asked one day, when he came to a session with dilated pupils, but he wouldn't tell me."

"Did he have any friends here?"

"In true Derald form, he got along with everyone else because everyone else wasn't worth noticing."

"He didn't mention anyone?"

"Nope."

Jack asked, "Did they do group therapy here? Maybe he said things—"

Bellamy was shaking his head. "Group with teenagers is largely pointless. They're all just posturing for the other kids. You have to be alone in a room to get anywhere. You have to have that one-on-one relationship.

That's what people don't get about therapy with juveniles. They think I can sit in an armchair on the other side of this plushy office and charge two hundred an hour to take a few notes about their relationship with their mother. It's a lot more than that."

"The drugs," Jack reminded him. "How do you think Derald came to overdose?"

"I don't know. I told him if he kept playing around the drug would be in control and not him, and he said that would never happen. Outside, maybe that was true, but in here where he had nothing else to do . . . no one has as much self-control as they think. Not even sociopaths. Especially not sociopaths."

"How long was he here before he died?"

"Three weeks." At their raised eyebrows, he said, "Yeah, not much time from nonaddict to overdose, but Derald was a hard-core adrenaline junkie. Besides, he couldn't buy from his usual source so who knows what the stuff he used had been cut with."

"So you don't find his death suspicious?" Jack asked.

Bellamy's eyes narrowed. "Suspicious how?"

"Just—unexpected?"

He spoke with a weary expression. "Everything about juveniles is unexpected and yet not surprising. This is the difficulty in treating them, restraining them, reacting to them—it's why theories and techniques come and go. Programs like this center try to quantify a person's life to a series of checkboxes on a form. It has to be done—how else to measure risk or success—but it's largely impossible. Could you do that with your own life? Why do we assume a child's life is exponentially simpler? Sorry, I'm wandering. Did it surprise me that Derald overdosed? Not really. He was a walking disaster hell-bent on destruction. I'm only surprised it happened sooner rather than later."

Jack and Riley thanked him for his time.

"What do you think?" Riley asked his partner as they descended the steps to the first floor.

"Believe it or not, I kind of liked him."

"Bellamy or Derald?"

"Bellamy," Jack said, jerking the stairwell door open. "Derald should have been drowned at birth."

Chapter 19

"Are you supposed to be here?" the pathologist asked Maggie, his words slightly muffled by a paper mask over his nose and mouth, with a plastic face guard resembling a clear welder's helmet over that.

The relatively small room with tiled floors hummed with its usual bustle. A female doctor at the next table sliced open an overweight man while an assistant stood ready with the long-handled pruning shears to cut through the ribs. The pathologist hovering over Damon's wisp of a body had not been out of med school for long, his caramel skin smooth and unblemished, whereas the diener assisting him had been rode hard and put away wet for decades, to judge from the broken blood vessels and pockmarks in his face.

Maggie explained her job and credentials, believing the pathologist wanted to know why a person who didn't work for the medical examiner's office stood in his autopsy suite. He interrupted with "Weren't you in that school shooting yesterday?"

"It wasn't a school shooting," she said. "I mean, it *was*, but not the way—"

"Doc Fielding is doing that autopsy," the diener told her, and added it wouldn't take place for another two hours.

"Yes, that's all right. I don't—"

"You don't need to be here for that one, though. You know how *he* died. Coupla bullets through the head. No mystery there."

"Exactly. It's Damon here that's sort of a—"

"'Cause you was there."

"Saw you on the news," the pathologist said, sketching the road-rash scrapes on the dead boy's thigh.

"Really? Me?" She hadn't spoken to any member of the media, and they'd gone back to their studios and offices by the time she'd left the building with Jack and Riley.

"Your mug shot," the diener explained.

Probably from HR, her personnel file photo, taken several years previously. "Did I look good?"

"Uh," the diener said.

"Uh," the doctor said.

"Yeah," the diener said. "Great."

She made a note to visit HR.

"What's the story with this one?" the pathologist asked, and she filled him in on the strange history of Damon Kish. Then she stood and watched as they gutted the poor boy like a walleye. It took two and a half hours, not unusual for a child's autopsy. First the external examination—any petechiae in the eyes or the inside of the lips (no), blood (no), bumps that might indicate a subdural hematoma (no), bruises (quite a few, typical of any young boy but especially unsurprising for one with Damon's habit of throwing himself at doors and people), minor scars (ditto), major scars (none), or tattoos (none). He had bruising on both sets of knuckles, but Maggie remembered how quickly he had thrown a punch at her, and a pretty solid one at that. No doubt he was just as uninhibited with anyone and everyone else.

The foam in his mouth might indicate poison, the doctor said, but could also be due to other causes.

Maggie explained about the missing EpiPens.

The pathologist noted the healing scabs on Damon's thigh, but whether they were from needles or merely fallout from the scraping and injury, Maggie would have to wait until he could explore underneath the skin. She wanted to bring up her theory about the scrapes disguising the needle tracks—those EpiPens had gone *somewhere*—but didn't say a word. No attorney would be able to say she had pushed the doctor toward a biased conclusion.

Then they opened the chest cavity and removed the organs. The diener worked with the photographer to document the various bruises from the inside of the skin while the doctor sectioned and examined the lungs (normal), liver (normal), and spleen (slightly larger than expected for the size of the boy, but within the normal range, probably due to infections left untreated during the course of his short life). He spread these out for his dissection on a half-inch-thick polyethylene cutting board that took up most of the counter area.

"There's a little bit of congestion in the lungs," the doctor said, adding that this, too, could result from a variety of causes. He squeezed pieces of the organs to show Maggie; she had no idea what she was supposed to be seeing but nodded anyway and told him that Damon had had strep throat. He said he knew that and had seen the remains in the throat. Though strep should not cause lung congestion possible complications from it might, but overall the congestion seemed too minor to play a factor in the boy's death.

Next came the heart. Maggie again brought up the missing EpiPens but the pathologist could not quite tell if the assumed bolus of epinephrine had pushed Damon into a heart attack. "It's not as easy to tell when an attack didn't happen for the usual reasons—blocked coronary arteries, pericardial fluid, hypertrophy, thrombi." He examined all the valves and ran a finger along the insides of the now-opened chambers, then removed cross sections into plastic boxes that were about two inches square each. The boxes were flat and the sides looked like open miniblinds; the whole item resembled a miniature suet feeder for birds. These would be given to the histology department for the heart muscle to be fixed in a waxy substance and then sliced with a microtome to create slides for the doctor to examine under a microscope.

The trachea and esophagus, aside from flecks of the aforementioned foam, were not irregular. If poison had been used it had not been caustic and didn't badly upset the stomach, fairly unheard of for a poison.

The stomach contents also did not support the poison theory. The doctor cut the flaccid bag open with a scissors and let what it held *sploosh* into a plastic measuring cup, while Maggie stood well out of splashing range. Then he rinsed off the liquid and spread the solid bits on the cutting board and yanked a magnifying lamp from its mount above the counter in order to take a closer look. Maggie peeped through it over his shoulder, occasionally rising to her toes for a better angle.

The pathologist kept up a running dialogue with himself as he worked and she strained to hear all his conclusions. "Oatmeal, some kind of berry, maybe strawberry, maybe cranberry . . . would they put cranberries in children's oatmeal, would need more sugar . . . something . . . lump . . . apple? . . . apple . . . brown . . . lot of brown . . . brown lump . . ."

"Brownie?" Maggie suggested.

"For breakfast? Who gets dessert with breakfast?"

"I always do."

"When you were ten?"

"Maybe not then."

"Brown . . . hard   brown . . . chocolate   chip? . . . chocolate chip muffin, I guess. . . . They think if they call it a muffin it's suddenly healthy . . . too many calories, too much sugar . . . that's about it." He swept it off the board into a plastic cup with an attached lid. The toxicology department would have to tell them anything more, if there were illegal drugs present or—

"Can Tox tell you if he had amoxicillin in his stomach?" Maggie asked.

This completely stumped the pathologist, who didn't know. Normally they looked only for illegal drugs and alcohol. Exotic drugs, heavy metals, and poisons would be found only if more specific tests were requested.

Because of the victim's age and unknown cause of death he went quickly through the intestines as well, but didn't find anything of interest. The air now smelled particularly rank, no longer just the vague smell of cold, dead flesh, but exhaust fans helped and her nose quickly adjusted.

The diener had sliced through the child's scalp just under the hairline and peeled it back to expose the

Lisa Black

skull, which he sawed through with a round blade about the diameter of an orange. With the bone removed, they could see the neat convolutions of the brain's surface. Unless physically damaged, a brain never looked as scary as the glistening red-brown organs of liver and lungs, dark entities with deep secrets. Its light gray colors highlighted with white seemed so innocent by contrast. A great anatomical irony, since it could hold more evil than all the gleaming offal in the world.

And now the pathologist patted it as if it were an obedient puppy.

"Are you going to want to bucket it?" the diener asked.

The pathologist patted again. "No. It's fine."

The diener said okay, then took a scalpel to the optic nerves and the spinal cord and the other connections that held the brain in its place.

"Bucket?" Maggie asked.

"The brains of the very young and very old can be extremely delicate, the consistency of Jell-O. To be able to work with them at all we have to 'fix' them—use a piece of string to suspend it in a bucket of formalin for two weeks. Then it can be examined. But a ten-year-old, yeah, he's fine."

"I'm sure he'd be glad to know that," Maggie said, and the doctor gave her an odd look.

While the diener gently removed Damon Kish's thought center from its resting place, the pathologist turned his attention to the scrapes along the boy's thigh. Maggie waited.

"Huh," the doctor said.

She continued to wait.

He prodded with his fingers, then the tip of the

scalpel, then made some small incisions among the tiny scabs. "You said there were EpiPens missing?"

"Yes," she said. "Four."

"Got needle tracks here. Tiny hematoma, the beginning of a bruise, but then the whole area is bruised from this fall he took so that doesn't tell me much. Four? No one would give a kid four EpiPens."

"No one who wasn't trying to kill him," Maggie agreed.

"EpiPens shouldn't kill anybody. They're not designed to do that. They're issued with a sort of 'when in doubt, use it' and 'if the first doesn't work use another' kind of advice," he continued to argue.

"I know."

The diener photographed the now-loose brain on a flat, light gray board, present only for that purpose. Once that had been done he turned it over to the doctor, who set to work on it, still mumbling about the harmlessness of epinephrine. "Might put someone into cardiac arrest if they had a weak heart, speeds up the pulse, or—necrosis."

"What?"

He had sliced through some of the boy's brain with a large bread knife and now ran his wet, gloved fingers over a section with bits of blood in it. "Little bit bloody, necrotic here."

He cut the slices more thinly and looked again. He held some parts up to the magnifying lamp. He cut off a few small chunks for the plastic histology frames. Meanwhile Maggie thought she'd burst.

Finally she did. "What does that mean? Necrotic? It means dead, I know, but—"

"Stroke." He kept slicing.

"And that—"

"No injuries to the head but there's bloody, necrotic tissue in the brain. That indicates stroke. Between that and the needle marks—a sudden influx of epinephrine would shoot up the blood pressure, heart rate. . . . The kid stroked out. Why would anyone give four adult doses to a child? Especially a skinny little one like this guy?"

He glanced at the boy who, truthfully, no longer resembled a child. With the scalp pulled down over the face, the torso unfolded and empty, the arms and legs fileted to determine the extent of the bruising and to reveal the needle tracks, he looked more like a half-boned chicken. And that made it all the more horrible. Maggie felt the bricks tremble inside the wall she kept in her head to separate the things she saw on the job from the rest of her world.

It didn't help that the "rest of her world" continued to, somehow, shrink, a little more every day.

She answered the doctor's question. "Because they wanted him to die."

While his ex-wife watched a child be cut open, Rick Gardiner sat with his feet up on one corner of his desk, using his own cell phone to call Jack Renner's former supervisor in Minneapolis, Minnesota. Though the Cleveland PD coming up on their caller ID might help with his story's verisimilitude, he had decided to do what he could to keep this investigation off all official records. Cops took a dim view of cops investigating other cops. If that was what he was doing . . . hell, *he* didn't even know what he was doing, a fact he reminded himself of approximately every thirty seconds.

However, when Lieutenant Howard Romero answered, Rick gave him the same story about the police chiefs association awards, to which Romero didn't seem to be listening, and Jack Renner, to which he did.

"Renner? Sure, I remember him. Great guy. He could be a pain in the ass, but a great cop."

"Really? Oh . . . well . . . that's good to hear. He was with you guys for a long time."

He heard a brushing sound as Romero covered the phone, incompletely, and yelled for some unnamed person to ask where the prisoner had been placed. "Yep, been everywhere, done everything in this city. I used to work details with him at the mall—you know, the Mall of America, helping out the Bloomington PD. I could tell you some stories from that place—"

"He's a native of the area, right?"

"Hell yeah! Mill City all the way. I knew his mother, actually. Best friend of my aunt. I never met Jack until we were in vice together, though. Did a lot on the north side—no surprise. Those stories wouldn't be suitable for publication."

"Got it," Rick said. "I see you gave him a great recommendation when he went to the Cleveland PD."

A guess, but a good assumption. Surely HR would have checked his references, right?

"I did, you betcha. Hang on—he's in one, take Chrissy in there too. Make sure the camera's on. Yeah, that came as a surprise, that he went back to work." It took Rick a moment to realize that Romero had returned to their conversation. "He'd been so determined to leave it all behind, move to his land in Tennessee and spend the rest of his days like Daniel Boone, hunting bears or some shit like that. But I see that with guys—they think retirement is going to be so great, and in two days they're jonesing to go back to work. Mistake, I always tell 'em. Give retirement a while to settle into your bones first. Don't put yourself back in the harness the minute you feel bored for a second or two. It's an adjustment, you know? Going to be me in another six months, and I'm making all sorts of plans. It's going to feel weird for a while. You have to know that going in; otherwise it freaks you out."

"Yeah," Rick tapped his pen against his coffee cup, trying to think of something else to ask. "This is going to sound crazy, but I need to make sure I've got the right Jack Renner. Tall guy? Dark hair?"

"I don't know if I'd call him *tall*. But I guess, yeah."

That didn't help. Romero might be six five and no one seemed tall to him. "Kinda quiet?"

"I don't know if I'd call him *quiet*, either. Did a few stakeouts with him—he half drove me nuts. Never shut up." He launched into a reminiscence about a drug house in the north side more heavily guarded than Bagram airfield and how he and Renner had had to sit on it until detectives could get a judge out of bed and the search warrant signed. He'd nearly asphyxiated on the smoke. Apparently Renner used to be a chain-smoker.

"I never saw him with a cigarette," Rick said.

"Yeah, I'm sure the docs made him give that up. Fat lot of good it did him in the end."

The pen slipped from Rick's fingers. "The end?"

"Yeah. The cigarettes. That's what got him. Hang

on, I gotta direct—well then give him a legal pad if that's what he wants. As long as he's confessing he can write it on toilet paper for all I care."

Rick asked, "What happened?"

"Cancer, I guess. I assumed that's why he left you guys or Tennessee or wherever the hell, came back home to be with his mom. Poor old lady, pretty much killed her, too, according to my aunt."

Rick's feet dropped off the desk.

"I always kinda felt bad I didn't go to see him, but I didn't even know where he was. And I figured he wouldn't want any of the old crew seein' him like that. I know I wouldn't."

"Jack *Renner*. Died."

"Yeah. Couple years back."

"There must be some mistake. The Jack Renner here is definitely not dead."

"Huh," Romero said, not too startled by this. "I *thought* it was Jack Renner with the emphysema. Maybe it was Andy Hastings—he also moved to Tennessee after he retired. . . ."

"Is there any way you could find out for sure?"

"Well, why? If your guy isn't dead, then obviously it isn't him."

"My guy is Jack Renner and listed you as his most recent supervisor at the Minneapolis PD. Unless you had two Jack Renners there—"

"That's possible, I guess. We've got about nine hundred cops."

"Both working as detectives with you as their supervisor?"

"Nope," he agreed as he shuffled papers, close enough

to the phone to be heard. Apparently the Minneapolis homicide division kept a man busy. "Definitely would have remembered that."

"Then I've got a guy here claiming to be Jack Renner, and he ain't."

This idea didn't startle the lieutenant much either. "Nah. I'm probably just getting him mixed up with Andy Hastings."

Rick scrambled to sound firm while within the confines of his cover story. "I need to make sure. Obviously, the muckety-mucks can't give an award and have the guy's bio all mixed up. My boss would have my head."

"Award?" Obviously he *hadn't* been listening. "What for?"

"Some big case from last year. That half of it isn't my job." Rick left that vague but clear on what he needed: "Can you please check on what happened to Jack Renner and get back to me?"

"Um . . ." Long pause while, Rick bet himself, Romero tried to come up with a good way to say he already had enough to do. "I don't know. I doubt anyone here would know. When he headed off to the mountains he cut all ties, didn't want no reunions or even a Christmas card. I only heard that he came back because of the family connection, but even there—his mom died, and last year so did my aunt. My mom's getting forgetful and never paid much attention to anything my aunt said anyway. But I'll *try*."

His emphasis on the last word made it clear that Rick shouldn't expect much.

"I'd appreciate that. When can I call you back?"

"I usually go over there on Sundays. I'll try to remember to ask."

Rick chewed the end of his pencil in frustration. He'll try to remember to ask? "That would be great. I'd really appreciate it."

"If it's for an award bio, why don't you ask the guy?"

"It's a surprise. Let me ask you something else. You ever have any weird murders there? All sorts of different scumbags dropped on the street with twenty-twos in the back of the head? None of the usual crew good for it?"

Romero guffawed. "In the north side? Every night."

"Ever get some you thought might be connected? Like, to each other?"

"Yeah. Turf wars, one of the leaders expanding his territory, got to take out the other leaders. Had a rash of it a couple years ago but then they all settled into their new organizational chart and have been fairly good since. No mystery. Why?"

"Long story. Okay, one more."

Romero's tone grew in snarkiness as his interest faded. "You always spend so much time on department awards? Wish I had that kind of time."

"You ever have a case of an illegal nursing home? Like this woman took in a bunch of old folks, cashed their social security checks, and then left them to rot?"

A long pause. Rick couldn't tell if Romero took the time to think or to tell a detective 'Get in there and make sure Chrissy asks about the money,' because he did that, too. But then he said, "That rings some weird kind of a bell. I'll ask around."

Rick said, "Thanks. I'll call you back in a few days if I don't hear from you."

"Do that," Romero said without sincerity, and hung up.

Chapter 20

Riley asked Ms. Cooper in the under-twelve unit if they could speak with Damon's therapist.

"I told you he didn't—"

"Didn't get too far, yes, we know. We're just covering all our bases," he told her.

"Oh. Well." Behind her most of the children seemed to be working in soft-covered workbooks, not uniform, probably specific to each child's age. Some had finished and closed the books, gathering pencils and erasers. One girl had her head down on her desk, crying as if her heart might break. "He's in early diversion."

"Did he do something bad?"

She didn't crack so much as the hint of a smile. "It's a voluntary playgroup for local children, separate from our resident and day programs. They're outside at the moment. Through the door at the end of the hall."

She shut the door with the soft thud of finality.

"I can't figure out if she doesn't like us or doesn't like child psychologist Hunter," Riley noted as they headed for the outside door.

"Don't be so sensitive. She thinks Hunter is over-rated. Besides, he gets playground duty while she's locked up in Bedlam."

"Good point."

The heavy metal push bar let them out into the fenced under-twelve recreation area. Patchy grass ran underneath a few picnic tables, a rusting swing set, a jungle gym that had once been painted in primary colors, and balls of all sizes and shades. The slender blond man pointed out a page in a coloring book to a girl at a table, called encouragement to an older boy showing a younger one where to kick the ball, and spoke to two girls sitting on the grass before noticing the cops. He came over to them immediately, perhaps wondering if yet another disaster—for example, another child's death—had occurred.

Riley assured him they only wanted to ask some follow-up questions about Damon Kish.

"Ah. Okay. I'm afraid I can't tell you much. I didn't get too far with him."

"So we've heard."

The man spoke calmly and reasonably, never ceasing in his surveillance of the children around them.

"Damon—wow. I had no idea how tough it would be trying to work with a child with no understanding whatsoever of *language*. A completely unique situation. Most of the time for our one-on-one therapy, I'd bring him out here. He had no clue why but didn't care. To run around in the open air was paradise for that poor kid. When I introduced him to kicking a ball it was like an epiphany."

"So you just—played?"

Hunter glanced at them briefly, back to the kids. "Play is vital to children. It's where they learn everything about socialization—making friends, being picked for the team, *not* being picked for the team, winning, losing, the ups and downs of life."

Riley now surveyed the children as well. "This is therapy?"

"Yes and no. Early diversion is an extracurricular activity for kids we've identified as at risk. They're not in any real trouble yet, their families aren't *too* bad— which means we haven't yet proven any outright abuse—but they're having issues that their schools and families don't feel equipped to handle. Play work can help define those issues."

"That's kind of vague," Riley pointed out, and Hunter laughed.

"It is, I'm sorry. Let me illustrate. You've heard that any kind of acting out is a cry for help, and that sounds simplistic, but it's true. Everything kids do tells us what's on their mind. You only have to know that and then ask a few questions. They'll tell you, in one way or another. For example"—he looked around—"Hector over there is the oldest in his family. You know how in a typical family each kid gets assigned a role? The smart one, the pretty one, the funny one. Hector is the sensible one. His father drives a truck and leaves for weeks at a time, tells Hector that he's the man of the house—terrible thing to say, by the way. You have kids?"

Jack had been pondering how many people would

have access to the infirmary on an average morning and had to snap back to the present. He shook his head.

Riley said, "Two girls."

Hunter continued. "Said with the best of intentions, make the son feel proud, that you have confidence in him. Very sweet. Except that we don't realize kids take everything literally, and making a ten-year-old responsible for the safety and well-being of his mother and sisters is putting a crushing amount of pressure on the kid. Not to mention the resentment of his sisters feeling bossed by a sibling who's barely a year or two older. He started pulling back in school, underachieving, avoiding the other kids. He just got bloody tired of being the grown-up and deep down he knew he was missing out on his own childhood. Here we're trying to give him that back. I don't give him any tasks or put him in charge of any teams, nothing like that. Here he can allow himself to be a child."

Over in one corner a boy held a ball away from a younger one as he spoke to an older one, apparently arguing with them both. "Stewart is my troublemaker. He's about to be expelled for a second time because he disrupts every class he's in—the kid's a genius at not only getting both students and teachers to argue with him, but also with each other. Both ends against the middle, that's Stewart. Of course, this all stems from Mommy and Daddy each drafting Stewart into their side in their daily battles. Stewart figured out that if he makes them argue with him, they'll stop screaming at each other. He extended this to making enough trouble for the whole class to live vicariously through his rebellion. He takes one for the team, every day. We're trying to get him out of his family role, but, well, it's a tough slog."

A wail drew their view to the other side of the yard. "Maddie," Hunter told them. "She's my crier. Every group has one, the kid who bursts into tears if someone looks at her cross-eyed, making mountains out of molehills until you want to choke the crap out of her. At first I thought she simply learned it from her mother, who when she comes to pick the kid up, is often in tears from the car not starting or the groceries being expensive or her boss's criticism of her use of margins. Turns out she's simply in a crisis of self-worth—her sister is younger but gets better grades, her BFF dumped her, her father left. She wants someone to comfort her simply to make her believe she still has value."

"They're like a cryptogram," Riley observed.

"Yeah, sorta! Kids' behavior is their communication. They're acting the way they are because they're trying to figure something out. A baby throws all his food on the floor, and Mom has to run around cleaning it up. Once that's done, he thinks about it and then deliberately does it again."

"I remember those days," Riley said.

"The kid isn't being a little shit. He's studying the phenomenon of Mom freaking out. Why did that happen? Let's re-create the circumstances and see if we get the same result."

"Actually, I'm pretty sure Hannah was just being a little shit."

"Hang on." Hunter left them to join a group of the three biggest boys in the yard, whose body language had become confrontational. Within minutes they had been dispatched, not too reluctantly, to other spots of the playground to move around equipment or help out a younger one.

The blond man retook his sentry position, continuing a lecture he apparently felt he had begun. "A good rule of thumb is however the kid is making you feel, that's how they're feeling. Kids who are overwhelmed by anger become aggressive and disruptive to make you angry. Cocky, experimenting-with-sex preteens make us feel uncomfortable, unmoored, because they're discombobulated by the changes that are occurring in themselves, and more than a little frightened by them. The kid who's constantly breaking the rules actually wants the restrictions made clear, because their life seems unpredictable and chaotic—we get that a lot with kids who get shifted from house to house with unreliable parents who disappear and reappear without warning. We worry over kids who mope around like they're worried sick."

"That one's moping." Jack referred to a little girl who slumped against the chain link, watching the other children without interest. Her face remained blank, changing only to a concerned frown if anyone came too near.

"And I'm worried. The boisterous, the aggressive kids can be a pain in the neck but at least they're still trying to have a relationship with other kids and adults. The withdrawn ones have given up all hope. They're the ones you really have to watch. I have to make sure she knows that I know she's here, that I care, that I'm watching out for her. Okay, Shonda?" He shouted the last two words to the girl. She briefly met his gaze, her only response.

"And Damon?" Jack asked, unable to see where all this information could get them, other than ready to schedule a vasectomy.

"Damon . . . Damon was a combination of many things. Damon was exactly like a man transported to a future world, overwhelmed by the new sounds, things, colors, smells, living beings in it. He was starved for human contact so he grabbed it with both hands. Literally. Every game was tackle, not tag. Most of the kids in the under-twelve residence have been abused, so they're hypersensitive to touch as it is. They'd pull away, push him away, or ignore him. All of which only sharpened his need, so he'd get even more physical."

The three men took two steps to the rear as a rubber ball skidded in front of them, followed by two boys running neck and neck and a third who seemed to be keeping up simply for the company, without any real interest in the ball.

"But of course Damon was also deeply angry."

"At his mother?"

"Certainly, if he could put that into conscious thought. His mother, society, the world. Children are born knowing that it's the job of us, the adults, to take care of them. When we don't, they know they've been cheated. Damon knew he had been wronged, and the flip side to being freed to live with normal, quote unquote, children is that he knew it more every day. This amazing world had been kept from him, so he'd bounce between joy at every new discovery and fury that it *was*, only now, discovered."

"Who did he take it out on?" Jack asked.

"Anyone who crossed his path. Especially anyone who rejected him. The desire for acceptance and the pain of rejection is so deeply ingrained in our DNA that language isn't necessary. Anyone who pushed him away could expect a blitz in return. He and Martina had a spectacular battle one day. A more neurotypical group of kids would be more understanding, if still terrified, than you'd expect, in the way they understand when their infant brother pokes them in the eye. But these kids have too many of their own issues to be sanguine about someone else's."

"Any adults?" Jack asked. "That he attacked?"

"Oh, all of us. Ms. Cooper, me, the lunch lady. Size didn't matter—he'd take you on without hesitation."

"He did."

"We passed the fourteen- to fifteen-year-old girls one time—we try to keep the age groups completely segregated, but this is not that big of a building and our routes are limited—and he jumped into them like the Tasmanian devil. Being presented with a *new* set of human beings overwhelmed what little self-control he'd been learning. He nearly twisted one girl's arm off."

"Rachael Donahue?"

"What, the girl who died? No, not her. Some skinny little thing. Name started with a *T*. She was okay, though."

"So he terrorized everyone, but was there anyone *he* seemed afraid of?"

The blond eyebrows shot up. "Damon? He was afraid of everything and nothing. It sounds condescending, but basically, he was a puppy."

"Are those kids fighting?" Riley asked, regarding the three boys Hunter had interrupted earlier. Two had started throwing punches, though none connected with flesh.

"They're play fighting. It used to be known as boys being boys when people used to let their kids out of their sight once in a while. It's how boys learn about their bodies and, believe it or not, show affection, but the flower children decided all aggression is bad and tried to breed it out of our genus. But it's good for them—until it turns into real fighting. Then I'm here."

"Puppy?" Jack asked.

"You know how puppies and kittens jump and run at the slightest movement? Then curiosity drives them back. That's how Damon viewed the world. Every new person seemed like Godzilla, but Godzilla fascinates enough to spawn countless sequels."

The sun had grown hot and Jack readied to leave. Damon's history with whoever had come to visit him in the infirmary had died in his mute, reeling, powerfully hungry brain.

One of the boys swung at his mate and this time it did connect. The *smack* of skin on skin rang up and down the street.

"That's my cue," Hunter said, and went to intervene.

Jack said to his partner, "Well, this was pointless."

Riley pulled the door handle, but it wouldn't open. They'd have to wait for child psychologist Hunter to let them into the building. The guy couldn't have a kid he supervised sneaking back into the building while he broke up fights.

While they waited Riley agreed with Jack's assessment. "All we know so far is that whoever murdered our wild boy is a coldhearted monster if they couldn't see the puppy inside the Tasmanian devil."

"Or a child," Jack said, "who can't see past his own issues."

Chapter 21

Maggie met them at the center.

Riley glanced at his watch. "Including the lunch we just ate, I think I've only had ten hours in the past three days when I *wasn't* at this place."

She said, "I have the prints we lifted and photographed yesterday. Will they let me have the applicant prints?"

"Yes," Riley said, "and no."

With that he meant that Dr. Palmer and the Firebird Center, not unreasonably, had no intention of opening their human resources records to the police en masse. Maggie would be allowed to examine the fingerprint cards collected from the staff when they were hired and compare them to the prints from the infirmary, but she could not remove them from the building or copy them. She could, of course, obtain copies from the state or federal system to which the applicant cards had been sent for their background check, but that would involve a little bit of red tape and a whole lot of time.

The detectives could examine the time cards of the staff members to determine who had been on the premises and when but would not be able to review their personnel files without a warrant. They didn't really want to anyway, as that would involve too much irrelevant information and if someone there had a history of abusing children that person was unlikely to list it on his or her resume. The only advantage the cops had in this case was a conveniently narrow window of opportunity, so they wanted to filter out the staff to who *could* have killed Damon, and go from there.

The center gave them a corner of the second-floor visiting room to work in. Maggie spread out at one round table while the detectives set up at another. She decided to wait until they'd narrowed the suspect pool down rather than compare her latent prints to the entire staff of thirty-one. Without the use of a computer program to create a database of the patterns she needed to search, and a corresponding database of the patterns of the staff to compare them to, it would be a long and laborious project. She didn't relish the idea of spending hours bent over magnifying loupes in a place where she couldn't adjust the height of the chair or the table. At least the windows gave her a decent amount of light.

While she waited she sorted out her latent print cards into piles containing fingerprints, palm prints, and both. Then she joined the detectives.

"Reese, F.," Riley read.

Jack checked the time card. "Clocked out at six a.m. Must be night shift."

"Bailey, G."

Maggie and Jack both shuffled buff-colored tickets. "Nothing for yesterday," Maggie said.

Across the room therapist Melanie Szabo led in a

parade of people of varying colors, genders, and ages, heading for a private meeting room off the main visiting area. She let the group find their own way and came over to the detectives and Maggie.

They explained their presence and she nodded toward the assemblees. "Family counseling. We make them come up with their own strategy for dealing with their problem child. Rules, schedules, custody, consequences."

"Wow," Maggie said.

"Yeah. These sessions can go really well or really bad. Or alternate between both. But most of the time they come up with amazingly precise and effective strategies. It works better in the long run than busybodies like me trying to tell them what to do. If the family isn't on board, nothing is going to change. Correction, on board *and* realistic. Even more frustrating than the parents who don't give a single shit are the ones who are totally dedicated to the kid but in complete denial. Not *my* kid. Not *my* parenting technique."

"That sounds like a thankless task," Maggie said.

"Sometimes yes. Sometimes folks think we did it all when it was actually them. This group isn't going to go that route, not today. They're extra uptight because their kid helped create the disturbance yesterday, helped Quentin smuggle in his gun."

"I thought they were day students," Riley said.

"They are. We're a full-service place; we counsel all involved families. Especially the day students. They walk out of here every day and go home to those same families. And the families are more motivated when the child isn't in custody—they want to keep them *out* of custody, but custody will be an inevitable outcome if things don't change. It gives us a stick to hold over their heads, in addition to the carrot of having a less troublesome kid. When a kid is in residence it's too easy for them to throw up their hands and wait for us to work magic."

"Melanie," a man called from the doorway to the private meeting room.

"Okay, just a sec."

"How is little Quentin doing?" Jack asked.

"He's in isolation—meaning his schedule is re-arranged to keep him away from any other residents. We try never to do that here. Isolating an already disturbed child only makes their problems worse. But shooting down an acquaintance in cold blood—yeah, we're not eager to give him another opportunity. On the plus side he's got the basketball court to himself. I've gotta go—a brawl may break out if I don't get them started." She hustled over to the meeting room, long skirt rustling around her ankles.

Maggie and the cops continued to work, narrowing down the possible suspects to roughly half of the total employees at the center.

Security officer Coglan stopped to chat as he made his rounds. "You guys making any progress on our poor little wild boy? I heard the ME said definitely murder. I thought poor Doc Palmer was going to have a heart attack. He threw a hissy fit at the DORC board and now they're going to be doing double time on the renovations. The cameras should all be operational by the end of next week."

"About time," Riley said.

"Tell me about it," he said. "For a high-risk, *ex-*

tremely high-risk, youth place the security infrastructure here wouldn't be acceptable at a 7-Eleven. But there was no place to put these kids while the work goes on, so—"

Perhaps because of the amount of body heat a large group of people created, the family in counseling had not closed the door to the private meeting room and snatches of their words carried into the visiting area. Officer Coglan stayed on his feet, pacing slowly around their table, obviously listening and obviously monitoring the stress level in the conference room. Violent children learn their violence from adults, after all.

Someone said something in a low tone and a momentary silence ensued. "That was *not* my fault," a gravelly voiced woman insisted.

A man spoke in a somewhat high and clear tone: "No, that'd be your new baby daddy."

"Ain't his gun."

"He know where to get one, though, don't he?"

"Where we living? Everybody know where to get a gun."

Riley said to his partner, "Is evidence obtained by eavesdropping admissible?"

"I don't see why not. It's voluntary admission."

"In that case we should be taking notes for Property. The gun used *did* come back to a burglary."

"But isn't it technically therapy?" Maggie asked. "So doctor-client privilege—"

A squeal rang out from the room as a chair pushed back. "You ain't never raised that boy with no discipline. When I was a girl I—"

"When you was a girl you still rode streetcars."

"So? At least my kids knew what respect meant."

"It meant their daddy hit them every day. After he was done hitting you."

"At least they knew who their daddy *was*."

"He's got to get back into that charter school. He ain't never going to get nowhere without that."

"Those teachers are insane. You see the amount of homework they give?"

"Why are you worryin' about where he going to *go*, when the court say he's got to be *here*?"

"He's doing good here. His grades are decent."

"He helped a boy kill another boy yesterday. That ain't decent."

"And where did he learn *that* from?!" a woman shrieked.

Melanie Szabo's voice calmly interjected. "We're here to talk about Donnell, not ourselves. What habits are going to serve him best to keep him on the path to a productive life?"

"The Johnsons and the Carters," Coglan said to the detectives. "They'll make you think the Hatfields and those other folks sat in a circle and sang 'Kumbaya' by comparison."

Szabo's voice murmured a bit more, then ended with a bald statement that they were all going to stay in that room until they came up with a mutually acceptable plan to schedule Donnell's time and agree on goals and consequences for all future behavior—for instance, deciding on a curfew, which social activities were curtailed when he violated that curfew, and so on. Until they had a written plan to which all factions could pledge cooperation, no one could leave.

"Melanie—you can't make us stay here!"

"No, I can't. But you will. Because no one wants to be the one who gave up on Donnell's future."

With that closing salvo she emerged from the room and shut the door behind her. After a shocked moment, the voices started up again, now muffled.

Coglan shook his head. "You are playing with fire, missy."

"Don't I know it. You'd better keep some flash-bangs handy."

Riley watched the closed door for eruptions. "Does that work?"

"You'd be amazed at what they can do. As I said, it has to be their ideas, or the whole process is doomed to failure."

Coglan kept shaking his head. "I give 'em five minutes."

Szabo said, "Nah. They're too stubborn to give in but they're also too stubborn to give up. I just do this to hurry them along a bit. Lock them in a warm room with no food or water and no bathroom. Don't you guys do this with suspects? Just wait them out?"

"It's less effort than bright lights and rubber hoses," Riley joked.

"I'll pull those out next if this doesn't work."

Jack didn't appear to have listened to any of this and glanced up from his time cards with a question. "Could a staff member come and go without signing in or punching the time clock or however you do it here?"

The security guard and the therapist exchanged a glance.

"They ripped the time clock out," Coglan said. "We just fill out a form now."

Szabo said, "When the key card system is installed

that will monitor everything—and not just for security but for billing our hours. Especially ancillary services like me. Efficiency studies, etcetera."

"But it's not operational yet?" Jack asked, though he clearly knew the answer and wasn't happy about it.

"Nope."

Coglan said, "Course there's only two ways in, through reception or through the day student entrance, so it's not like you could sneak in a back door without anyone seeing. There is no back door except to fenced areas and the fire doors have no outside handles." Understanding dawned in an uncomfortable grimace on his face. "You think someone on *staff* killed Damon?"

"You think it's more likely one of the juveniles?" Riley asked him.

Szabo said, "They *are* here for a reason, you know. And it's usually a violent one. Don't look at me like that—that's not disloyalty to my clients, it's reality. And we're all about reality here. Rehabilitation doesn't stand a chance without it."

"Okay, okay," Riley said, holding up his hands in mock surrender. "But the juveniles here are supervised twenty-four/seven. How would one have the opportunity?"

The therapist thought about that as voices raised in the private meeting room. The family rumble grew to full swing. "We let them go to and fro for short errands, such as coming for an appointment with me. Especially the older ones. As long as they're behaving. If they're not being oppositional or suicidal or something."

"We noticed that."

A thump sounded from the meeting room. Coglan

straightened up but the therapist held up her hand. "They always do this. They'll be okay."

"Facilities just patched the holes in the wall from the last time."

"I know."

"Mitch ain't gonna be happy if he has to pull that blue paint out again."

"I know."

Jack said, "So any of them could have been any-place in the building without a record of it. And once you're inside, this place is a free-for-all. Residents, staff, visitors can go anywhere."

Dr. Szabo said, "And teachers and therapists know when a kid steps out. They can't get into each other's age units. Only common areas."

"Most of the kids would have been in class," Maggie pointed out.

Jack said, "We'll have to get with the teachers. And most of the visitors come in the evening."

Riley said, "Still can't see it. How would a kid find the EpiPens?"

Maggie said, "Perhaps there's a few who spend a lot of time in the infirmary. They'd have time to explore when the nurse took bathroom breaks or responded to emergencies."

Riley made an oral note to check with the nurses for recent extended stays in the medical office. They packed up the time cards and lists and left Maggie to deal with her stacks of fingerprint cards and the in-evitable neck strain and went off to find Dr. Palmer. Coglan went along as escort. Melanie Szabo flopped down in Jack's abandoned chair.

"Don't mind me," she told Maggie. "I'm just on fire

brigade duty. Here to run for buckets if there's an explosion."

"Otherwise you just wait?"

"A great deal of therapy is waiting."

"A great deal of forensics is, too."

Doctor Palmer juggled a phone in one hand and a newspaper in the other, standing behind his desk. The office looked as if a strong wind had rippled through it, though Jack couldn't be certain what had changed. An unfamiliar secretary squeezed past them to plop a set of stapled papers on top of the small mound of similar items already covering the desk blotter, and through the window Jack saw the silhouette of a lone basketball player practicing his free throws. The day was warm but overcast, comfortable without a lot of UV exposure.

The doctor said into the phone, "It's not as bad as it could be. I thought the article was fair, more or less. Of course, any bad publicity . . . but that's to be expected . . . that's not really reasonable, though, is it?" He murmured a few more things before both sides apparently gave up and ended the call without any real resolution and turned to them. "Gentlemen."

"Doc," Riley said.

"Thank you for keeping me posted on the ruling regarding Damon's death. Of course, you have our complete cooperation. The poor boy. We've come so far as a society and yet we seem to be going backward when it comes to dealing with our own children." He slumped into his chair as if his knees had given out.

"We're going to need to interview everyone who

was in the building that morning," Riley said, gently but firmly.

"Everyone?"

"Yes. Every staff member and perhaps the . . . patients . . . as well."

"*Ever*—of course that's fine, it's just going to take a lot of time and time away from their duties. We're stretched thin as it is. We always are, of course, starved for funds and personnel—that's the lot of social services—but *really* thin at the moment with all the disruption. The students are restless, agitated by the drama. Besides the construction workers stomping all over the place, they can see the press vans outside."

"We'll be as discreet and quick as possible," Riley promised, adding that they had no alternative.

"Murder. I can't believe someone *killed* Damon."

The boy on the basketball court, Jack realized, was Quentin Sherman. He wondered if the court had a padlock on it, or if a guard had been stationed out there to keep an eye on the kid. He said, "I thought you said nearly every resident here had killed someone."

"I may have overstated," the older man said, but then, compelled to be truthful, added: "Slightly. But usually in a fit of rage. That's what traumatized kids do—they erupt. They scream, fight, throw things."

Outside, Quentin made a perfect shot, the ball sailing through the netless hoop without even touching its sides. He whooped to himself, gave a triumphant leap, and then ran toward the chain link that separated the roof from the open air above the street.

"They don't use medical supplies in a methodical manner and then carefully conceal—"

Jack heard a short yip, an animal cry of surprise and

pain. Quentin had launched himself onto the fence over the street in his usual celebratory taunting of death, but this time death taunted back. The entire section of chain link fell outward, loosened from its mooring, and it and the boy tumbled over the side and disappeared from sight.

Jack was up and out of the office before his mind could catch up. He knew only that Quentin Sherman had probably just died—and that he had watched it happen.

Chapter 22

So far Maggie had identified twelve of her unknown latent prints. Ten of them belonged to one of the two nurses. She had also picked up on who in the Johnson clan felt that Donnell should be allowed to attend his prom and who in the Carter clan opposed this on the grounds of teaching the boy a lesson, when Jack sped into the visiting area with that look on his face. He glanced at her but didn't slow, and she immediately abandoned her latent prints in violation of all chain-of-custody rules. But she had to know just what the hell had happened now.

To her surprise he continued outside through the day student entrance and ran around the street corner. There, in the middle of the mercifully empty street, Quentin Sherman lay underneath an eight-by-eight section of chain-link fence. A September sky beamed overhead, pieces of cobalt blue peeking out from behind gray clouds. On the next block a bird sang. A car drove lazily through the far intersection.

Maggie stopped to stare, her brain processing. Jack

never slowed. He grabbed the fence section and flung it off the boy.

A voice in the back of Maggie's mind said, *There go any fingerprints on those inches of pipe.* And then she also stood over Quentin Sherman.

He lay faceup, eyes staring into that peaceful sky. They swiveled in their sockets to her and Jack, and his lips twitched.

Maggie crouched, putting a hand to his cheek. Blood seemed to be leaking from everywhere and she had no idea what to do. "Quentin!"

He tried to say something to her, his expression urgent.

She spoke his name again, desperately begging him not to die. It felt as if the day before had never happened, or happened to someone else. She didn't see the dangerous predator who had so terrified her and nearly killed Jack. She saw only a young boy clinging to his life as it slipped away from him.

Then a faint rasp, and the face went still. His gaze lost any sense of concern.

Jack put two fingers to the boy's carotid. "He's dead."

"What *happened*?"

Jack straightened and gazed upward, where each window had young faces pressed to it, witnessing yet another violent sight in the long history of their short lives. "Someone loosened the fence section. Riley is up there, making sure no one touches anything."

Maggie took a deep breath and consciously turned her focus to the crime. She made a phone call to Denny to ask for reinforcements, and told Jack she would get her camera from her car. Returning with it she documented the scene, the dead boy, the fence section. Her heart pounded oddly but she ignored that, reasoning that she wasn't accustomed to her victims being so fresh—or having held her as a hostage, either. But she had a lot to do and couldn't coddle herself right now.

Quentin Sherman wore a T-shirt, wet with sweat from his boisterous playing, and a pair of baggy, shiny athletic pants. His shoes probably cost a hundred bucks or so and had all the normal knicks and marring of a teenage boy's footwear. A gold chain rested against his chest, a thick twist with a single pendant that read *Mom* in script. His face showed a few small scrapes on the right temple, probably from yesterday's tackle by several law enforcement officers. His otherwise perfect skin stretched over high cheekbones and long lashes framed his eyes.

His pockets contained a contraband cell phone—which she instantly placed in a Faraday bag to prevent remote wiping by anyone who might have Quentin's passcodes—and a pack of Juicy Fruit.

"He had been arrested," Jack said. "Why wouldn't the phone have been confiscated?"

"Maybe he'd hidden it before shooting Luis, just in case he got caught afterward."

A close-up look at the fence brackets bore out Jack's theory—none seemed to be twisted or deformed. The brackets and the loose screws she located showed little damage, only some clean nicks at the tips of the screws from the final wrenching as the fence connections came apart and at the indented crosses in their heads where a tool had been used.

"All they had to do was loosen the bolts," she said.

"And wait," Jack added.

"Could it be some kind of escape attempt? Some kids planned to tie their bedsheets together after dark but didn't let Quentin in on the plan?"

"It *could*," Jack conceded. "But I doubt it. I think someone knew this kid liked to climb the walls and knew he'd be temporarily banished to outdoor exercise. And I doubt anyone here would leave a number four Phillips lying around, so getting a tool to use took some planning."

She looked again at the large bolt. "They might use a coin. If they had strong fingers. But *why*? Revenge for Luis?"

"Maybe. Most likely. But what did Damon have to do with Luis? What did Derald?"

"Jack."

He turned to her.

"Just what the hell is going on here?"

He gazed up at the roof again. "I wish I knew."

At the top of the building, Riley guided her through the crime scene: a knee-high brick wall that rimmed the edge, with chain link atop that. The forty-by-thirty roof space included an electrical machine room (locked), a patio with three round tables with chairs, and the basketball court. More chain link provided a barrier to keep the game players from bumping into anyone sitting at the tables or emerging from the stairwell, but not the machine room. Its door had suffered copious dents from balls and bodies.

She approached the gaping, now fenceless section. The remaining fence sections were quite sturdy, connected to their posts with tight, weathered brackets.

The two involved posts showed only fresh scrapes similar to the tips of the bolts where their oxidized surface had been scratched as the brackets pulled loose.

In the street below she saw Jack, and Amy, who had arrived from the forensics unit to help her process the scene. But again, there wouldn't be much processing to do. Structures constantly exposed to the elements were not good for latent prints. Dirt, rust, and oxidation coated a not-that-smooth-to-begin-with surface and made finding visible ridges nearly impossible. Not *completely* impossible, however.

"Three stories isn't necessarily enough to kill," she observed to Riley, who stood well back of the edge.

"Yeah. If he had landed on his feet he might have made it. Of course he'd be several inches shorter."

"He'd have a better chance on grass, but asphalt?" She surveyed the surroundings, wondering if occupants of neighboring buildings had seen something. But though still downtown the structures had flattened out in that sector and only two stories had been built across the street to the east. To the north sat the lake and a municipal parking lot, leaving her only seagulls as witnesses.

Even if there had been skyscrapers around, the killer had since the last basketball game to loosen the bolts. The kids would have been in school all morning, so that had probably been the night before. Cover of darkness, a few quick turns of a tool—she felt like screaming in frustration. Someone had been executing children right and left without leaving her a single clue.

Her gaze fell on Jack.

Jack, who had made a shadow profession of exactly that sort of work only a few short months before. Jack, who had been in and out of the Firebird Center for several days, who would be allowed access to any part of the building by virtue of the badge he wore on his hip.

She shook her head, throwing her hair out in an agitated halo.

"What's the matter?" Riley asked from behind her. He had inched up but still avoided the edge. Vertigo did not seem to be his friend.

"Nothing," she said aloud, firmly. It was ridiculous. Rachael and Derald had already been dead before Jack ever heard of this place, right? Granted, perhaps they were not murders at all . . . but she couldn't picture Jack injecting ten-year-old Damon with EpiPens. Damon's mother, certainly. But not the small boy who had been so terribly unfortunate. Damon had been damaged—he hadn't been *evil*.

Quentin Sherman, on the other hand . . .

She felt a sudden chill. From the lake, she told herself. That touch of coming frost.

Chapter 23

Maggie did what she could. That included processing the door leading to the roof with portable superglue wands that turned it white and illuminated the slapped handprints of dozens of teenage boys pumped up with youth and testosterone. This took an hour with camera and tripod and adjusting the light every which way while curious staff members kept catching curious children in the stairwell trying to get a glimpse of the crime scene. Some of the kids wheedled for more time, some ignored commands to move, and one thirteen-year-old pushed his social worker down the steps. The social worker managed to catch himself on the railing, or Maggie might have had another bizarre but accidental death to investigate.

She could hear noise and raised voices from the classrooms. Yesterday they had a murder occur in science class and today a fatal fall. She couldn't blame them if geometry didn't hold their interest.

Amy had carefully collected the bolts and superglued the fence section in the street after having the traffic diverted. It would be impossible to move it back to the lab without grasping the frames and possibly smudging prints that would be delicate and problematic to begin with. They didn't even have a vehicle large enough to transport it and Maggie didn't feel sure it would fit through the door into the lab. Better to process it on scene and then it could be loaded onto a flatbed as roughly as necessary. As bulky, heavy, and basically uninteresting as it was, it was evidence of murder and would have to be kept at the police department as long as the case remained open.

But photographing the wisps of latent prints Amy could raise on its frame was a pain and a half. At least the roof door had been a flat surface. Trying to photograph faint white prints against the curved dull metal of the frame in broad daylight proved an exercise in frustration. Struggling to hold them still in the breeze off the lake, Maggie held tarps up to block the intermittent sun so Amy could adjust the light source to sidelight the prints. This simply had to represent the best they could do. They couldn't leave the piece in the street overnight for the superglue to oxidize so they could drip the prints with dye stain and use an ultraviolet light source to make the dyed prints glow, and they couldn't get the section back to the lab without disturbing the superglue.

Maggie doubted the killer would have left prints anyway—he, or she, had been careful enough to wipe off the EpiPens and their box. But perhaps he, or she, counted on the elements to destroy any prints, so Maggie couldn't make herself give up on the idea.

But once back on the roof she thought of something else.

The sections of fence were held to their poles by round brackets that looped around the pole and then protruded to secure the section frame on either side. The ends of these brackets were held by carriage bolts, which had obviously been loosened until hanging on by a single thread, easily torn away by the weight of a fifteen-year-old boy.

The brackets were spaced out along the pole so that the upper two were well out of reach from the roof. The killer had to have been a climber like Quentin to get to the upper bolts and would have had to cling to the pole to steady himself, or herself, as he, or she, used the tool. Even if the killer used a ladder or stacked up the chairs he, or she, probably held on to the pole as well as the still-solid neighboring section of fence.

Riley came up behind her as she stared up at the top of the remaining fence. "Don't even think about it."

"He got up there somehow." She grasped the mesh of chain link and pumped it in and out. It barely moved. "I need a ladder."

"I thought you said prints were impossible."

"I said *nearly* impossible. Besides, I'm not going to try for prints. I'm going to swab the pole and links for touch DNA. I'll bet those bolts didn't turn easily after all these years. He would have had to work hard to budge them, he had to be nervous, risking being seen. He would have been sweating. Maybe even if he wore gloves they were cloth gloves and the sweat would have soaked through. Maybe they were an old pair of leather gloves and had a decade of skin cells built up from being pulled on and off."

"That's a lot of maybes," Riley observed.

She crossed her arms. "I need a ladder."

Two ladders were located within the building, both eight feet high and unable to reach to the top of the chain link. Maggie propped one against the pole and went to the top step. The right side of her body faced the links of a secure section of fence, the left side, nothing but open air. She had a nice view of the lake and the city as it spread to the east.

The pole is steel, buried in the brick wall, she told herself. *It's not going anywhere.* No reason for her heart to pound and her knees to quiver as they did.

Even though the pole was buried in old brick that had been there for decades, sun and snow and wind working on its mortar, possibly loosening bits of it.

She should probably have a safety harness, something to tether her if the fence gave way, but no such item existed in her current crime scene kit. She might make the suggestion to Denny—

A burst of wind seemed to push at her, and she grabbed the links. Deep breath.

"You sure you should be up there?" said a voice below and behind her. Justin Quintero. She didn't turn to look.

"Quite sure. Just tell me the bricks into which this pole is set aren't going to suddenly fall apart."

He sounded as if he were speaking from the center of the roof, apparently not too fond of heights either. "Um . . . I hope not."

"That's not reassuring."

"Sorry. But it's been my job to point out the deficiencies in this building so we can give the state an itemized request."

"Oh," she said, not terribly interested at the moment.

"There're so many aspects that make a place more conducive to rehabilitation that we currently"—he sighed—"lack. More interior space. More windows, more natural light. Enough outdoor spaces—like this one—for each age group so they can be accessed at will without scheduling. Better colors, kid-proof decorations."

She half listened to him. With the ladder's help the uppermost bracket appeared at eye level. Still she couldn't tell if the killer had borrowed a ladder as well; she saw distortions in the links where he, or she, could have grabbed or stuck in a shoe during the climb to the top. Besides, the ladders were stored in a dust-coated cubby in the limited basement area, to which only maintenance had the key. Even if someone could have broken in they would have had to lug the thing up four flights of steps, or one floor and take the elevator for another three and all without being seen by staff or residents. The construction workers had ladders as well but they removed all their equipment at night to a van parked outside, and it had not been disturbed.

The chairs wouldn't stack, and one by itself wouldn't even lift someone to even the middle of the fence, so they were useless to the killer.

"At least our furnishings are moveable so we can scoot tables and chairs around for different purposes. And we have both big and small rooms, so that variety apes what the outside world is like more than places where they're either in one big dorm or one big mess hall or one big exercise auditorium. But we need more sound-absorbing materials in those spaces, especially when you get a bunch of teenage girls chattering."

She still imagined this being done at night, when perhaps the climb wouldn't have been as nerve wracking, when you couldn't see every crack in the sidewalk far below or how small the cars seemed as they crawled along South Marginal.

"And furniture that isn't designed primarily for suicide prevention, because there is such a thing as self-fulfilling prophecy. It's not easy. We got a good design out of last year's budget. Now all we need is the money to go ahead."

Maggie kept her body as still as possible and twisted the tiny blue cap off the vial of sterile water, then tossed the cap back over her shoulder. A bit of littering could be tolerated at this juncture.

"Detectives," she heard Quintero say. "Are they going to remove the body soon? I would really like it *not* to be there when the state budget board members arrive. It might put them off their baby carrots."

Riley said, "ME just got here."

"Fabulous." She heard the relief in Quintero's voice and the swish of his clothing, testament to his hasty departure from the aerie.

She moistened the swabs and ran them along the pole where the boltless bracket remained and the links to the side where a killer might have held on while loosening that bolt. It was a long shot—touch DNA usually was—but a slam dunk if it worked. Kids climbing the fence wouldn't go this high . . . would they? . . . and presumably not in the last twenty-four hours.

Now she heard Jack's voice from below. "What are you doing?"

"DNA," she said.

"There you have it," Riley said. "DNA."

"Peachy," Jack said.

She felt a tremor under her feet and saw that Jack had grasped the ladder to steady it, though it had not shifted. Funny how he always seemed determined to protect her, even when she remained the only fly in the ointment of his calling to make the world a safer place.

Something in the still-firm bracket caught her eye. A thin filament protruded, caught between the pole and the brace. A hair, or a fiber. She slid the swabs into their clean box and then into a manila envelope she had tucked into her belt, then gingerly made her way down.

"Done?" Jack asked.

"No. Perhaps our guy did use gloves, because he may have left a thread up there. And then I need to do the other side." She nodded toward the opposite pole at the other end of the gap.

"Oh boy," Riley said. "You two have fun. I'm going to gather up another set of time cards from the last basketball game until now. How anyone's going to get paid this week is beyond me."

Maggie gathered a tiny manila envelope and climbed into the sky once more.

Another hour passed at the crime scene and Maggie at last conceded that they had done all they could. The medical examiner investigator had arrived and taken

Quentin's body away. Riley had gone to observe the autopsy, not that they expected any surprises to come of it since the cause of death seemed pretty damn apparent. Amy had transported the loose brackets and bolts back to the lab after supervising the removal of the fence section. The fire department came to handle the biohazard—Quentin's blood—in the street and reopen it to traffic. Dinnertime approached and Maggie's stomach growled.

Melanie Szabo came looking for her once the crime scene tape had been removed from the top of the stairwell. "Trina would like to see you. She said she has something to tell you. She won't tell me what it is. So if you have a minute before you leave—"

"Sure," Maggie said, with less enthusiasm than she felt. She still had no idea how to be supportive and mentoring to a juvenile violent offender. Especially one who had apparently tried to kill her own mother. Of course, if Trina's mother had been anything like Damon's, that might not be so hard to understand. "Let me lock my stuff in my car and I'll be back in."

They descended the steps, voices bouncing off the concrete walls. "I have no idea what it is; she wouldn't give me a hint. Anyway I told her she could wait in my usual counseling room. Second-floor visiting area, where you were this morning?"

"Got it. Dr. Szabo—"

"Just Melanie, please. Even the kids call me that."

"How did the Johnsons and Carters make out?"

Melanie Szabo stopped dead, one foot hovering over the landing. "Uh-oh."

Maggie halted as well. "What?"

"With all the excitement—poor word, let's say *bustle*—of Quentin's accident and getting the kids settled down and more emergency sessions—"

"Yeah?" Maggie said, drawing the word out.

"I totally forgot about them!"

The therapist flew down the next flight in a swirl of skirt, her low heels clattering on the treads.

Chapter 24

Maggie shut the hatch on the mini city-issued station wagon, clicked the door lock button, and turned around to bump into Jack. "Jeeze! I wish you wouldn't do that."

He took no offense. "I'm thinking."

"That's a good thing." Then she remembered other details of Jack and added, "Usually."

"The building is still locked down. So far no one cares because it isn't yet quitting time, but eventually we'll have to put some teeth into it."

"Uh-huh." They walked along the sidewalk. The sun had finally burst out of the clouds and heated the back of her neck until sweat poked out of its pores.

"If you could identify that fiber and I could get some reinforcements, we could toss the building for the gloves."

"Simple but effective." It would take a long time for a thorough search of the large structure, but finding the gloves would give them cast-iron proof of the killer's identity. Or nearly cast iron, depending upon the type of fiber. "In truth the fiber *could* have been there since the fence was constructed, though that's pretty unlikely. If it's cotton or some natural fiber, the elements would have worn it away long ago. Making a murder case on that alone would do a lot for my poor neglected science of fiber comparisons. It would be the biggest thing in fibers since the Wayne Williams case."

"I'm not really interested in making forensic history," Jack said. "I just want to catch whoever is slaughtering these kids. With a building full of people who have the means, opportunity, and whatever they want to pick for a motive—I'm desperate," he summed up. "I don't even know it yet, but I'm desperate."

Those weren't words she often heard a man say. Especially cops, who had that invincible image to protect. For a man who had taken the cause of justice into his own hands in the most outrageous way, Jack could be remarkably un-self-conscious. She found herself wanting to give him a hug. Or maybe, after the events of the past few days, she just wanted one herself.

She said, "First I need to identify the type of fiber and the color that we're looking for—and I can't do that without a microscope. Let me say hello to Trina for a minute, and then I'll hightail it back to the lab and find that out. She says she has something to tell me. I'm hoping it might be about Rachael."

"Make it quick. I'm going to muster an invading army."

She asked about Rachael's father. Jack told her the man had claimed the ring was his, though Jack still had his doubts, and could not positively identify the kids in Rachael's two photos. He thought they might be children from their old apartment complex but didn't know their names, making them impossible to track down.

He and Maggie went inside and climbed the stairs to

the second-floor visiting area, by now finding their way without hesitation.

Maggie said, "The staff won't be happy when you seal the exits."

"Tough. A boy was murdered here today. They'll have to suck it up."

"Good luck with that."

Jack surprised her again by saying, "I don't expect too much pushback. The people here make a lot of sacrifices to help these kids—work long hours, stay overnight, get threatened, screamed at, occasionally have the snot beaten out of them by pint-sized maniacs. I'm pretty sure they'll take it in stride."

He continued to the third floor to inform Dr. Palmer of the plan while she stopped on the second, passing the Jackson and Carter clans on their way out. Since they had not been on-site until immediately before Quentin's death and had had no contact with anyone else at the facility except Melanie Szabo, they could be allowed to leave. To Maggie's surprise they now seemed relaxed, chatting and laughing together easily, followed by the beaming therapist. Apparently she had been right—let them work out their own plan and they'll not only get but stay on board.

The second-floor visiting area sat empty, all afternoon appointments rearranged for immediate crisis counseling. Trina had been arranging chairs just outside the door to Szabo's therapy room and greeted Maggie with carefully controlled enthusiasm. She showed her inside as if it were her own living room, shutting the door behind them.

Maggie sat down at the tiny round table, nearly tripping over a bucket filled with what smelled like a strong solution of ammonia. A plastic bottle rested on the floor by the wall. "I'm on bathroom cleaning duty," Trina explained. "It's pretty gross."

"I know what you mean. I worked as a maid in a hotel while in college."

The girl wrinkled her nose. "Lots of toilets."

Maggie agreed, then leaned forward over the magazine and assorted toys that had been left on the table. "I had one overflow once. With *stuff* in it."

Being a teenager, the delicious disgustingness of this image tickled Trina. She burst into giggles with an "Oh *no!*"

"Oh yes." Maggie let the girl chuckle for another moment, then, with ice sufficiently broken and Jack's plan in mind, said, "So, what did you want to talk to me about?"

The laughter disappeared. "I know you only care about Rachael."

"No—that's not true. But we would still like to know what happened, why she died. Don't you? Do you have anything else to tell me about her?"

Trina jumped up and paced, as much as she could in the very small room. "Rachael really wasn't nice."

"I've heard that." Maggie kept her voice calm and warm. Talking did not come easily to Trina—that had always been obvious. She would have to let the girl get to it in her own way, even if the staff had to stay locked down a few more minutes.

"She'd say mean things."

"Uh-huh. Like what?"

"She told me I was ugly and that boys would never like me."

An uncomfortable thought began to hover in Maggie's mind. "That was mean."

"It was! Ms. Washington made her apologize but she said it like it was a joke—the *I'm sorry* part—and then she was supposed to help me with a homework assignment. That's what they make you do when you hurt somebody—you have to help them with something and that's supposed to make us feel like helping is good instead of hurting."

"That's a very good idea."

Trina stopped in her pacing to snarl, "It's *stupid*."

"I think it's supposed to encourage you—*us*—to empathize, to put ourselves in others' shoes."

The agitated pacing started up again, Trina pausing only to gnaw at a cuticle. Two fingers already showed pinpricks of blood. Trina seemed to be prodding herself into an angry mood, and Maggie continued to worry. Was she working herself up to a confession? If so, what should Maggie do? She wasn't a cop, couldn't advise her of her rights or—

"We had to draw the photosynthesis process and Rachael could draw pretty good. But she purposely made it bad, made stupid stick plants that didn't look real and this dumb sun that looked like a baby drew it."

"She was still being mean." What could Maggie do, other than sit still and listen carefully? So she sat still and listened carefully.

The ammonia from the bucket tickled her nose and she stifled a cough.

"That's what I'm *saying*! You're not *listening*."

Maggie wished she had asked Melanie Szabo to sit in. "Tell me."

Trina threw her body into the other chair for a brief

rest. "She said she had a boyfriend who was going to sneak her out of here and they were going to live in Manhattan in a penthouse and I couldn't come because I was just a kid."

"Okay, but that probably wasn't true, right? You figured Rachael made a lot of stuff up."

"It doesn't *matter*! That's not *important*!" The lithe form bounced up again, resumed the movement, moving from wall to wall like a pinball in a machine. Only instead of working up to a point she seemed to be getting farther from one, her thoughts more dispersed. "It's what I'm *told*."

"Told by who?" Maggie asked.

"Told by them." Trina picked up the bucket by the handle, moved it closer to the door, and set it down again to continue on her erratic course.

Maggie asked who *them* might be. The air had gotten close in the tiny space, the ammonia smell thick.

"The voices." Trina stopped abruptly to stare down at the bucket, as if wondering what it might be and how it had gotten there.

"Whose voices?" Maggie deeply regretted starting this conversation. She had no more business trying to mentor Trina than she had pressing vitamins on a cancer patient.

Trina didn't answer. Instead she picked up the plastic jug, twisted off the lid, and began to add it to the solution.

"I think that's strong enough already," Maggie said. "I hope you're wearing rubber gloves when you use that. The chemicals will do a number on your skin."

Trina didn't answer. The liquid made a soft *glug glug*.

Maggie tried again. "I didn't like to wear them either when I was your age. But harsh cleaners will really dry out the epidermis. Do you have any hand lotion? I could bring you a bottle."

No answer. Yet the girl's back, the shoulders, her waist began to round and relax. She might have been adding eggs to a quiche for all the stress her body showed. Perhaps this motion soothed her, even as it choked the air.

"Really, Trina, I think that's enough. Let's at least open the door, okay?"

No answer. The last of the liquid dripped from the bottle.

Maggie rose very slowly, but before she had completely straightened Trina whirled, her face screwed into an unrecognizable mask. "*Sit down.* You have to stay here!"

Her voice as gentle as she could make it: "Why?"

"This is what I have to do," Trina said, and in one smooth motion she opened the door, stepped outside, and closed it behind her.

Maggie jumped up and reached for the latch knob. It had no lock; all she had to do was turn it to open. But Trina had already wedged a chair under it, the chair she had moved out of place to position next to the door. An old-fashioned technique, as old-fashioned as loosening a bolt or pushing someone over a railing. Simple but effective.

"Trina!"

Through the high window in the door the girl watched her, a triumphant grin creasing her face. She rocked on her toes and clapped her hands in delight at her accomplishment.

Maggie pulled, to no effect. The chair under the latch didn't budge. She'd have to either take the hinge pegs out or break the whole door down. Neither would be impossible for a lightweight, interior door whose purpose had been more for privacy than security, but that would be a bit of an overreaction. She wasn't in any actual danger and Jack would come looking for her, eventually.

She coughed. The air had turned acrid. How much ammonia had the kid poured into this bucket?

That's when she noticed the emptied bottle lying on the floor.

Bleach.

Bleach + ammonia = chlorine gas. Chlorine gas, which had killed over ninety thousand soldiers during the First World War. If it didn't flat-out suffocate it would damage the respiratory epithelium and cause a toxic pneumonitis, not to mention chemical burns. There was no antidote.

However, Trina used stuff she stole from bathroom duty, not a weapons armory. Even commercial strength bleach wouldn't be much more than typical household fare, a 5 percent solution, the ammonia perhaps up to 10. The reaction would produce hydrazine, with a melting and boiling point close to water. No explosion of fumes, then, and if she—

Outside the door Trina watched, her feet shuffling beneath her as if dancing a small jig. Then she launched onto the chair, both holding it in place under the knob and giving her a front-seat view of the show.

Maggie coughed. And then she coughed again.

Then she held her breath.

While doing that she picked up the bucket by the

handle and moved it about two feet to the center of the room. She slid the chairs out of the way and upended the entire small table. The magazine and toys slid to the floor. Heavier than she expected but manageable; she flipped it upside down so that the skinny legs pointed to the ceiling. Then she set its flat top onto the top of the bucket, straining to keep it steady. She didn't want to either crush or tip the bucket, which would leave herself worse off instead of better.

Her lungs reached the limit of their ability to freeze and she sucked in a half breath. The air felt like a living thing, reaching deep into her alveoli with tiny stabbing knives of pain, but she stifled another cough long enough to get the table situated. The bucket held. The flat surface of its top covered the bucket and would hold in the fumes; they wouldn't generate much pressure to speak of and definitely not enough to shove the table off. And the pour lip would act as a vent. The lip also made it impossible to completely seal the top but still the fumes would be largely contained. She debated setting a chair on top of the overturned table for good measure but decided that would be unnecessary and possibly destabilizing and she really wanted to breathe *now*.

She returned to the door, not that the air was any fresher there, and drew in a deep breath.

Trina had been watching all this activity, and her smile faded. Her plan to create a mini gas chamber had possibly been foiled. A mighty frown creased her brow.

The breath made Maggie cough, long and deep. Her stomach roiled until vomiting seemed a possibility.

This made Trina smile. "You're going to die! You're going to suffocate."

Maggie made herself stand tall. She stood back from the door and faced its window with crossed arms. "I'm not going to die, Trina. The solutions aren't strong enough. At worst I might get a headache."

The girl's face fell as she spoke. Perhaps if she convinced Trina that the plot would never prove fatal no matter how long she waited, she'd give up and let her out. Maggie didn't have time for attempted murder. She had a fiber to identify.

And her lungs burned. She tried another shallow breath; it caused a cough that made her want to double over but she fought it, stayed upright. Her eyes watered with the effort. For all her calculations of percentages and cubic air space, perhaps she had gotten enough in that first snootful to give her a case of instant bronchitis. Or worse.

But she could do nothing but stand there and breathe it, one tiny mouthful at a time, until Trina gave up.

A shape moved behind Trina. Maggie heard Jack's voice, asking the girl something.

Trina turned away, her face melting into that same feral mask Maggie had seen. Then the girl threw herself at Jack with all the force in her tiny frame.

Maggie rushed to the window. Jack saw her and had one quarter second to sum up the situation before Trina was upon him.

She beat at him with her fists, kicked with both legs. Though twice her size and twice her weight, Jack had not been trained in hand-to-hand combat with a child. He hesitated, not knowing what or where to grab, and in that instant the girl launched herself up and slashed at his face with both hands. The chewed nails couldn't do much, so she clung to the front of him and bit his neck. Maggie saw his face contort in pain.

"Jack!" she shouted.

In her distress she forgot to keep her breaths shallow and sucked in enough chlorine-tinted air to double over in coughing. It felt as if she might leave a lung on the carpet. Five percent was still too damn much.

The door flew open, and Jack stood in the open space. Blood flowed from the wound on his neck. Beyond him she saw Trina's still form, prone on the linoleum floor of the visiting area.

"Jack," Maggie wheezed, "what did you do?"

He grabbed her by the shoulders and yanked.

Chapter 25

The black, portly, chatty EMT who cleaned and patched the wound over Jack's carotid asked if he had been attacked by a vampire. And he didn't seem to be kidding. When told it had been an undernourished fourteen-year-old girl, the guy said only, "I hope she had all her shots."

"Me too," Jack said.

Two seats away from him, Maggie coughed again. She had an oxygen mask strapped over her nose and mouth and her watery eyes watched him, the brows pointing down in a heavy frown. Then she ripped the mask off to demand, "Where is she?"

"Keep that oxygen on," the EMT ordered. Maggie gave him a darker look than Jack had ever seen from her, ignored the demand, and repeated the question, complete with cough.

Jack told her, "She's in the infirmary, getting ice on her jaw. She'll be up and attempting murder again in no time."

"You didn't have to hit her so hard."

He held up the bandage, now soaked with his own

blood. "*Hello!* I'm going to have to get twenty-one shots now—"

"It's not that many," the EMT corrected. "It's only four or five now. And—"

"Not to mention the fact that she was trying to kill you. You're welcome, by the way."

Maggie said, "I wasn't in any danger. All I needed you to do was open the door—" Her shoulders ducked and she spewed out coughs that sounded deep and wet. She slapped the oxygen mask to her face.

The EMT continued, "And it's not necessary unless her blood turns up abnormalities. A course of antibiotics—"

"I didn't know that, did I?" Jack guessed that he sounded silly and that annoyed him even more than his bleeding neck.

Maggie took away the mask long enough to ask the EMT if he had seen Trina.

"No, my partner's got her. She didn't lose consciousness, just had the breath knocked out of her and a goose egg on her jaw—"

"What do you think, I killed her?" Jack demanded, even while not believing he would say such a thing out loud and in front of a witness. But, more importantly, Maggie's glare told him that, yes, that had been exactly what she'd thought.

As if that would have been a *bad* thing. Trina was a crazy, homicidal menace.

He didn't bother trying to explain that to Maggie. These days there was a lot he didn't bother trying to explain to Maggie, he thought sourly.

"We'll have to start *her* on antibiotics, too—" the EMT mused. "I'm sure you don't have any communicable diseases, dude, so don't take it personally. It's just the accepted protocol to avoid infection from the usual mouth bacterias—"

"All right," Maggie said, and took one last suck of the oxygen before hanging the mask over the tank and turning to Jack. "Are you ready?"

The EMT stuck one more piece of medical tape to Jack's neck. It felt as if the guy had used most of the roll. "For what?"

"To find out if Trina has succeeded in anyone else's murder."

"Sweetie!" Carol exclaimed. "What are you doing here?"

"I have to identify a fiber," Maggie wheezed.

"Can't anyone—well, no. I guess you're it, huh?"

Maggie didn't bother to agree, only moved to the microscopy bench and got out a glass slide, a glass cover slip, and a heavy brown bottle of liquid mounting medium. Fiber and hair comparisons were rarely done anymore in a field that preferred the certainty of fingerprints and DNA. No one new had been trained, which left Maggie the only fiber analyst within a hundred miles.

"Can you breathe okay?" The older woman hovered. "You sound wheezy. We heard that some little juvenile delinquent tried to gas you."

"Bleach and ammonia."

"Fabulous," Carol said. "Hydrazine. How are your eyes? Will you even be able to see through that microscope?"

"They're still burning a little, but not too bad. Mostly it just gave me an instant case of bronchitis."

"Which will probably turn into pneumonia."

"You're not cheering me up." Maggie pulled out the tiny envelope with the fiber and made a concerted effort to stop coughing. She had one, tiny fiber. If she blew it away into the oblivion of the lab's floor, their chance to stop the murders of children would be lost.

"Sorry. Can I get you anything? Coffee? Tissue? Z-Pak?"

"Coffee would be great. The EMTs have me covered for the rest."

Carol moved off and Maggie took a slow, tentative breath. She had to think and move calmly, slowly, deliberately. Her lungs would have to cooperate until she got the fiber stuck in the liquid Permount. Then it would be secure even in case of a typhoon.

Her lungs were having none of it. So she let them hack while she put a few drops of the clear viscous liquid onto the slide. Then, fine-tipped tweezers in hand, she flipped open the top of the envelope. The slender thread had at least been dyed a helpful dark color and even with watering eyes she could see it nestled in the bottom. Another shallow breath, and she plunged the tweezers inside.

A tickle sprouted at the bottom of her right lung. It quickly spread to the bronchia.

She moved hands, envelope, and tweezers to just over the slide, reducing the distance the fiber needed to travel to about two inches. She willed her torso to freeze, commanded her lungs and even her blood to stop all movement just until she got the thing in the sticky stuff *please*.

It didn't listen. The alveoli went into a quivering

frenzy, wanting to cough, wanting to breathe in and out and up and down, all at once.

She pulled the fiber from the envelope. It seemed to have lost half its mass inside the manila and seemed barely visible. But perhaps that was only her irritated eyes. Move it to the tiny puddle of Permount—

She sneezed.

No, no, *no*!

It had disappeared. No—the spasm had made her hand dip and clench, so that the tweezers held the fiber but had also dipped into the Permount and now the fiber wouldn't come off the tweezers. She used its predicament to take a moment to cough the tickle out of her body, then used another set of tweezers and a solvent to get the fiber both freed from the tweezers and stuck enough in the Permount, dropped on a cover slip, and that, thankfully, was that. After, of course, she cleaned the sticky stuff off both sets of tweezers before they were ruined for good.

She moved the slide under the light microscope and promptly determined that the miniscule piece of thread consisted of two fibers, a thin cotton and a wider synthetic. They were both the same shade of brown. A trip to the polarizing microscope made the synthetic fiber glow with the pale pinks and greens of polyester. Probably a pair of cheap work gloves.

Maggie made a quick note of the polyester's diameter and cross-sectional shape. If their crime scene had been a home, a pair of work gloves wouldn't be much in the way of evidence. Every home owner needed a pair. But in a school–slash–jail–slash–office building, they would be harder to explain away except for the maintenance man or the construction crew. Someone—perhaps Ms. Washington—had said that the children didn't maintain a winter wardrobe as they didn't have the storage space. There had been no construction work under way on the roof and it didn't appear to get a lot of maintenance, either.

Maybe this would lead to the killer. He or she couldn't have known to get rid of them, had no reason to think they would turn into damning evidence.

And Trina. Did Trina have a pair? Maggie could easily picture the girl scaling the chain link as if she were in Cirque du Soleil. She would barely have dented the links.

At some point she would have to deal with the fact that the little girl she had befriended had tried to kill her. She knew she shouldn't take it personally—obviously Trina had severe issues—but when her eyes still burned and her lungs ached it was damn hard not to.

Carol returned with a steaming, fragrant mug, proclaiming, "Caffeine. It cures all ills."

"I'm eternally grateful. But can I get it to go?"

Chapter 26

Jack had begun to wish he'd accompanied Quentin Sherman's body to its autopsy instead of Riley. Jack felt much more comfortable around dead bodies than convincing a live judge to authorize the search of a building full of county employees and disadvantaged children. He'd made Jack strike out the part that included computer data and cell phones, saying that to his knowledge technology had not advanced to the point where a pair of gloves could be hidden in cyberspace.

But at last the guy had signed the thing so Jack only needed to pick up his car keys, which he had stupidly left on his desk blotter, and get out of the building before Maggie realized he'd gone. She didn't need to sit in on a search, coughing all over creation and providing a target for any other murderous teens.

Speaking of Maggie, her ex-husband sat at his desk in the nearly empty homicide unit. Gardiner seemed to spend a lot of time at his desk. Crimes were solved mostly by legwork but you would never know it from watching Rick Gardiner.

As Jack's fingers closed over his key fob, he looked

up and said, "Where you from, Renner?" in a friendly tone that didn't fool Jack in the least.

"Huh?"

"You're not from Cleveland, originally, right? So where you from?"

"Minneapolis. Why?"

"You don't have an accent. Like in *Fargo*, yah?"

"Didn't grow up there."

"Oh yeah?"

Jack couldn't figure out if Gardiner was just wasting time, at which he excelled, or had some bug up his butt. Jack had never spent more than two seconds trying to figure out Gardiner, and began to wonder if he should.

"Where you from before that?"

"I've got to go, Gardiner."

"I was talking to an old pal of mine in Minneapolis the other day."

"Fabulous. Still got to go. We have a bunch of dead kids and no answers."

"Howie Romero. You remember him?"

Yes. He'd better start spending some time figuring Gardiner out. Jack picked up his keys, fixed his gaze on the other man, and asked, "You call him Howie?"

Gardiner's smug look faltered. "You didn't?"

"Not unless I wanted to get stuck on night shift on the north side."

Gardiner's mouth fell slightly open. Jack left the room with his keys, his search warrant, and a slight smile.

He made it as far as the hallway before running into Maggie.

"Brown cotton/poly," she said.

He moved past her and aimed for the bank of elevators, still hoping for a quick getaway. "Good. I've got the warrant and Riley's going to meet me—"

She grabbed the cuff of his sleeve, pinching an inch firmly between thumb and forefinger and not letting go even after he snapped to a halt. "Kind of like what you're wearing."

He met her gaze, giving the words a moment to sort out into some kind of sense. They didn't.

"What?"

A surreptitious glance around to be sure they were alone in the hallway, and she stepped closer.

"You—" She stopped, swallowed, and started again. "You kill to prevent future crimes. These kids are all future criminals, unless all the classes and therapies and structure turn them around, and for many the odds aren't good. That's right up your alley."

"You think *I* killed all these kids?"

"Why not? You helped in Derald Tyson's arrest, knew the difficulties of keeping him inside due to his age. You might have gone there looking for him and found all these other kids who were never going to peacefully reenter—"

"And how would I be getting in and out of the Firebird Center without being noticed? All the exits are monitored. The staff all know each other and they have a set routine for coming and going—"

"The *kids'* movements are regimented. Adults can roam at will, and there're always family visitors, attorneys, parole officers in and out. We've been all over that place for the past week and never once did anyone challenge us or even ask what we were doing there."

He couldn't believe this. This weird—arrangement— between himself and Maggie couldn't continue if she was going to suspect him of every murder that took place within city limits. Even if she sometimes hit the mark.

He put his hands on her shoulders. "Maggie. I didn't kill these kids. I didn't even know these kids existed, and even if I had, you're missing the important point. *They were already in custody*. They weren't out on the streets, hurting innocent people, impervious to law enforcement."

That at least stopped her flow of words. He could see the wheels turning as she considered this.

"Oh," was all she said.

"Exactly. They'd already been caught."

"But they might have gotten out," she tried.

"Sure. But not likely, and not without heavy monitoring. Besides, no matter what you think of me, Maggie, I would never kill a mute ten-year-old. For God's sake." He felt like adding, *How could you even think such a thing?*, but then admitted to himself she had good reason to.

"But, Jack—"

He dropped his hands. "*What?*"

"I'm right about one thing. The adults in that building have much more freedom of movement than the kids."

"What, now you don't think Trina is our killer?"

"I'm just not sure." She headed for the elevator and waited there for him. Jack sighed. Obviously he wasn't going to get back to the Firebird Center without Maggie Gardiner.

As he turned he caught sight of her ex-husband, watching them from the entrance to the homicide unit.

*   *   *

There was a lot to be said for having crimes occur within the inner downtown area. They reached the Firebird Center in ten minutes flat and the receptionist, gobsmacked by all the goings-on, showed Maggie and Jack to Dr. Palmer's office. Through the window Maggie could see the gap in the chain link where Quentin Sherman had plunged over the side.

"Ah, Miss Gardiner," Palmer said. "I can't begin to tell you how sorry I am—"

"It's okay. Really." She slipped into an empty chair as Dr. Palmer fussed about how much better Trina had seemed to be doing, and what a setback this represented.

"What *is* her story?" Jack asked. Maggie didn't. She felt almost afraid to know.

"Trina," Dr. Palmer said heavily, "is mentally ill."

Jack said, "No shit."

"No, you don't understand. Ninety-nine point nine percent of the children we treat and school here were born healthy, neurotypical children who now have emotional and behavioral issues due to abuse, neglect, violence in the home, and other outside influences. Trina suffered no abuse, neglect, or violence. But she was not, apparently, born healthy."

"A bad seed?" Jack asked.

The little man frowned. "That's a glib but somewhat accurate explanation. Her parents were lovely people who wanted more than anything for her to be happy. But from birth her life has been a battle between light and dark."

"Like I said, born bad."

"Trina isn't *bad*. She's *ill*. She's quite ill. And her illness is difficult to treat because we don't know its cause. It's some form of psychosis, but not a straightforward biochemical imbalance as in schizophrenia."

"So she's a psychopath. That doesn't exactly come as a surprise."

"*No*, Detective. Psychotic is very different from psychopathology. Psychotics are delusional. They hear voices, they suffer from paranoia. Their thoughts and emotions are so impaired that they lose touch with reality. They live in a frightening, confusing world."

That described Trina, Maggie thought.

"A psychopath, or sociopath, is not at all delusional in the medical sense. They see reality exactly as it is— they just don't care, because no one else matters except them. They are not frightened, depressed, or anxious. They have no insecurities or neurotic torment."

"No remorse," Jack said.

"Exactly. Derald Tyson was a psychopath. Quentin Sherman was a psychopath—virtually all gang leaders are. Not gang *members*, who are usually kids looking for a substitute family or dullards who are looking for some self-actualization, but to have the calculated cruelty necessary to turn *those* kids into killers and pawns, yes, that requires a complete absence of empathy."

"That's not Trina," Maggie said. She couldn't point to what made her believe that, but believe it she did.

Dr. Palmer nodded. "We've used a combination of cognitive therapy and Thorazine to try to keep her on an even keel. Justin warned me that this may not be the right facility for her, but she had been doing so well. It's been months since her last outburst."

Jack asked, "What'd she do last time?"

"Um . . . attacked Dr. Szabo. With a chair. Nothing as clever as what she tried on you, Ms. Gardiner. I can't tell you how sorry—"

"I'm all right, Doctor," Maggie said, this assurance somewhat mitigated by another coughing fit.

As it subsided Palmer said, "No doubt the trauma with Quentin and Luis undid much of her progress. I should have seen that coming. It's an example of Trina's capacity for empathy, Detective, that she worried over Luis. He missed his stepbrother terribly. We think of siblings, especially stepsiblings, as feeling nothing but rivalry and competition. We forget that when the parents are absent or abusive, the kids often have only each other to depend on. They're the only ones who know what each other has been through."

Jack said, "So she had a crush on Luis, until Rachael came along and screwed that up. Dr. Bellamy, Derald Tyson's therapist, said he had taken on a girl from the resident flower child. I assume that meant Dr. Szabo. Was he talking about Trina?"

Dr. Palmer frowned, perhaps at the change in topic, but then said, "Yes. As I said, Trina's condition fell outside our usual purview, and her father took out a loan to hire Jerome. I believe he's only had a few sessions with her, however, and she still sees Dr. Szabo as well. I—anyway, you still feel you need to search the building?"

Jack said, "We will be looking for a pair of gloves or perhaps the sleeve of a jacket or sweatshirt. It's—"

Maggie said, "Brown, cotton-polyester."

"Yeah. That."

This perplexed the good doctor, but he didn't spend much time working it out. "Um—fine. I'm sure my staff will be cooperative. And again, Ms. Gardiner, my apologies. She wants to see you, by the way. Trina. I'm sure to tell you how sorry she is. She always does, after one of her . . . episodes."

Maggie didn't know what to say to that. Mentally she knew the poor girl suffered from forces she could not control, but emotionally she wasn't quite ready to trust herself to remain 100 percent understanding when face-to-face.

"Of course, that is entirely up to you, and you shouldn't push yourself. You've had quite a dramatic day already— we all have. Now, Detective, what will be the procedure for this—"

"Wait," Jack said.

Maggie and the doctor looked at him.

"Let's talk to her first."

"What?" Maggie asked.

"Trina just became our number-one suspect. She didn't like Rachael, Damon apparently attacked her in a hallway a while ago, and she had more than enough reason to want Quentin Sherman dead."

Maggie opened her mouth to protest, if she could only have thought of a valid argument for Trina's innocence. Ridiculous to feel so protective of the girl who had so gleefully tried to murder her, but there it was. Trina scared her but she couldn't make herself blame Trina, the real Trina, that shy, tentative soul searching for someone to make her feel safe, even from herself. Especially from herself.

Dr. Palmer said, "You think *Trina* killed Quentin?"

"I think it's an excellent possibility. You said she has to take medication. Does she go to the infirmary for that?"

The little doctor looked as if he might be sick. "Yes."

"Okay." Jack turned to Maggie. "You need to talk to her. Can you do that?"

"Of course I can." But her stomach plunged at the thought.

"Maybe what she wants to tell you is a confession. And after that, don't forget to ask about the gloves. We might save ourselves a lot of time here."

"Wouldn't that be fabulous," Maggie said dryly.

He leaned closer. "I'll be right there. No small rooms or closed doors this time."

She couldn't help but soften, though he had misread her apprehension. "That's unnecessary. I appreciate it, but I'll be okay. Forewarned is forearmed."

"You can't be forearmed enough when it comes to that bitch," Jack said.

Chapter 27

Maggie met with the girl, who now appeared more pale and waiflike than ever, in the middle of the visiting area. The room had been cleared and Officer Coglan stationed himself at one exit, with Jack looming in the other. Justin Quintero hovered as a stand-in for Dr. Palmer, nicely dressed for company in a blue suit coat, until a worried kitchen staff cook came and told him of some emergency in the catering plans for the reception. Next to Trina sat a court-ordered attorney from the Public Defender's Office, a young woman nearly as pale as Trina in an ill-fitting suit jacket and skirt. Melanie Szabo occupied a fourth chair. Maggie failed to see how the girl could be put in a confessional mood in this fishbowl, but it could not be helped. No one intended to take chances, neither with Trina's legal safety nor the physical safety of anyone around her.

Trina slumped in the hard chair, knees up to her chin, arms around her shins. Her dark hair fell over her downturned face.

Maggie sat. When Trina didn't move she looked to the lawyer and the therapist for guidance.

"Trina?" Melanie Szabo spoke quietly. "Did you have something you wanted to say to Ms. Gardiner?"

The girl shook her head up and down in short, spasmodic movements. Then she murmured, "I'm sorry for trying to kill you. I'm glad you're all right."

"She's not admitting any wrongdoing," the lawyer put in.

Maggie didn't bother pointing out that Trina had just done exactly that. The lawyer had the unenviable task of protecting Trina's rights in the murky world of juvenile law, with a client who resided in an even murkier land between a hospital and a prison.

Instead, Maggie considered responses. *Me too* would not sound very forgiving. *That's okay* would be neither true nor helpful. "I understand that you've had some difficulties in the past."

A glance up from under those dark brows, lasting only a nanosecond. "Yeah, I have a lot of difficulties." She began to chew on one cuticle.

"You can tell me about them," Maggie said. "If you want."

A bit broad, but she figured *Are you now or have you ever been a serial killer?* might be too harsh.

Trina shrugged, still working on the cuticle.

"I know what happened yesterday must have upset you terribly."

Longer eye contact this time. "I liked Luis. He was always nice to me. He gave me a sticker once."

"That was horrible when he died. It threw everyone's equilibrium for a loop."

Szabo put in, "But we don't excuse hurting other people in response."

"Yes," Maggie said. "Of course. Did you have anything else you wanted to tell me?"

Gaze on the floor, the finger—now with a spot of blood around the edge of the nail—in her mouth.

"Trina?"

The quick, agitated shake—but now from side to side. "No."

"Are you sure?"

"If she needs to talk about her feelings, that should be with her therapist," the lawyer ventured. Maggie could guess her thought process. Since the therapist had set up this meeting she must feel it would assist in Trina's road to health, so the attorney wanted to cooperate, but at the same time didn't want her young client talking herself into any more charges.

Trina turned her head just long enough to give the woman a mighty frown. "I *do* talk to Dr. Szabo."

"Yes. And that's fine." Because it was privileged, of course. But this answer confused Trina, who shook it off and repeated that she had nothing else on her mind.

"Did you want to tell me about Quentin?"

"I'm glad he's dead now." Trina might have expressed an opinion on the sunny day or the way she liked her pizza.

Maggie's thoughts bounced around as she wondered how to respond to this. Asking the girl if she had helped the boy get that way might scare her back into her shell. On the other hand, she seemed quite comfortable discussing the issue. "Do you know how he died?"

"He fell off the roof."

"Do you know how?"

"She doesn't have to answer that," the lawyer said.

"I *can*. The fence fell out. He bounced onto the street."

Bounced. Did she refer to Quentin's habit of throwing himself onto the chain link? Maggie asked if Luis had liked to play basketball. If Trina had a little crush on him, she might have gone up to the roof or snuck up there to watch him in action. But the girl said the teenage day students didn't stay there for rec (recreation). They left right after classes.

"Do you know why the fence collapsed?"

"She doesn't have to—"

Trina's feet nearly hit the floor, clearly annoyed by the interruptions, before refolding into her standard position. "I *can*! Someone loosened the holder things. Someone killed him. I'm glad they did."

"Do you know who?" Maggie asked.

"Trina, don't answer—"

"Shut *up*!"

Szabo said calmly, "Trina, that's not how we speak to people with respect. This lady is trying to look out for your legal status. You understand that that's necessary."

The girl's shoulders slumped, in pique more than in defeat. She gazed at Maggie and said clearly, "I don't know who did it but I'm glad they did."

"Okay. What about Damon Kish? Did you know him?"

Trina took to rolling her head as if her neck hurt. "Who?"

"The little boy who didn't talk."

"Oh, him."

"Who's that?" the lawyer asked.

"Shut *up*!" Trina said again, more forcefully.

"Trina—" Szabo began.

"Make her go away!"

The lawyer explained, her tone hovering around impatience, "I can't do that, Trina. I am here to protect your—"

"I don't care."

"You're agitating her," Szabo said to the lawyer, gently. "She—"

"Well, she's going to have to be agitated, then. I'm not going to let her talk herself into a murder charge—"

"Shut *up*!"

Maggie tried, leaning forward, hoping to pull Trina into a world where only the two of them existed. "Trina. What can you tell me about Damon?"

"It wasn't my fault, okay? It just wasn't my *fault*!" Her eyes filled with tears and she clutched at Maggie's collar and shoulder with one hand, tiny mouse fingers plucking the material. Maggie willed herself not to flinch.

"Honey, I don't understand what you're trying to tell me."

"Trina, don't—"

"Go away!" Trina jumped up, skittering back from the table and knocking over the chair in her haste. "I want you all to go away!"

She backed away from them as the lawyer and the therapist also rose. Maggie stayed down, still hoping to calm the girl enough to talk. But Trina had had enough; she turned her back on them and made for the hallway. Unfortunately, Jack stood in her way, glowering as if he itched for a rematch.

The girl stopped, her tennis shoes squeaking against the linoleum. The arms encircled her own body again, and she sidled toward Officer Coglan. The therapist and the lawyer continued to bicker, their client hovering unnoticed in the background.

"Keep her here," Jack called to the officer.

"You've got it."

"Come on," he said to Maggie.

Chapter 28

"What do you think?" he asked her as they beat a quick path to the third-floor girls' area.

"How could I possibly know what to think? I know nothing about mentally ill children."

"She knew who Damon was."

"We *think*. There could be other boys here who can't or won't talk."

He went on as if she hadn't spoken. "And then said it wasn't her fault. Meaning she had to kill Damon only because the voices told her to?"

"Or Quentin wasn't her fault? Or me?"

"You have a point," he admitted, and knocked for Ms. Washington to admit them.

"I don't feel qualified to interpret Trina."

"I don't think anyone is qualified to interpret Trina. That girl is in her own little universe."

The dorm mother opened the door and gave them access to Trina's room. Jack had a search warrant that applied to the entire building but didn't bother to produce it. The Firebird Center was both Trina's prison and her school, and in neither type of place could she have an expectation of privacy. For the children's own safety more than anyone else's, Maggie knew, but figured it must still suck for the girls there.

Classes had ended for the day and the other girls were in various states of doing homework, freshening up, closeting themselves in their rooms, or talking in the conversation area. At least they had been, until Maggie and Jack walked in. Then they all went still, and watched the progress with the sharpest of eyes, missing nothing. It reminded Maggie of lions and antelopes scattered across the plain in a frozen tableau, but she couldn't have said which camp were hunters and which were prey.

Maggie had not expected Trina's room to be so stark, since she had been at the center much longer than Rachael Donahue. Despite what she knew about the girl she'd still expected a typical teenage girl's room—a jumble of clothes and magazines and makeup and maybe a kitten poster.

The cubbyhole wall unit had one or two items of clothing, neatly folded, on each shelf. The bedding had been removed from the mattress, but folded neatly at the bottom of it. The shelves were bare. The top of the desk was bare. Every other item in the room—clothes, books, pens, a towel—rested in a pile in the corner on the other side of the desk from the bed.

Maggie sighed, got down on the floor with her legs folded underneath her, and went through it piece by piece.

"What's with the bed?" Jack asked Ms. Washington.

"She did that every single day. I have no idea why."

"Some OCD thing?"

"Unlikely," Maggie said. "Or she wouldn't have been able to stand this pile o' stuff in the corner."

Jack asked, "Where was she last night?"

"Here," Ms. Washington said.

"All night? Are you sure?"

"Yes and yes."

"How can you be sure?"

"Because I have to let anyone in or out, and I didn't. If they somehow jimmy a door after bed check it will sound a claxon. It would wake me. It would wake anyone within two blocks."

"What about before bed check?"

Reluctantly, she said, "It's possible. Not probable. We maintain only fifteen girls, as you can see, so it's not hard to realize when one has gone missing. And I don't remember Trina being missing at all. I was keeping a particular eye on her, of course, after the goings-on yesterday."

"Luis's murder."

"Yes. Some of the other girls still have a heart and they were trying to sympathize with her about it, but she went in her room and shut the door. It worried me a little, but it hardly seemed odd after what had happened. She'd had adults talking to her all day long so I figured she needed a break. I did check on her just before lights out, and she seemed fine. Fine for Trina, I mean. Dry eyed, but wouldn't say a word."

So far in the pile the clothes had proved unremarkable, and Maggie folded them to one side. She also found a powder compact in a shade too dark for Trina, and a silver necklace with a St. Dymphna medal. The patron saint of those with mental illness.

"Did she spend a lot of time on the roof?" Jack was asking.

"Girls' exercise periods. And we let them hang around out there for an hour every other evening, alternating genders and age groups."

"Did she play basketball?"

"Trina? She didn't play tiddlywinks. Not a joiner, I'm afraid."

"She didn't get along with Rachael?"

"No one got along with Rachael."

Other items were unearthed: a piece of ribbon, a crumpled photograph of a younger Trina and a woman—her mother, perhaps. Nothing had been written on the back. A small spray bottle of cheap perfume.

"She's not supposed to have that," Ms. Washington said. "We can overlook a little eyeshadow or lipstick, but nothing flammable."

Then, underneath a pair of lightweight jeans, Maggie found a pair of gloves. Brown. No tag but the material felt like the standard cotton/synthetic blend.

"There we go," Jack said.

"They're too big for her," Maggie said.

"She probably stole them from the construction crew. They were installing the cameras in the girls' common area two days ago—not that they *work*, of course; they're merely *installed*."

"You're sounding awfully petulant these days."

"I am petulant. They've got a building full of killers here and security is a joke."

Ms. Washington had had enough of Jack. "These kids aren't cold-blooded murderers. They have painful reasons to explain the things they do." But truth compelled her to qualify: "Most of the time."

"That's comforting."

"And our priority here is rehabilitation. These are *children*—"

"*Dangerous* children," Jack said.

"—who have suffered the worst society has to offer—"

Maggie had bagged the gloves and reached the bottom of Trina's pile of stuff. No other items suggested foul play. She interrupted the two to say so.

Jack got back to specifics. "What about Monday?"

Ms. Washington raised one eyebrow.

"Monday, say ten to eleven. Where was Trina?"

"She would have been in class."

"Are you sure?"

"As I'm not her English teacher, no."

"We'll need to talk to her," Jack said.

Maggie corrected, "Him."

Rick Gardiner got Lieutenant Howard—apparently not Howie—Romero back on the phone. The good lieutenant immediately opened with, "I'm so sorry."

"I beg your pardon?"

"It was Andy Hastings, died of cancer. I always did get him and Jack mixed up."

Rick's stomach seemed to plunge. He didn't often get gut feelings but he had one now. He had a theory he couldn't define and didn't even know if he wanted to prove and yet felt disappointed that none of the facts wanted to cooperate. He wasn't getting anywhere, not with the vigilante case, not with his career, not with Maggie, not with anything. "So you haven't heard anything about him since he left there?"

"Nope. Went off to be a hermit in Tennessee. Then you guys called for a reference, so I guess the hermit thing got old. Figured it would."

Might as well justify his time. "And the illegal nursing home thing? Did you have a case like that?"

"That's the weird thing," Romero said, and then paused to have a conversation with someone at that end regarding the unit's coffee order and the bizarre fact that one of the guys had requested decaf. This led to Romero debating how many packets of decaf coffee the whoever at that end should order until Rick wanted to scream.

"*What's* the weird thing?" he finally demanded.

"We did. Have a case like that. Some of my guys worked it and the gal in the Elder Crimes unit remembered it real well. Bunch of old folks left to rot. Hell of a thing. It takes a lot to disgust me after this many years, but that did."

"Did you get the guy?"

"Nope. The victims were nearly all dead when we got there and those that weren't, we couldn't get any sense out of. Checks were deposited to an account by night depository and no one had time to sift through twenty-four hours of video. The gal that cleaned out the account had a big hat on, so you wouldn't even recognize your own mother in the photo."

"Huh," Rick said. "Listen, if I send you a photo, could you tell me if—"

"I just said you wouldn't recognize your own mother."

"Not of the woman with the old folks. A photo of Jack Renner."

Rick heard a rushing sound as Romero exhaled his

impatience. "Now we're back on Jack Renner. He didn't even work that case. What does Jack Renner have to do with this old folks case?"

"As God is my witness," Rick said, "I have no idea."

Chapter 29

Paul Lewis, Maggie thought, didn't quite deserve the judgment of nonhotness that Trina had bestowed. Yes, his nose had been broken at some point in his past, but the tousled hair melded with the sparkling eyes to give him a boyish insouciance. Sniffing, she couldn't detect any sausage-like odors. But she guessed him to be over forty, which in the mind of a fourteen-year-old girl might as well be 103.

Students shuffled in and out of the room, changing classes just as they would in any school. Some gave the interlopers sharp looks while some appeared bewildered by the change in routine, but most reacted as teenagers did, with complete indifference. Whatever the adults were up to couldn't possibly be as interesting as what they themselves had to discuss.

Still, Maggie couldn't help keeping her back to the wall and watching the natives for any sign of restlessness. She noticed Jack did as well.

"Ah," Lewis said, "Trina—I heard she went on quite the rampage yesterday. Pity. She's a fairly good student. Surprisingly articulate, in writing. I can hardly get her to speak a word, but on paper she turns into Proust."

"What does she write about?" Maggie asked.

"That's hard to describe. Her topics are eclectic but usually loop back to death. Pretty dark."

"Murder?" Jack asked.

The guy frowned in thought. "Not really. Just death. End of life, taking one's last breath, the brink of moving from this world to the next. But she never talks about that next world, only the one on this side of that chasm. Her imagination has limits, I suppose. Or she's more interested in the process than the result."

Jack interrupted. "Was she in class on Monday?"

"She's always in class. As I said, she's a fairly good student. As you can imagine, that's not common for this group."

"Did she leave during the class for any reason?"

"On Monday?"

"Yes." Maggie could feel his annoyance vibrate through the syllable. It didn't seem to affect Lewis, but then he spent all day surrounded by violent teens. It would take more than a snippy homicide detective to rattle him.

Of course, he didn't know what Jack was.

"I don't think so. I keep her right in front"—he pointed to a desk second from the end in the first row—"because she gets agitated if the other students get chatty and distract her. But she does have to duck out once in a while; I don't know if it's a weak bladder or she just gets overwhelmed. Might have been on Monday, but I don't know. She could have."

"What—" Jack began.

"Let's ask my co." He turned to the door of the room, where a slim black woman spoke with two boys. "My co-teacher, Jacqueline."

"Co-teacher?"

"We have two teachers in every class, one to teach, one to handle discipline. Jacqueline teaches science and we tag-team each other. You'd be amazed what a difference it makes to be able to focus one hundred percent on teaching and let the other person break up the whispering, sleeping, contraband, escorting kids to Dr. Palmer's office, etcetera. She'll remember if Trina had to leave. But let her finish with those two first. She's much better with the superaggressive kids than I am. I have to fight the appealing temptation to rip their heads off their shoulders and hang them from the ceiling like Christmas ornaments."

Maggie felt her eyebrows crawl toward her hairline. "How's that working out for you?"

He laughed. "Okay, only *sometimes* I feel like that. On the whole, I get these kids. School is all about uncertainty. You have to learn stuff you don't know, take tests you might not pass. Secure kids, happy healthy kids with parents who love them, they can approach uncertainty with a little bit of trepidation but also curiosity and a feeling of challenge. At worst school is tedious and annoying. But to maltreated kids, uncertainty is terrifying. It causes great distress, which securely attached children learn to tolerate because they have faith that it will be relieved. They'll figure it out, as they have before, and if not Mommy or Daddy will help them. A child who never had that security can't tolerate distress. It's not annoying, it's life threatening.

But they can't fight a math problem or take flight from it, so they freeze or freak. Tantrums, throwing chairs, screaming are not unheard of around here."

"They believe they can't learn it," Maggie said. Jack turned to check on the co-teacher, but the two boys still held her attention.

"Yes, but it's not that simple. Maltreatment in early life can physically alter cognitive development, the skills necessary to read, write, do math. Tissue in the brain originally available for these functions can be diverted to defense in an abused or neglected child. Instead of exploring its world the brain has to focus on staying alive. This can also affect executive abilities, which manage emotional and behavioral functions as well as cognitive. Tuning out distractions, keeping the instructions in mind and doing the work at the same time, staying aware of the time allotted, monitoring their own work for mistakes and correcting as they go—some don't do it at all and others do it so obsessively that they never finish. Trina is the latter, by the way. She's such a perfectionist that she never finishes anything, gets lost in a ball of self-criticism because her margins aren't exactly equivalent."

Maggie thought, *No wonder Trina felt so angry at Rachael for slacking off on the photosynthesis illustration*.

"And of course this difficulty snowballs as they get older and more and more behind their own peers. By this age most of them have given up hope of ever having a brain. Meanwhile schools, which are in a unique position to recognize these situations, have gone to zero-tolerance policies and expelling any kid they think is a problem—and/or, not coincidentally—a low achiever who might drag down their standardized test scores. The juvenile justice system becomes their dumping ground."

"How do you treat that?"

Jack griped to her, "You're as bad as Riley."

She didn't know exactly what he meant, but ignored him anyway.

Lewis did too. "What gets them through the distress is a relationship with the teacher. Their primary attachment—to parents—has gone awry, so they need teachers to make them feel safe and stable enough to learn. Because of the early trauma they can't tolerate frustration, are overanxious, have to work at their own pace, and all that makes them attention seeking. *Constantly* attention seeking. They interrupt, disrupt, try to usurp our authority, poke, prod, fight. They're desperate to know that adults are actually going to do their jobs this time around and take care of them. Regular old teenagers rebel to establish their independence, but these teens—they're rebelling to bring adults *closer*."

"To see if you'll stick," Maggie said.

"Exactly."

"Sounds, um—"

"Challenging?" Lewis suggested.

"Nightmarish."

He laughed. "Sometimes it is. But I'll take these kids any day over some suburbanite who whines that his mom won't do his homework for him. Each and every one of these kids is a walking, talking unique cipher, each with a unique key. What opens one won't open another. And then the hour's up and I get a whole new set."

"Speaking of which—" Jack said.

"Yes, Detective. Let's get with Jacqueline."

The two boys had moved off with pats on their departing shoulders and the young woman listened to Jack's question. A wrinkle creased her perfect skin as she tried to remember. "Monday . . . Monday . . . Joaquin came in with a black eye, and oh, yes, we sent Laquisha home for smelling of pot."

"Yeah, that's right," Lewis agreed.

"Yes, she did," Jacqueline said. "Trina, I mean, left to use the restroom. Gone about five minutes. Maybe a little more, because I got distracted texting the paperwork about Laquisha. Trina leaves a lot—she gets anxious whenever she has to write—but she's real good about coming right back. I can trust Trina."

Jack said, "You realize she tried to kill Maggie yesterday."

Without pause, Jacqueline qualified: "As long as she isn't in one of her moods."

Maggie felt her shoulders slump. She knew she shouldn't be surprised. Trina had tried to kill someone doing her best to be her friend—how much more irritated would she get at the supremely annoying Rachael and the wild Damon? Derald—if he had been murdered at all—had probably conflicted with gang rival Luis, and Quentin had been lucky to live through the night after his transgression. But even knowing all this, she couldn't form a cohesive portrait of Trina as a serial killer.

Maggie thanked the two teachers as they turned their attention to the milling, nearly full classroom, and she and Jack headed for the stairwell.

"Could she really have gotten over to the other side

of the building, down the steps, into the infirmary, found the EpiPens, injected Damon, and then gotten back to her desk in five minutes?" She kept her voice low, knowing how it carried in a concrete well.

"Yes. She was quick and light, and it was probably more like ten minutes."

"How could she even catch Damon? He bounced off walls under the best of circumstances. A strange child enters his room, he'd either charge her or hide under the bed."

"Who knows? Maybe he was sleeping until the first injection. He *did* have strep throat. Or maybe she enticed him with something."

Like a brownie," Maggie suddenly remembered, and told Jack how the boy had had chocolate crumbles in his stomach. If those had been eaten with his breakfast they should have been more digested.

"A few people have said he'd do anything for sweets."

"That's how they got him to sit still for the Epi-Pens," Maggie said. "They enticed him with the brownie, got him close enough to get a good grip on him. That's all you'd need. *I* could have held him down, he was so skinny. It was catching him in the first place that was the hard part, and the brownie took care of that."

"That's how *she* did it, not *they*. Trina's a little thing but she's still bigger than he was."

Maggie persisted. "Though they might give the children midmorning snacks here. Most schools do. That would explain the lack of digestion."

"Fine, we can ask the nurse. But Trina had motive, means, opportunity, and a record of homicidal violence. And we already know she killed Quentin."

"We don't know that. Anyone could walk into Trina's room and plant those gloves. They had all night and most of the day to do it."

"It's a locked-down unit. You seriously think someone *framed*—"

"Why not? She's psychotic. No one is going to believe anything she says."

"Including me," Jack snapped.

The nurse established that she had not given Damon a midmorning snack but the kitchen staff established that they *did* provide snacks around ten o'clock to the under-twelve group, and they had indeed been brownies on Monday morning. "They're not bad," one of the cooks said. "I eat them all the time. Don't tell Palmer, though, okay?"

That seemed to make Maggie think of something. "Does the staff eat with the kids? Or do they brown-bag it?"

"Yeah, most of them take a plate along with the kids. Promotes bonding, all that crap."

"What about therapists? Teachers?"

"They just walk through and help themselves. One of the perks of the job."

Another added, "They have to bring the plates and tableware back, though. This ain't a damn Marriott."

"Got it," Jack said, and he and Maggie escaped the steamy room.

He seemed ready to call it a day. He said they had done all they could. It only remained to get an arrest warrant sworn out for Trina, though that wouldn't be easy. He had no smoking gun. He had no physical evidence other than a generic pair of gloves and an unreliable narrator as a suspect. He—

Maggie started up the steps.

"Where are you going?"

"To see Trina."

He caught up with her. "Why? You can't trust anything she says, and between Ms. Washington and the public defender, they're not going to let you ask her any questions."

"Then I won't ask. I'll just listen."

"You can't be a witness even if she makes any spontaneous statements. She tried to kill you. You're biased in the eyes of the court."

"I know. But I can't shake the feeling there's something she wants to tell me."

"I'm sure there is. But it probably took place in the ninth dimension."

"It can't hurt to try." She knocked on the door of the girls' fourteen to fifteen area. "Besides, it's a secure building. What's the worst that could happen?"

"She could nick my other carotid."

"So get Riley to come with me."

"He's at the autopsy. And after that he's got a date, believe it or not."

She shook her head at him. "Why would that be hard to believe?"

Ms. Washington opened the door, only to tell them Trina wasn't there. She had gone for a session with Melanie Szabo.

"Again?" Maggie asked.

"Yeah, Melanie's putting in some overtime today.

The joys of limited resources." She shut the door as behind her the girls in her care craned their necks for a
glimpse of the outsiders.

"We can't interrupt her therapy," Jack said, and
Maggie reluctantly agreed to give it up. They followed
the stairwell back down to the ground floor. As they
made their way outside her feet dragged with every
step. She didn't want to leave Trina in that building.
She shouldn't leave Trina in that building. Kids were
dying in there.

A perfect fall afternoon turned the asphalt an inky
black and the sidewalk to bleached silver. She felt a
breeze lift the hair around her face. She thought of the
troubled children involved with the Firebird Center
and her pace ground to a halt.

Jack reached the car without her, noticed, and re-
traced three steps. "What now?"

"I know what he's doing."

The look on her face seemed to erase his impatience—partly, at any rate. "What who's doing?"

"The killer. He—or she."

"And they're doing . . . what?"

Now she met his gaze. "Triaging."

He paused. "I'm waiting for those words to make
sense."

Maggie said, "These kids need intervention in every
area of their lives, physical, emotional, cultural. This is
an intensive, hands-on program for the residents, and
to a lesser extent the day students, because without that
nothing is going to change. Each one is different, has a
different story. You can't warehouse them or dole out
treatment in an assembly line."

"Yes? Your po—"

"But resources are limited. Everyone here keeps saying that. The minute a bed is open, it's filled. They have to fight every minute to keep their funding without letting the state force them to overcrowd."

He raised an eyebrow. "So—"

"So every spot here is incredibly valuable. They can't waste space or time on a kid who's—"

The words now made sense. Jack said, "Hopeless."

"Yes. You can never know what might turn a kid around or when that might happen, but after years and years of working with them the staff here had to develop a good ability to guess as to who's going to respond to treatment and who isn't."

"Rachael wasn't responding."

"Not in the slightest. They couldn't budge her out of her fantasy world."

"All someone would have to do is grab her ankles, tip her over the edge. No weapons, no evidence. Not even a fingerprint."

Maggie went on: "Derald didn't want to change. Why would he? He had to believe Mom and Dad's money would always get him out of any trouble he could get into."

"But Damon," Jack said, as if the idea of someone murdering Damon simply to get a bed open truly pained him.

She'd been wrong to ever suspect Jack of killing Damon. Very wrong. "Damon would always have had severe difficulties in adapting to society. His brain had been neglected too early for too long."

"All that stuff about early childhood development—"

"Yes. And Quentin, of course, he proved in the most dramatic way possible that rehabilitation wasn't working for him. And—Trina!"

"Trina's psychotic," Jack agreed.

"They can't even put a name to it, so they can't treat it with any hope of success. Jack, we have to find Trina. *Now*." She dashed up the steps to the ancient building.

"Wait!" Jack called.

She didn't.

He went to follow but heard his name called from behind.

Rick Gardiner had pulled his car to the curb and got out as his ex-wife disappeared into the building. Jack opened his mouth to tell the guy that whatever it was it had to wait, but Rick Gardiner said, "Just tell me she didn't help you."

Jack shut it again.

Chapter 30

Maggie didn't know where to run first. She asked the receptionist, who had no way to know precisely where Trina might be right then and anyway had her hands full greeting DORC board members. Maggie left her to it and ran up the steps as quietly as she could, to the fourteen-to-fifteen girls' area. Ms. Washington stepped away from introducing two board members to her charges and told Maggie, rather tersely, that Trina had been put on kitchen duty. But just washing dishes, of course; no food prep, given her penchant for poisons.

Like Cinderella, Maggie thought, as she galloped back down the stairs, *the unacknowledged child banished from view while her more presentable stepsisters partied*. That might be unfair, of course. More noise and bustle and even well-meaning questions from strangers could hardly do Trina much good at the moment.

She burst into the cramped, dim kitchen and felt immediate relief. Trina stood at the sink, washing pots nearly as big as she was, quite alone and apparently unharmed. Steam wafted up from the basin of hot water.

Already cleaned ones were stacked in a precarious heap on a rubber-matted counter. A blender and an electric food chopper crowded the girl's elbow. The oven gave off a delightful smell and the microwave hummed with a distinctly less pleasant odor.

"Trina," Maggie said.

The girl looked up without surprise. "Oh. Hi."

Maggie moved closer. Now that she had found her, she didn't know quite what to say. *I think your life is in danger. I think someone is going to try to kill you.* Probably not the best thing to tell a teen suffering from psychosis. So she asked what the girl had probably already been asked at least thirty times that day: "How are you feeling?"

"Okay."

"Stuck on kitchen duty, huh?"

"I think it's punishment for acting out," the girl said without rancor. "Because I wasn't supposed to do kitchen until next week."

"Where are the cooks?"

"They have to stay in the visiting area in case they run out of something. That nice man in the blue jacket told them so, but they didn't seem to mind."

Probably not, Maggie thought. Anything to get out of that dungeon of a place. The smell from the microwave had grown stronger—ammonia-like, again. And through the glass square in the door she could see something begin to spark.

"Trina," Maggie asked, "what's in the microwave?"

The girl glanced over at it with the same lack of interest she'd shown in Maggie's presence. "I don't know. Something Dr.—"

In one fluid motion Maggie pushed her away from the sink, switched on the food chopper, and knocked it into the filled sink. When it hit the water it gave a snap and a pop, blowing whatever fuse the kitchen operated on. The microwave died along with the lights.

Trina screamed at the sudden dark, but Maggie grabbed her arm and pulled her toward where she knew the door to be. She walked into a counter instead, slamming her hip against it, just as the oven blew up. An explosion of hot gases, flame, and debris drove them to the ground, and after that Maggie could not see, hear, or breathe.

"What are you talking about, Gardiner?"

Maggie's ex-husband said, "Did she help you fake your prints?"

"I don't have time for this." He turned toward the building, but Rick Gardiner scooted in front of him to block his path.

"Because I don't know who the hell you are but I know you're *not* Jack Renner from Minneapolis."

Jack worked hard to keep his voice level. *No tics, no tells, don't let him know how close to the bone he's slicing.* "Gardiner, listen to me. There's someone in this building killing kids. Maggie's in there trying to protect the next victim and I—"

Rick didn't bat an eye. "I know because I sent them your ID photo, and Howard Romero, the guy you listed as a reference, the guy you say you worked under for years, hasn't got a clue who you are."

Jack's stomach, already pitching, slid toward his ankles. But he didn't let himself look away. "Yeah, that sounds like him."

"The real Jack Renner retired to Tennessee. Does he know you're using his name? They had to run your prints when you got here. Did Maggie help switch them for you? That's all I want to know."

Jack thought, and thought fast. Problem was he had never been good at thinking fast; that's why he always did a great deal of research and planning before stepping out of bounds. Rick Gardiner had just knocked him over the line without warning and any story he came up with would have holes big enough to drive a spaceship through and once Gardiner kept looking he could rip all sorts of additional gaps in his fictional history—

He said, "I've been here three years. I just met your wife—*ex*-wife—a few months ago and you were there when I did. I don't know what the hell you're talking about and don't care. Everyone knows you'd rather sit around on your ass than do any actual police work. That's probably why she dumped you. Now get out of my way."

"You can't talk your way out of this one, buddy. I saw your little huddle this morning."

"Huddle?"

"You put your hands on her shoulders."

Jack had to have stepped into the Twilight Zone. *Had* to have. "What? *That's* what you're on about? Seriously?"

"I know Maggie. That's what you all forget—I *know* Maggie. She's never been the touchy-feely type. If any other cop had done that she'd have shook his fingers off in a split second and probably broken a few of them. You're *special* to her. And I bet I know right where that started—last month when that maniac throttled her and you carried her off to her rescue like some sort of damn knight in real shiny armor. And who was sitting at the hospital ready to hold her hand? You were."

Jack didn't know how to stop this wall of words. But he remembered the waiting room, and he realized just what he had said to tip Rick Gardiner off, start him on this journey to prove Jack Renner was a complete fiction.

Which, of course, he was.

What should he do?

Maybe he should tell the guy he was sleeping with his ex-wife. That might distract him from his digging.

It might also spur him on to ruin Jack in any way he could.

Focus on the biggest threat. "Of course Howard Romero told you he didn't know me. He was the department prankster for thirty years—facing retirement won't slow him down."

Rick's face turned a deeper shade of puce. "You think I'm going to believe—"

But before he could describe what he thought Jack expected him to believe, the building beside them gave a rumble and a groan, and Jack swore he could feel the vibration through the sidewalk.

The smoke didn't do Maggie's lungs any good. Every breath she sucked in only tickled them more with dust and soot and burnt chemicals until white spots began to appear in front of her eyes—not from concussion but asphyxia. She plowed through this miasma, heading away from the explosion and toward the less smoky part of the hallway, dragging Trina with an arm around the girl's shoulders. Parts of the wall had scattered along the linoleum to trip her.

Trina's waiflike form felt abnormally heavy, as if her feet had been encased in cement. Or as if the kitchen still had a tentacle wrapped around her ankles, pulling her back to finish the job it had started. Maggie looked down to kick at the rope-like tendrils, and knew then that she had lost touch with reality. She couldn't take another step. The kitchen and the smoke would take them both.

Justin Quintero, however, strode through the swirling dust and swept up Trina without any apparent struggle against cement or vine.

"You okay?" he asked either her or the girl. She heard his voice as if from a long way off, her ears still ringing—either from the sound of the explosion or from all the blood leaving her head and concentrating in her muscles. But she managed to take another two steps, just enough to find a patch of clear air and get a breath. She immediately coughed it out, of course, but at least the white spots began to fade. She slumped against a wall and Justin carried Trina off around the corner.

"Wait," she called, but it came out in a squeak, quite unrecognizable as human speech.

Maggie concentrated on expanding and constricting her lungs a few more times, flipping onto hands and knees and locomoting that way until two pairs of feet appeared in front of her and two different voices said, "*Maggie!*"

She looked up. Rick and Jack stood shoulder to shoulder, each looking concerned and annoyed in such equal measures that she thought this must be some bizarre form of double vision.

"Oh, *hell*," she said.

Chapter 31

She found Trina. Justin Quintero had dumped the girl in the infirmary, logically enough, and Nurse Brandreth had tilted her head back and applied gauze to a bloody piece of scalp by the time Maggie staggered into the room, followed by the two cops. The nurse looked up with a forced calm.

"I've called EMTs. She's breathing but she's not conscious. I think she took a blow to the head. There's nothing I can do for her here. She needs a hospital."

"Of course," Maggie said. "Good idea." And she sat in the chair next to Trina's bed.

To her eyes the girl already looked dead, utterly limp and as pale as a piece of copy paper. But the chest rose and fell a millimeter or so every few seconds.

"What happened?" Jack demanded.

"What were you doing?" Rick demanded.

"Kitchen blew up," she told them, as if that should be obvious. Then she added, because of course it would *not* be obvious, "Someone put a mix in the microwave, turned it on."

"Who?" Jack asked.

"What do you mean a mix?" Rick asked.

Voices rose in the hall, adult tones, no doubt the visiting DORC bigwigs. She heard Quintero's excited words explaining what he could to Dr. Palmer, and Melanie Szabo's shriek of horror.

"She was just about to tell me who it was when I figured out it was a bomb. I shorted out the GFI to kill the power, but it was too late. It blew."

"*What* blew?" Jack demanded.

Maggie explained. By now she barely noticed her own habit of coughing every few words. "I thought I smelled ammonia when I first found Trina, but that's just because I had ammonia on the mind where Trina is concerned. It was vinegar. Put vinegar in a cup, drop in a ball of steel wool, like the kind Trina was using to scrub the pots, and pop it in the microwave. The steel and the vinegar react to form hydrogen gas, the confined space creates pressure, and when the steel sparks it lights the fuse."

"Kaboom," Jack said.

Rick didn't care about a microwave bomb. "Tell me what you're doing with this guy."

Maggie rubbed her face and her fingers came away bloody—slightly bloody, nothing life threatening. No doubt scratches and small cuts from the flying debris. "What guy?"

He jerked his head toward Jack, scowling, his expression furious. She had seen it often enough during their marriage. "*This* one. The supervisor he used as a reference in Minneapolis has never seen him before in his life."

That didn't clear it up any, as far as she could see. And though she recognized that Jack—and by extension herself—were deeply threatened by Rick's interest, she couldn't make herself care right at that moment. Much more than a jail term stalked Trina, and perhaps them all.

"I *told* you—" Jack began.

Behind them two EMTs hovered in the doorway, torn between responding to the infirmary as instructed or dealing with the chaos in the hallway beyond. Nurse Brandreth flagged them down.

Rick said, "*Maggie*. This guy's lying to you about something. His name isn't even Jack Renner."

"Wait—what are you doing here?" she asked.

"Trying to figure out what this asshole's gotten you mixed up in!"

Maggie tried to suck in air, but her lungs could not expand. She choked.

"We need some room to work here, people," one EMT said as the other affixed an oxygen mask to Trina's face. "We need you to leave."

Maggie told him, "Not on your life. I'm not letting this girl out of my sight. Someone wanted her dead."

"Yeah, but—"

"And now they *need* her dead."

The man studied her gaze with intelligent brown eyes as Jack hovered and Rick went on and on about phone calls and e-mailing an ID photo to someone named Howard Romero.

"Okay," the EMT said. "But I need to get on that side of her."

Maggie immediately stood, moved her chair, coughed, and collapsed into it again, as Rick told her that something called cooies were important.

"Coo—eze?"

"Coues. They're small deer," he told her with desperate intensity.

She blinked at him.

Then she shook her head, stood up, and moved toward the door, before Dr. Palmer and assorted personnel began to crowd into the tiny infirmary. "Rick, let me explain this: I have no idea what you're talking about, and I don't care."

"But, Maggie—"

"I can't even put into words how much I don't care."

Jack said, "Get out of here, Gardiner. You—"

"No," Maggie said. "Stay."

This silenced both men, albeit briefly.

Rick said, "You have to tell me what's going on with him."

Jack said, "Gardiner, just because you're off on some tangent—"

Maggie said, "Someone in this building is killing kids, and right now this building is full of agitated, unstable, frightened persons, one of whom is very guilty. We need all the manpower we can get. Dr. Palmer, the EMTs have got Trina. You need to get everyone to the visiting area and away from the kitchen before anyone else gets hurt."

"But what happened? Is she going to be all right?"

"She's going to be fine. But they need to transport

her now." Maggie herded the fussing older man and the rest of the staff out of the infirmary door, as Jack stared and Rick continued to sputter about personnel records. Dr. Palmer told his assistant director to take the guests to the visitor's area and start the presentation. He would reset the breaker so that the projector would work and meet them there.

Maggie shut the door behind them and turned. "Rick, stay with Trina. Don't let anyone other than hospital staff come near her, got it?"

"But his file—"

"Still don't care."

"You *have* to listen to me!"

"And I will. Just not now."

"But—"

"*Her!*" Maggie said, grabbing his arm and wheeling him around to look at the tiny form now being lifted onto a gurney. "She's only fourteen years old. Someone just tried to kill her, and she knows who that person is. Now whatever you do, *keep her alive*."

Her ex-husband groaned with frustration. "*Fine.* Okay. But this is not over."

"Yeah yeah, I know." To Jack she said, "You, come on."

They escaped into the hall. Firemen were arriving to deal with the kitchen, but the horde of staff, visiting adults, and select teenagers had moved away.

"What is Rick talking about?" Maggie asked as they hustled up the west staircase.

"It might be a problem," he said, and even with so much else to think of, his words terrified her. She got that tingling at the nape of her neck, that patch of skin that recognized mortal danger when it approached.

Then he asked, "What are *you* talking about?"

"Who just tried to kill Trina," she told him. "I think *I* know who it is, too."

Chapter 32

The visitor's area, lit almost brightly by the emergency light units, thronged with people. Those in suits or dressy versions of business casual numbered perhaps ten, plus double that number of staff and fifteen resident children whose expressions veered from fear to worry to a trembling excitement. Justin Quintero tried to get the guests to sit in the neatly aligned seats but like cats they didn't want to be herded.

He stood in the center of the room apologizing for the disruption. "The explosion created a small fire but it's already under control. There's no problem in any other part of the building. We've lost the last tray of hors d'oeuvres, I'm afraid, but that's all. One of our students was injured but she is receiving medical care."

That's a sunny outlook, Maggie thought. With Jack on her heels she glanced at the crowd from the stairwell.

Even in the midst of chaos, Quintero had not lost sight of his overall goal for the gathering. "I'm afraid this only illustrates the sad condition of this old structure. This is why we need a complete renovation, so we can provide a safe, efficient, and healthy environment for the reemergence of these young people while still complying with all judicial mandates. Now we're going to hear from two of our young people. Gentlemen, will you come up here?"

"But what happened?" one of the suits asked, refusing to let dogs and ponies distract him from the drama.

"Some malfunction with the kitchen equipment, I suppose. The fire marshal will have to determine the cause."

The suits, staff, and children in the room erupted into questions. Maggie kept going, up the next flight of stairs to the third-floor landing. Emergency lights burned dimly in the offices along the hallway but she ignored them and pushed open the door to the roof. Instantly the night turned black and quiet, the din of the crowd cut off by the heavy metal door. The missing section of fence that had plunged with Quentin to his death left an inky black hole in its place. The only light out there, other than that of stars and distant skyscrapers, came from a small flashlight that Dr. Palmer used to see inside the mechanical room.

Maggie strode over to it, kicking a lonely basketball out of her way, Jack at her shoulder.

She heard a loud click and light flowed out of the office windows behind her, illuminating the roof just enough to avoid basketballs, but not enough to prevent startling Dr. Palmer when he emerged from the shed, the breaker reset.

"Oh, my!" he said. "Oh—Miss Gardiner, and . . . are you all right? I feel so terrible about—"

"Trina told me."

This silenced him for a moment. "I don't know what you—"

"Trina was meant to be the scapegoat for all the deaths, and that would be so much easier to pull off if a homemade IED in your kitchen took her out. You told Justin to send the rest of the staff to the reception, then went in and set up the bomb. Trina told me a doctor had done that—"

"I'm not the only doctor in this building! There's Justin. There's—"

"She didn't know who Quintero was. She hadn't become a patient of Bellamy's yet. And she calls Dr. Szabo 'Melanie.'"

The man grew stern, as if Maggie had flubbed an easy question on a pop quiz. "You remember that I told you Trina suffers from psychosis."

"That doesn't mean she hallucinates."

"That's *exactly* what that means."

Maggie ignored this. She repeated the theory she'd outlined to Jack. To keep the resident-to-staff ratio at the correct proportions, to give every child the space and attention he or she needed, Palmer had decided to separate the chaff from the wheat. They were getting nowhere with Rachael, too damaged to repair, or Damon, too damaged to develop. "You keep complaining about the lack of security measures, but these kids are kept on a pretty tight leash. They occasionally move from place to place unaccompanied, but not often. It would be impossible for Trina to slip out enough times to tip Rachael over a railing, inject Damon, slip high-powered heroin to Derald, and unscrew fence brackets on the roof to kill Quentin without anyone noticing. But you could. You're all over this building the whole day long, overseeing every aspect."

The man audibly scoffed. "Trina nearly killed *you* without anyone noticing. You really think it would be that difficult? This is ridiculous. I'm calling your superior right now."

"Go ahead. It will save me the trouble."

But he didn't move, didn't try to push past Maggie to the roof door.

Jack stirred at her elbow, but said nothing, letting her play this her way. She had already jumped in with both feet and now he just had to hope she provoked a confession, because proof wasn't exactly lying around loose on the ground. So she kept talking. Anger wouldn't have let her stop.

"Derald was the first, right? He wasn't some poor, neglected, traumatized child of his circumstances. He was a friggin' spoiled brat, as sociopathic as they come, and unlikely to change. Why should he? Mummy and Daddy would keep him out of jail and he could continue his criminal activity as long as he pleased, provided he took care not to get arrested after his eighteenth birthday. You couldn't have slipped him the drugs, that would be too risky. He could have told someone, bragged to the other kids—he had nothing to lose, after all. My guess is you simply left them in his room."

Even in the minimal lighting she could see his eyes widen. She had guessed right.

"You knew the boredom would be driving him out of his mind and he'd jump on that little baggie like a drowning man to a raft. He had no way of knowing the dose was overpowered."

He tried to rally, clearing his throat. "That's a complete guess, and an insulting one. Where would I even *get* heroin?"

"Oh, please. You run a boarding school for juvenile delinquents."

He snapped, "They're not delinquents!"

"Rachael was," Maggie said. "Wasn't she? A messed-up kid, ping-ponging between Pollyanna and Lolita, refusing to even consider facing reality. Did she run into you in the stairwell, maybe come on to you? Or did you wait there for her, knowing she had to emerge for kitchen duty? Did you push her or just pick up her ankles and swing her over?"

He said nothing, the night breeze lifting his shaggy locks, the light too dim for her to tell if he was even breathing.

"Then there was Damon."

His shoulders slumped under the worn blazer.

"I'm sure you felt very sorry for Damon, but really, what could have been done with him? He'd most likely never learn to speak, much less read. Custodial arrangements for the under-twelve set are few and far between and most are priced out of range for anyone except the very wealthy."

"You *have* been listening to me." He gave her a weary smile, and almost seemed genuinely pleased.

Still Jack said nothing. She could feel the slight warmth from his body along her back. She was spouting off a bunch of stuff she probably couldn't prove, and he was letting her do it. He didn't point out that she might be endangering any case the police department tried to bring, that Palmer hadn't been advised of his rights, that any spontaneous utterances would be called into question. Perhaps, like Maggie, he just really wanted to know for certain who had killed those children.

Or perhaps he didn't expect a trial to be necessary.

She kept going.

"You're often in the kitchen, concerned about safety and keeping the kids on a schedule and keeping the two giggly girls in there on track. You picked up a brownie, heard Nurse Brandreth rushing out to the little kids' play area. You went into the infirmary. This center is your life, you oversee every aspect—so who else besides the nurses would have known about a stock of EpiPens?"

"Now, really—" he protested, but weakly.

"You gave Damon the brownie, which distracted him long enough to jam in the first, maybe the first and second at once. Did he make that grunting scream? Did he try to run away or did the sudden pounding of his heart keep him in place? Then two more. It was quite a risk. You couldn't have known if it would even kill him, or if the nurse might return at any moment or if the receptionist might pop in or maybe a kid with a paper cut. But one thing you were sure of. He couldn't tell on you."

Even in the dark she could see that his eyes had grown moist.

"Damon—" he began, then stopped.

Maggie took a breath, which of course made her cough. She glanced at Jack. His expression told her nothing, but he turned up a palm as if to say, *Go on.*

"You had to put the caps in your pocket so we wouldn't connect the EpiPens to his death, but then tossed them into the recycling bin, probably on your next trip through the visitor's area. You really believe in recycling, don't you? Everyone here does, but at your direction."

He murmured something she had to strain to hear. "It's such a habit." Not an admission of guilt, exactly, but getting there.

"Quentin didn't require a lot of debate, did he? Rachael and Damon were unfortunates, but Derald and Quentin, they were just plain evil. Anyone who could shoot another boy in the face in cold blood, in your *schoolroom*, well, no sense wasting a bed on *him*. And he was the easiest to figure out of all." She pointed to his dark office window, which reflected back her own image against the black night. Her hair unruly, her hand outstretched, she looked like an avenging angel demanding justice. Or a witch laying a curse. She did not know which would be more appropriate.

"You watched him play every day. You knew of his habit of jumping on the fence. You told Justin Quintero to keep him on the roof, isolated from the other kids—a way of locking him up without locking him up. You knew Justin wouldn't go close enough to the edge to notice a wobbly bracket. All you had to do was give Quentin a ball, and wait."

Palmer swayed on his feet, running his hands through his hair. He took a step to the side, then back again, as if trying to walk away from her voice and knowing he couldn't.

Jack leaned forward and whispered into her ear, "How did he get the bolts—"

"He climbed," she said aloud. "He can't weigh much more than I do, maybe less. The metal mesh would have easily held him; the links would only bend a little at his footholds. And he would know when all the other staff would be tied down to bedtimes or punched out. The dedicated doctor works late nearly every night."

Thin fingers swept over the doctor's face, temporarily smoothing out the wrinkles.

Maggie waited.

"You can't prove it," was all he said.

"We can. There's something called touch DNA. We can obtain a genetic profile from a fingerprint, or skin cells, or sweat. You wiped off the pens and the box, but you had to have thrown away those caps with your bare hands. You wouldn't have been walking around the building in latex gloves—that would attract attention."

Even in the dark haze, she saw him blanch. He moved again, walking toward the roof edge, where the gap in the fence left an area open to the night.

Maggie shouted a short exclamation and she and Jack both advanced on the man, but he held up a hand as he turned to face them. "I'm not going to jump, Ms. Gardiner, Detective Renner. I just want to sit down."

And he did, a slight *oof* escaping as he lowered his hips to the brick wall. He slumped forward, elbows on knees, shoulders sagging.

Maggie did not let up. "And the gloves as well. We routinely get DNA from used clothing now, and I'm sure your hands were sweating as you clung to that fence. I know mine were and I had a ladder."

He looked up, then, light from the far windows illuminating his face just enough to show her the hopelessness. He knew now that he had been caught in his own web. He would not get out of it.

"Trina, of course, Trina had to go. She would be your scapegoat. You put us all in the visiting area so that you'd have time to plant your gloves in her room when you went there to warn Ms. Washington of the impending search. Then you had her put on kitchen duty, knowing that the reception would tie up the kitchen staff—on your orders—so that she would be alone in there. One pass through the kitchen with a makeshift bomb and everything could be blamed on Trina. As an added bonus the explosion would force the state to come across with the funding to renovate the kitchen. Win-win."

He sighed, or perhaps it was only the wind. "I felt bad about Trina. I'm glad she'll be all right."

Maggie opened her mouth to say that could not be certain yet and then snapped it shut so hard her teeth rattled. She wanted the guy to believe Trina could identify him as the one who put the foul-smelling bomb into the oven. She wanted him to believe that he had been found out and she could prove her theory, even with an emotionally unstable witness and the ofttimes insufficient type of DNA known as "touch."

"But my assessment is correct, I'm afraid. There is no cure for Trina's psychosis. We can try to minimize it, but she will shuttle back and forth between institutions for the rest of her life. How much more sensible to expend our resources instead on a boy like Luis or a girl like Martina. She came to us as a bundle of violent impulses at war with each other, and now she can learn to control them and channel them in constructive ways."

"She didn't seem much of a sweetheart to me," Jack said, "when she was beating the crap out of Dr. Hunter in the under-twelve unit yesterday."

Palmer switched his upturned gaze to Jack. "We're

not trying to turn her into Sandra Dee, Detective. We have to keep our goals reasonable. If she can function in society, hold a job, maybe even raise a family someday, that is a *triumph*."

"You're triaging," Maggie said.

His eyes lit up, as if delighted with the term. "Yes! That's it exactly. We can only do what we can. I—I simply wanted to do the most we could for the most children."

"But your victims," Maggie said. "They were children, too."

The doctor gazed up at the night sky. "I'm well aware of that, Ms. Gardiner."

And then lifted his feet and fell backward over the low wall, into the night.

Chapter 33

Maggie jumped for the edge, and so did Jack. But he didn't grab for Palmer as she did; he grabbed Maggie, making sure that momentum would not carry her over.

Neither could have caught the man anyway. He was already gone.

He fell in silence. No scream, only a faint thud when he hit the pavement. He had executed a perfect backward dive, taking no chances, aiming to end up as dead as Quentin had. She looked down on the small form, motionless in the street, searching for any sign of movement or suffering. She saw none.

Jack was there, of course, speechless with shock, just as she was. After they gazed over the side they looked at each other, helpless, angry, and accepting all at once.

Trina, at least, would be safe. If she survived.

Maggie moved to slump onto the low brick wall. Perhaps Jack thought she might faint like some kind of Victorian maiden because he grasped her shoulders and asked if she was all right, and though she did not feel the least faint she let herself lean against him. Completely unnecessary, but she snaked her arms around his waist and pressed one ear to his chest to feel the comforting solidness of him. She could let herself have one moment of peace before the all-night processing, the reporting, the affidavits, the hundred myriad tasks that make up a crime scene. Just one.

"I knew it!"

She opened her eyes, and past Jack's elbow saw her ex-husband step onto the roof.

"Only coworkers, my ass!" Rick shouted. He apparently didn't care if all of downtown Cleveland heard him, and most of it probably could. He had always considered subtlety to be useless.

Maggie stepped away from Jack, relying on anger to see her through the unwanted feeling of embarrassment. "Where's Trina? Why aren't you with her?"

Jack pointed out, "Guarding Trina is no longer necessary, now."

"*He* didn't know that!"

Rick had been barreling toward them but stopped, as if repulsed by some invisible force or a very bad smell. "You two are fu—"

"*Trina*," Maggie said.

"I left a patrol guy with her! Doc says she'll be fine anyway, just a bump on the head. Do you know this guy isn't who he says he is? Jack Renner is an old retiree who lives in a cabin in Tennessee."

His words died off into the dark sky, disappearing into the breeze from the lake, and Maggie's heart seemed to pause in its rhythm. Jack, too, had just been caught in his own web, and would not get out of it.

She stared at her ex-husband because she couldn't bear to look at Jack. Her world was about to crash in on her, these past few months of secrets and lies and wondering every single waking minute if she had done the right thing and why. She should feel relieved, to have the decision taken out of her hands. Now she and Jack would both be exposed, she would be fired and possibly go to jail, but she would no longer have to lie to her coworkers, her brother, or herself.

But instead of relief or even fear, she felt devastation.

All of this flew through her mind in the split second before Jack opened his mouth to speak. And when he did, he said, "You're right."

She blinked.

So did Rick. He hadn't expected an easy capitulation. "So who the hell are you, then?"

"I'm Jack Renner—yes," he went on, seeing Rick's expression, "that's exactly *why* I joined the Minneapolis force, because they already had a guy named Jack Renner and that would make it easy to appropriate his history."

"So what are you hiding? Are you even a cop?"

Jack spoke without anger, as if saddened by his own actions and the necessity of them, but Maggie could see the wheels in his head turning fast enough to smoke. "Oh yes, I'm a cop. But I knew if I was up front about the reason I went to Minnesota, and the reason I left there and came here, no force would hire me."

He waited, forcing Rick to ask, "And what's the reason?"

"The vigilante killer."

Rick frowned. So did Maggie.

"He killed fourteen—I believe—in Chicago. But Chicago—well, it's an unusual place. I couldn't get my chief to listen to why I thought a bunch of dead low-lifes were killed by the same guy. He laughed me out of his office. Then they seemed to stop, so I thought okay, he was right, it was all in my head. Except that a few months later I went to training out of state and a guy from Minneapolis started telling me about these dead scumbags turning up. I went to my boss. He thought I was crazy, so I turned in my badge and packed up my stuff.

"At the MPD I tried to get a handle on him, but couldn't. There was no way to predict who he'd hit next, or where. Just like here, he didn't leave any evidence. When they stopped, I scanned the rest of the country for similar killings and found them here. I knew it would take forever to get into the detective unit since I hadn't been at MPD that long, so I used the other Jack's longevity to fast-track myself to promotion. That part was wrong. I'm sorry."

Maggie studied her ex-husband. He had his arms crossed over his chest and didn't appear to be buying a word of it, but his lack of interruption told her he was. Sorta. A little bit. But not enough to let her believe that Jack could talk his way out of this.

However.

Rick said, "So you lied because you wanted to chase this vigilante?"

"Yep."

"Who is he?"

Jack attempted to look sheepish, a condition so alien to his makeup she could have laughed. "I have no idea. I'm no closer today than I was ten years ago. It seems like all I can do is follow him around like some weird kind of groupie."

"Then why didn't you ask for the case instead of letting Patty and the chief dump it on my desk?"

"When do they ever let us pick our cases?"

Rick snorted. "True."

Maggie felt the straightjacket around her lungs begin to loosen, just slightly.

But then Rick said, "And what about that woman he killed? The one who left all those old folks to rot? MPD had a case like that."

Jack shrugged. "Don't know. That sort of thing is popping up all over the country."

It chilled Maggie how smoothly he could lie. He had barely told Maggie anything about his past—of that miniscule amount how much might be true?

Perhaps none.

Not that it mattered, right? She kept silent to protect herself, not him.

But still the doubt burrowed into her heart like a grub, leaving painful, hollowed-out trails behind it.

"And what about Phoenix?" Rick asked.

She could see a muscle jump in Jack's cheek, but he merely nodded slowly and told Rick, "Yes. There too. I've been following this guy all over the country. My chief in Maryville said I was obsessed and said I could resign or be fired. I tried to go over his head and now they won't admit I was ever on the payroll. After that I learned to keep my theories to myself."

"I *knew* it," Rick said.

As if the idea had just occurred to him, Jack said, "Maybe we should convince the chief—assuming he doesn't fire me—to assign the vigilante killings to me. I have the history and I'm willing to follow him to the next place he turns up. *If* he's done here, of course, which remains to be seen. At least you could get it off your desk."

Rick's eyes narrowed, checking this offer for catches—of which, of course, there were many. It would look funny to IA, to anyone, really, if revealed within the department. If Jack actually solved the case there would be no glory for Rick. It would leave Jack free to continue dating his ex-wife. On the other hand, it would make Rick's life easier and his clearance rate, never stellar, improve. But would that be enough to buy his silence?

"I still gotta tell the chief, you know," he said, a triumphant gleam in his eyes.

Jack shrugged again, as if didn't matter. "Sure. I get that."

Maggie held her breath. She didn't have Jack's acting skills and couldn't begin to behave as if it didn't matter. Rick might not see all the implications, but if anyone started looking at Jack, really looking, that person might stumble into the black vortex of his actions over the years. And that cesspool could suck her right in as well.

"Or maybe you could," Rick suggested. "Make a clean breast of it all."

"Good point," Jack said, waiting, as Maggie did, for the deal, the tit for tat.

It didn't come. Perhaps the glut of information had simply confused Rick, or maybe he really did only care about one thing. "So are you two sleeping together?"

Jack's mouth began to form the word *no*.

Maggie said, "Yes."

"Well, *shit*," Rick said.

"We've been divorced for years, Rick. What do you care anyway?"

His face screwed up into a disbelieving grimace. "Seriously? *This* guy?"

"Seriously. Not that it's any of your business." The best defense, after all. "Now do you mind if we call the medical examiner and do something about the dead body in the street? Or have you forgotten that—"

"How long?"

She hadn't so much as glanced at Jack during this exchange. "A month. Anything else? Would you like an itinerary or maybe a checklist? Or would you like to do your job for a change?"

"Fine," he said. "Whatever." And walked away. At the door he turned as if for a parting shot, but if he expressed his disgust at the thought of the two of them entwined in passion, the words were lost in the rising wind. He lurched through the opening and disappeared.

Maggie let out her breath.

Jack seemed aghast. "Why did you tell him that?"

"He wouldn't have believed a denial. Besides, I know him. He ignores anything he doesn't like: criticism, CNN, sending out birthday cards. Let him think I'm sleeping with you. It's the most effective way to keep him out of your life."

"Oh."

"You're welcome." If she hadn't been so worried she might have enjoyed the discomfort on his face.

"But—are you sure you want to do that? I mean . . . people at work . . . if you have anyone else in your life, they might . . ."

Now she did grin. "Are you worried about my *reputation*, Jack?"

"No . . . it's just . . ."

"No one is going to care except Rick—just because he shaves doesn't make him any less of a Neanderthal where women are concerned. Don't worry about that. Start worrying about what you're going to tell the chief."

He snapped his attention back from the impact of Maggie's imaginary sex life on her career. "You think he'll report me anyway?"

"Rick?" she asked, pulling out her phone. "Absolutely. Now, let's get Dr. Palmer's blood off the street before classes start in the morning."

Chapter 34

Maggie sat at her keyboard, trying to pack all the events and discoveries of the past week into one comprehensive report. It wasn't going so well.

Carol came by with fresh, hot caffeine and hitched one hip over the edge of the desk. "How'd he take it?"

"Not good."

"Can't say I'm surprised."

"Me neither." Maggie sipped the steaming liquid. "He learned how to give a guilt trip from our mother. First he said I'd been working too hard and needed a trip to Disney to get in touch with my inner child."

"You have an inner child?"

"Nah, I packed her off to boarding school years ago. Then he put the girls on the phone to tell me about all the things they wanted to do with me in Mickey Mouse Land. That conversation got confusing—turns out he and Daisy do limit their access to commercial media so I'm not sure they understand exactly what Disneyworld is. They seem to think it's a cross between a huge movie theater and the food court at the mall. But they damn sure knew that getting a tiara makes one a princess, so there's no way Alex is leaving that park without shelling out for a mess of rhinestones."

"It's required, I'm afraid."

"Then he tried to put Daisy on, but she refused. I could hear her in the background telling him to tilt at his own windmills. Then he reminded me of how Mom and Dad wanted to take us when we were kids but could never afford it."

"Ooo, the parent card. Brutal."

"Eventually I wore him down with tales of murdered children and mountains of paperwork."

Carol played with her coffee stirrer. "All of which could wait for you until you got back."

"Yes, but . . . I'm staying in touch with Trina. Melanie thinks it would be good for her to have someone outside the center to talk to. She won't speak to her father."

"That's kind of you. But you know, Trina's not your flesh and blood—"

Neither is Jack. But I feel the same reluctance to leave him, when I think he may be in trouble. "Don't *you* start."

"What can I say? I learned from my dear old mom, too. And your brother is right that you need a break. This has been a rough couple of months for you." Carol watched her over the rim of her coffee mug, eyes too perceptive, concern too genuine. "You've been almost killed what, twice? Shot at, gassed—"

"I wasn't gassed."

"You're still coughing."

"Hardly at all." Of course, right then her body betrayed her with a hacking rasp.

Carol abandoned the gentle route. "It's changed you.

All these experiences—I know at your age you tell yourself you're invincible, but . . . it accumulates."

Maggie kept her gaze on her keyboard, where her hands were still. Carol didn't know the half of it. Maggie's experiences during the past five months had definitely changed her and almost certainly not for the better. She'd become lost in a murky world where beliefs and assumptions changed with the wind, and if she had ever been on solid ground, she no longer knew how to find her way back to it. And she couldn't tell Carol that. She couldn't tell Alex. She couldn't tell anyone.

Except Jack.

Maggie lifted her face to her friend. "I'm fine. Just too worn out for Dizzyworld right now."

"Huh," Carol said. "Okay."

She did not even pretend to be convinced.

Jack pulled the chief's office door shut behind him and moved along the blindingly white hallway. The official boss of the homicide unit liked the prestige and working conditions of the position and didn't care so much about doing any actual work, so it hadn't been hard to convince him to shuffle aside a resume exaggeration. The PD didn't need bad press; best to dispense with the matter quietly. Jack would have to correct the record, of course, which he knew would require some good forgery skills and maybe some outside help, but he could do it. Good thing he hadn't had to speak to the de facto boss of the homicide unit, Patty Wildwind, or the meeting would have had a very different outcome.

Jack had fessed up to only a fraction of what he'd told Rick, but the chief would never deign to go into details with Gardiner so Jack felt fairly safe in doing so. As a bonus, the chief promised to have the case transferred to Jack. Now he would be the official investigator of his own handiwork, in which he would, sadly, fail to make progress. This left Rick Gardiner free to focus his attention on other things. Jack hoped it would be *any* other thing besides Maggie and Jack.

He figured Gardiner could go two ways. He might redouble his efforts to ruin Jack, keep poking and prodding until he found something actionable. Or he might prefer to keep everyone's attention off the fact that his ex-wife preferred another man's bed to his and, as Maggie had predicted, ignore Jack's existence. Jack bet on the latter.

At least he *hoped* for the latter.

Jack knew he couldn't count on either Gardiner or the chief keeping every word to themselves. Cops didn't keep *anything* to themselves. This meant he'd have to tell Riley something, an even more abbreviated version, in case rumors got back to him. Partners could forgive anything except being left in the dark. With luck Riley would be too occupied with his new girlfriend to spare Jack's situation much thought. With a *lot* of luck she'd turn out to have the body of a Barbie doll combined with the brain of Marie Curie and the cooking talents of Rachael Ray, because Riley didn't distract easily.

And if his patch job didn't work, if nothing worked, his go-bag remained packed, an untraceable vehicle waited in storage, and he could be out of town in any direction in a half hour. Without the woman who had started it all to pursue he could head anywhere he wanted, to any place where future victims of bad people needed protection. He could even go home. The only flies in the ointment of relocation would be where to find decent pierogi, and not being able to say good-bye to Maggie.

He didn't particularly want to say good-bye to Maggie.

He stumbled over that thought, both mentally and physically, and as he put out a hand to catch himself on the corner of a trophy case, his phone rang. The burner phone. He checked the number.

He answered it, saying, "Emma."

She didn't bother with a "good morning" or even berate him for missing Giles's funeral. She said, "Tell me why my boss just showed me your picture and asked if I knew who you were. He says some cop in Cleveland sent it to him. What d'ya think about that, cuz?"

Jack leaned against the trophy case.

ACKNOWLEDGMENTS

As always I had the help of many people in writing this book, but in particular I'd like to thank the esteemed Dr. Doug Lyle and my nurse sister, Mary, for their help with the medical topics.

Not having children myself, much research was required and so I turned once again to my local library, reading *Burning Down the House*, by Nell Bernstein; *A Playworker's Guide to Understanding Children's Behavior*, by Andrea Clifford; *Small Criminals among Us*, by Gad Czudner; *Lost Boys*, by James Garbarino; *Positive Youth Justice: Children First, Offenders Second*, by Kevin Haines and Stephen Case; *One Small Boat: The Story of a Little Girl Lost, Then Found*, by Kathy Harrison; *Warning Signs: How to Protect Your Kids from Becoming Victims or Perpetrators of Violence and Aggression*, by Brian Johnson; *Ghosts from the Nursery*, by Robin Karr-Morse and Meredith S. Wiley; *Savage Spawn: Reflections on Violent Children*, by Jonathan Kellerman; *Psychotherapists as Expert Witnesses*, by Roger Kennedy; *Born, Not Raised: Voices from Juvenile Hall*, by Susan Maddon Lankford; *Juvenile Crime: Opposing Viewpoints*, Andrew C. Nakaya, Ed.; *Girls & Sex: Navigating the Complicated New Landscape*, by Peggy Orenstein; *The Spiral*

Notebook, by Stephen and Joyce Singular; *Raised by the Courts: One Judge's Insight into Juvenile Justice*, by Irene Sullivan; *Nowhere to Go*, by Casey Watson; and *Healing Emotional Wounds*, by Nancy M. Welch.

I also utilized many online articles and resources from the Ohio Department of Youth Services, the U.S. Department of Justice, the Native American and Alaskan Technical Assistance Project, and the American Psychological Association.

I'd also like to thank Michaela Hamilton, my wonderful editor; publicist Lulu Martinez; social media specialist Lauren Jernigan; and the rest of the fabulous staff at Kensington Press.

And as ever, my fantastic agent, Vicky Bijur, and Alexandra Franklin at the Vicky Bijur Literary Agency.

Don't miss Lisa Black's next enthralling Gardiner
and Renner thriller

LET JUSTICE DESCEND

Coming soon from Kensington Publishing Corp.

Keep reading to enjoy a suspenseful excerpt . . .

Chapter 1

Sunday, November 4
58 hours until polls close

"Well. That's not something you see every day," Maggie said.

The woman's body stretched along the walkway to her door, her feet, still in stylish heels, on the concrete slab and her back along the flagstones. Dead eyes stared up at the gray November sky, and a few colored leaves had fallen onto the neatly buttoned but damp suit coat. A briefcase and an overstuffed tote bag had fallen from her left hand, and her right clutched a knot of keys. No blood dried in the crisp air, no struggle had mussed her perfectly curled hair, nothing about her gave the slightest clue to her demise—save for the black streak on her right hand.

"First time I've ever seen something like this,"

Riley agreed, gazing not at the woman but at her front door.

Jack, as usual, said nothing.

Maggie Gardiner had already taken her "overall" photos—the yard, the exterior wall of the house, the body—and now turned to what had killed the woman. The front door to the woman's house had a heavy metal screen door with a design of curlicues and latticework, made to fit its surroundings, a brick century home. Its front yard seemed more like a courtyard, ringed by an eight-foot-high brick wall with a matching gate that led to the street, where the victim had parked her car. No driveway, no garage, but only one street from the lake and surrounded by other old-money homes on the edge of Cleveland's city limits. The cute courtyard, with a few wrought-iron bistro tables, mini lights, and even a Beer Meister kegerator under the protection of the elms, gave Maggie and the homicide detectives the ability to work in isolation. The high wall kept the dead woman's situation from both offending the delicate sensibilities and feeding the prurient interests of neighbors, media, and onlookers. A mourning dove sat in the branches above them, cooing a morose sigh to complement the scene.

From the woman's ice-cold body and complete rigor, she had apparently lain there all night, unseen, until staff had arrived to escort her to her first appointment of the day and had found her.

The woman's own home had killed her. Someone had cut the extralong cord to the squat kegerator, then peeled the wires inside the cord away from one another. A black-coated one had been snaked up the side of the metal screen door as far as it would reach, about three-quarters of the height. Its end had been stripped to the bare wire and wound firmly around one of the curlicues—quite visible in the daylight but tough to see in the dark, and Maggie assumed it would have been dark. The clothing told her the woman had come from work or some professional event, and the days had grown short. Tired, approaching her own door in the night, she would not have noticed the black wire.

Maggie noted the motion-sensor floodlight over the door, but it either wasn't functioning or had a light sensor so that it didn't come on during the day, because it didn't light up now.

From this same plug cord, the killer had taken the white-coated wire and connected it to a metal grate with the proportions of an undersized welcome mat. This he placed on the concrete slab in front of the door.

Then all he had to do was plug the cord back into the wall . . . and wait.

Jack Renner, homicide detective with more secrets than most of his suspects, had materialized at her elbow without a sound. It made her start, but not as much as it used to. Jack was tall, dark, decidedly not handsome, and a killer. She knew that and yet told no one, a fact that, even after six months, still astounded her when she woke to it each morning. "I get it," he said aloud. "When she stepped on the grounded plate and then touched the handle, her body completed the circuit."

His partner, Thomas Riley, stared down at the body. "I'd expect more . . . more. Wouldn't she, like, burst into flames?" Maggie raised one eyebrow at him, and his fair skin colored until he protested: "Well, we had a guy on a construction site who got tangled in a live wire, and he wound up practically cut in half."

"She's got the mark on her hand, and she'll probably have a similar scorch on one or both of her feet," Maggie said. They couldn't move or examine the body until an investigator from the Medical Examiner's office arrived. "That's fairly typical. Electrocutions can vary quite a bit, depending on how much power and where it goes. Frankly, it seems like an iffy method of murder."

Jack said, "Maybe. Wearing those probably helped." He gestured to the woman's fashionable shoes. "Thin soles, no rubber. Plus it rained last night."

Maggie examined the grate and the concrete slab without touching it, though the fire department had already pulled the plug from the outlet. The surface had sagged over the years, caving until grime accumulated in its shallow depth, providing the perfect resting spot for the grate. "It was already dirty, so she didn't notice the grate against the dark area. He could have even brushed some leaves over to disguise it. But wouldn't it have been, like, humming? How did it not set the house on fire?"

"They're not touching—the screen door and the grate." Riley stepped closer and pointed to the door's sill, two inches above the ground. "Each one alone is static, perfectly safe until—"

"Until she grabs the screen door handle and completes the circuit."

"Exactly. Then she dies, gravity takes over, her body falls back, her hand pulls away. The circuit is broken, and the door goes back to being a mere door. No fire, no sparking, no wildly zinging electric meter. Kind of ingenious, really." He caught her look. "Don't glare. It's, um, definitely different. Iffy, like you said. If that light worked and she noticed the wires. If the leaves blew away so she wondered why there was a metal grate in front of her door. If she had been wearing tennis shoes, or felt some static just before she touched the latch, or if some unlucky UPS guy came to drop off a package—assuming she left the outer gate unlocked during the day, anyone could have wandered in here— or if the outlet had a ground fault interrupter, it might not have worked."

Maggie glanced toward the covered outlet under which the cord lay among the scattered leaves. After nearly being blown up a few weeks earlier, she knew everything she had ever wanted to know about ground fault interrupters. "Frost-free refrigerators don't plug into outlets with GFIs because of the freezing-warming cycles. And aren't they two-twenty?"

"A small one like that, I don't know," Riley said. "Even one-ten could have killed her, what with the wetness, thin shoes, no gloves, and at her age her heart might not be that great any more. She's sixty-two, eight years older than me, and my doc's already giving me a hard time about cholesterol and coronary arteries. So electrocution might have seemed a pretty safe bet, as methods of murder go."

"Please don't sound so admiring," Maggie said without meaning it. By now, she knew Thomas Riley better than that.

He continued as if she hadn't spoken, still thinking the scenario through. "Even if it didn't work, he wasn't out a lot of work or effort. He didn't have to enter the house or bring anything with him except wire strippers and this metal grate, which—correct me if I'm wrong, Miss CSI—doesn't seem to have a spot on it wide enough to get a decent print from."

Maggie looked again at the latticework of metal strips, none more than perhaps an eighth inch wide. "Probably not, no, especially after the rain."

"Or the plug?"

"Rubber covered and exposed to the elements? Unlikely. I'll swab for contact DNA, but if he wore gloves—"

"And he's an idiot if he didn't. So he doesn't set up a slam dunk but then he doesn't leave us any clues, either. Unless our dead lady has surveillance cameras set up, and I don't see any. Or if the neighbors saw someone dipping into this yard, and they haven't even poked their heads out to see what all the cop cars are for, so I'm not too optimistic."

"The perfect murder?" Maggie wondered.

"There's no such thing," Jack said. And he, of course, would know.

Within a half hour both the ME investigators and the search warrant arrived. It never ceased to amaze Maggie how finding a dead body on the stoop was *not* considered sufficient probable cause to enter a home, but there it was, and in any case she had been too busy with the scene to be in much of a hurry.

The kegerator fridge did not yield any fingerprints, not even with superglue—only a lot of water marks and dirt. Ditto for the outlet and the decorative grill of the screen door, where the black wire had been attached. The white one had been snaked along the edge of the house in the crack between the foundation and the concrete stoop, and accumulated dirt in the crack helped hide the white rubber coating. In terms of fingerprints, the dirt scarcely mattered, since the wires were too narrow for any usable latents, but she collected the length anyway, planning to take a much closer look at it in her lab. She did the same with the metal grate. The blanket of leaves, charming in their reds and browns and golds, made her nervous. The killer could have dropped his glove or his wallet or his business card on his way out and they might miss it in all that debris. But she didn't particularly want to rake the entire yard, either.

Meanwhile the detectives took the keys from the dead woman's hand and confirmed that the fob did, indeed, unlock a newish sedan parked at the curb. The front seats were tidy, but the rear ones held a variety of papers, folders, and brochures, all having slid around willy-nilly until no order could be detected. Three empty paper coffee cups, each rimmed with the same dark red lipstick as on the face of the victim, sat on the floorboard in front of the passenger's seat. The trunk held only a spare tire and an unopened set of jumper cables. Maggie photographed all of this but left it in place until they could decide what might be of significance.

In the grass behind the large oak, she found a black rubber mat with an open weave design—obviously what had been the victim's welcome mat. The mat was larger and thicker than the metal grate, but what with the leaves, the dark, perhaps hurrying through the rain, the victim did not notice the difference. She would have felt it with that last step, but in that instance it became too late, her hand already on the electrified door handle.

On a whim Maggie looked inside the small refrigerator, but it didn't seem to be missing a black wire shelf. It held a pony keg, shiny and secure and—she shook the entire unit—apparently empty. The fridge had probably been unplugged now that the season for outdoor parties had faded, but Maggie wondered why the owner would leave it outside. But then she didn't have a garage and would have needed help to lug the thing inside or down to a basement, or maybe Diane Cragin simply hadn't gotten around to it. Diane Cragin had been very busy and spent a great deal of time out of town, because Diane Cragin was a sitting U.S. senator, R–Ohio.

And that meant, Riley informed her as if Maggie hadn't already figured that out for herself, that this case was going to be a snafu of epic proportions.

"She had enemies?" Maggie asked.

"She's a politician. Would you like enemies listed alphabetically or in order of importance?"

He seemed to have paid more attention to politics than either Jack or Maggie, so he filled them in on what he could as the ME investigator, and Maggie examined the body. Diane Cragin had been the duly elected senator from Ohio for twelve years.

Diane Cragin had been campaigning on the usual issues of bringing jobs back to the rust belt and cleaning up food stamp requirements, didn't hire any tax-free domestic help, didn't sleep with her interns, and hadn't created any major scandals that Riley could remember, but . . .

Maggie looked up as the ME investigator removed the senator's shoes. "But?"

"A Cleveland guy has been running for her seat, Green. He's head of economic development or something like that. It's been a pretty nasty campaign—par for the course these days—and he's accused her of taking kickbacks, promising Ohio one thing and then flying to DC to agitate for the complete opposite, being paid under the table to lobby for the pharmaceuticals with the large hospitals, trading jobs for votes, basically all the same things she accuses him of doing. Politics as usual, in other words."

"You're a cynic," Maggie said.

"Impossible not to be these days."

Riley told her the unhappy man standing outside the courtyard had been Cragin's assigned Secret Service agent for this week. He had dropped her off still breathing the night before and had told anyone who would listen that escorting her only as far as the courtyard had been standard procedure for a senator who put a premium on her privacy and, after two terms in office, was accustomed to getting her own way. She had earned a reputation as an uncooperative client, and it got worse during stressful periods—such as these crazy days before Tuesday's election. So he had left her alive and inside the gate the night before, then saw the body that morning and had to break the gate door to get in.

"Is that it?" Riley asked Maggie.

"That's it." A scorch mark along the bottom of the woman's right foot had burned through her nylons and peeled a small amount of skin, with only a single round burn on the sole of the shoe.

The ME investigator, a young woman with dark skin and dimples, told them, "It doesn't take much, especially with AC power. Hey, bird," she said to the dove in the tree, which had been heaving its heavy sighs nonstop, "knock it off."

Sudden silence, save for the rustle of leaves in the breeze.

"We'll see if she had any medical conditions that made her more vulnerable. Do we have doctor information?"

"Not yet. We haven't been inside or done any notifications," Riley said.

"She's wearing nylons," the investigator said, as if she found this more perplexing than using a screen door as a murder weapon. Nylons and pantyhose had been out of style for years. Women now left their legs bare, cutting industry sales by more than half until nylons were rebranded as lingerie or "sheer tights." Or worn by older women like Diane Cragin, who wished to wear skirts without exposing every age spot, scar, and mole to the public, always so harsh on women's looks once they passed twenty-five or so.

"It's gotten chilly," Maggie pointed out.

The investigator, who had yet to see an age spot mar her perfect skin, shrugged and put Tyvek bags over the late senator's hands, pulling the drawstring tight to keep them from slipping off. The manicured fingernails would be scraped for trace evidence, not that anyone expected to find it—there had clearly *not* been a struggle or physical confrontation. She and Maggie turned the body to one side, but nothing waited underneath it except more dead leaves.

"That's it, then," the investigator said, pulling off her latex gloves with a definite *snap* as the body snatchers moved in to load up the earthly remains of Diane Cragin. "You have a fun Halloween? I wanted to wear my sexy vampire costume all last Wednesday, but my supervisor said such frivolity wouldn't be in good taste."

Maggie said, "That's a pity. One does hate to see a good sexy vampire costume go to waste. To be honest, I can't remember the last time I dressed for Halloween."

"That's sad," the investigator said, and Maggie agreed that, yes, it was. But her life had changed that year, and perhaps such frivolity was no longer in good taste. Either that or she no longer had the taste for it.

She went to photograph the interior of the house with Jack and Riley.

Uniformed officers, armed with guns and the usual strict instructions not to touch anything (except doorknobs, as needed), had used the dead woman's keys to go inside and "clear" the house. The knob and keyed deadbolt had been securely latched. No one waited there, not family members, pets, or the killer. So the detectives walked behind Maggie as she entered, camera at the ready, hoping that Senator Cragin had left them some clue as to who had wanted her dead.

The bird started up again.

Connect with Us

Visit us online at
KensingtonBooks.com
to read more from your favorite authors, see books
by series, view reading group guides, and more.

Join us on social media

for sneak peeks, chances to win books and prize packs,
and to share your thoughts with other readers.

facebook.com/kensingtonpublishing
twitter.com/kensingtonbooks

Tell us what you think!

To share your thoughts, submit a review,
or sign up for our eNewsletters, please visit:
KensingtonBooks.com/TellUs.